Windover

Jane Aiken Hodge

Thorndike Press • Thorndike, Maine

Library of Congress Cataloging in Publication Data:

Hodge, Jane Aiken.
   Windover / Jane Aiken Hodge.
      p. cm.
   ISBN 1-56054-553-4 (alk. paper : lg. print)
1. Large type books. I. Title.
[PS3558.O342W56   1993]   92-29408
813'.54—dc20   CIP

Thorndike Large Print® General Series edition published in 1993 by arrangement with St. Martin's Press, Inc.

Cover design by Studio 3.

The tree indicium is a trademark of Thorndike Press.

This book is printed on acid-free, high opacity paper. ∞

Windover

1

'Is it really true?' She looked up at him, dark eyes wide with amazement, dark curls wind-ruffled around the small, vivid face.

'True as I stand here. The Bastille has fallen; a whole age of tyranny has ended. It's a great day for the world, Kathryn.' He had no right to call her that, but neither of them noticed. He was the tutor, she the daughter of the house, but who cared now?

Teaching her along with her younger half-brothers, Mark Weatherby had taught his pupil to share his passion for liberty and the rights of man. 'What a day!' He held out both hands and she put hers into them as if it were the most natural thing in the world. 'Only think! If King Louis plays his cards right, it should mean democracy in France, an end to the threat of war between us. A whole new world.'

'A new world! Oh, Mark —' Their eyes met and held. 'I should not be calling you that!'

'Why not?' Pulling her towards him. 'Today, everything is possible.' After the long, gentle first kiss, he loosed her a little to look down at her. 'How long have we loved each other? I didn't know, did you?'

'No.' Smiling. 'But, oh, how happy I am. I'll never be frightened again.'

'Kathryn!' He kissed her desperately now, beginning to be afraid himself. For her, for them both.

'You're hurting me!' She pulled away, gazed up, taking him all in: fair hair, brown skin, blue eyes under firm dark brows. Hers. 'What are we going to do?'

'We can't talk here.' He had met her in the walled garden as he walked up from the stables, back from Scarborough with the amazing news. By a miracle, none of the gardeners was working there, but one might appear at any moment. 'Come out to the cliff garden; we'll be safe there.'

'Safe?' Now she held back, all her upbringing crying out against it. 'I should not.'

'Too late for that.' He said it almost ruefully. 'It's happened to us, Kathryn. You're mine now. We neither of us meant it; it's happened just the same. We are one, you and I. For always. We both know it. Both knew it, really; what we have to think is what we are going to do about it.' He had her arm

8

now, gently encouraging her towards the gate to the wild garden that lay outside the walls, in a slight depression of the cliff edge. Kathryn's mother, the heiress of Windover Hall, had planned the shrubbery there to occupy herself while her husband was away, fighting the American rebels. It was to have been a surprise for him. When the news came, shortly after Kathryn's third birthday, that he had been killed in a skirmish on the Heights of Haarlem, Lady Charlotte had lost all interest in it; and in anything else for a while, and work had stopped. Battered by wild northeasters for thirteen years, only the hardiest of the planting had survived along the cliff path; nobody came there now to disturb the rabbits and sea birds that had made it their own. And it had the signal virtue of being screened from the Hall's observant rows of windows by the high walls that sheltered the vegetable and cutting gardens from winter gales. Even now, in July, the wind blew fresh here, with a tang of the sea. 'Will you be warm enough?' She seemed to him infinitely vulnerable, infinitely precious.

'Of course. You know I love it here. But whether we should — without the boys.' They came here often with her two half-brothers, children of the second marriage that had changed everything.

'We must. You know one can never be alone in the Hall. Where are the boys?'

'Out riding. My mother has had one of her spasms, said she must have some quiet.'

'I'm sorry.' But it was an old story. Everybody knew that Lady Charlotte had taken refuge in illness three years and two sons after her headlong remarriage to a charming curate some years younger than herself. She had not liked the change in her position in the county, but she had liked even less what she gradually learned about her overpowering husband. She did not like childbirth much either. After Roderick was born, she grumbled; after Jeremy, she banished her husband from her bed, took to her *chaise longue* and stayed there, leaving him to pursue what interests he pleased elsewhere.

For a while, Windover Hall had been efficiently run by the housekeeper who had grown up along with its young mistress, but as the two boys grew noisier, and their father drank deeper on the nights he was at home, Mrs. Burrows began to pine for the urban comforts of Scarborough, and in the end left suddenly one morning after the second maid had found her master fast asleep in the dining room, his head in a pool of wine, an overturned candle beside him. 'We might all have been burned in our beds,' Mrs. Burrows told her mistress, and went to keep house for her brother.

There was muddle at Windover for a while, but Kathryn ended it on her fourteenth birthday by announcing that she would take over the housekeeping herself with the help of her maid Sally, who had been with her from childhood, came from a nearby village, and was afraid of nothing. 'The servants will mind me,' young Kathryn had told her mother, and it proved true. Her father had been popular enough, but her grandfather, Lord Eskdale, had been the great man of the small district, active and merciful both as magistrate and landlord. Kathryn had her dark hair and firm chin from him. She was loved as much as her step-father was deplored, and had been running the Hall successfully for two years, much assisted in the last one by the new tutor who now walked beside her.

He had been thinking about it all as they walked, silently, hand in hand, down to the cliff edge and her favourite view of the turbulent sea. A man-of-war lay off-shore, north, towards Scarborough. Too far to be a threat, but a reminder, just the same. 'I'm ashamed.' He dropped her hand, faced her. 'I should not have let this happen. Will you — can you forget it?'

'No.' She smiled at him with love. 'I knew

you were going to say that. And I know what you are going to say next, too. That you cannot support a wife.'

'It's true, God help me. The moment I speak of this, I lose both position and character.'

'And a good thing too.' Bracingly. 'You know perfectly well that you are fitted for much more rewarding work than bear-leading two cubs, have only stayed here because you were sorry for us — the boys and me.'

'How did you know?'

'Of course I knew. I'm not stupid. I have seen how you yearn to be at the heart of things, how you have plied Mr. Wilberforce with questions on his rare visits. About parliamentary reform, the slave trade, all the great issues. You want to do something in the world, and so do I. Mr. Wilberforce will help us, I am sure. He is an old family friend. He will give you a start if we ask him, and then, it is just to wait, dear friend, while you make your way. And I shall have some money of my own when I am twenty-one.'

'And what a miserable creature I would be to be counting on that!'

'I knew you were going to say that too, and it is the most complete nonsense, as you very well know. Have you taught me all this time about the equal rights of man and now go back on your own arguments? If I let you work

12

for me, why should not you let me share what I have with you? We shall do excellently well, I promise you, when you are Mr. Weatherby, M.P.'

'Oh, my darling, I love you so much.' All else forgotten, he swept her into his arms.

'What's this? What in damnation's name is this?' They sprang apart at the furious words and turned, hand in hand, to face Kathryn's step-father. Oliver Morewood had come out, mildly befuddled as usual, for a breath of air to cool his head after his early dinner. Tall, and broad with it, he had long since shed any trace of the clergyman. A formidable rider to hounds, he was better known among the cock fighters and badger baiters of the district than with its men of God. He was a passionate devotee of the gentle art of boxing and it was rumoured that he had killed an unlucky young man who had questioned his judgment at a cock fight years ago. It had been hushed up, of course, by his fellow magistrates. The boy had been a vagrant, it had simply been too hard a blow from a powerful right hand, but no one had risked questioning Morewood's opinions since that day, most certainly not when he was drunk.

'What's the meaning of this, you doxy?' He turned first on Kathryn. 'A chit! A child! Kiss-

13

ing and canoodling in the open air for all the world like the strumpet you're setting out to be. Get indoors, girl, where you belong. I'll speak to you presently.'

'You've said too much already.' Mark stood his ground. 'Sir, we have just discovered that we love each other. It is not, I know, the match you and her mother would have wished for Kathryn, but it is truly what she wants for herself. All we ask is your patience. If you wish it, I will leave at once, this very day, and go to carve out a career for myself, make myself a fit husband for her. I shall always be hers, she must be free as air to do what she pleases with herself. When I can support her, I will return to ask for her hand in marriage. Kathryn,' he turned from Morewood who was actually gobbling with rage, unable to get out anything but random curses, 'I'll always love you. You know it.' He took her hand, kissed it. 'Go to your mother, love. This is no place for you.'

'But — you really mean to go?'

'I must, I think. But I'll come back, Kathryn. From the ends of the earth I'll come back to you.'

'And we'll talk before you go?'

'Of course. I must speak to your mother. Go now, please, my dearest love.' He was aware of Morewood's rising wrath, liable momently to burst into speech that Kathryn must not hear.

She paused for a moment, irresolute, looking from one to the other, afraid to go, afraid to stay lest she make things worse. 'Papa —' She seldom called him this and it was in itself an appeal.

'Get out of this, you bitch! Or I might do something we will all regret.'

'Yes, please go, Kathryn,' put in Mark. 'We have to discuss this, man to man.'

'Man to milksop!' But Kathryn had turned reluctantly away and did not hear.

The two men stood for a moment in silence, watching her slight figure vanish among straggling shrubs. Mark purposely let the silence lengthen. He had not heard the rumour about the youth Morewood had killed, but knew him for a dangerous man, when drunk. The worst thing that could happen would be for it to come to a fight. He could give as good as he got, he knew, training and science making up for Morewood's bulk, but what could be more disastrous than to knock his future father-in-law down?

'I'm truly sorry, sir,' he said at last. 'We did not intend it, either of us. It just happened. I came back, you see, with the news of the fall of the Bastille. It's a great day for the rights of man, sir.' If he had hoped to ease the sit-

15

uation by turning the talk to general topics, he could not have picked a worse one.

'Rights of man, eh! Your right to debauch my daughter? Whippersnapper of a tutor! Always did think the boys would be better at school, learning to be men. Let myself be overridden by Lady Charlotte. Won't let that happen again. Mushroom, come-from-nowhere tutor fondling and fumbling our girl as if she was a drab from the gutter. Which she doubtless will be, by the time you are done with her.'

'That's no way to speak of Miss Pennam!' Mark was angry now.

'So it's Miss Pennam now, is it? Remembered your place, at last, did you? Too late for that, boy. Too late to say "sorry" like a puling girl. Only one thing for you to do. Get out of here. Now!' He moved a threatening step forward as if to drive the other man along the narrow cliff path that led, in the end, to Scarborough.

'You cannot be serious. I offered to go today, but — my things. And I must say goodbye to the boys, to Lady Charlotte, to Kathryn . . .'

'Oh, you must, must you?' Another step forward. 'Want another couple of kisses and a squeeze or two, do you? Well, you're not getting them, cully, and that's my last word. Oh

— never fret for your two shirts and your bag of shabby books. I'll have them sent after you, all right and tight. To the kennel we got you from. Just remind me where it is. Some backslum in London, was it not? Son of a bitch!'

'We'll leave my family out of this.' Mark lost his temper at last. 'But my birth is better than yours, as you well know. On that count, I have every right —'

'To seek Kathryn's hand,' he would have said, but he had caught the other man fatally on the raw. Morewood lashed out with his famous right, caught Mark entirely off his guard, and sent him headlong.

'That'll teach you!' He stood over him for a moment, breathing satisfaction. 'Come on then, don't lie there, faking it. Get up and take your punishment like a man.'

Not a word; not a motion. The young man lay still on the close turf, and Morewood, bending down, saw a slow trickle of blood from his temple, saw the sharp outcrop of rock that had caused the wound and knew a moment of absolute panic. 'Weatherby!' Sharply. 'Pull yourself together, man. Speak to me!' Nothing. He bent to fumble drunkenly for a pulse in the outflung wrist, felt nothing. A quick look about him, but the cliff top was deserted as always, the rise of the path each way sheltering it from distant view. He bent again over what he began horribly to fear was a body. Was there breath coming from the flaccid mouth? He did not think so. He could not let this happen. It had been bad enough when he killed that boy at the cock fight, but then there had been witnesses, friends to help him. Facing facts for once, he knew he had few friends now. And no witnesses, except Kathryn, who might tell a damning tale. 'Weatherby!' He turned the body over and felt it limp under his shaking hands. 'Weatherby!' Nothing. In the windy silence, he could hear the waves lashing the rocks below. A quick glance confirmed that it was high tide, the water deep against the cliff. No time for thinking. One desperate glance around and he bent, with something between an oath and a prayer, and rolled the helpless body to the cliff edge, and over. Done! He was safe. Another wild glance around. Still not a soul in sight. Now, to think of a story. He must be cool; he must be calm — sober. He turned to follow the cliff path, away from Scarborough, the walk he had meant to take. No problem about his story. Not the slightest need for anxiety. He had sent the young man about his business; told him to walk to Scarborough. Would the chit believe him? She must. He must make her. How?

Half an hour later he returned to the Hall by a path that took him in through the stable yard. His two sons were there, unsaddling their own ponies, a practice on which Mark Weatherby had always insisted, and grumbling as they did so. 'No need for that.' He suddenly felt a great longing for friends, for allies. 'Let the groom do it; it's his job, dammit.'

'But Mr. Weatherby says —' Jeremy, the younger, began the protest, but was cut short by his father.

'Be damned to Weatherby! And no need to be fretting about what he says any more. I've given him his marching orders.' With an attempt at a laugh. 'Sent him packing down the cliff path to Scarborough for an insolent dog of an upstart revolutionary. New world, indeed! Fall of the Bastille! I won't have such seditious nonsense talked in my house, and so I told him.'

'But, papa, who is going to teach us our lessons?' asked Roderick.

'You're going to school, boy, and not before time.' It had struck him that to take the boys south and enrol them in his old school against the autumn term would get him very comfortably away from any local talk there might be about Weatherby's sudden departure.

'School! Huzza! But will mother —'

'Yes, she will. I'll see to that.' He left them and strode into the house, feeling very much the master of the situation. The next question was, had the child told her mother? Sparing Lady Charlotte from upset when she had had one of her spasms or indeed at any time was such a family habit that he thought it safe enough to assume that Kathryn would have said nothing. After all, so far as she knew, there was no hurry about what was bound to be an uncomfortable revelation. He went straight to the room he called his study and sent for Kathryn.

'You wished to see me, sir?' The child was looking anxious, as well she might.

'Yes. I have a message for you. But, first, I trust you have had the good sense not to trouble your mother with this nonsense of yours.'

'Hardly nonsense, sir, but, no, I thought it would be time enough to discuss my engagement with my mother when she was feeling more the thing. But, sir, a message? — Mr. Weatherby has not returned with you?' She must have been on the lookout.

'Returned with me? I should rather think not. A blood-red revolutionary! I'm surprised at you, Kathryn, and on more counts than one, but least said soonest mended, after all. I'm glad you were wise enough not to go running to your mother. It's what Mr. Weatherby would wish, I am sure. Not that I care a damn for that. But the last thing he said to me was that though he would consider himself bound, you must be free as air. I'll give him credit for that,' he added, as if reluctantly.

'The last thing? What do you mean?'

'He's gone, child, and good riddance. If I had had any idea of the seditious nonsense he was talking, he'd have been gone long since. Rights of man indeed! Fall of the Bastille! I'm sending the boys to school as soon as I can, to get the nonsense knocked out of them, and if I were you, my girl, I'd set my mind to forgetting the young cub.' He raised a hand to quell her protest. 'But fair's fair; I told him I would deliver his message, and I will. He says he'll always love you. You're free, he's bound. Believe it if you like. Absence never made any heart I knew grow fonder, but maybe he's the exception. Oh,' casually, 'I asked for his promise that he would not get in touch with you for six months. He didn't like it, but I'm glad to say he recognised, in the end, how badly he had behaved to you, to us all, and gave me his word.'

'Six months! But, papa — And his things . . . You sent him away just like that? Walking?'

'Yes. I'm a little sorry now. I was angry

21

with him you see — rightly so. Making up to an innocent chit of sixteen! But we are not going to set that about the neighbourhood, for his sake as much as yours. You can see what harm it would do him as he makes the new start in the world that is to make him worthy of you.' Sardonically. 'So, it's as a revolutionary he's turned away, and that's all there is to it. And as for his precious things, I undertook to send them to London for him — to the Crown and Anchor, I'll have you know, that revolutionary meeting house. You may have the charge of packing them up, if you like. But no little love notes tucked inside the shaving kit. Do I have your word for that?'

'He's gone. Without saying goodbye?' She was finding it hard to believe the extent of her disaster.

'I told him it was that or fight me. Craven to the last, he went.' He knew that she would look on it in a totally different light.

'He'll be benighted.' It was only one of the host of protests that thronged her mind. 'It's miles to Scarborough. And that path's dangerous at night.'

'Don't be more of a fool than you are, girl. He'll stop soon enough when it begins to get dark. There's plenty of cottages will give a young man a bed for a night along the way, and taverns too, if he wants to drown his sorrows.' He was congratulating himself that she had already thought of the danger of the cliff path, his explanation if the body should be found, when she opened another problem.

'But — money?' she asked anxiously. 'He lives so carefully —' She could not bring herself to start thinking of Mark in the past tense, as having truly gone.

'I'm not a monster,' Morewood took refuge in bluster. 'Fool of a girl! Naturally I paid him his wages; turned off without a character, paid him to the end of the month, and a month over. It was all the cash I had on me.' He felt triumphantly that this gave a fine note of conviction to his tale and indeed she showed not the slightest sign of doubting it. Well, why should she? Why should anyone?

Nobody did. He had always known himself for a lucky man, and when no inconvenient body was washed ashore he was more sure of it than ever, and left to take the two boys south with a comfortable feeling of a great danger cleverly avoided. Lady Charlotte had created such a rumpus about the boys going to school that she totally failed to notice her daughter's pale cheeks and hollow eyes. Nobody knew what tears Kathryn shed as she packed up Mark's few possessions. She had given her word that she would not include a note, and she kept it. Only, at the last moment, she copied out a Shakespeare sonnet that she had read with Mark one day, a century ago it seemed. 'Let me not to the marriage of two minds . . .' He would understand the implicit promise.

And so she set herself to wait out the six months of enforced silence. August passed in a whirl of activity, since Morewood had arranged for his sons to begin at Harrow in the autumn and everything was to be prepared for them. Lady Charlotte was much too busy bewailing their going to do anything about the necessary apparatus of shirts and socks. As usual, the whole burden of the operation fell on Kathryn, and she was grateful for it.

2

If Kathryn had hoped to hear some casual word about Mark, she was disappointed. Nobody spoke of having seen him in Scarborough; nobody took any notice of his departure. The boys were too excited about their trip south and their school plans to miss him much, and it was only after they went in September that Lady Charlotte began to notice the gap in the family circle. Mark Weatherby had always been ready to make a fourth at whist when the vicar dined at the Hall, to read to her when her head troubled her, or do her errands in Scarborough. In some ways, Kathryn thought, her mother missed the tutor more than she did her sons. She certainly complained about his going as much if not more, which Kathryn, silent herself, found hard to bear.

But everything was hard to bear that slow autumn. For the first time, as the northeaster lashed the windows, and Lady Charlotte grumbled through her days, Kathryn was becoming aware of how isolated their life was at Windover Hall. The winter before had been the first one when she had been expected to join her mother in society, and she had been so happily occupied with Mark Weatherby and her studies that she had not noticed just how little society they actually had. Mr. Tench, the vicar, came faithfully for his dinner and game of cards once a fortnight; a few female friends called on Lady Charlotte when the weather was good, but all they talked about seemed to be servants, and fancy work, and the latest novel from the circulating library.

Kathryn's longing for news of the outside world became so great that she finally put it into words one day when her mother was complaining of being dull. 'You are quite right, mamma. We are moped here, you and I, for lack of company, now the boys are away. Nobody invites us, because we do not entertain. I remember, when I was a child, watching the guests arrive for one of your dinners, and coming down in my best dress for dessert. I remember how beautiful you looked, and the gentlemen clustering round you when they came in from their wine. You would still enjoy it, you know you would, and I would be delighted to make all the arrangements, so it need be no trouble to you. Did you hear Mr. Tench say the other day that Mr. Wilberforce is expected in Scarborough about some electioneering business? Would it not be civil to invite him, and a few friends to meet him?' She smiled. 'I remember how kind he was to me last time he came, talking as if I was a rational being. I liked him.'

'He's a good friend,' said Lady Charlotte. 'He would come, I think, if I were to ask him, but, Kathryn, who would give him the meeting? It's been so long — I don't rightly know — Besides, your father don't much care for that kind of entertaining. To tell truth,' she surprised her daughter by pulling herself bolt upright on her *chaise longue*, 'I have been quite in a worry about how I was to launch you in society, my love, and it has just this minute come to me what I should do. I shall take you to Scarborough next summer, for as much of the season there as I find I can afford. The bathing will do you good, I am sure. I think you have been growing again, my love, and you look pale with it. I shall tell Mr. Morewood that we must go for the sake of your health. I might even decide to bathe myself, if the weather should smile on us. Now is not that a delightful plan, dear child? Just you and I together, if your father does not choose to come.' They both knew that Oliver Morewood detested what he called the social flimflam of the summer season at Scarborough.

'It's a lovely idea, mamma.' What else could she say? 'But next summer is such a long time off.' She had quite other plans for next summer. 'It's now I am thinking about. Do let us have a party. It would be good for the servants too. They are getting idle and tiresome. Mr. Wilberforce and just a few friends, nothing elaborate. Just to get back in touch.'

'Oh, my poor pet,' said her mother. 'You don't understand. They wouldn't come.'

'Wouldn't come? What can you mean?'

Lady Charlotte's fingers writhed in the fringe of her shawl. 'We have to talk about this, you and I. You are a grown girl now, a young lady, and such a sensible child. We have to think what is best for you as well as everything else. Of course I would have wished to give a coming out ball for you, as my father did for me, here in the Hall. To launch you in society, to introduce you —'

'To some eligible young men?' Kathryn smiled at her mother. 'I'm very happy as I am, you know.' Was this the moment to tell her mother about her engagement? It had been on her conscience all autumn that she had not done so, but the moment had never seemed just right, and she had found, to her cost, that the longer a revelation is delayed, the more difficult it gets.

'But you shouldn't be,' said Lady Charlotte.

'And anyway, you're not, you know. Not happy at all. I'm your mother; how should I not notice that you are looking pulled and wan! Of course you need some young society, but don't be setting your heart on Mr. Wilberforce, I beg. He's quite the confirmed bachelor, they say, and must be thirty, if he's a day. And gives all his time to politics and good causes since he came down with those evangelical notions. But that's beside the point. The thing is . . .' She hesitated. 'Oh dear, what can I say? You must know, dear child, that your father has unluckily put up some backs among our neighbours. He's not just in the ordinary line, you know.'

'He most certainly is not,' said Kathryn. 'And not my father either. Let's be honest with each other, mamma, since we are talking about it at last. You are telling me that the neighbours won't come to the house because of my step-father?'

'I am afraid they are just a little prejudiced against him. You do see how difficult it makes everything.'

'Yes,' said Kathryn. 'Dear mamma, I do.'

Balked of a visit from Mr. Wilberforce, who might or might not have seen Mark in London, Kathryn had to resign herself to the total silence into which he had vanished. She knew him well enough to know that having given his word to her step-father, he would make no move towards getting in touch until the end of January, when the promised six months would be up. She had a little hoped that he might write a farewell note to her mother, perhaps after finding that Shakespeare sonnet among his things. When it had not come, she had told herself she should not have expected it. But January seemed an infinitely long way off. She threw herself into the studies he had directed. All her hopes were centred on the earliest possible marriage; she must prepare herself to be a useful companion to him in the political career on which she hoped he was now embarking. But in this, as in so much else she was inevitably frustrated by the isolation of Windover Hall. When she went into Scarborough to change her mother's book at the lending library and buy household necessities, she spent all her own pin money on the latest sheaf of political pamphlets to read what the world said about the extraordinary events in France. She would have liked to order her own newspaper, but her step-father, learning of this, put his foot down. He was not having her turn into a political bluestocking, he told her.

Without Mark, the literary studies she had enjoyed so much with him to guide her began to pall. She turned instead to the one subject in which she had always surpassed him. Soon after he had arrived at the Hall, he had discovered her natural aptitude for mathematics and had laughingly, but in all seriousness, handed over the boys' instruction in this field to her. Her step-father had told her, with some surprise, that their new masters at school had been astonished at their aptitude in this area. It had not pleased him in the least. 'Time I got rid of that young counter-jumper Weatherby! Turning them into a couple of banker's clerks!'

Kathryn had said nothing. To claim the credit — or discredit — would only turn his attention to her, and this was the last thing she wished to do. She had found him, once or twice that autumn, looking at her in a way she did not at all like.

Sally had noticed it too. 'Miss —' She was brushing Kathryn's hair. 'There's something I'd like to say to you, if you'll promise not to be angry with me.'

'When was I ever angry with you, Sally dear?'

'Not often, since you grew up and mastered that temper of yours. But it's you growing up frets me, miss. Since we've had to let all your gowns down at the hem and take them in at the waist this autumn, you're grown into quite a looker, and, to tell truth, that's something I never thought to see. There's something about you, these days, I can't put my finger on.' Their eyes met in the glass, and Kathryn found herself wondering, not for the first time, whether Sally, who knew her so well, had not recognised what had happened between her and Mark. But not having told her mother, she most certainly could not tell Sally. It was her secret, warm always at her heart as the slow months passed, and the day when his letter would come drew nearer. Then she would tell everyone. 'Something — what?' she asked now, considering herself in the gold-framed glass. Dark hair, brown eyes, wide forehead, high cheekbones, all just what she was used to, but pulled together somehow, grown coherent, a face to be reckoned with.

'You're not exactly a beauty, miss. I wouldn't say that,' said loving Sally. 'But you catch the eye, somehow. I'm just a little anxious lest you might have caught the master's.'

'Sally?' It was both question and rebuke.

'We've known each other a long time, Miss Kathryn. Long before you knew him. And an unlucky day that was for us all. Miss, what I'm making a mull of saying, is, try not to be alone with him, with the master.'

'But, Sally, how can I help it? You know, half the time my mother has her meals sent up? Of course I'm alone with Mr. Morewood.'

'That's not alone, miss. There's always servants to and fro at meals. Banks and I had a word a while ago, he's seeing to it you're well served.'

'Banks?' He had been butler at Windover Hall as long as she could remember.

'He remembers your father, miss. *And* your grandfather. He's not going to let anything unchancy happen to you if he can prevent it. They all love you in the servants' hall, don't ever forget it if you should find yourself in need of a bit of help. But there's places we can't go. They're the ones you want to stay out of when your step-pa is about.'

'But, Sally!'

'I know, miss, it's not a bit nice, and I'm sorry to have to tell you, but why do you think Bella left so sudden? And Nan. He comes up after you in passages, miss, and he's strong.'

'After you, Sally?' She had to ask it.

'Oh, yes, when I was younger, when he first came. I soon sent him to the rightabout.' Smiling. 'To tell truth, I bit him, hard. He didn't like that; left me alone after. But that was long ago, before the mistress took to her sofa. It's worse now.' They exchanged a long, silent glance. 'I wish you had friends you could go to, miss, for a while. Is there no one?'

'Not that I can think of. You know my

father's people stopped writing, years ago, after mother remarried.' I shall marry Mark, she thought, just as soon as possible, and get away. 'I will be careful, Sally, it's horrid, but I'll be careful, and I do thank you for warning me.'

The boys were to spend their Christmas holiday with Mr. Morewood's sister who was married to a clergyman in Brent. At the last moment their father announced that he was going to take what he described as 'a bolt to town' to see a little life and take a look in on his sons. 'I'll be putting up at Limmers,' he told his wife. 'Not at all the thing for you, but then I know you wouldn't fancy the journey at this time of year. It would be bound to make you ill. But I'll do any commissions for you,' he said handsomely. 'And for you, too, Kathryn. Any frills or furbelows you need? The latest thing in shoe roses, maybe? A touch of town bronze?'

And where would she wear them? She thanked him civilly, longing to ask him to bring her the latest pamphlets from London, but this would be almost as useless as to beg for news of Mark, which pride forbade. And it was not two months now until the end of January when Mark would feel free to write to her. She had discussed with herself, in the long watches of the night, whether he would feel he could write a couple of days ahead, so that she would get the letter on the anniversary of their parting, but knew in her heart that such an idea would never occur to him.

To her relief, and, she rather thought, her mother's, Mr. Morewood did not return until the middle of January, when he arrived unexpectedly, looking tired and jaded, and took at once to his bed, with what he described as an influenza.

'Burning the candle at both ends *and* the middle, if you ask me,' said Sally robustly. 'And what it all cost him I'd rather not think about. He had Stokes the bailiff in before he took to his bed, and Banks heard them going at it hammer and tongs. I doubt there will be more timber sold off the estate come spring.'

That afternoon Kathryn found her mother in tears. 'Oh, my poor darling, I don't know how to tell you —'

'Tell me what?' Kathryn had a moment of pure terror. Her step-father had brought bad news of Mark and left it to her mother to break it to her. Absurd, she told herself. But: 'What is it, mamma?' Her voice shook on the words.

'Oh, my poor pet, I don't know how to begin —'

'Just tell me, mother. Please —'

'It's our trip to Scarborough. I know how you have been looking forward to it, and now, I am afraid I shall not be able to afford it.'

'Is that all!' Kathryn could not conceal her relief. 'Of course I am sorry, mamma. I know you had been looking forward to it, too. But —' she went to the heart of the matter, 'what has happened? Why do you suddenly find you cannot afford it?' She knew the answer as she asked the question.

'It's your papa, my dear. I'm afraid he found his trip to London sadly expensive. Only think, he might not even have been able to get back to us if he had not found a most obliging lawyer in London who contrived to do something I do not quite understand about my portion.'

'Your jointure? Your little income? But, mamma, is it all gone?'

'Oh, no. He would never do such a thing to me. He says it was very inconvenient to him not to, and he had to leave ever so many tradesmen's bills unpaid, so tiresome, but he paid all his debts of honour, and half of my income remains untouched, and you know we can manage very well on that for what we need from day to day, but as for any hope of saving up for a holiday, which I had truly meant to start doing just as soon as Christmas

36

was over . . . Well, you can see, my poor love, that is quite out of the question now.'

'I do see. Never mind about Scarborough, but this is monstrous. You mean the money is gone for good?'

'I am afraid I did not find it quite easy to understand what your papa was telling me. He was so wretched about it, and wasn't feeling at all the thing because of this dreadful influenza.'

'I'll talk to him when he is better, mamma. This must be understood, and you must have some guarantee that it will not happen again next time he goes to London and risks his money — or yours — gambling at the clubs.'

'Oh, my dear, I do beg you will do no such thing. Why the very thought of it makes me feel quite unwell! Ring the bell, quick, love. I am afraid I am going to have one of my spasms.'

Oliver Morewood left his room for the first time the next day and joined Kathryn and her mother for an early dinner. He was putting himself out to be agreeable, Kathryn thought, making a point of describing the improvement school had made in the boys' behaviour and telling of his visits to the theatre, where, he said, Mrs. Jordan was carrying all before her, since her great rival, Mrs. Siddons, was refusing to act until Mr. Sheridan paid his Drury Lane actors their long overdue wages. It was so unlike him to provide his wife with the town gossip she loved that Kathryn was afraid to think how much his extravagance must have cost her. After a good deal of anxious thought, she had decided to leave remonstrating with him until she had heard from Mark. It would be easier with him behind her. And it should be very soon now. She was counting the days.

It had never for a moment occurred to her that there might not be a letter from Mark. But January moved wetly into February, day followed wretched day, and still none came. At first, she blamed the post, the weather, anything but Mark. Then, as the miserable days dragged by, she began to blame herself. She must have misunderstood what her step-father had said. There was no way in the world she could believe that Mark might not have been faithful to her. That almost wordless understanding had gone too deep for doubt. She was as sure of this as she was of anything. But was she sure of anything?

On a stormy mid-February morning she found her step-father alone in the breakfast room. She herself had breakfasted long since, and had been returning from her morning ride when one of the grooms rode into the stable yard with the mail bag he had picked up from

Scarborough, where the cross post from York arrived late in the evening. 'Anything for me, Ned?'

' 'Fraid not, miss.' Everyone knew she had been watching the post, everyone wondered about it, and everyone was sorry for her. It made nothing any easier.

She went straight to the breakfast parlour and found Oliver Morewood there, enjoying a convalescent feast of kidneys and bacon.

'Papa.' She always found it difficult to call him this, but knew he liked it. 'You did say Mr. Weatherby promised he would not write to me for six months?'

'Yes.' He poured himself more coffee. 'Oh.' He seemed to think about it. 'Time's up, is it?'

'At the end of January. You're sure there's not been a letter for me?'

'Hold hard, girl!' He looked at her angrily. 'I hope you are not suggesting I've suppressed it. Besides, how could I?'

It was perfectly true, as she had just proved by asking Ned for it. 'I'm sorry, but I'm getting so anxious. I know Mark would have written to me.'

'Mark is it?' he blustered. He had spent sleepless nights wondering what he would do when this moment came; suddenly made up his mind. 'Try for a little conduct, girl. Mark indeed! Mr. Weatherby gave me his word he would not write to you or get in touch in any way for six months. He gave me no promise that he would do so when the time was up. I warned you last summer that you were in a fair way to make a fool of yourself. Now I hope you will put your mind to forgetting all about Mr. Mark Weatherby and be properly grateful to me for keeping mum about the whole unlucky business. Least said, soonest mended, after all. I'd been letting myself hope that you had had the good sense to forget him as he seems to have you.'

'What do you mean? Did you see him in London? You've said nothing, so I thought —'

'Of course I've said nothing. Fool of a girl! And, no, I didn't see him, how should I meet a young nobody like him? But it did just happen that I heard his name spoken one day — somewhere I was . . . Let me think . . . Cocoa Tree? Coffee house? Yes, I think that was it. One near the General Post Office where we northerners sometimes meet waiting for our mail . . . I was reading the *Morning Chronicle,* passing the time, and I chanced to hear his name. "Mark Weatherby," someone said. "Saw him the other night, but with such a delightful bit of goods on his arm, I thought it best not to speak to him." I hadn't meant to tell you —'

'I don't believe it,' she interrupted him. 'Oh, there must be some mistake. Another Mark Weatherby —'

'They came from these parts, the men who were talking. The accent was enough to prove that.'

'You don't know them?'

'I'm afraid not.' He meant to keep as far removed from this piece of misinformation as he possibly could. But how should she ever prove it false? His luck had held. The body had never been found, and he had received no enquiries about Mark Weatherby's whereabouts, which confirmed his comfortable conviction that he was a young man without close family or friends. A couple of letters had come for him, and he had simply readdressed them to the Crown and Anchor Tavern where they were doubtless lying unclaimed along with Weatherby's possessions. If he could just put a stop to his step-daughter's inconvenient enquiries, he would be able to congratulate himself on a lucky escape from what might have been an awkward enough business. The girl needed distraction; well, she should have it. Indeed, it would be a pleasure. Being crossed in love, poor fool, seemed to suit her; she had grown into quite a little beauty this winter.

3

February dragged gloomily on, and still Kathryn would not believe it. They were one, she and Mark. With those few words, those two kisses, they had committed themselves once and for all. She knew it. And did not know it. Memory is a treacherous thing. Now, when she tried to recall that short, passionate scene on the cliff edge, it would not come clear for her. She even found it hard to remember Mark's face, the tones of his voice. Had it all been a dream, an illusion? And worst of all, if she, who had nothing to do but remember, found memory betraying her, how much more might not he have done so, busy as he must be making his way in the world?

'Such a delightful bit of goods.' Her stepfather's words echoed cruelly in her mind. What did she know about men? Perhaps they were all the same, all like Oliver Morewood. Her mother's conversation certainly suggested this, and such novels as she had read were hardly encouraging. There was Lord Orville, of course . . . But, Lovelace in *Clarissa Harlowe*, Mr. B. in *Pamela* . . . Mark thought nothing of novels. She was back to Mark again and where did that get her? If only she could talk to someone . . . Passionately, now, she wished that she had told her mother and Sally about her engagement. What engagement? She had not told them then; she most certainly would not do so now. There was nothing to tell. Just something to be got over as best she might. If he had forgotten her, then she must set herself to forgetting him.

But something in her cried out that this was all wrong. Mark was ill; he had met with an accident. How could she find out? She loved him with all her heart; knew so little about him. He was an only child, she knew; his father was dead, his mother had remarried, somewhere down on the Welsh border. He did not much like his step-father, they had shared an unspoken sympathy on this count. And the worst of it was that she did not know his mother's married name. If she had, would she have tried to find her? Ask her if all was well with Mark? She thought she would. Easy enough to think so when it was manifestly impossible.

Her thoughts went round and round like this, bitter, useless, unproductive. 'A delightful bit of goods.' Was that really all women were to men? I shall not marry. This was where the viciously spiralling thoughts always ended. I shall never marry. Not give myself up into the untrustable hands of any man. Did something, deep in her heart, suggest that this way, if by some miracle Mark should return, she would still be there for him?

Think ahead. In five years, less, four and a half, she would be twenty-one and inherit the two thousand pounds her unknown god-mother had surprised everyone by leaving her. Carefully invested, this should yield her a competence, and she had thought about investments. Mark had been surprised and a little amused at how seriously she thought about them. Oh dear God, she was back at Mark. Don't cry. Think about something else.

Obvious enough. How was she to get through the years until her twenty-first birthday freed her? She must plan for that freedom, for the new life that would follow. What would she do with it? Her life, her unmarried solitary life? Something useful, something with people in it. There were women, she knew, in London, leading lives of their own, or almost their own. Her step-father had made a slighting, casual reference to a group he called the blue-stockings. What he said about one of them, Hannah More, had caught her attention partly because Morewood had said she was a friend of Mr. Wilberforce. 'Can't think what he sees in her,' he had sneered. 'Little dab of a woman, calls herself missis, no more married than you are. No looks, no countenance, and behaves as if she were lord of creation. Lady?' he had added, surprising himself.

So far as Kathryn could make out, Hannah More had made her way with her pen alone. She had written poems, pamphlets, had plays put on at Drury Lane by her friend Mr. Garrick, and had moved as a result into the first circles of society. What she had done could surely be done again. But how? What weapon had she to use against the world? And could she afford to wait until she was twenty-one to leave Windover Hall? The tacit conspiracy of the servants and a good deal of evasive action on her own part had protected her so far from any actual molestation by her stepfather, but she was increasingly and unhappily aware of his eye on her. She had taken to studying in her mother's room, rather to Lady Charlotte's surprise. The trouble was that she got so much less done, and what but study would get her away from Windover?

'Beth is leaving, I'm afraid.' Sally was helping Kathryn dress, an office she insisted on combining with running the house.

'The new maid? That attractive child? I'm sorry.' Beth was from Sally's own village, a cousin of hers, and had come to the Hall as her protégée. 'Not — ?' She boggled at the question.

'I'm afraid so. He came to her room last night. She jumped out of the window. Lucky for us it was on the ground floor.'

'Oh, dear!' Their eyes met in mutual, admitted hopelessness. Oliver Morewood was absolute master of the household; there was no one to whom they could appeal against him. The idea of speaking to meek Mr. Tench was, simply, laughable. And there was no one else.

'It will be better, come spring,' said Sally, looking on the bright side. 'When he can ride in to Scarborough. There's a house he goes to there — several for all I know. But in the mean time — don't forget to bolt your door at night, miss.'

'Believe me, I won't.' The bolt had been part of the tacit conspiracy. Kathryn had found it on her door one day when she returned from one of the rare trips to Scarborough she had managed since Christmas. It was a heavy door, and a strong bolt, and she was glad of both, and of Sally's company when she went up to bed. Sally always stayed up to help her undress, and, downstairs, Banks equally waited to hand her her candle and wish her pleasant dreams. 'It's all very well to say it will be better, come spring.' She faced it.

'But does it mean I won't be able to walk in the gardens alone? Sally, it's intolerable. Do you think if I spoke to him — ?'

'Oh, miss, don't chance it. Or — in Lady Charlotte's room?'

'I think we have to leave my mother out of this.'

'I suppose so.' They both knew it would mean a spasm, or worse.

The sun came out at last. Jem returned from Scarborough with a pile of letters for Oliver Morewood and news from London. 'There's talk of a bill for reforming Parliament,' he told Kathryn, always eager for news. 'No, miss, nothing for you, I'm afraid.'

Something in the post put Morewood into a towering rage. After questioning Jem about the state of the road, he sent for his horse, announcing that he would ride to Scarborough. 'And spend the night there,' he told Lady Charlotte. 'Or, more like, several. Jem shall come too with my cloak bag.'

'Yes, Mr. Morewood.' Lady Charlotte never asked questions, and if it occurred to her that it was hard on Jem to have to do the ride to Scarborough three times in a day, she did not mention it.

When they had ridden away, the whole Hall seemed to breathe a sigh of relief. Lady Charlotte picked up Mrs. More's *Thoughts on the Importance of the Manners of the Great to General Society,* a tract that Kathryn had recently bought. It had been published anonymously the year before but everyone now knew its author and was amazed at her outspoken attack on the frivolous habits of the society that had welcomed her into its ranks. Since Lady Charlotte was not able to join in the dissipations of the élite, she was very much enjoying Mrs. More's attacks on them. 'Pour me a glass of ratafia, dear child,' she said to Kathryn, 'and run along into the garden. The sun is out at last and you should be making the most of it.'

It was good to be out. There was a shine of spring about the walled garden, green in the grass walks, a few violets budding under the neglected pear trees against the south-facing wall. If the fine weather lasted, they might be in bloom tomorrow and she would pick a few for her mother who had not been in the garden for years. Kathryn began to think hopeful thoughts; to plan. She must find help. She had faced it by now that she was not going to conquer London single-handed, but help must be there for her somewhere, if she could but think where to turn. She would ask her mother about her father's family. Now was a good moment, with her step-father away.

48

But her mother was discouraging. 'I never could like them, my love. To tell truth it was almost a relief when they cut the connection after I married Mr. Morewood. Your father's mother was long dead, you know, and his father an old Welsh tyrant if ever I met one. He liked my fortune well enough, but that was all there was to it. And as for the women — Miss Lavinia and Miss Janet — they thought me a shocking worldly little miss. My dress was cut too low for their starched notions, and I couldn't talk their kind of highfalutin' nonsense. A parcel of prosy bores! I can tell you a week was too long for me. When you were born next year Henry wanted me to call you Lavinia, ask your aunt to stand godmother, but for once in my life I refused him. I ask you, what use would they have been to you, two old tabbies stuck down at the end of nowhere?'

'And that is all the family?'

'All I know of. If they are still alive. You could write to them, I suppose, if you feel such a need to know your father's people.'

Kathryn had made her suggestion simply on the basis that she felt sad to be so entirely out of touch with the other side of her family, and it was hard now to see what she could do next, but she wrote down the address that her mother proudly dug out of an old and battered memorandum book. Suppose she wrote to the old ladies, and they were alive, and invited her to stay. The Welsh border; Mark's mother lived there somewhere . . . Was she hoping again?

If they had anticipated a long relief from Mr. Morewood's presence, they were disappointed. He came back next day in a worse temper than ever. It was remarkable how rapidly the word spread through the house.

'He's gone straight to Lady Charlotte's rooms.' A breathless maid had found Kathryn picking violets. 'Sally sent me; she says you're bound to be needed. The state he's come back in, she'll be in hysterics in no time.'

'Oh, dear!' Kathryn wiped damp hands on her skirts. 'I'll go at once. Put these in water for me, would you?'

She was relieved to find her mother merely crying quietly. 'Oh, Kathryn, thank goodness. Your papa wishes to speak with you.'

'With me?' Once again obstinate hope leapt and once again she quelled it.

'Yes, we have to talk business, you and I,' said Oliver Morewood.

'Business?' She did not at all like it, and it showed in her tone.

'Kathryn!' Her mother's voice was rising. 'Please . . . For my sake? We're in such trouble. Oh, I don't believe I can bear to hear it all again. I feel one of my spasms coming on; ring for Priss, Kathryn, quick! And my medicine!'

Inevitably, her maid was lurking outside, and Kathryn was sad and relieved to hand her mother over to her loving ministrations. Her own had been rejected since a fatal day when her mother had become aware that her apparently dutiful daughter suspected her of working herself up into the frightening spasms.

'We'd best go to my study,' said Oliver Morewood. 'Your mother has had as much as she can bear.'

He was obviously right, but Kathryn, ahead of him on the wide stair, was wryly aware of Banks busy doing nothing in the downstairs hall. Well, at least, entering on this unwelcome interview, she knew that if it should go wrong, the slightest sound from her would bring instant help.

Morewood closed the door behind him and handed her to a chair. She was actually more alarmed by his cool, unusual politeness. The crisis, whatever it was, must be serious indeed.

'I've been to Scarborough,' he said unnecessarily. 'To see my man of business.' He paused as if unsure how to go on.

'And how is Mr. Renshaw?' She had always liked the busy, friendly country attorney, who

51

had served the family for years.

'An idiot! A soft-spoken, smiling, mealy-mouthed idiot! I'm only sorry his stupid obstinacy forces me to trouble you, Kathryn.'

'How is that?' But as she asked it, she knew. Mr. Renshaw was trustee of her godmother's legacy to her.

'It's those damned London lawyers,' blustered Morewood. 'Promising what they could not perform. Making me sign things I should not have, did not rightly understand. I tell you, Kathryn, I had not the slightest intention of harming you; merely thought I was using your name as security; the least a daughter could do for her father; all to be right and tight years before your coming of age. And now they come down on me like — like the devils they are, demanding this, demanding that, threatening me with I don't know what . . . You have to help me, Kathryn, dear child, or we are all disgraced.'

'All of us?' She would not let him see how very much afraid she was.

'How would your mother feel if I were to be sent to prison, Kathryn? Answer me that! I still can't believe it, but Renshaw seems to think it a serious possibility if you refuse to help. I tell you, the shame of it would kill your mother.'

She was silent, gazing at him with large,

52

thoughtful eyes, trying to assess the situation. He had done something illegal about her legacy, and counted on her to stand his friend. And the worst of it was, she thought he might be right about her mother. Every instinct of her own shouted that this was the chance to get rid of Oliver Morewood, once and for all. But if the disgrace really were to kill her mother? She knew she could not risk it.

'Say something, Kathryn.' Morewood was getting impatient. 'Don't just sit there looking at me with those baby big eyes. Tell me I'm a fool, you've the right to. An honest fool who wanted to buy trinkets for his wife and daughter. But say you'll help me.' He was actually beginning to convince himself, she thought, and knew what she must say.

'I certainly don't say that I won't,' she told him. 'But first you must see that I have to go and talk to Mr. Renshaw myself, to learn precisely what this is about.'

'But I've told you! You're saying you don't believe me? Surely you know how much I have always been your friend, Kathryn. Think how faithfully I have kept that schoolgirl's secret of yours. Imagine the lamentations if your mother knew about that! You know how she is, Kathryn, how she suffers. We have to put our heads together to spare her any more anxiety.'

'If you feel like that, perhaps it is a pity that you did not speak to me first,' said Kathryn dryly.

'You're right, of course, but man and wife is one flesh you know. Only let us tell her that all is going to be well, that she won't see me led off by the constable to stand my trial at York Assizes, with all her friends looking on and condoling with her.'

'It could really come to that?'

'That's what Renshaw seems to think, damn him. I thought he would know a way of brushing me through without anyone's being the wiser. After all, what is one's attorney for but that? But he pulled long faces at me all morning and practically ordered me to come back here at once and speak to you. You're the one can save me, Kathryn, with a word, a stroke of the pen. Just to back me up.'

'And what will it cost me?'

'Why, nothing, nothing at all. There are years before your coming of age; plenty of time to see everything right for you. It is only to make a few economies, fell a few more trees. You know you can trust me, dear child.' He put a hand on her shoulder and she flinched away from his touch.

'It's too late today,' she said. 'I'll go and see Mr. Renshaw tomorrow.'

'Send for him to come here. No need for

you to be jauntering about the countryside, and the roads are too heavy still for the carriage.'

'I like the ride. And Mr. Renshaw is old enough to be my father. I would not dream of asking him to ride out here.' They both knew she wanted to be sure of seeing Renshaw alone, without risk of interruption.

'As you wish.' Carelessly. 'And you'll say something to comfort your mother? We don't want her making herself ill with anxiety.'

'No.' She was trapped, and knew it. She had as good as committed herself to backing him in whatever lies he had told. All her visit to Renshaw would achieve would be the exact knowledge of what Morewood had done to her. But that she must have. Time enough to think about it all later, when the immediate crisis was past. Because Morewood was right. Her mother simply would not survive her unpopular husband's appearance at the next York Assizes. She talked sometimes of happier years, when her first husband had been alive and they had gone to York for Race Week, and the Assize Ball, and she had been the belle of it. The contrast would surely kill her.

'My dear child.' Morewood had obviously been thinking along much the same lines. 'You shall never regret your goodness to me. I'll make it up to you, you see if I don't. The next time I go to town, you shall come too. Father and daughter, what could be more suitable? We'll find you a beau worth ten of that young milksop, Weatherby.' He was looming over her now, too close for comfort, bending for a 'paternal' embrace.

'No!' She whisked herself away from him. 'If I'm to help you, we'll have no flummery about it. We're not father and daughter, thank God, and you know perfectly well that anything I may find myself constrained to do for you, is done for my mother. I must go to her now.' She had made him angry again, she saw, and regretted it.

'Vixen!' He restrained himself with a visible effort. 'But you're right. Your mother comes first, now, as always. We'll talk again, you and I, when you have seen Renshaw, but remember, please, that the man has never liked me, always resented my coming into the family. You'll hear no good of me from him.'

'I do not expect to.' She regretted it when she saw him begin to turn purple, and got herself quickly out of the room.

'It's all gone?' She had listened to the attorney impassively, now broke in to make it easier for him.

'I am afraid so. I cannot begin to tell you how unhappy I am about this, Miss Pennam.'

'You don't need to. And what you are really trying to tell me is that even if I should resort to the law, I would ruin him, but would have no chance of recovering my fortune — such as it was.'

'Thank God for a woman who understands.' He had spent a wretched night in anticipation of this interview. 'You can't get blood from a stone, Miss Pennam. He was penniless when your mother married him. Worse. The estate had to pay off his debts. But what else could I do? If your grandfather had only left things differently. I did try to suggest to Lord Eskdale that he tie up the estate, set up a trust, but he was always sure he would have a son in the end, there would be no need. So when he died the estate came to Lady Charlotte absolutely. Well —' He paused. 'Your father was the soul of honour. He would not sell out, when he married your mother. He had no expectations of his own, said he must earn his living. And then that wretched war broke out in America. At least he let me write his will before he sailed. And again I suggested a trust, for the children, but he was young and very much in love. He said it would be an affront to Lady Charlotte. I think his family had rubbed him up the wrong way about the marriage, you know.' He felt he owed this grave young woman the whole story just because

57

of her admirable restraint. No tears, no hysterics. He thought of her mother for a moment. 'He wanted to show his entire confidence in Lady Charlotte,' he told her. And what a mistake that was. But they neither of them said it. 'I did my best, when she married Mr. Morewood, but she did not understand, and he would not help.'

'Of course not. So —' She summed up for him, surprising him again. 'My legacy is simply gone. My mother's income is halved?'

'He's very proud of that.' Renshaw allowed himself the dry comment.

'Boasts of it, does he? But, Mr. Renshaw, what will happen next time?'

He had thought about this too. 'There must not be a next time, or your mother will lose Windover Hall.'

'It's as bad as that?'

'Quite as bad. I am so very grateful to you, Miss Pennam, for taking this all with such calm good sense. It makes it possible for me to propose a plan of action . . .'

So he had expected hysterics. She smiled at him. 'Yes?'

'You agree to back his claim that he was in a position to act for you. But on conditions.'

'I see. Which would be?'

'A firm promise that the rest of Lady Charlotte's income remain untouched. And,

I'm sad to have to say it, but you know as well as I do that the boys must leave Harrow. For one thing the fees are quite beyond your mother's means as they now stand, and for another —' He paused, embarrassed.

'It's a pretext for Mr. Morewood to go south.' She said it for him. 'Poor boys. It will come hard on them.'

'Not so hard as to grow up to no inheritance.'

'No. But we must be realistic, Mr. Renshaw. My step-father will promise anything, today, to persuade me to save him from prison. And forget it tomorrow.'

'Yes.' He was more pleased with her than ever. 'So I have drawn up a paper for Mr. Morewood to sign. Here it is: a full admission of the crime he has committed, and the debt he owes you. Tell him, with my compliments, that he has only to come to me tomorrow and sign this in front of me and my clerk and his immediate troubles are over. Then he and I can draw up a plan for retrenchment that should at least safeguard the remainder of your mother's jointure. The boys will need a tutor of course.'

'I could teach them.'

'It wouldn't do, Miss Pennam.'

'I suppose not. Mr. Renshaw, I have to think of some way of earning my living.'

'But surely, an attractive young lady like

you — if you will allow an old friend the liberty of saying so?' And as he said it, she saw a cloud cross his face as he recognised the handicap she suffered in the marriage stakes. 'Your mother does not entertain much these days?'

'She does not entertain at all. People do not willingly come to meet my step-father.'

'No.' He thought about it. 'Have you no relatives, Miss Pennam? On your father's side? No, stupid of me, there are only the two ladies down at Ross.'

'Who could hardly launch me in society.' She said it for him. 'But that is no loss, Mr. Renshaw, because I do not mean to marry. That is why I have to think of some way of earning a respectable living, and would welcome your suggestions.'

'Mine?' He was totally at a loss.

'You're my only adviser. I could say my only friend only that it would sound like a shameless bid for sympathy.'

'I'd do anything to help you.' But he looked miserable, and she could not blame him.

'It's depressing, is it not, that the obvious alternatives for a girl in my position are to go as a governess or as an old lady's companion. Frankly, I'd rather die than do either.'

'You would set up as a school teacher then?' He named the only other possibility he could think of. 'I happen to know the two ladies who run the most genteel establishment here in Scarborough. I would be happy to mention you to them.' Once again that look of doubt clouded his face. 'Unless you think it might be better to go further afield?'

'Very much better. Besides, I do not wish to be a schoolmarm. I am hoping to make a living by my pen, Mr. Renshaw, and for that I think it will have to be London.'

'Miss Pennam!' He looked at her between pity and horror, and she got up to take her leave.

Morewood blustered and raged, and signed Renshaw's damning document. His wife had taken to her bed and his step-daughter had refused to enter into any further discussion after delivering her ultimatum. The boys were to stay at Harrow until the summer and Kathryn was sorry for this. Their presence would have provided some kind of buffer between her and Oliver Morewood. Inevitably, he blamed her for all his troubles, and she was beginning to find herself actually afraid of him. He sat longer and longer over his wine and the household kept out of his way as much as possible.

Kathryn always took a groom when she rode out now and never walked alone in the garden except when Morewood was away on one of the visits to Scarborough that were rare now that he was, as he put it, 'so damnably short of the ready'.

He went there one fine morning of late June, and the household breathed its usual sigh of relief. When she had finished her work for the day, Kathryn picked up her shawl and went gladly out to her favourite walk along the cliff top. This was where she came to think about Mark, and when she heard the sound of a horse being ridden rapidly along the path that led to Scarborough her first thought was of him. Perhaps, by some miracle . . .

The horseman came over the brow of the cliff, riding dangerously. Oliver Morewood. 'You?' He jumped from the saddle, strode over to where she stood, stock still with surprise.

Best not show fear. 'Yes.' She stood and faced him. 'We did not expect you back so soon.'

'I did not mean to come! It's all your fault, damn you! They say my credit's used up! I thought them my friends. Only a week until that scoundrel Renshaw doles out my own funds to me again. And they won't trust me! Call themselves friends. Bloody women! Won't trust me for three days.' As he loomed over her, she could smell spirits on his breath.

'You're a woman!' He made it sound like a discovery. 'Almost. Better than nothing. All your damned fault anyway. Bitch of a girl. Turning everyone against me. Wife won't let me into her room. Your mother.' He thought about that for a moment, reached out to grasp her shoulder. 'You owe it to me, for her, for everything.' He looked about him. 'Never did like this place. Never mind.' He was forcing her back and down with ungentle hands.

'No!' She remembered Sally, turned her head and bit him savagely.

4

Kathryn was still shaking, with fear, with anger, with relief, when she reached the house and found Sally looking for her. 'Mr. Renshaw is here, Miss Kathryn. He's with your mother, wants to see you too. Miss,' with a quick look, 'are you all right?'

'Yes, but I must change this gown.' It was torn. 'Tell my mother I'll be with her directly. She must not face more bad news alone.' It did not occur to her that it could be anything else.

But when she reached Lady Charlotte's room she found her beaming with joy. 'Such news, my dearest child. Such a thank as we owe kind Mr. Renshaw! And I have decided just what we are going to do with it. We are going to Scarborough, my love, for that season I promised you. Nothing is going to stop me!'

'But — I don't understand.' She turned to Mr. Renshaw. 'You have contrived to save something for us after all, sir?'

'Not precisely, Miss Pennam. I have been

confessing to your mother that I took a great liberty and bought a share in a lottery ticket in her name.' He paused, and Lady Charlotte broke in.

'And only think, dearest love, it has brought me in two hundred pounds. Just the kind of windfall sum one feels entitled to use as one pleases. And I mean to spend it on a trip to Scarborough for you and me. Mr. Renshaw has very kindly undertaken to hold the money for us and let us have it as we need it. And he is going to hire my usual lodgings for us. Can you be ready next week, dear child? Anything we need, you know, we can buy when we get there. Oh I don't know when a piece of news has done me such good!'

They had settled it all between them, and Kathryn could not find it in her heart to protest. Questions surged in her mind. Had Mr. Renshaw really bought the ticket or was it all a kind pretext to help her to the Scarborough season that was supposed to find her a husband? Intolerable thought. But what could she do? If the ticket was indeed a fiction, it was one her mother had gladly accepted. She could not question it any more than she could tell kind Mr. Renshaw how much she would rather have had the two hundred pounds for a start in life. Nothing for it but to say pretty things to him, and when he had gone, let her mother enjoy the planning of the trip. She had been glad to agree to the earliest possible date. At least it would get her away from Oliver Morewood, whom she had left, bleeding and speechless with rage, on the cliff.

'And I confess that I shall be glad of the chance to take the waters.'

Kathryn had been half listening to her mother's happy plans, but this phrase caught her attention. Dr. Forsyte thought the waters did Lady Charlotte good, but she disliked them and had most certainly never volunteered to take them before.

'Mother! Are you not feeling well?'

'Dear child, how could I be, after such scenes as I have been going through. You and Mr. Morewood just do not understand how I suffer from your brangling. It will do us both good to have a change of scene, but do you know I believe we will not tell your step-father about it until the very last minute!'

'An admirable idea. And I promise I will do my very best not to fall out with him in the mean time.' She could not help the note of bitterness, but luckily her mother had already plunged into a happy consideration of what new clothes she would need for Scarborough.

To Kathryn's silent relief, Oliver Morewood

did not come back to the Hall that night, arriving next day with a bandaged hand and a tale of being bitten by a savage dog. 'I shot it of course.' He spoke to his wife, his fulminating glance for Kathryn. But at least he now seemed to be avoiding her as much as she did him.

'The master's in a very strange state,' confided Sally. 'I'm truly glad you are going away, miss.'

'If only you could come too! But there is no one I can trust to manage things here at the Hall as I can you.'

'That you can, miss. And Priss will look after you well enough, I am sure, so long as Lady Charlotte keeps well.'

It reminded Kathryn of her anxiety. 'Is Priss worried about my mother, Sally?'

'A little, I think. She keeps herself to herself, does Priss, but she did say something made me wonder. About Dr. Forsyte being sure to call when he heard Lady Charlotte had come to town.'

'So he will,' said Kathryn relieved. 'Much better than sending for him and putting her into a fret.'

Kathryn had meant to break the news of their trip to her step-father the day before they left, and had not been looking forward to it, but he got wind of it the day before that. Kathryn, summoned by a frightened maid, arrived to find her mother hovering between spasms and hysteria, with her husband looming furiously over her. 'What's this I hear?' He turned on Kathryn. 'A trip to Scarborough and I am not even consulted! What kind of a household is this?'

'A very ill-conducted one.' Kathryn looked him in the eye. 'But let us not go into that, Mr. Morewood. The thing now is that my mother has been so fortunate as to win a prize in the lottery, and proposes to treat herself to a rest and change, and the waters in Scarborough, which you know always do her good. She certainly needs it now.' Priss was bending over Lady Charlotte with the smelling salts. 'Is your hand better, where the dog bit it?' With a very straight look. 'I am glad that you have suffered no ill effects from it — so far.' It was the first time that the scene on the cliff had been referred to between them, and she meant it to be the last.

'Not the least in the world.' He recognised the quiet threat. 'I'm delighted to hear about the lottery, of course.' With an effort to be agreeable. 'How much did your mother win?'

'Not enough.' It was all she meant to say.

The sun shone. Lady Charlotte's favourite lodgings on the cliff had proved to be vacant, and the landlady had an obsequious welcome for an old and valued client who had not, as she put it, 'honoured them enough with her presence of late'. There was a huge bouquet of flowers from Mr. Renshaw in their sea-view drawing room, and a note awaiting them to say that Dr. Forsyte would give himself the pleasure of calling next day.

'Very civil of him.' Lady Charlotte was in a mood to be pleased with everything.

'Yes, indeed.' But it made Kathryn just a little more anxious.

They had decided to spend a few quiet days in refurbishing their wardrobes before they made their first appearance in the Rooms, where they had heard that company was still thin so early in the season. Miss Jones the dressmaker confirmed this when she arrived next morning to check their measurements. 'Just as well I came,' she told Kathryn as she left, burdened down with bandboxes. 'Your mother has lost a deal of weight since I last made for her. I'm taking these gowns for alteration. It wouldn't at all suit me to have her wearing them as they are.'

'I suppose not.' Kathryn was very glad indeed when Dr. Forsyte paid his promised call, and made a point of walking downstairs with him when he took his leave. Yes, he said, Lady Charlotte should certainly take the waters, but begin gently and increase the dose day by day. And, no, he would not at all recommend that she bathe. 'I would not advise such a shock to the system. I will send round a draught for you to take the night before you begin bathing, Miss Pennam, but you must not think of letting your mother.'

'Dr. Forsyte,' she stopped to face him in the downstairs hall, 'is there something seriously wrong with my mother?'

'I sincerely hope not, my dear, but I must tell you that I am not quite happy about her condition. The nervous spasms to which she is liable place a considerable strain on the heart. I am afraid it is beginning to take its toll. I am more relieved than I can say that you have been able to bring her here for some peace and quiet. She tells me that you mean to stay for several weeks, and I am glad of it.'

'Is there anything we should do, or not do?'

'Just keep her calm and cheerful, Miss Pennam, that's all. No bathing. No shocks of any kind.'

He left Kathryn facing up to the new anxiety. Had she been hoping just a little that there might be some of the two hundred pounds left over after this trip? If she had, she gave up the idea. They would stay until the last penny was spent. But then they must go back to Windover Hall, to Oliver More-wood, and inevitably, more spasms, and the risk she now knew that they carried. She surprised Mr. Renshaw with a visit next day and told him bluntly what the doctor had said. 'What am I to do, Mr. Renshaw?'

He was surprised and touched by the appeal and gave it a serious moment's thought. Then, 'Marry,' he said. 'It takes a man to deal with a man. And not, I am afraid, one in my way of life. A son-in-law; a young man in a position of authority, of power, might be able to exert some kind of control over Mr. Morewood. And of course you would have a house of your own, could have your mother to stay . . . The trouble is,' with a very straight look, 'that I have tried in vain to persuade Lady Charlotte to make a will.'

'I see.' They exchanged a long look, sharing the knowledge that Morewood might feel he stood to gain by his wife's death. 'Thank you for telling me that, Mr. Renshaw.'

Kathryn bathed for the first time at seven next morning, and very cold the water was. 'But exhilarating,' she told her mother, joining her in the pump room. 'I think I shall indulge myself in a ride on the sands later on, if you can spare me.'

'Of course, dear child. This is to be your

holiday just as much as mine.' She drained the last drop from her glass. 'I declare it is nastier than ever! What a blessing Dr. Forsyte says I am not to take too much of the horrid stuff at first. Shall we go back to our lodgings now? I met dear Lady Rampton as I came in and she positively urged me to pay her a visit. She says the place is deplorably thin of company and it will be a miracle if we find partners for you at the dressed ball. But at least I am sure of my party at cards. Such a comfort to have found an old friend.'

Had it also been a comfort to find that the old friend did not intend to cut the connection? Kathryn rather thought so, and thought too that they must be grateful for the dearth of society that made Lady Rampton welcome her friend, despite the fact of her friend's husband. She wished that she did not also remember Lady Rampton as someone who liked to play high.

'I warned Clarissa she would find me sadly out of practice,' Lady Charlotte's next remark suggested that she had been thinking on similar lines. 'The vicar is a good enough sort of a man but no one could say he was a challenging player.'

'No.' It gave Kathryn the opening she wanted. 'So I do hope you warned Lady Rampton that you would play only for small stakes, mamma.'

'Oh, my dear, how could I seem so shabby? It would quite spoil her pleasure. And you know it will be only a few days before I get my old skill back. Who knows? I may end up by winning enough to extend our stay.'

Kathryn, remembering the past, thought this unlikely, but no good would come of prolonging the discussion in this public place.

She returned from her ride to find her mother just back from visiting Lady Rampton and full of Spa news. 'Only think, Mrs. Milbanke is here with that little niece of hers she dotes on so. She's a Noel, you know, and her husband is heir to Sir Ralph Milbanke. He is in Durham, busy about the elections, but he visits her when he can, and of course she is always surrounded by young men of the very first stare. Did you see her on the sands perhaps? Clarissa says she rides out for two hours every morning with quite a little band of cavaliers.'

'I think I must have.' Kathryn decided not to mention that they had passed her at a gallop with an inconsiderate flurry of sand.

'It would be beyond anything if she were to welcome you into her set,' said Lady Charlotte. 'Clarissa half promised that she would try to present us. It is the most unfortunate thing that I have never met Judith Milbanke, though your dear father was on the best of terms with her father-in-law. But then, Clarissa says there is not much love lost there. Though it seems Sir Ralph is helping to pay his son's election expenses, which are bound to be considerable. Do you know, my dear, I quite think that if Miss Jones brings our gowns home we should change our plans and attend the undressed evening tonight. Clarissa is desperate for a fourth at whist, and I believe Judith Milbanke is a great card player too. Clarissa says there is often a little dancing on these evenings; very casual, you know. Quite the thing for you to make your début.'

Kathryn, who was looking forward to this début with very mixed feelings, was wondering whether to protest at the change of plan, when her mother clinched the matter. 'I promised Clarissa that we would pick her up in our carriage, since she has not brought her own. Some little difficulty with her husband, I understand, who did not choose to come. Clarissa was most grateful for my offer.'

But Lady Rampton had bad news for her friend. She came out with it at once, meaning to have any unpleasantness over with before they reached the Rooms. 'I am so very sorry, my dearest Charlotte.' She spread her skirts comfortably and Kathryn, sitting bodkin between her and her mother, tried to shrink into half her size. 'I am afraid I have bad news.

I did contrive a word with Judith Milbanke, but I am afraid she had heard some sad tales about that husband of yours. No use beating about the bush between old friends like you and me, my dear. I thought you and the child would like it best if I came right out with it. Nothing in the world to do with you two, of course, but she says she has most absolutely to be Caesar's wife. For her husband's sake, naturally. He must not be associated with any kind of shabby business. As a Member of Parliament, you know, up for re-election.' There was an awkward little silence and she plunged on, hoping to make things better. 'It makes no difference between you and me, of course, Charlotte dear. I told Mrs. Milbanke so, and she said she respected me for it. As a childhood friend, you know. So that is all right. And she tells me there are some very good sort of people here. Bankers . . . that kind of thing. From Hull perhaps?' She pronounced the word with a faint hint of distaste. 'I don't think I ever met anyone from Hull, but I believe it is a very thriving prosperous sort of place. Anyway, she said she was sure there would be plenty of charming partners for you, dear child, without her exerting herself, which you will quite understand she feels she cannot do, granted your unfortunate connection. And here we are.' With obvious relief. 'Such a commodious carriage! I do hope I have not been inconveniencing you, child.'

But Kathryn was too angry to speak, which was perhaps as well. It made her even angrier to see how meekly her mother took her old friend's snub. She had never gone with Lady Charlotte to the Rooms before, having been left at home as too young the last time her mother had been able to afford the season. It did not need Lady Rampton's whisper to identify Judith Milbanke as the morning's inconsiderate rider. Resplendent now in half dress and pearls, she was holding court in the centre of the first room, while the musicians tuned up for the dancing next door. Every unattached young man was hopefully gathered round her. It was obvious that to be cut by Mrs. Milbanke was to be cut with a vengeance. Kathryn was resigning herself to an evening spent watching her mother at cards when she saw Mr. Renshaw enter the room piloting a tall, frail old lady hung about with diamonds.

'Good gracious.' Lady Rampton had seen them too. 'What a display! And on an undressed night, too. My dear,' to Lady Charlotte, 'is not that your man of business? Can he be meaning to present her to you? That figure of fun? Because, if so, you will excuse me. Join me in the card room, pray.' She turned away just as Mr. Renshaw joined them.

'Lady Charlotte.' With a low bow. 'And Miss Pennam. Welcome to Scarborough. I am so pleased to find you here tonight. May I have the honour of presenting Mrs. Comyn and her son Mr. Thomas Comyn.'

Kathryn had not connected the young man with the other two before, since he had hung somewhat back from them in the crowd. Now, as the first civilities were exchanged, she had a chance to study him. As tall as his mother, he was more broadly built, with fair hair and a fresh face somewhat marred by a small, anxious frown. He was taking her hand now, in a firm grip, as Renshaw introduced him. 'It is not often my young friend can be persuaded to leave his bank,' Renshaw said. 'You probably do not know, Miss Pennam, why should you, but Comyn's Bank is the oldest and most respected house in Hull. A very heavy responsibility to inherit so young.' He turned to Mrs. Comyn. 'But too good a son, ma'am, to allow his mother to take the waters unaccompanied.'

'I should think not.' She had been considering Kathryn through her lorgnette, now seemed to come to a conclusion and turned to Lady Charlotte. 'Mr. Renshaw gives you a great name as a whist player, ma'am. Shall we leave the young people to their dancing — I hear them striking up for the cotillion in the next room — and see if he can find us a fourth?' She took Lady Charlotte's arm as she spoke and began to steer her gently but firmly towards the card room.

'Will you do me the honour?' The young banker was bowing over Kathryn's hand.

'Thank you.' Curtseying. Her mother would probably think a banker from Hull a sad comedown for Lord Eskdale's grand-daughter, but she found herself liking the look of this anxious young man. And at least he did something in life, unlike most of the beaux who surrounded Judith Milbanke. 'With plea-sure.' She accepted the outstretched hand and let Thomas Comyn lead her to the next room where the sets were now forming. One of her many thoughts was a hope that at least Mr. Renshaw and Mrs. Comyn might play for more reasonable stakes than Lady Rampton.

She had never danced in a public place be-fore and was occupied for a while in watching her steps, keeping an anxious eye on Judith Milbanke at the head of the set and doing as she did. To her relief, her partner shared her concentration, explaining at the end of a fig-ure, when they paused for a moment side by side: 'Forgive me, Miss Pennam. I have never been here before. I would not wish to disgrace you.' His frank, engaging smile smoothed away the frown.

She smiled back. 'Why, no more have I!

I have been watching Mrs. Milbanke as best I might and hoping not to shame you.'

'And I her partner.' With a laugh. 'What a comfort to be newcomers together. Our assemblies at Hull are not on this scale at all. We are a city of plain people, Miss Pennam, and proud of it. Hard workers too. I am afraid I am more at home in my shop than in the ball room.'

'Your shop?' She could not help liking him for the frank admission of trade.

'My counting house, I should say. My mother won't have me call it my shop, but I like plain speaking. My father always called it the shop. And my mother never contradicted him! Nobody did.' Something changed in his face. 'He was a great man, my father, in his own way. He started in general trade, you know, was one of the first to see the possibilities of banking. His notes were accepted from the Baltic to the Mediterranean. There was near panic in Hull when he died so suddenly last year. I have been hard put to it to take the reins into my hands. My father never talked about the business, you see. Fortunately I have a perfect trump of a chief clerk, or I am not sure I would have dared to take this little holiday, even though my mother needed it so badly.'

'Your mother is not well? I am so sorry.'

'An affliction of the nerves merely. My father's death was a terrible shock to her. I was away at the time, just gone up to Cambridge. Of course I came home at once. To tell you the truth, Miss Pennam, I was glad to. They seemed an idle enough set of fellows there.'

'So you never went back?'

'Quite impossible. This is the first time we have been away, my mother and I, since it happened, and I confess I shall be glad to get back, though Scarborough strikes me as a pleasant enough sort of place. Do you ride, Miss Pennam? May I hope to see you on the sands in the morning?' They had exchanged these sentences, piecemeal, as they mastered the intricacies of the dance. Now, as it ended, he breathed a sigh of relief. 'May I find you some refreshment, Miss Pennam? I think we have done very well for a couple of beginners, do not you?'

'Extremely well.' Impossible not to like this forthright young man. 'And, yes, I think I have earned a glass of lemonade. Would you be so very good as to take me to the card room? My mother is not in the strongest health either.'

But they found Lady Charlotte in high spirits. The cards were going her way and she did not at all wish to be distracted by her daughter.

5

Lady Charlotte ate a hearty breakfast. She had won six guineas at Crown Whist, which almost made up for the shock she had suffered when she reached the card room and saw her dear friend Lady Rampton already established at a table with three other players. 'Calls to me across the room, cool as you please, to say she had quite given me up. And had made other arrangements for getting home!'

'Well,' Kathryn poured chocolate for them both, 'we should be grateful for that really, since she was obviously meaning to stay until all hours, and you know you were glad to come away when you did.' It had worried her more than she liked to admit to see her mother, so obviously enjoying herself, turn suddenly white with fatigue. Luckily she and Thomas Comyn had just returned from the second dance she had allowed him and she had been deeply grateful for his swift understanding and practical help in calling the carriage and seeing them into it.

'Just what I would have done for my own mother.' He had shrugged away her thanks. 'I have to thank you for a very pleasant evening, Miss Pennam, and hope I shall see you on the sands in the morning.'

'If my mother is well enough to be left.'

Lady Charlotte had decided to spare herself the waters and take a quiet morning, but insisted that Kathryn keep what she described as her engagement. 'A very good sort of young man, I thought, and rich as whoever it was. Mr. Renshaw told me a little about them. The father was nobody of course. Built up the bank from nothing, made a fortune and married well; she is some kind of a connection of the Howards. Remote enough, I imagine, though you'd not think so to hear her speak of them. Now, off you go, child, and enjoy yourself. What a fortunate thing we brought Ned with us and he can escort you. I would not want that cat Judith Milbanke to be able to say you were not properly chaperoned.'

'I doubt if she has even noticed I exist.' Kathryn picked up her plumed hat.

She found Mr. Comyn waiting for her at the riding stables by the sands and it was pleasant to see his face light up at sight of her. 'You were able to come, Miss Pennam, which has to mean that your mother is feeling more the thing today. I am so very glad. Now, we have a little problem about horses, which I hope you are going to let me settle for you. I did not like to take the liberty without your approval, but I found your man having a few words with the proprietor here. It seems Mrs. Milbanke and her party have taken the horse you asked for, and there is nothing but a perfect slug for you. I hope you will let me intervene on your behalf; it's monstrous how a lady on her own is always taken advantage of.'

'It's true, miss.' Ned was looking sour as curd in the background. 'You might as well ride your mother's sofa, but they wouldn't listen to me nohow. I was here first too! They just took Firefly from under my nose. Wouldn't listen to a word. What Mrs. Milbanke wants, she gets. It's either not to ride at all, or to let the gentleman speak for you.' Ned's tone told her that he had inspected and approved Thomas Comyn.

It was a bright, breezy, sunny morning. Intolerable to be deprived of her ride by Judith Milbanke. She smiled at Thomas Comyn. 'It's most kind of you. If you think a word from you will really settle the matter.'

'Oh, yes.' He vanished into the yard and returned a few minutes later with the proprietor himself leading a handsome bay and profuse in apologies. A total mistake . . . most certainly would not happen again . . . Miss Pennam had only to decide which suited her best, Sultan here, or Firefly, and the horse should be reserved for her for the rest of her stay, which he sincerely hoped would be a long one.

'Well, you certainly are a worker of miracles.' Kathryn smiled at Comyn as he helped her mount, showing a toughness of muscle she had not expected.

'Miracles are my business.' He vaulted into the saddle and they set out at a brisk trot across the sands.

It was pleasant to ride with a companion other than silent Ned. Pleasant too that, like her, Comyn was an enthusiastic rider and happy not to talk too much.

'Do you ride much in Hull?' she asked as they slowed to rest the horses after an invigorating gallop along the water's edge.

'On business, mostly. To see clients of the bank, you know; that kind of thing. Hull streets are no place for a carriage. You wait till you see the High Street where we live, it's nothing but a narrow lane.' He spoke as if he expected her to do so. 'But I have a little place my father bought upriver on the Humber. I like to go there now and then for a few days, to fish and ride and get the cobwebs out of my hair. Not a mansion at all,' he hastened to explain. 'Just a pleasant farm-house that was going to ruin for lack of an owner. My father enjoyed putting it in order and I treat myself to a weekend there from time to time. I'm lucky in my chief clerk, who can really run the business better than I, though I wouldn't dream of telling him so.'

'He's been with it a long time?'

'Oh yes, for ever. My father was thinking of making him a partner before he died, and I expect I will in the end, but one thing at a time, you know; one has to take things slowly when one comes in as such a tyro as I did. My father never told me about the business.' He had said this the night before, and again it puzzled her. What had been wrong between him and his father? Something, she was sure.

'I was always away, you see.' He leaned forward to pat his horse's head. 'Harrow and Cambridge. Father meant me to be a gentle-man.'

'But you are.' And then, horrified, 'Forgive me!'

'On the contrary: thank you. But Mrs. Milbanke wouldn't say so, and I expect your mother has her doubts. But what I am trying to say, Miss Pennam, is that if there has to be a choice I'd rather be a good banker than ever so fine a gentleman. Bankers are some use in the world.'

'I do so agree with you.' They returned to the stables in great charity with each other. But that night Kathryn dreamed, all night long, of Mark Weatherby.

Sure of a partner for the first two dances, and more than satisfied with the new gown Miss Jones had brought home the day before, Kathryn found herself actually looking forward to the dressed evening at Mr. Newstead's Rooms. Her mother was feeling better and had resumed taking the waters, and she herself was increasingly enjoying her morning rides on Sultan, with young Mr. Comyn in attendance. She was honestly interested in hearing about the problems he had encountered in taking over the bank, and he was delighted to have so perceptive a listener. But she did find herself wondering, more and more, why his father had sent him off to school, to be miserable, instead of training him in the ways of the bank he would inherit.

Rather to her surprise, Lady Charlotte and Mrs. Comyn seemed to have taken to each other too. They shared a dislike of the waters, but drank them in amicable distaste, and when Lady Charlotte learned that this was in fact Mrs. Comyn's first visit to Scarborough she was delighted to act as guide and adviser. And then, the Comyns' carriage was a miracle of modern comfort and it soon became the accepted thing that any excursion was made in it rather than her own stately but shabby vehicle. Busy with her new friend, she took Lady Rampton's continued defection with more philosophy than Kathryn had feared. 'I understand she plays for the most frightful stakes,' she confided. 'And a very sharp group of players too. I am very well as I am.' She went on winning more than she lost, and was very well satisfied with a companion in Mrs. Comyn who treated her with what Kathryn thought almost toad-eating respect.

This was not true of her son. One of the things that Kathryn increasingly liked about Thomas Comyn was his comfortable certainty that he was quite as good as the next man. Not better, just as good. He would never assert himself, but he would never give meekly in either. In any situation, he knew precisely how to get value for his money. When the four of them drove out together in his luxurious carriage to explore the beauties of the surrounding countryside, they always found an elegant nuncheon awaiting them, ordered in advance at some well-chosen hostelry, a rustic dinner at Hackness for a look at Lady Hilda's ruined nunnery, or a more lavish meal of local mutton and fish at Filey. Lady Charlotte loved the feeling of being looked after and even

Kathryn had to admit that she found it remarkably pleasant.

The best of everything,' sighed Lady Charlotte when they returned from Oliver's Mount. 'What a delightful young man.'

'Yes, but mamma, is it right to let him stand the shot like this, wherever we go? What in the world can we do in exchange? We can hardly invite him and his mother to Windover Hall, with things as they are there.'

'No,' said Lady Charlotte. 'But why should we do such a thing? Pray do not forget, dear child, that being seen with us gives them a consequence to which they could not otherwise possibly aspire. Do you know, I really believe Lady Rampton is beginning to think of asking to have them presented to her.'

'Is she so?' This was unwelcome news to Kathryn.

'Did I forget to tell you? She came slap up to me in the pump room this morning, just after dear Mrs. Comyn had left me, as friendly as could be. Her friends are leaving Scarborough today, she very much hopes to see us at the dressed ball tonight. It was just a little awkward, I am afraid. I had to explain that we no longer use our own carriage to go to the Rooms.'

'You mean that she had the effrontery to ask us to pick her up?'

'Not precisely ask, dear child, she's too much the lady for that, but she did contrive to make it clear that she would find it convenient.'

'I hope you made it equally clear that we could not!'

'So awkward,' sighed her mother. 'And, you see, she has lost her whist four too. I was truly sorry to have to tell her I was promised to Mrs. Comyn.'

'I am delighted you did.' Not that anything, she thought, would ever make her like Mrs. Comyn, but that was something else again.

'Well, of course. A lady's word must be her bond. But I do a little wonder what will happen tonight.'

Whatever happened, Kathryn had the comfort of knowing she looked her best after a series of battles with Miss Jones over what a young lady should wear for her full dress début. She had insisted on muslin rather than silk and a becoming fall of curls rather than the hideously high heads that were all the rage. No ship in full sail for her. The results had satisfied even Miss Jones who had surprised them by coming to assist at their toilette.

'She never did that before,' said Lady Charlotte, making her rustling way downstairs. 'Now, I wonder . . .'

Mrs. Comyn was formidable in grey satin

and even more diamonds than the first time they had met, but Kathryn was delighted to find that her son was as plainly as he was perfectly dressed. A series of mutual compliments got them to the Rooms where they found such a stream of carriages blocking Long-Room Street that the musicians were already striking up for the first dance when they entered.

'Don't you two young things stay for us old people,' said Mrs. Comyn, unusually bland tonight, Kathryn thought. 'We'll make our own way to the card room, will we not, dearest Lady Charlotte? You children must not lose your place in the set.'

Kathryn was glad that they had come twice already to the more casual undressed evening, once here and once in Mr. Donner's rival establishment down the street. She no longer felt the complete newcomer as they joined the set; she knew the form, she knew quite a few faces, received smiles and bows, and had a comfortable certainty that she would not need to spend much time tonight watching her mother at the card table.

Thomas Comyn, too, had been making friends, and they had to pause several times on the way to the dance floor for a passing word, an introduction, a request for a dance. Judith Milbanke was at the top of the set as usual, partnered by a smart young officer from the small garrison at the castle, but Kathryn was a quick learner, she no longer felt the need to watch her every movement.

'Do you know,' Thomas Comyn took her hand for the prescribed moment as they moved up the set, 'I am actually enjoying myself.' And then, shocked at what he had said: 'Forgive me! I meant to say —'

'I know just what you mean.' She smiled at him as they parted. 'And so am I!'

'I feel quite an old hand,' he told her as, the dance ended, they moved by mutual consent in the direction of the card room.

A surprise awaited them on the way. Judith Milbanke had left her military partner and now approached them on the arm of a handsome, confident-looking young man a few years her senior. 'It's Comyn, is it not?' He held out a friendly hand. 'I was so very sorry to hear of your father's death last year. May I make you known to my wife, who has an apology, I believe, for your charming partner.'

'I'm quite ashamed of myself,' said Judith Milbanke, the introductions completed. 'I had no idea in the world that that rascal at the stables had given us your mount, Miss Pennam. You will forgive me, I hope.'

Kathryn could only blush and acknowledge, angry with herself that she could not equal Comyn's coolness in the face of this outbreak of aristocratic patronage.

When they parted after the exchange of a few more civilities, Comyn smiled down at her. 'My mother will be pleased,' he told her. 'She sets rather more store by these social niceties than I do. Well, across the counter in my shop there's not much distinction between a lord's son and a sugar baker's. It's their credit I care about, and the sugar baker's is often the better. Will you be affronted, Miss Pennam, if I tell you I suspect that apology of Mrs. Milbanke's owes more to her husband's election expenses than to your charms?'

She laughed. 'Not in the least in the world, but should you tell me so?'

'I want to tell you everything, Miss Pennam.'

She gave him a quick, startled look. This was going very much too fast for her, and, besides, she did not believe him. But they had reached the card room, where she was disconcerted to see that Lady Rampton had replaced one of the members of her mother's four.

Lady Charlotte was in tremendous spirits. 'I told you all I needed was a little practice, did I not, dear child? Mrs. Comyn and I are in a fair way to make our fortunes tonight.'

After those few words with the Milbankes,

Kathryn found herself thronged with potential partners. Impossible not to enjoy it, but irritating to know the reason.

'You are quite the belle of the ball,' said Thomas Comyn, who had applied too late to take her down to tea.

'Now I have been officially approved, thanks to you.'

'But you were always the most beautiful woman here, Miss Pennam. And the most elegantly dressed. Even my mother —' He paused, blushing crimson, and she found herself liking him very much. But she was glad, just the same, to be handed down to the refreshment room by a handsome young military rattle from York, who entertained her with tales of all the battles at which he wished he had been present. 'These times of peace are death to a man's ambition, Miss Pennam. I just hope we'll get a chance to teach those revolutionary dogs of Frenchmen the lesson they need. Then there will be some chance of glory.'

'And of promotion?' She smiled at him to take the sting out of the question. 'I can see that times of peace must be hard on a man with his way to make in the army.'

They were both relieved when Comyn appeared to claim her hand for the next dance. 'And after that, Miss Pennam,' he was leading her smoothly through the crowd, 'I think maybe we should take our mammas home. I went to speak to my mother just now and Lady Charlotte is looking tired again. Besides, entirely between ourselves, I do not quite approve of the stakes they are now playing for. I have heard a thing or two about Lady Rampton. Will you be very disappointed at going home so comparatively early?'

'Of course not.' She smiled at him warmly. 'I am only grateful to you for thinking of it.'

To her relief they found her mother still winning, but ready enough to go home before the luck changed. With a sinking heart, she heard the four ladies engage themselves for the next night at Mr. Donner's rooms. 'No need to ask you young people if you wish to come,' said Mrs. Comyn with an arch look for Kathryn. 'After such success as you have had tonight, dear child. And in such looks too. I always did say happiness was worth a whole armoury of beauty aids. Did I not, dear boy?'

'I am sure you did, mamma. But our carriage will be blocking the way.'

Since this was an unforgivable sin in the crowded little resort, the ladies made haste to say their good nights, but Kathryn heard Lady Rampton promise herself a change of partners and 'revenge' for the next night which would be Monday, since this was Saturday. They would all meet, of course, for the eleven o'clock service at St. Mary's next morning, and all occupy the rest of the long, sober day as best they might. Lady Rampton even suggested 'a quiet game of cards' at her lodgings, but this was sternly rejected by the other ladies, much to Kathryn's relief. She had no particularly strong views about Sunday observance herself, but certainly would not shock other people's sensibilities by playing cards, any more than she would ask any work beyond the necessary minimum of the servants. She and her mother would need the carriage to take them up to the church close to the castle at the top of the town. But there would be no ride on the sands, and that was particularly disappointing because Saturday had been a day of sea mist, when riding was considered dangerous.

6

The next day was brilliantly fine, and for the first time Kathryn found herself homesick for Windover Hall, where, church over, she would have had the freedom of the gardens. But, no, she reminded herself, she would not have been free; not if her step-father was at home. He had gone south to fetch the two boys from a last visit with their cousins, but the three of them were expected back any day now. She just hoped that, since London would have been empty of company, Oliver Morewood would return this time comparatively free of debt.

Mr. Hewetson, the underpaid curate of Scarborough, gave them a precisely timed sermon about brotherly love, and they emerged, soon after twelve o'clock, into the high, breezy graveyard with its wide views of harbour, sea and closely looming castle. It had been hot in church and the high crown of her new bonnet was tight on her forehead. She had dreamed of Mark again. It was over a year now since the day she lost him, but in her dream he had taken her in his arms . . . She would not think about it. How could she stop?

'Such a beautiful day.' Thomas Comyn and his mother had shared their pew. 'And such a pity there is no riding, now when the tide is right and the air clear. But I did wonder — I am sure you are a good walker, Miss Pennam, coming from the country as you do.'

'Why, yes.' Doubtfully.

'Well, here we are, at the top of the town, with the castle just a footpath away. You must have been longing as I do to take a closer look at it, and the views to both sides of the promontory.' He turned to Lady Charlotte. 'May I beg the great pleasure of Miss Pennam's company for an hour or so? I am told there is a footpath with delightful views on the North Bay, where the more venturesome take the air of a Sunday. We won't think of going to the castle itself of course. Just get a view of it.' He anticipated her objection. 'And my mother will send the carriage back to await us at the corner of High Tollergate, so there will be no need to walk through the town. And, forgive my saying so, but it seems to me that Miss Pennam looks this morning as if she was a little feeling the dissipations of the last few days. I know I am! A breath of air would do us both good.'

'An admirable notion.' His mother seconded him. 'And if you would give me the pleasure of a visit, dear Lady Charlotte, I could show you the book of fashion plates I spoke of. Kind Mr. Schofield the bookseller in Newborough Street obtained an advance copy for me; nobody else has seen it yet. Then the young people could join us for a nuncheon later on.'

'I'll take the greatest care of her, Lady Charlotte.'

'I'm sure you will.' Lady Charlotte's heart yearned for a particularly delicious cordial that Mrs. Comyn produced, with great pledges of secrecy, when the two of them were alone. 'It's not as if it were Brighton or one of those crowded sort of places.' She convinced herself. 'It's true, dear child, you do look a trifle hagged this morning. I am afraid I have been letting you do too much. If the walk will really do you good . . .'

'I'm sure it will.' If only she could go alone. She was suddenly sick to death of the crowded pavements, the bows and smiles, the constant pressure of friendly, inquisitive glances. They were standing now at the churchyard entrance and she was aware that they were blocking the way.

'You had better get started then,' said Mrs. Comyn, also aware of this.

She doesn't approve, thought Kathryn, but

her son has overruled her. What a fuss about nothing. I wish I was a farm girl, with her cows to milk. I wish . . . Oh, what do I wish?

But she turned a smiling face to Thomas Comyn. 'I admire your strategy,' she said as they began to climb the steep brow of the ridge. 'You should be a general at the least of it.'

'It's useful in a bank too.' He took off his Sunday hat and ran his hand through irrepressibly curling fair hair which he wore in a short modern cut. 'Do you feel escaped as I do, Miss Pennam? From the eyes, the comments, the constant observation?'

'Oh, yes!' She had never felt more in charity with him.

'Then let us by all means make the most of it. That must be our footpath, I think. I wonder if it will really give us a view of the North Bay.'

'Who cares, so long as it takes us away from the town.'

The sun shone, larks sang overhead, sounds of the town and the garrison at the castle came to them muted now, mixed with the long sigh of the sea. He had not taken her arm, leaving her to pick her own way over the rough path, and she was grateful to him for recognising her need to walk free. Her Sunday shoes would be ruined, of course, but much she cared for that.

They walked steadily for a while, pausing from time to time to remark on a bush blown sideways by the prevailing wind, or a blooming burst of gorse. 'You walk like a man.' He had paused to hold a bramble back for her on the narrowing path.

'That is a compliment?'

'Oh.' He thought about it. 'I suppose I meant it as one. You are wonderfully good for me, Miss Pennam, you make me think about what I say. It's why I so much want . . . It makes it easy . . . Miss Pennam, you must know why I have contrived — why my mother helped me to get you to myself at last.'

'I thought she didn't approve.'

'Well, of course not. Which just goes to show how very much she approves of what I am trying to say to you, Miss Pennam.' He paused in a turfed clearing of the scrub, turned to face her. 'You must know . . . you must have been aware . . . You must feel how very much I admire and respect you.'

'Why, thank you.' She gazed at him for a moment, taking in the flushed, anxious face, the Sunday hat clasped under one arm, the cravat ever so slightly awry. And suddenly she was back on another cliff, facing another man. No talk then, no time for it. No time for anything. Just that brief, eternal moment in each other's arms.

'Not just respect.' He had taken her words for encouragement. 'Liking . . . love.' He got it out at last. 'Miss Pennam, I am asking you to be my wife.'

'Oh dear!' She could not help it. 'I had no idea . . . I had not expected . . . I really thought we were going for a walk!' It came out as just slightly reproachful, and he reacted at once, quick as always to sense what she was feeling.

'And I respect you for it, love you for it, Miss Pennam.' He found the words easier this time. 'If I have been too quick for you, I can only apologise and ask you to take time and think about it. The thing is . . . situated as we are . . . I do not think my mother and I will be able to stay much longer . . . And she was telling me something your mother said about how you are situated at home . . . Forgive me, but I would feel so much happier if you would give me the power to care for, to protect you.'

'You are too good.' She meant it. She was near to tears because she was sure that he did not love her, but meant every other word he said. 'But, Mr. Comyn, I can't. You see, I love someone else.' She had not meant to say it, but the very honesty of his hesitations had been too much for her.

'What?' Now she had entirely astonished

him. 'It's not possible. It can't be true. Who?'

She was in for it now. She told him. It seemed the only, the decent thing to do. She told him the whole story, as quickly and as simply as possible, and at the end, like the practical man he was, he pounced on the basic issue. 'He disappeared a year ago; you have heard nothing from him since; and you still say you love this man?'

'I don't just say it. It's true.' At least she had managed not to tell him about her dreams; they were most entirely her own affair.

His fresh face had clouded. He put his hat back on his head. 'I still find it hard to believe. And, Miss Pennam, everything I have said still stands. You are letting yourself live in a young girl's dream. When you wake, I shall be there, waiting for you, ready for you, working for you. I need a wife, Miss Pennam. I need you.'

It came over with the ring of truth, and she found herself wondering just why he wanted a wife so badly. 'You'd be such a help to me.' Once again he seemed to have read her thoughts. 'It's a lonely business, being master of one's own banking house. And the other bankers so much older . . . Oh, they've been kindness itself. The Smiths . . . the Peases . . . Mr. Thompson . . . they were all good friends of my father's, but you see that just makes it more difficult; they still think of me as his son, young Comyn. You are the first person who has really listened to me, Miss Pennam.'

'Surely the chief clerk you speak of?'

'Oh, Robertson is part of the problem. Well, of course,' fairly, 'my father's death was a terrible shock to him, as it was to us all, but he seems to me to be trying to keep me at arm's length, to keep me out of the business.'

'Should you, perhaps, have made him a partner when your father died?' She was glad of the practical turn the talk had taken.

'You have put your finger on it, Miss Pennam, as you always do. Yes, I had meant to. But when I got home from Cambridge and he kept me at a distance, treated me like a child . . . Well, how could I?'

'Awkward, I can see . . .'

'I think I've always been lonely, Miss Pennam. An only child . . . My mother . . . I had a friend once . . .' His face whitened, closed in a way she was learning to know. 'At Harrow I was ragged for being a banker's brat, as they called me, and Cambridge was not much better. It's no pleasure to know your friends are your friends because they count on you to pay the shot. I cannot begin to tell you how much I have enjoyed our rides, our talks . . . Miss Pennam, won't you please think again?'

'Mr. Comyn, I wish I could. But it has to be no. I have always promised myself that I would marry for love or not at all.' She smiled at him. 'I just wish you could find me a place in your bank.'

'You're living in cloud cuckoo land.' Impatiently. 'Marry for love! Work in a bank! What kind of a world do you think you live in?' He pulled the gold watch from his fob. 'I've kept you talking too long! We must make the best of our way back, or the horses will be cold and our mothers anxious. Just remember, please, that I have meant everything I have said, and will stand to it.'

'Thank you.' It was a business man's commitment and she respected it as such, noticing at the same time that he had said nothing more about loving her. It made things easier, somehow, and after a few moments of walking side by side in silent constraint, they were able to get themselves safely launched back into indifferent topics, the latest news from France, and the trouble with Spain over a remote place called Nootka Sound that might even, he told her, carry a threat of war. 'That's partly why I feel it time my mother and I went home,' he explained. 'Mr. Robertson and I do not quite agree as to the action to be taken in case of war, the inevitable panic and possible run on the banks.'

'And you don't feel you can trust him to pursue your policy if you are not there to insist?'

'That's exactly it, Miss Pennam!' He was delighted with her.

'It's no concern of mine.' Diffidently. 'But feeling like that, do you think you should keep him as your chief clerk?'

'What else can I do? I've thought about it over and over. If someone else would only offer him a partnership! But he is always talking of his devotion to Comyn's Bank. He's been with it for ever, of course, from a boy. I even thought of offering him our factorship at one of the Baltic Ports, but I am afraid he would take it as a moral affront. Factors are not quite the figures of power now that they used to be, you know, since the countries we trade with are beginning to have trading structures of their own.'

'You trade, then, as well as banking?'

'In a small way, now. But my father began in the Baltic trade and had, I think, a kind of romantic fondness for it. I wanted to go there, as factor, as supercargo, as almost anything, rather than waste my time at Cambridge, but he would not have it. I still hope to get there some day. They say St. Petersburg is a most beautiful city, as much the Venice of the North as Stockholm.'

'Oh, how I should love to go there!'

'Miss Pennam!' Was he going to make another appeal?

But they had come back into sight of the castle and were suddenly surrounded by a group of officer acquaintances, also out for a Sunday stroll. Aware that she was being quizzed from under many a military headpiece hurriedly doffed in her honour, Kathryn suddenly saw Mrs. Comyn's point. This walk with Thomas Comyn would have been all very well if she had come back from it an engaged young lady. As it was she had to recognise it as unfortunate, to say the least.

But Thomas Comyn was standing no nonsense. He had taken her arm for the first time and steered her firmly through the lively little group, with a civil bow here, a firm nod there. 'My mother's carriage is waiting for us in High Tollergate; we must not keep the horses standing.' They both heard the remarks: 'Lucky devil,' 'Bankers have all the luck,' but ignored them, though Kathryn felt the blood rush to her face, but not, thanks to his firmness, until they were safely out of the little crowd.

'I'm sorry about that.' They had both been glad to see the carriage waiting.

'Not your fault.' She smiled at him. 'I thought you dealt with them admirably, Mr. Comyn.'

'Oh, I can manage men,' he said. 'I've learned it the hard way, but thank God I have learned it. It's women defeat me.' But to her grateful relief, he left it at that.

'You refused him?' Lady Charlotte did not want to believe her ears. 'I was afraid of it, when the two of you came in so quiet, but I could not bring myself to think you could be such a fool. Young, handsome enough, anyone can see you like him, you've been in each other's pockets ever since we got here; I'd have said a word if it had not all seemed so suitable. And, rich. Child, have you any idea how rich he is?'

'I don't think I want to know, mother.'

'Don't want to know! What kind of answer is that? Fool of a girl, what do you expect? What are you waiting for? One of the royal princes to come and beg your hand? Oh, I shall have one of my spasms, I know I will!'

'I'm truly sorry, mother. But you see, ever since I have been grown up I have promised myself that I will never marry except for love.'

'For love? As I did, you mean? Oh, it was the world well lost for me, all right! And look where it has got me!'

'Where it has got us,' said Kathryn. 'But, don't you see, mother, it's just because I like Thomas Comyn so much that I don't feel I can marry him without loving him.' And that was a bit of sophistry if ever there was one, when she was sure that he did not love her either. A business arrangement; he needed a wife; she needed money; or rather, face it, her mother did. Her mother who was crying now, hiccuping into her handkerchief, working her way towards a spasm.

'Don't, mother. I do beg you, don't work yourself up.' She knew the words were fatal as she spoke them.

'Work myself up! You think that's what I'm doing! With all I've planned and hoped for in ruins thanks to your selfishness. We had it so charmingly arranged, Sarah Comyn and I. She doesn't — she didn't,' with another hiccup, 'she didn't mean to stay on in her son's house. Not when he was married. He has another one in Church Lane, close to the Hull Grammar School. An excellent school; I could have stayed with her, sent the boys there, what could be more suitable? And you — you say you cannot marry without love! I tell you, child, money is a commodity that lasts a great deal better than love. Oh, how shall I bear it, and how angry Sarah Comyn will be!'

'Oh, poor Thomas,' said Kathryn, surprising herself by her use of his Christian name.

'Poor Thomas indeed! What about me? I shall be ill; I know I shall be ill. Fetch me my cordial, child, and the vinaigrette, but it will be no use. You'd best send for Dr. Forsyte and be done with it. I shall never get over this; never.'

'I did advise against shocks,' said the doctor reproachfully an hour later, when he had finally composed his patient with a sedative draught. 'She'll sleep now till morning, and I think we can hope to brush through this with less damage than I had feared, but I must most seriously warn you, Miss Pennam, that any further upset of this kind might prove fatal.'

'Fatal?' She stared at him for a moment, wide-eyed. 'You truly mean that, doctor?'

'I would not say it if I did not. I have thought a great deal about your mother's case and have decided that I would not be doing my duty if I did not give you this warning. I respect you, Miss Pennam, as a young woman of great good sense. That is why I am telling you this.'

'What you are saying is that you do not feel you can tell my mother.'

'Precisely so.' He was grateful for her quick comprehension. 'That, too, might well prove fatal. She needs rest and calm, Miss Pennam, rest and calm. Or, best of all, some happy project to occupy her mind.'

'She has told you of what happened today?'

'Yes.' He was looking earnestly into the

crown of his hat, held in his lap. 'Lady Charlotte did say something. I gather that hopes had been raised . . .'

'Not by me,' said Kathryn bleakly. 'Or, not intentionally.'

'Ah, but you must see, Miss Pennam, that that makes no difference in this case.'

'But she is better for the moment?' She was not going to yield to this silent blackmail if she could help it.

'Yes.' He rose to take his leave. 'I can honestly say that she is better than, in the circumstances, I would have expected.'

'Thank you, Dr. Forsyte.'

When he had gone she found her mother sleeping peacefully, and sat for a while by her bed, fighting with herself. Dr. Forsyte had said, without saying anything, that he thought she should marry Thomas Comyn for her mother's sake. Get her to the rest and quiet of the life she and Sarah Comyn had planned in the house in Hull. All planned, all settled without her knowledge or consent. It stuck in her throat. It would not do. She could not do it. And the doctor had been honest enough to tell her that her mother had come better through the present attack than he had expected. Surely it must be possible to contrive rest and quiet for Lady Charlotte without sacrificing her own future in the process?

7

Lady Charlotte looked better next morning, but said plaintively that she did not feel well enough to go to the pump room. 'I do not think I shall go out tonight either. How can I face Sarah Comyn after the way you have treated her son? We would neither of us for a moment have dreamed of letting you two young people go off together like that, in public, and on a Sunday too, if we had not been sure you would return an engaged young lady. What I am to do with you now, the good Lord only knows!'

'I mean to earn my living, mother.' She regretted the words the minute they were spoken.

'Earn your living? Are you gone entirely out of your mind, Kathryn? Oh, what is it now?' A knock on the door.

'Mr. and Mrs. Comyn have called, my lady,' said the servant. 'They are in the parlour. I told them you are not well today, but Mrs. Comyn says she very much hopes for a word.'

'Oh dear! I shall go distracted! And so early too! I'm not dressed for company. What shall we do, Kathryn?'

'I think we should see them. They would not have called so early if it were not important. Mr. Comyn said something yesterday about their meaning to return soon to Hull. It may be that they are come to take their leave.' And what a blessing that would be.

'Going to leave? Oh, I can't bear it! They can't be — Sarah Comyn said nothing . . . Oh, very well,' to the girl. 'Tell them we will be down directly.' She turned to Kathryn as the door closed behind the girl. 'What am I going to do, Kathryn?'

'Do? What do you mean, mamma? Say goodbye to them, I suppose.'

'Oh, I should never have done it.' Wringing her hands. 'But what else could I do? And she said there was not the slightest need for me to pay her back. Not until they were leaving, and long before then of course the luck would have changed.'

'Mother, what do you mean? What are you telling me?'

'You must see I could not let a debt to Lady Rampton go unpaid. And how could I think of taking you home when everything was going so swimmingly, as I thought, between you and young Comyn. And then, yesterday, when the two of you went off together, she said of course we would forget all about it. And you refused him, Kathryn! Oh, what shall I do? What shall I say to them?'

'I thought you had been winning at cards.' The horrid truth was dawning on Kathryn, but she tried to resist it.

'So I was, until just the other day. We changed partners, you know. Lady Rampton wanted her revenge, she said. And then the luck changed. It happened so quick, Kathryn. We were talking, and playing, and suddenly Lady Rampton said something and I realised I owed her more than I could possibly pay.'

'So what did you do?'

'What could I do? Went on playing, of course. I could hardly break the game up, tell her I could not afford to go on. It would have been all over town, and then where would your chances have been? Of course I hoped I would make a recover, but by the end of the evening I was so badly dipped I did not know what to do, and then Sarah Comyn took me aside, on a pretext of pinning up my lace, told me she saw how it was with me, handed me enough to pay my debt. What could I do but take it? And what shall we do now?'

'Go down and see them,' said Kathryn bleakly. 'But, first, I will tell you one thing, mother. I don't know what Mrs. Comyn intended when she lent you the money, but I know her son well enough to be certain that he will never dream of letting you repay it.'

'You think not?' Hopefully. 'But — a debt of honour, child. You know I must.'

'I know we must go back to Windover.' She had been swiftly and efficiently making the necessary adjustments to her mother's hair and toilette as they talked, now picked up the essential vinaigrette. 'And now we must not keep the Comyns waiting a moment longer.'

When they entered the parlour, it was clear that they had interrupted an argument. Mrs. Comyn's colour was high under the rouge; her son's eyes sparkled. With rage, Kathryn thought, and thought she had never seen him look so nearly handsome.

'We are come to take our leave,' announced Mrs. Comyn, when the first awkward greetings were done. 'My son feels it is more than time he returned to his duties. We go this afternoon, and are only sad not to have one more pleasant evening at the Rooms with you.' Her tone proclaimed it for the lie it was. 'You must be sure to come and see us if ever you should find yourselves in Hull.' They all knew how unlikely that was. 'I trust you will enjoy the rest of your stay here. You must make my apologies to Lady Rampton tonight.' To Lady Charlotte.

'I don't know what to say.' Lady Charlotte was wringing, her hands again. 'This is so sudden. I had not expected . . .'

'You are not to let it put you out in any way, Lady Charlotte.' Thomas Comyn took a firm step forward between the two older ladies. 'It is entirely my fault that we must leave so suddenly; it must not be allowed to inconvenience anyone else. And, to speak plainly with you.' Now his colour was high. 'As to the trifling matter over which my mother was able to assist you, it is to be forgotten, if you please. For good.' He smiled at Kathryn. 'You will let me do this small thing for you, Miss Comyn?'

'Why, thank you.' Her eyes, meeting his, were full of tears.

'But I cannot —' Lady Charlotte's protest was interrupted by a commotion on the stairs. The parlour door burst open and Oliver Morewood stormed into the room. He was in riding dress, dusty from the road, had made no pretence at tidying himself for ladies' company. 'So here you are!' He looked from his wife to his step-daughter. 'Enjoying yourselves, entertaining your friends, spending my money! And no welcome for me — or for your sons — at home, no preparations, no observance.' He paused for breath.

'But I told you we would still be away. And

I know Sally had everything ready for you and the boys. How are my dear boys?'

'No thanks to you that they are safe at home. Well, Kathryn,' turning on her. 'No greeting for your father? No daughter's kiss?' He swept her into an unexpected embrace that both hurt and frightened her. 'You're in looks, I see. Been spending money like water, you two, that's obvious. Well, your time is up. You are coming home today.' And then, as an afterthought: 'Make me known to your friends.' He greeted Mrs. Comyn with a curt nod that was just short of rudeness, favoured her son with a long, thoughtful look, turned back to his wife. 'Best get to your packing; I've told the old madam downstairs you are leaving this afternoon. If you will excuse us, ma'am.' To Mrs. Comyn. 'Lady Charlotte has much to do.'

'We are leaving this instant.' Mrs. Comyn was scarlet with fury. 'I have never in my life — Goodbye, Lady Charlotte. I am sorry that it will not be possible to continue our acquaintance.'

'On the contrary.' Thomas Comyn had stood quiet so far, watching, now stepped forward to face Morewood. 'My mother and I return to Hull today, sir, but when I have seen her safe home I shall give myself the pleasure of calling on you at Windover Hall. Just to make sure that Lady Charlotte and Miss

116

Pennam have also reached home in safety.' He turned to Lady Charlotte. 'You must not let yourself fret about anything, ma'am. I shall hope to call on you early next week. If you should wish to see me sooner for any reason a message to Comyn's Bank in Hull would bring me post haste.' He took Kathryn's hand. 'I shall not say goodbye, Miss Pennam, but *au revoir*. Come, mother, we are delaying the ladies. Goodbye, sir.' A curt nod and he ushered his fuming mother from the room.

'Young fighting cock,' said Morewood. And then: 'Comyn's Bank, eh? Not been wasting your time after all, miss. Pity they are leaving, or I'd have suggested we stay on a few days after all. As it is, best get to your packing, the two of you. The carriage is ordered; I shall ride ahead and prepare a welcome for you that you did not give me.' To his wife. 'But you do seem to have been spending your time more profitably than I could have imagined. No wonder you are in such looks, girl.' He loomed over Kathryn as if for another of his paternal embraces, but that last one had shaken her badly, and she ducked swiftly behind her mother. 'Well, well,' shaking a finger at her. 'Turning the coy miss are we? Saving our favours for the favoured man? I shall look forward to hearing all about it when we get back to the Hall. For the moment, I must have a word with Renshaw. Try not to keep the carriage waiting.' To his wife: 'Your sons are eager to see you.'

Left alone, the two women gazed at each other for a long moment, then, 'Well,' said Lady Charlotte, 'what do you think about that, dear child?'

'I don't know,' said Kathryn slowly. 'I just don't know.'

'He's going to offer for you again. I'm sure of it. Kathryn, dearest child, think about it, think about it all? Please?'

For the rest of the day, Kathryn was too busy to think. It fell on her to soothe the outraged landlady, and pay her the compensation she demanded for their early departure and the inevitable vails. Naturally, Morewood had not done this, and it was disconcerting to know that but for Mrs. Comyn's generosity, or rather her son's, they would have been quite unable to pay. Then there was their packing to be supervised, and Priss to blandish out of a fit of the sullens. Priss had found herself an elderly admirer in Scarborough and was far from pleased to be leaving so suddenly.

The one good thing was that through all the drama of the morning Lady Charlotte had shown no sign of a spasm. But did this mean that she was indulging herself in false hopes?

That she really believed Thomas Comyn would propose again and be accepted? Kathryn did not, though she was immensely grateful to him for his generosity and moral support. It had been interesting to see Morewood cowed by his firmness. But then bullies were often cowards. And how long would the effect last?

The future looked bleak indeed. If Comyn should surprise her with a renewed proposal, she would refuse him. She had told him she loved someone else. She could no more take him now for his money than she could cut Mark Weatherby out of her dreams. Talking about him had brought him back with agonising vividness, and the return to Windover did not help. Memories lurked in every corner. I must get away, she thought. How?

It was disconcerting to find how like their father her half-brothers had grown in the year they had been away. Had the likeness always been there, unnoticed, or was it partly the effect of spending so much time with Morewood's relatives? They were furious at being taken away from school, where they had soon graduated from bullied to bullies. Any dream she had been nourishing of taking over their studies and so earning her keep vanished at sight of their cross red faces and sound of their angrily raised voices as they blamed their mother for making them leave school in order to indulge herself and Kathryn in their Scarborough holiday. Their father had got his version of the story in first and there would be no shaking it. Kathryn was surprised and disconcerted to find herself thinking that Thomas Comyn would not have sons like them.

She did not see Sally alone until it was time to dress for dinner, and then the bombshell dropped. 'It's like a fairy story, miss,' said loving Sally. 'Oh, I am so happy for you.'

'What in the world do you mean?'

'Why, your engagement, miss, to this rich young banker. Oh, I know the master said it wasn't official yet, but he told Stokes that the young man is coming here next week to make his formal proposal. Very suitable, he said, that he would wait for your papa's permission before he spoke. Tell me about him, miss. Is he really so rich and so handsome?'

'Rich, yes. Handsome, not precisely. But, Sally, my step-father has it all wrong. Mr. Comyn has proposed to me and I have refused him.'

'You never? Oh, miss!' And then: 'But if so, why is he coming next week?'

'Sally, I don't know. Or, maybe I'm afraid I do. He saw the way Mr. Morewood behaves to my mother and me. He is trying to help us, to protect us.'

'But, miss, how can he if you won't have him?'

'He can't. But that makes no difference. I don't love him, Sally. I told him so.'

'Oh dear,' said Sally.

'I'd not be surprised if he never came after all,' Kathryn told her. 'He may well feel he has done his best for us by just proposing it, suggesting to my step-father that we are not entirely without friends.' But we are, she thought. 'And, besides, his mother does not like me, made no secret of the fact that she wished to cut the connection. She will have had a whole week to work on him. No, I'll be surprised if he comes.' And relieved? She was not sure.

Her confidence to Sally had an effect she should have expected. Sally told her friend the cook, the cook told Banks the butler, who told Stokes the bailiff, who, inevitably, told Morewood.

'What's this I hear?' He had kept away from Kathryn so consistently for the first couple of days that she had felt happily free for her old walks in the garden. Now he had found her in the shrubbery, during the gardeners' lunch hour, and she shrank into herself at sight of his face with its strange mix of emotions. 'Servants' gossip, I expect, and not a word of truth in it.' He loomed over her, very close so that she could smell the brandy on his breath. 'But I would be glad to be sure. It cannot be true that you have been such an idiot as to refuse that young banker of yours?'

'Not mine.' She was in for it. 'Yes, I am afraid I did.'

'Idiotic.' He put both hands on her shoulders and stared down at her, breathing brandy into her face. 'Lunatic. But the kind of thing you would do, I suppose. It's time for some straight talking, miss, between you and me. You know as well as I do how things are here at the Hall. Just don't fool yourself that your being here makes them any better, because it doesn't. If you stay, no good will come of it. I'm warning you of that and you should listen to me. I'm only a man, after all, and your mother . . . an invalid for years . . . What's a man to do? And you're a stunner, girl. No wonder that young Comyn is mad for you. And rich! Imagine the settlements . . . Just what we need . . . And you'd better take him, girl, for all our sakes. If you don't, we'll be dirt poor; I'll have to stay home. No trips to Scarborough. It's the nights, how is a man to endure the nights? And here you are, such a little beauty, with that don't-touch-me look of yours. It's enough to drive a man mad, and it will, and so I am telling you.' He was pushing himself against her and she felt something that terrified and roused her. Horrible. 'Not now.' He let her go. 'Not here. But never say I didn't warn you. Stay here, and I'll have you in the end, one way or another, and then where will we all be?'

'But I can't —'

'Why not?' He interrupted her. 'It's a woman's privilege to change her mind. No problem there. And what else can you do? I saw the doctor in the street after I left you the other day. Old full-of-gloom Forsyte. He read me a lecture about your mother. Wrap her in cotton wool; no frights; no shocks. What do you think she'd do if you went for a governess? She'd die of it, Kathryn. Do you want that on your conscience? Anyway, you're far too pretty for a governess; no one would have you. And —' He stopped, thought for a moment. 'If by any crazy chance you are still moon-dreaming over that young Weatherby, I've news for you. Didn't much want to tell you, but if it will bring you to your senses . . . Saw him myself, in the Haymarket, with a prime article on his arm. Didn't see me, just as well, embarrassing for everyone. You had better believe me, Kathryn. That hope is dead.'

It came over with a complete, deadly ring of conviction. He watched her take it to heart. Then: 'Young Comyn's worth ten of him,' he told her. 'You've always been one for facts and figures; well, here's your chance. Being a banker's wife should suit you down to the ground, and, who knows, I might even decide to agree to that crazy idea of your mother going to live with his so the boys can go to school in Hull. She's no use to me. It's not a bad notion, not if it was to be made worth my while. Think about all I've said, Kathryn. Think about it hard. And here's a reminder for you.' His lips came hard down on hers; his tongue was in her mouth. She would be sick; she would scream; she was helpless. 'You see.' He let her go at last. 'You can do nothing. Least of all tell anyone. Be grateful for the warning, girl, and act on it. I won't be able to let you go next time, and it will be entirely your fault.' He turned and strode away towards the house just as the gardeners came straggling back to work.

Her mouth hurt; her own body betrayed her. She turned away from the house and almost ran down the path and through the gate to the cliff garden. Safely alone at last she sat down, stared at the sea, let the tears come, tried to think, tried to plan, tried, in vain, to hope. In the end, she faced what she had to do.

8

Thomas Comyn made everything easy. 'I'm glad,' was all he said when she accepted him. 'Now you will leave everything to me.' He made no attempt to embrace her, and she was not sure whether she was relieved or disappointed. It was all strange beyond belief, and she moved through the few weeks between engagement and wedding half conscious, in a kind of walking dream. Everyone was pleased with her; everyone congratulated her. Except perhaps Mrs. Comyn, who merely sent civil messages by her son.

Mr. Renshaw was more delighted with her, she thought, than anyone, but when she tried to ask him about the financial arrangements making between Thomas Comyn and her stepfather, he shook his head and told her they were no affair of hers. 'I need not tell you that your future husband is the most generous of men. I hope you know what a lucky young lady you are, Miss Pennam.' Was there a hint of self-satisfaction in his voice? Increasingly,

Kathryn felt herself a puppet, a marionette, dancing to someone else's tune. In a way, it helped. All she had to do was behave, do the prescribed, the expected thing.

She was fitted for wedding clothes, received and answered notes of congratulation and a scattering of presents from friends and neighbours. She broke down once, when a piece of antique silver arrived with the good wishes of the two ladies in Ross-on-Wye. They had read the announcement in the *Gazette*, wrote Lavinia Pennam, and were delighted at the chance to get back in touch with their only relative. Was it too much to hope that Kathryn and her new husband might consider a bridal tour among the beauties of the Wye Valley? Much more suitable than to venture abroad with things on the Continent in such a distressing state. They would so much like to entertain dear Henry's child and her husband, to whom they sent their kindest regards. Theirs was a small and simple establishment, but if the young couple would take them as they found them, it would make them very happy indeed. And then, in a hastily scratched postscript: 'Janet has not been very well, and would dearly love to see Henry's daughter.'

Kathryn showed the letter to Thomas next time he rode up from Hull to see her. 'I haven't answered it yet; I thought I should consult you first.' Nothing had been said about a wedding tour and she had begun to think that he must plan simply to go back to Hull. Neither had any further mention been made of the house Mrs. Comyn had spoken of sharing with Lady Charlotte, and the prospect of a honeymoon spent with her mother-in-law was not one to which Kathryn looked forward.

'Indeed yes.' Thomas read the letter quickly, pausing over the postscript. 'It sounds as if Miss Janet is not long for this world. You are their only relative?'

'My mother says so. I have never met them.' One of the things she found increasingly comfortable about Thomas Comyn was his total, tacit understanding of her circumstances.

'Then I think we should accept their invitation. In fact, it comes most timely. My mother and I were discussing, just this morning, what would be the best plan for us. I had thought of a short stay at Scarborough, but this is better, this is almost a duty.'

'You think so?' She must not let him see how much she minded that he had begun by discussing their honeymoon with his mother rather than with her.

'I certainly do. It reads like an appeal to me. Two old ladies living alone, and one of them far from well. They must feel the need of a man in the family. A man of business.

I shall be happy to look into their circumstances for them while we are there. Write to them, my dear, accept their invitation. Tell them we will spend a few days with them, maybe take one of the boating trips down the Wye I have heard people praise so highly. You would enjoy that, I am sure. A real holiday for you.'

'Yes.' He had never called her his dear before, and she could not help linking it with his discovery that she had two elderly aunts with a house of their own and no other kin. Or was she being hideously unfair to him?

'It's hard on women alone,' he said now. 'Some rascally country attorney may well be taking advantage of them. Yes, we will certainly go. Let me think. We could go up the Trent to Nottingham — there's a man I need to see there — you will bear with me for that? And then by easy stages across country to Hereford and so down to Ross. Write them that we will hope to be with them at the end of the month, my dear. That should give us ample time for a leisurely journey.'

'You mean to start from Hull rather than from here?'

'Oh, I think so. I'd like to see my mother safe home after the fatigue of the wedding. She is not so young as she was either, and there must inevitably be adjustments to be made. You can have no idea of how hard she is working just now, getting everything at home into apple pie order for you. I never saw such a spring cleaning. She is quite delighted when I ride up to visit you because she says it gives the servants a freer hand than when I am there getting under their feet. There's not been such a turnout since she came home as a bride, thirty years ago. I would not let her move out of their room when my father died, but of course she is now.' He was blushing. 'There's a wing of the house runs down to the river. She says she will be snug as can be there.'

'She is not moving to your house off the Market Place then?' She made herself ask the question. Face the worst?

'Well, no.' His colour was higher than ever. 'Rather a quixotic idea that, don't you think? I cannot imagine that your step-father would possibly have approved, and, quite between ourselves, I am not sure how well our two mammas would get on if they were actually to find themselves sharing a house. Are you?'

'Well, no.' She had to admit it, and to admit to herself that in some ways it would be a relief as well as a wrench to leave her mother behind at Windover. But to have her mother-in-law, snug as could be, in a wing of the house? That was another question. Her own mother had never thought of interfering in the running of Windover; it was hard to believe the same would be true of Mrs. Comyn.

'But I mean to be mistress in my husband's house,' she confided to Sally.

'As you should. And you are not to fret yourself for a moment about things here. I shall manage admirably now the money is going to be less tight.' Sally must stay at Windover Hall as housekeeper and had been busy training her cousin Beth to supply her place as Kathryn's maid.

'Sally, do you know how much — ?' Kathryn left the question unfinished, but Sally understood it well enough.

'I do not. And you should not be thinking about it. He's a very rich man, your future husband, and if he is prepared to make things easier for your mother, you must just be grateful.'

'I know.' But it was hard not to feel that she was being bought.

At least they were getting what Thomas Comyn paid for. Oliver Morewood was behaving like a model of a husband and stepfather. There had been an awkward moment when he had suggested that he himself should take the marriage service, but Thomas Comyn had persuaded him that his part was to give away the bride, leaving Mr. Tench to perform the ceremony. 'A quiet village occasion, with just our close friends about us.'

Kathryn had been a little surprised at just how few of his and his mother's friends he proposed to invite, but he explained that Mrs. Comyn's friends were too old to make the journey, and most of his own too busy. 'I am afraid you will find us a nose-to-the-grindstone lot, my dear. But my Cousin George has agreed to come up from Beverley and give me his support. I am only sorry it will not be possible for you to meet him before our great day.'

'Your cousin?' This was the first she had heard of Cousin George.

'Yes. My first cousin.' Something odd about his tone? 'My father was his father's older brother, but George is older than me. He's an only child too. We were together always when we were boys. George did everything better than I did.' He paused, changed tack. 'Then his father left the bank, bought a small estate outside Beverley. George's mother was a Miss Folliott, your mother must know her. Above our touch. George has been brought up a country gentleman. We have not seen much of each other since we grew up; our lives are too different.'

'How sad. After being such friends.' Something strange about this. Thomas had his closed look again. 'Will his parents come to the wedding?'

'His father is dead, and his mother something of an invalid; I doubt she'll think of coming.'

'I see.' He doesn't like his aunt, she thought. Or is it his mother who does not? She was not sure whether she was glad or sorry that there would be no chance to see Mrs. Comyn before the wedding. It was even doubtful now if she would feel able to come to it. She had been overdoing things a little, her son explained, thought it might be best to stay home and prepare a warm welcome for them.

Suddenly, it was upon her. Tomorrow, she would be Mrs. Thomas Comyn. Preparations were made, the new portmanteaus packed, the wedding dress ghost white in her closet. Thomas was to spend the night at the Rectory, his Cousin George making the shorter journey from Beverley next morning. It was her last day of freedom and for once there was nothing to do. She slipped out into the autumn sunshine, down to where the first leaves were beginning to turn on the cliff path. This was where she must say her last goodbye to Mark Weatherby whom her step-father had seen with a very prime article on his arm. He had forgotten her. It was more than time to forget him. If she could. And she must.

Returning reluctantly to the house, she found Thomas with her mother. 'Good news.' He greeted her with one of his cool kisses. 'My mother is feeling so much better she has decided to come tomorrow after all. She cannot bear, she says, to be missing on my great day. She is spending tonight with my Aunt Matilda to break the journey, and promises to see to it that she and Cousin George are here betimes in the morning. George has never been an early riser,' he explained. 'And we must keep strictly to our timetable for the day if we are not to be uncomfortably late home to Hull.'

'You rode up then?' The plan had been that he would come in the carriage, which would take the two of them back.

'Yes, I enjoyed it, this fine day. My mother will have a pleasant drive of it over the wolds, it will do her good, I am sure.'

'I hope so.' Mechanically. It had dawned on her that Mrs. Comyn must inevitably drive back to Hull with them. An odd way, surely, to start one's married life? But she said nothing. What was there to say?

It was good to feel the little church crowded with friends as she entered it on her stepfather's arm. Farmers and their wives, neighbours from nearby villages, the fabric that had supported her life. Tonight she would be in Hull, where she had never been, where she knew no one but the Comyns. And Beth, of course; she was glad about Beth. But now, advancing down the aisle, she saw Mrs. Comyn in the front pew, across from her mother, with an unknown beanpole of a woman beside her. It must be Cousin George's mother, the invalid Aunt Matilda, and she supposed she should be flattered.

But here was Thomas awaiting her, Cousin George, floridly handsome, at his side. Mr. Tench stepped forward, cleared his throat. It was happening. Nobody leapt up to forbid the banns. Had she really dreamed that Mark Weatherby would appear at this eleventh hour? For a wild moment she imagined answering 'No' to the inevitable question; heard herself whisper 'Yes'. It was over; she had done it; the least she could do was put up her head and smile at friends and neighbours as Thomas gave her his cold hand to lead her down the aisle.

People kept kissing her. Mrs. Comyn smelled of camphor, her sister-in-law of peppermint, Oliver Morewood strongly of brandy, triggering an alarm somewhere at the back of her mind. No time for that. No time for anything. Back to the house on her husband's arm . . . she was changing into the maroon travelling dress . . . Sally was looking anxious, urging her to leave as soon as possible: 'Mr. Morewood . . .' No need to say any more. She must go down, and smile, and smile, and smile.

'Time to go.' Thomas, her husband, was suddenly at her side. 'Say goodbye to your mother, my dear. We must not keep the ladies waiting.'

'The ladies?' She looked about, saw no sign of Mrs. Comyn.

'They have made their adieus, said their thank yous. They thought it best to slip away and await us in the carriage. My aunt spends the night with us, of course.'

Of course? Why? They would pass through Beverley on their way to Hull. She kissed her mother, who was crying, let Sally ease her into her pelisse, looked about for her step-father, who was nowhere to be seen. 'Mr. Morewood is resting a while.' Sally interpreted the glance. 'I'll say your goodbyes for you, madam. And don't worry.' It was both promise and reassurance.

'Thank you. Dear Sally.' With a loving kiss. 'And the boys?' They, too, had disappeared.

'Run out into the garden, I think. I'll tell them —'

'Thank you.' She felt Thomas rigid beside her as he led her out of the house, down the shelving front steps to where the Comyn carriage waited, white favours on the horses' harness.

'There you are at last, my dears.' Mrs. Comyn leaned forward to greet them. 'We were getting a little anxious.'

'I'm sorry, mother.' Thomas helped Kathryn up the step and seated her facing Mrs. Comyn. 'I know you don't much like driving in the dark, but this is a special occasion after all.'

'Indeed it is.' As her son went round the carriage to get in the other side, Mrs. Comyn leaned forward to pat Kathryn's hand. 'I knew you young things would not mind sitting with your backs to the horses.'

'Of course not.' They always had in Scarborough. Nothing had changed. Everything had changed. Thomas was beside her now; her husband. She was caught, trapped . . . The carriage was beginning to move; she leaned forward for one last, long look at Windover Hall where, now, a little group stood on the steps, waving pocket handkerchiefs.

'Well, that went off well enough,' said Mrs. Comyn, as if surprised.

'Excellent bride-cake,' agreed her sister-in-law, whom Kathryn had noticed helping herself to a lavish second slice. 'All very suitable . . . very pleasant . . . But what a surprise, Tom, to see you taking the plunge before my George.' Something in her tone Kathryn did not understand. 'All very agreeable and very exhausting.' An elegant little yawn into her gloved hand. 'Do you know, if you will excuse me, I believe I will have a tiny nap.'

It was the cue for a general silence and Kathryn could only be grateful. In her wildest dreams, she had never imagined a bridal journey like this. The carriage windows were tightly closed, no doubt on the old ladies' instructions, and it was already beginning to smell faintly but distinctly of camphor and peppermint. And something else. Of course, the pomatum Thomas used on his hair. I shall get used to it, she thought. I shall have to. And then, his aunt called him Tom, and he did not much like it. Odd to be so sure of this.

Everyone woke up when the coachman stopped to light the carriage lamps and a little desultory conversation broke out from which Kathryn learned that Matilda Comyn was planning to stay some time with her sister-in-law. 'Such a chance to do a little shopping in your splendid shops . . . And I know how you will be missing your son, Sarah, after all the happy years together . . . All the way to Ross-on-Wye . . . Such a venturesome journey . . . Such a lucky girl . . . Two spinster ladies? . . . Such sad lives . . . How they must be looking forward to it . . . And so must you, child.' Reaching forward to pat Kathryn's knee with a bony hand. 'Never left home before? Never further than Scarborough? The great world opening before you . . . Ah, to be young again.'

I wish I was dead, thought Kathryn, and then was angry with herself, made herself lean forward and say something friendly. But there was something about Matilda Comyn that she could not like.

Soon Matilda Comyn was snoring again, in little ladylike grunts, but she woke up when they passed through Beverley and told Kathryn all about her family's tomb in the Minster. 'You and dear Thomas must come and visit me some time and I will show you our beautiful town.' The invitation did not carry conviction and Kathryn was glad when Matilda nodded off again, finally fell asleep herself.

She was waked by what must have been a question from Matilda.

'No, we go this way, since the new dock was built,' Thomas had his arm round her, Kathryn found, and her head was on his shoulder. 'We are almost there, my dear.' He had felt her stir against him. 'This is Whitefriargate now. I only wish the High Street were as wide and handsome.'

'But it's home,' said Mrs. Comyn. 'And about time too. You must be quite exhausted, Matilda.'

'I am a little tired. A pity, perhaps, that we could not make an earlier start, but, thank goodness, here is the High Street at last.'

The carriage had turned sharp left into a street so narrow that the manoeuvre had been an awkward one. Peering out, Kathryn saw houses looming high, close on either side, fitfully illuminated by the carriage's lamps and flares here and there at house doors.

They stopped at last before a lighted door on the right hand side, and Kathryn saw it swing open. Liveried servants streamed out. 'It's very late,' said Mrs. Comyn. 'No ceremony, Thomas, tell them. What we all need is our beds.'

Kathryn's heart sank. Surrounded by talkative well-wishers, she had achieved none of the bridal feast; even her slice of bride-cake had been snatched from her by one of her hungry half-brothers. Her first thought, on waking, had been of food.

But, thank goodness, there was Beth among the bowing and curtseying servants on the step. Poor Beth, who had come ahead with the heavy luggage, looked small and frightened. Well, thought Kathryn, it's how I feel.

A sombre hall panelled in dark wood; stairs rising at the far side, a confusion of servants, and good nights being said at last. Mrs. Comyn had her sister-in-law by the arm, was leading her towards a doorway to the right. 'You'll be as glad of your bed as I am, Matilda, after such a long day. How strange it all seems.' She looked up at her son as he bent to kiss her. 'You'll let me know as soon as your plans are made in the morning.'

'You know I will.' He was shaking his Aunt Matilda's hand. 'Sleep well, both of you. And I do thank you for coming.' He turned to Kathryn. 'You must be tired, too. This way, my dear.'

'Plans?' she asked, as they moved towards the broadly sweeping stair.

'Stupid of me; I quite forgot to tell you, in all the excitement. I'll lead the way, shall I? The ship I had meant us to take upriver has been delayed. I must go out first thing in the morning in hopes of finding another. I am afraid it may mean less comfort than I had intended for you, Kathryn. I hope you will bear with me.' He had led the way across a handsome upstairs hall, swung open a door as heavy as the panelling. 'Here we are at last.'

A big room, dark panelled like the rest of the house, dominated by a vast four-poster bed, curtains looped back, the handle of a warming pan gleaming in the firelight. 'Good to have a fire.' She moved towards it, found she was shivering. 'May we not be able to leave tomorrow then?'

Heavy red window curtains matched those of the bed; enormous clothes presses were as dark as the walls; everything in the room was solid and old. She imagined generations of Comyns in this room, being born, being married, dying.

'Oh, I hope so.' He bent to prod the fire. 'We don't want to fail of our engagement to your aunts. If you won't mind a little discomfort? To tell truth, I'd as soon be out of the house while my Aunt Matilda is in it, though I am sorry to leave my poor mother bearing the burden.'

'Burden?'

'Aunt Matilda thinks herself too good for the likes of us. She has never forgotten she was a Folliott; never will. Or let George. She made my uncle sell out of the bank, has always resented the fact that it has done so well since. Mind you, my father was glad to see him go. No man for business, my Uncle George. Aunt Matilda thinks she is dirt poor. She will take my mother shopping in town tomorrow, choose everything of the best and then find she has left her purse at home.'

'And your mother will pay?'

'Of course. That's what we Comyns are good at. And now, you must be as tired as the rest of us.' He pulled the heavy bell rope . . . 'I'll leave you to your maid, just go and make sure that my mother is comfortably settled in her new quarters. Ask for anything you need. My dressing room is through there.' She had noticed the door beyond the bed. 'I'll be as quiet as I can.'

'Thank you.' What did he mean her to understand by that? Left alone, she went quickly to look into the dressing room, saw that it had a cot bed, returned to be taking off her pelisse by the fire when Beth appeared.

'Beth, I'm so hungry!'

'Oh, madam! Mrs. Moss went straight to bed after you came, she didn't much like waiting up so late. She's a proper tartar; things are tight in the servants' hall. I couldn't, Miss Kathryn — madam, I should say — I honestly couldn't.'

'No, I can see.' She picked up a candle. 'There must be something. Yes, look!' A solid biscuit barrel stood on a table between the dressing room door and the huge bed. 'Ginger knobs. Delicious. Have one, Beth.' She had seen the girl's wistful look as she ate her first one.

142

'I shouldn't, miss.' But she could not resist.

The little cakes were finished before they knew it. They exchanged a long, silent, guilty look, then went swiftly to work to get Kathryn into bed. That done, 'Good luck, miss,' said Beth. 'They all like him ever so much in the servants' hall.' Was there the hint of a doubt in her voice? But this had gone quite far enough.

'Good night, Beth, and thank you.'

The bed felt cold, despite the warming pan, which had been on the other side. The tiny buttons of her new nightgown stuck into her. She had never worn a nightgown before, but her mother had said she must. Her mother had not said much else, when she had tried to ask. 'Just do what he wants. It's a wife's duty.'

Bought and paid for. But the bed was amazingly comfortable. She must stay awake. Odd to feel a shared dislike of Aunt Matilda drawing her closer to Thomas. He was taking a very long time with his mother and aunt. She must keep awake. Must she? Could she?

9

Kathryn woke at first light, imperative sunshine finding its way through a gap in the curtains. A warm bulk against her back was her husband. How enormously strange. His breath was easy, regular. Fast asleep. She lay very still, listening to the sounds of the docks waking up; staithes, they called them in Hull. They had their own, at the bottom of the garden, Thomas had told her. He stirred a little, and she concentrated on making her own breathing regular, relaxed, the convincing sound of sleep. Presently she felt him slip out of bed and tiptoe to his dressing room. The door closed softly behind him. She gave a little sigh, moved her head out of the intrusive sunbeam and slept again.

When she next waked, Beth was drawing back the curtains, beaming at her. 'You have had a good sleep, madam. The master said I was to let you lie, but it's near nine o'clock. Mrs. Moss says would you like your breakfast in bed?'

'Oh, Beth, could I?'

'I think it might be best, miss. Ma'am, I mean. The old ladies had theirs sharp at eight and the breakfast room's been cleared. Rolls and hot chocolate I could get for you easy, ma'am.'

'Wonderful. Plenty of rolls, Beth!'

'Yes, ma'am.' She looked as if she would like to say something else, thought better of it and left the room.

Kathryn was out of bed on the instant, found a shawl in the looming clothes press on her side of the bed, wrapped it round her shoulders and went cautiously to look out of the window. Immediately below, a formal walled garden showed signs of neglect. Beyond the wall, a forest of masts, here and there a sail being hauled up into view. To the right, a wing of the house stretched down to the wall, presumably Mrs. Comyn's snug new home. To the left lay what must be the stable block. Familiar horsy sounds mingled with those from the river. Below, a gardener shambled into sight, began without enthusiasm to trim a shaggy box hedge. This is my home, she thought; how very strange.

'That's right!' Thomas found her finishing the last crumb of roll. 'You must have been starving. So was I! And not a biscuit in the barrel. I had a pretty sharp word for Mrs. Moss this morning, I can tell you. She won't let that happen again in a hurry. Now, can you and that girl of yours bustle about and be ready to leave by noon? There's a sloop sails then, will get us as far as Gainsborough. Not luxurious, I'm afraid, but wind and tide are right and I am sure you will find the mode of travel interesting. I rather hope we can find one of the modern passenger-carrying long boats to take us on from Gainsborough to Nottingham.' He paused. 'Don't, I beg you, mention that to my mamma when we say goodbye. She thinks I have a bee in my bonnet about canals and am bound to bankrupt myself in them, whereas I am quite sure that is the transport of the future. At least here in England.'

The *Rowena* was up from Yarmouth with a cargo of smoked fish and grain, and smelled strongly of the fish. The cabin space was as cramped as Thomas had said, but what did she care for that when she could stand, out of the way, on deck and get her first real sight of the town that was to be her home. A tumble of red brick houses was crammed into the corner where the Hull met the wide Humber. 'We are sadly confined for space,' Thomas told her. 'That's the tower of Holy Trinity where we worship. And there, further down, is St. Mary's.' They were rounding the point into the Humber. 'You can't see the Theatre Royal, it's behind there in Finkle Street, but look, there's what's left of the town walls that kept out Charles I. We've always been an independent lot in Kingston-upon-Hull. You know the story, of course?' She said 'yes', but he told it to her just the same. They were well out into the broad Humber now, moving briskly upstream with a following wind. 'Would you like to come below?' he asked. 'I'd like a word with Captain Peet, now he'll have the leisure.'

'Oh, may I not stay here?' She had never been in anything larger than a rowboat before, and was fascinated by the precision with which this large ship was handled, by so few men. 'I'll stay still as a mouse, I promise, and keep out of the way.'

'I don't see why not.' She rather thought he was glad to leave her there.

That journey was sheer delight. She enjoyed the admiring glances of the friendly crew, and watched with fascination as they manoeuvred the *Rowena* through the crowded traffic of the busy Humber and at last in at the mouth of the narrower Trent. Now fields stretched away on either side of the river, with here a church tower, there a clutch of cottages or a mill. Cows grazed in the meadows, or stood ankle-deep in the shallows, gazing meditatively at the passing ship. Kathryn thought she could happily have sailed like this for ever.

'I don't know when I have enjoyed myself so much.' She greeted Thomas warmly when he rejoined her much later, having found friends in the cabin.

'I knew you would make a good traveller.' He smiled back at her. 'I shall be interested to see what you think of our narrow boats.'

When a shower of rain forced her down to the cramped little cabin at last, she found Thomas deep in talk with their few fellow passengers, and was happy to sit quietly and listen. Aside from Beth and the captain's wife, she was the only woman on board and was relieved to recognise that nobody knew how recently she had been married. They treated her with a courteous lack of interest that she found infinitely reassuring.

They were talking about canals, and she enjoyed hearing Thomas make his case for the new passenger-carrying boats that would soon, he said, make it possible to travel from York to London entirely by water. There were problems still to be solved, he admitted, stretches of canal to be built suitable for passengers, but the enthusiasm was there, the money would soon be forthcoming. He spoke of fortunes made from investment in the Duke of Bridgewater's canal; told them the Birmingham Canal had paid twenty-three per cent two years ago. Locks and tunnels did add to the expense and make water travel slow, he admitted, but then think of the comfort of a passenger-carrying boat with its own cabins. No need to sleep in unaired sheets at uncomfortable and expensive posting houses. Once one had paid one's fare on the canal boat, one had paid for everything. And no risk from highwaymen either. It was just a question of building the passenger boats and getting the public used to the new way of travelling.

He was much the youngest of the little group of men and Kathryn was impressed by the respect with which they listened to him. Comyn of Comyn's Bank was someone to be reckoned with.

Nobody seemed to mind that when the bottle passed from hand to hand Thomas seldom filled his own glass, but presently he came over to Kathryn in her quiet corner. 'You must be tired. It is maybe time you left us.'

'Yes.' The laughter was indeed getting louder. 'Beth will be tired too.' Thomas had persuaded the captain to let Kathryn use the tiny cabin of the supercargo, who had gone ashore to his family in Hull, and Beth was to sleep on a pallet on the floor. It was close quarters enough, but Beth, too, was enjoying herself and they had a giggling, cheerful night of it. Drifting off to sleep at last, Kathryn found herself thinking about Windover Hall, a world and a lifetime away. Oliver Morewood had frightened her into leaving, into marriage. Into what a strange marriage. Her husband was out in the cabin now, sober, but cheerfully listening as the talk grew louder. He had arranged for her to spend the second night of their marriage with Beth. She could not quite decide how she felt about this, and fell asleep at last, while the noise in the cabin outside grew louder still, to dream about Mark Weatherby again and wake angry with herself.

They were lucky at Gainsborough. One of the new long boats was to leave only half an hour after they docked, and Kathryn was impressed once again by the efficiency with which Thomas got them and their luggage and servants on board. There was a ladies' cabin at the front of the long barge, and one for the gentlemen at the stern. Between them, a load of Baltic timber lay among traces of the coal the barge had brought down from Nottingham, and the air was full of its dust. Kathryn, shaking it out of a handkerchief, thought, but did not say, that this might prove a serious disadvantage of passenger-carrying barges. A first small doubt about Thomas Comyn's business sense crept into her mind.

And nobody could have said that the barge

was crowded. She and Beth were in the happy position of being the only ladies in the forward cabin, with eight berths to choose from, but the gentlemen's was well enough filled, Thomas told her, and again he had met friends. As for her, she found travelling at ground level like this even more fascinating than the higher view from the *Rowena*. Now, she was on a level with drooping willows and drinking cows. Mills and churches were high points beyond the banks, and, best of all, she could watch both sides at once from the stool a friendly crew member had found for her. She was amazed at how few there were of the crew, and thought this a great point in favour of her husband's scheme. Anyway, she was enjoying herself enormously, and so, she rather thought, was Beth, who seemed to have made firm friends with the crew. She liked the solid meals that were served in the gentlemen's cabin, and enjoyed lying in her narrow cot at night listening to the slap of the water against the side of the boat. It was a peaceful time, and she was grateful for it.

They were to take to the roads at Nottingham, and she was sorry, but Thomas had explained at some length why it was impossible to go further by boat. What it came down to, of course, was that there was no arrangement yet for individual travel on the canal network, no form of travelling post, which was what they would do from Nottingham on.

Kathryn thought Nottingham a dirty town, and the crowded inn was noisy after the peace of nights spent tied up against the river bank. They arrived late in the afternoon, and Thomas ordered a supper to be sent up to their private parlour. For the first time, she thought him out of temper, perhaps because there had been no message waiting for him from the man he was to meet. He had asked for a bottle of the hotel's best port wine and insisted that she join him in a glass, though she did not much like it, and thought it tasted odd with the huge porterhouse steaks and hashed potatoes he had ordered. She gulped it down to get it over with and was taken aback when he refilled her glass before she could stop him. 'We must drink to each other,' he told her.

'Yes, of course.' She raised her glass, sipped at it. 'To us.' And then, smiling at him. 'I am enjoying this journey. I do thank you.'

'Kathryn.' He reached out for her hand. 'I'm glad I married you. We are going to do very well, you and I. I'm sure of it. You're so easy, so sensible; you won't mind . . .' He emptied the dregs of the bottle into his glass. 'I've never . . . I don't know . . . You'll bear with me?'

'I'm your wife,' she said. 'I married you. But,' she paused, 'mother wouldn't tell me . . .' The wine was working strongly in her, and part of her wanted to say, 'I know we don't love each other.' She would not say it. 'I'm your wife,' she said again. 'Mother said it's my duty . . .'

'Duty!' He was suddenly angry. 'I've done it all my life. This is my duty.' Could he be crying? She tried very hard not to think so. 'There has to be an heir, Kathryn. An heir for Comyn's Bank. Do you see? Do you think if we try? Kathryn, you're so good, so strong; help me?'

'Of course I will.' She had never felt less good, less strong, but reached out, took his hand and felt it rigid in her own. 'It will be all right; of course it will.'

'Then —' He let go her hand, drained his wine, stood up. Did he really say, 'Let's get it over with?' He seized her hand again, pulled her into the next room, bolted the door. 'I'll be your maid.'

After that, it was all muddle. All misery? It took a very long time, and in the end she was not sure if anything had really happened. But at least he was fast asleep, his back to her again as it had been on the first night. She would not cry, but it was a long time before she slept.

When she waked, he was gone, and she was glad. Breakfast was brought to the parlour and she felt a little better after she had eaten it, but not much. She went downstairs, found Beth, found she could not meet her eyes.

'The master's gone out,' Beth told her. 'His friend came. He said we should go and look at the castle. He means to see us at dinner time. He says you must not go out alone; it's market day and the town is as full as it can hold of people.'

'Well,' said Kathryn. 'We have our orders then.' But they enjoyed walking round the castle ruins on their hill above the town and trying to decide whether the woods they could see from this high point were Sherwood Forest, home of Robin Hood. Walking back to the hotel, they found the town more crowded than ever; factory bells had rung and the streets were full of exhausted-looking women.

'They are stocking weavers,' Thomas explained over the lavish dinner he had ordered. 'It's the great trade here, and I'm afraid they have a hard enough life of it, poor girls. Long hours and low pay, but of course prices must be kept down.'

Kathryn rather longed to ask why, but remarked instead on the impression of independence the girls had given her. She laughed. 'You should have heard the things they shouted at Beth and me!' It had been disconcerting at the time, but in retrospect she rather liked to think of how the girls had swung boldly along the streets, arm in shabby arm, shouting their comments at the strangers.

'I should have been with you.' Thomas was conscience-stricken. 'Don't, I beg, ever mention to my mother that I let you expose yourself to such rudeness. She would be shocked at me.'

'And give you a scold?' She was sorry, when she saw him colour, and changed the subject. 'Have you finished your business? Did it go well? Can we leave this afternoon?' She very much did not want another night in that unpropitious bedroom.

'Yes, I've ordered the carriage. I shall see Brierley again on our way back from Ross and I am sure by then my arguments will have had time to convince him. He's always been a cautious man, John Brierley, that's just why I want him at my side in this venture. His name on our list of share holders will be worth ten other men's. At the moment he keeps talking about the difficulty of co-ordinating a service. I don't think he quite appreciates the advantages of the passenger-carrying boats. I'm rather sorry now that I did not contrive for you to meet him; such a fine little enthusiast as you are for them.'

'I'm sorry too.' She had found herself wondering whether John Brierley even knew that her husband was on his wedding trip. It was more and more evident that this was not something about which he felt inclined to boast.

The post chaise he had hired was comfortable and the horses the best, like everything else he ordered, and they made good time, travelling long days, with one pause in Burton-on-Trent, for another meeting with a business associate. It was raining hard in Burton-on-Trent and the whole place smelled so strongly of ale that Kathryn was glad enough to obey her husband and stay, as he put it, snug in the hotel with her needlework. Once again, she did not meet Thomas's friend, but this time he returned full of cheer from his conference. Mr. Bradshaw had agreed at once to have his name added to those willing to put up capital for the venture. 'He's a man of sense, is Sam Bradshaw; I knew he'd see things my way. He says he'll write a note to Brierley too. He knows when he is on to a good thing. And I am sure Wilberforce will back me. As Member for the East Riding he is bound to see the advantage of a direct passenger service by water between York and London.'

'Direct?' She could not help asking it.

'Well, as direct as possible! What a sharp

little thing you are, to be sure. I think I had best take you on as my business partner!' He laughed at his own joke, and pulled the bell in their comfortable parlour. 'We must drink to that!' He ordered steak again, and a bottle of port, and she thought, not for the first time, how much she would have liked to be consulted. Oliver Morewood usually drank claret, provided by the smuggler who used their bit of cliff, and she had quite liked the occasional sips she had had of that, found the port intolerably sweet and cloying. But she drank it. There was another night to be got through.

10

Kathryn had learned by now that her husband was not a great enthusiast for scenery, so she kept her pleasure to herself as they approached Ross-on-Wye. It had been good to get away from the industrial Midlands and into untouched country. There were valleys she longed to explore, enticing lanes leading off into woods, but Thomas was reading the *Morning Chronicle* and it was only two days until the end of September, when she had said they would arrive. They pressed on and finally drove up the hill into Ross-on-Wye towards the end of a fine afternoon, pausing by the pillared market hall to ask the way to Wye House.

'I hope they don't dine at four.' Thomas looked at his watch as the post chaise started up the steep street. 'You'd think with a name like that the house would be down near the river.'

But they had been directed up to the church at the top of the town. The chaise turned sharply into a driveway and the horses sweated up a last steep slope, turned left again to draw up on a gravelled sweep. To the right, lawns and terraces sloped down towards the great curve of the Wye. 'That explains the name.' Thomas jumped out and helped her alight. 'It looks well enough cared for.' The drive was smooth, the grass of the terraces closely scythed. 'I'm glad we came. Good gracious, what an old-fashioned house!'

It was low and rambling, beam and plaster, with small-paned leaded windows, the whole effect oddly out of keeping with the handsome approach. But the front door had opened and two women appeared.

They were not at all what Kathryn had expected. For one thing, they looked much younger than either her mother or Mrs. Comyn. They were both tall, one fair, one dark, both handsome in a fine-boned, brown-skinned way, and both dressed in elegant, mannish riding habits. She could feel her husband's surprise, as great as her own. These were not at all the two frail old ladies whose affairs he meant to set to rights.

'Dear child.' A kiss that smelled of lavender from the dark one. 'I'm your Aunt Lavinia and this is my dear Janet. We are so very pleased to see you. And you, Mr. Comyn,' she held out a hand and gave his a firm shake.

'You must be tired out, the pair of you. Annie will take you to your rooms. We dine at six. You must rest until then. Janet and I always spend the hour before dinner in study.' She smiled, and Kathryn loved her. 'Pray don't put on your bridal finery for us, child. You will wish to change, of course, after your journey, but we two dine as you see us.'

'Well!' said Thomas, safe in their room, which looked across the graveyard to the church. 'What an amazing couple. You gave me no idea, Kathryn.' A note of reproach in his voice.

'I had no idea. I do wonder what they study. I like them, don't you?'

'Like?' He thought about it. 'Most unusual. Dine in riding dress! I don't know what my mother would think.'

'No.' And I don't care. But she did not say it.

Dinner was simple but delicious. Kathryn was ashamed to be amused at her husband's face as the old servant poured him claret to drink with his Welsh mutton and batter pudding.

After the syllabub and the strong, delicious local cheese, Aunt Lavinia rose to her feet. 'I have told Piers to bring you a bottle of my father's port, Mr. Comyn. You will enjoy that, I am sure. He was a great judge of wine, your grandfather, Kathryn.' And then, with a brilliant smile. 'Not of much else, I am afraid.' She led the way to the tapestry-hung drawing room, where a huge log fire burned on the hearth, and shut the door. 'Now, dear child, you had best tell us why you married him.'

'I had to,' said Kathryn.

'That's obvious enough, but why? Not, I think for the usual reason.' The two old ladies (but she was not thinking of them as old any more) exchanged a brilliant, speaking glance. 'She doesn't even understand us,' said Lavinia. 'How old are you, child? I should know, but remind me.'

'Seventeen. He's very kind.' Something made her feel she must stand up for Thomas.

'A very good sort of young man,' said Janet. 'But not the man you wanted.'

'No . . . You see . . .' She wanted to tell them everything, but how could she?

'It's all right, child. We're safe for half an hour at least. I told Piers to see to it.'

'He's so kind —'

'Yes, but we are your family. More so, perhaps, than you know.' The two of them exchanged a sharp, questioning glance.

'What do you mean?' Kathryn looked from one brown, interested face to the other.

'You don't know.' This was Lavinia again.

'I told Janet that woman would never have told you.'

'You should not call her that,' said Janet. 'She is her mother after all.'

'More's the pity.' Lavinia smiled at Kathryn and again she felt the strong bond of kinship. 'Nobody told you (how should they?) that your father was engaged to my dear Janet before he met your mother. Oh, nothing published, but everything understood. Janet was my friend at school. She should have been my sister. And now she is. He'd not have stayed in the army if he had married Janet, poor Henry. He'd still be alive.'

'But I wouldn't,' said Kathryn, taking it all in. Not sisters. Friends. And no one had told her.

'That's perfectly true.' Another exchange of speaking glances. 'You take after Henry, I can see. He was no fool. Except when he let himself be bamboozled by that woman.'

'You should not say that,' protested Janet, who was not her aunt after all. 'Not to her daughter. And don't forget what a good match it was for him; how pleased your father was. He was stationed at York, you see,' she explained to Kathryn, 'met your mother at a race ball there. She was a great beauty, and heiress to Windover Hall.'

'And decided to have him,' said Lavinia.

'We were not engaged, you understand. We had just always known that one day we would be. Or that is what I thought. What is it, Kathryn?'

'That's what happened to me! I want to tell you about it. His name's Mark Weatherby; he comes from round here somewhere; I was quite certain. We were quite certain . . .' It was good to tell her miserable tale at last.

'And you never heard from him?' This was Lavinia, when she had finished.

'Not a word. I can't understand it! But my step-father has seen him twice.'

'Says he has?' suggested Janet.

'No reason why he should not be telling the truth,' said Lavinia. 'But — we'll have some enquiries made. They're from the north of the county, the Weatherbys. We live very quietly here, as you can see, two old maids together, but what we want to know, we always find out.'

'I'm sure.' She looked from one to the other, aware of a strength, a clarity about them. 'You like being old maids!' It was not exactly a question.

'Yes,' said Lavinia. 'Janet came to me when father died. It was the happiest day of our lives, I'm ashamed to say. We are our own mistresses, you see. I wish we had known about you. More than your mere existence,

I mean. I am ashamed that we let ourselves lose touch. And you still have not told us why you married Thomas Comyn.' A warning look. 'Here he comes.'

Over tea, Kathryn listened with awed amusement as the two ladies applied themselves to drawing out Thomas. They soon had him happily talking about canals, and he was their friend for life when they promised him an introduction to a landowner of their acquaintance who had shares in the Severn Waterway. 'I'm sure we could arrange for you to go over and see him, if you would like it,' Lavinia told him. 'We were asking dear Kathryn how long you feel able to stay with us.' They had been shocked, Kathryn thought, at how little she knew of her husband's plans.

'I should not be too long away,' he said now. 'I promised my mother.' Colouring. 'It's the first time I have left her since my father died. But if Mr. Sandborn is really experimenting with a new system of lock gates; if you think he would show me —'

'I'm sure of it.' Lavinia rescued him. 'I'll have Piers ride over first thing in the morning to make the arrangements. And Janet and I would dearly love it if you would consider leaving Kathryn with us for the few days you would need to be away. After all, you can look forward to a lifetime in her company, and we are so very much enjoying getting to know her.'

'Yes,' put in Janet. 'We thought we might take her on a few sightseeing excursions, while you are hard at work. You ride, of course, Kathryn?'

'Oh, yes!' She had been badly missing the daily exercise to which she had been used.

'The rector's wife has a charming little mare,' said Lavinia. 'He was telling me just the other day what a problem it was to get Sprite exercised. His wife is increasing again, and the doctor has forbidden her to ride.'

'Fool of a man,' said Janet. 'She would be much better riding, but it is lucky for us. To tell truth, Mr. Comyn, we had had it in mind to warn you that the excursion down the Wye you spoke of might not be quite the thing for a young lady like Kathryn. The company, you know, not always of the most elegant, and the conditions so cramped. I am not absolutely sure that your mother would approve of it.'

'Oh, my goodness.' As he thought about it, Kathryn surprised a look of entirely wicked amusement between the two women.

'Very often the passengers are all members of the male sex,' Lavinia explained. 'And some of the arrangements, I believe, not of the nicest.'

'A delicately nurtured young lady,' said Janet.

'And so recently married.'

'You must go and take a look at the excursion boat,' Lavinia ended the discussion, 'and come to your own conclusion. But if you should decide that your time would be more rationally employed in studying Mr. Sandborn's locks and sluices, we would be happy to show Kathryn something of our Wye countryside. The distances are so much shorter on horseback than on our winding, delightful river. It would be a rare pleasure to two old hermits like us.'

'You are more than kind.'

Later, in their comfortable bedroom, he put down the candle and turned to Kathryn. 'Would you be very much disappointed if we did not make the trip down the Wye? If the ladies do not look on it as quite the thing I cannot believe that my mother would approve.'

'No indeed. I would not wish to do anything she would not like.' Unspoken between them was the knowledge of the very similar conditions Kathryn had cheerfully endured on their journey. But then they both knew his mother would never be told about that.

Things went better in bed that night, and though it hurt, and she could not exactly say she had enjoyed herself, Kathryn was relieved for her hostesses' sheets. She found a spot of

166

blood on her nightgown in the morning, but that was easily washed out in the handbasin. And there was a kind of glow about Thomas that she found endearing.

She liked him less when he began what she could not help thinking a vulgar cross-questioning of the two ladies about their affairs in the course of breakfast. But they did not seem to mind it.

'Oh, we are as poor as church mice,' said Lavinia cheerfully. 'Janet's family cut her off without even a shilling when she came to live with me. This isn't our house, you know. My old home had to be sold when my father died, to pay his debts. The lawyers managed to save me two hundred pounds a year out of the wreck, and a good friend offered me this house, rent free, for my lifetime. He sees to the upkeep too, fortunately for us, and you can see how comfortably two single ladies can live on an annuity of two hundred pounds.'

'An annuity?' He took her up almost sharply. 'So what would happen to Miss Janet if you were to predecease her? Forgive the question.'

'Of course. It's what we worry about, why we try to save, though it is not exactly easy. But we have the best of friends and neighbours. They never kill a pig but we receive a side of bacon. And you are not to be worrying, Mr. Comyn; that mutton last night was a gift too, and of course we keep our own hens. Your breakfast egg was straight from the nest and cost us nothing.' She was teasing him a little now, Kathryn thought.

'But you must let me —' He looked miserable, uncertain how to make the offer.

'We'll let you earn your keep, don't worry.' Her smile was very friendly now. 'And Kathryn too. You are going to look through our accounts for us and see if there is any saving we can profitably make, and Kathryn is going to help old Annie, who came with me from home and is not so young as she was. You won't mind, Kathryn?'

'I shall love it. But, please, tell me, what is it you are studying?'

'Our project? Ah, that is our pride and joy, and we do let ourselves hope it may even be of some advantage to us one day. Janet speaks the Welsh, you know, and her family had a great collection of Welsh poetry and legend. We are hard at work translating it and hope that in a few more years we may have it ready for publication. There seems to be a growing interest in that kind of thing and we really hope that in the end we may make a little profit from our happy labours. You look doubtful, Mr. Comyn?'

'Someone told me the other day that Miss

Burney only earned twenty pounds for her *Evelina*.'

'How very sad. But surely she must have made a better bargain for *Cecilia?* And our friend Mrs. More has promised that when we have finished our *Gest of Sir Cradock*, she will send it to Mr. Cadell, her own publishing bookseller, who has done great things for her.' And, when he still looked doubtful. 'She told us, last time we saw her, that he sold seven editions of her *Thoughts on the Importance of the Manners of the Great to General Society* in a few months.'

'And very interesting it was,' said Kathryn. 'Tell me, is there any copying I could do for you? I write a plain, clear hand and you cannot imagine how I would like to do it.'

'We will tie you to your desk,' promised Lavinia.

They all rode to Goodrich Castle that afternoon, though Kathryn suspected her husband would really have preferred to spend the day going through the two ladies' account books. He did not share her enthusiasm for the ride over wooded hills with its varying views of Wilton Bridge and the castle ahead, and had to make an obvious effort to seem interested in what the two ladies told him about its history. He did not much care that William Marshall, Earl of Pembroke, had held it against the Welsh for King John, or that it had been surrendered after a short siege during the Cromwellian wars and then been destroyed by order of Parliament. 'They made a thorough job of it,' was his only reaction to the romantic prospect of ruined keep and winding, wooded river. Kathryn thought they were all relieved when they reached home to find that Piers had returned with an invitation from Mr. Sandborn, urging Thomas to come and inspect his locks next day, and promising him a bed 'and bachelor fare' for as long as he wished to stay.

'Your husband's name is clearly one to reckon with in the business world,' Lavinia told Kathryn. 'Mr. Sandborn is not usually so pressing in his invitations. I never for a moment thought he would ask him to stay, but it makes everything much easier.'

'Yes.' There were whole chapters unspoken between them.

Thomas worked her hard that night, in the lavender scented sheets, but she was not sure that they either of them really enjoyed it. 'I do not like to leave you for even one night.' He rolled off her at last. 'But it's bachelor quarters . . . And maybe you will be able to learn a little more about these two odd ladies, alone with them. This friend, for instance, who so kindly lends them the house. I would like to know something about him. Meet him, if possible. It would be an awkward enough business if your Aunt Lavinia were to die and he should choose to turn Miss Janet out. What is her other name, by the way?'

'I don't know. It's never come up.'

'Find out, if you tactfully can. Because, I am afraid we must face it, if something untoward should happen, we might well find ourselves in some way responsible for the poor lady, now we have acknowledged the connection. It's an odd enough sort of business. I do not quite know what my mother will think about it.'

In the end, he stayed four days with Mr. Sandborn, and Kathryn thought she had never been so contented in her life. It was not the wild happiness of loving Mark, but it was wonderfully comfortable to find that she could talk to Lavinia and Janet as she had to him, tell them everything, her plans, her hopes, and what had become of them.

'You have to make the best of your Thomas,' Lavinia summed it up when she had heard the whole story of the marriage. 'And there is a great deal of good. Will you be able to make a friend of his mother, do you think? It is obvious that he cares very much for her, respects her opinions.'

'Yes,' said Kathryn a little doubtfully. And then, 'I do hope so. I shall certainly do my best.'

'And apply your good mind to his work,' said Janet. 'Men do like to be listened to.'

'And will sometimes even take advice,' smiled Lavinia. 'If it is tactfully enough put.'

'You write a very good hand.' Janet picked up the page Kathryn had been copying. 'I wonder if Mr. Comyn would let you copy documents for him sometimes. There must be a mass of paperwork in a business like his, and it would be the best way in the world to understand what concerns him.'

'I don't know.' Kathryn sounded more doubtful still. 'There is a chief clerk, Mr. Robertson, who seems to be very much in charge. I only met him for a moment, the day we came away, but I did not feel that I was welcome in his domain. The bank is in one of the front rooms of the house, you know.'

'And Mrs. Comyn is in the wing,' Lavinia smiled at her. 'You will have to make friends of both. That's a problem?'

'I didn't like Mr. Robertson,' confessed Kathryn. 'And I rather thought he did not much like me.'

'Try again,' urged Janet. 'With both of them. And now, we must get back to work if we are to finish this canto before your husband returns. I don't need to tell you what a help you are being to us, dear child.'

'I'm enjoying it so! It is better than a novel any day. I had no idea that one of King Arthur's knights was supposed to have lived in a cave by the Wye.'

'Dear Sir Cradock. He certainly cuts a much more interesting figure in this collection of tales than in Mr. Percy's *Reliques*. The story there is all about his wife's chastity, not much of a remembrance for one of the heroes who helped Arthur fight off the incoming hordes of Saxons.'

'I like the tale of how he got his sword the best,' said Kathryn.

'Not from a stone, but from reading a rune. Yes, so do I. What is it, Annie?'

'It's a letter, Miss Janet. For Mrs. Comyn. Jem at the post office ran out with it when he saw Piers in the street, thinking it might be important.' She handed it to Kathryn. 'I hope it's not bad news.'

'I must go home!' Kathryn had recognised her step-father's sprawling hand, anticipated the bad news he conveyed so briefly. 'It's my mother. She's had one of her spasms . . . She's asking for me.'

'It's bad?' Janet put a loving arm round her.

'I'm afraid so. The doctor said . . . The next one . . . No excitement . . . Oh, if only

I could start at once.'

'You must wait for your husband, child. He said he would be back tonight, remember. I will send to the inn to be sure there are horses first thing in the morning.'

'Thank you. But it will take days. Excuse me!' She fled for her room and the scant relief of tears.

Left alone, the two ladies looked at each other. 'Poor child,' said Lavinia. 'From what she didn't quite say, I imagine she married for her mother's comfort. And now, I'm very much afraid, no mother, only the husband, and his.'

'She'll manage,' said Janet. 'I have great confidence in Kathryn, have not you?'

11

Returning from four happy days talking canals, Thomas was slightly miffed to find that arrangements for their return had already been set on foot, and thanked Lavinia pompously enough to make her see the error of her ways. Then he became human again. 'I'm really sad not to be able to stay longer with you two kind ladies, and meet your friends, but Kathryn would be wretched with anxiety, and my mother will be looking for us to come home.'

'Particularly if she has heard the sad news from Windover,' said Lavinia. 'You will go straight there surely?'

'Oh, I hardly think so.' Judiciously. 'It's such a small detour to Hull. My mother will be expecting us, and indeed may feel she should accompany poor Kathryn at this sad time. We have to be prepared for the worst, I fear. Lady Charlotte's doctor held out little hope, when I talked to him, of her recovery from any future spasm.'

Lavinia looked quickly round, but Kathryn

was out of earshot, talking anxiously to Janet. 'You have discussed Lady Charlotte's health with her doctor?'

'Oh yes, I had to. I was settling an annuity on her, you see.'

'And he got a bargain,' Lavinia told Janet angrily, safe in their own room. 'He is quite sure that, hurry as they may, they will arrive too late.'

'And is glad of it.'

'I am afraid so.'

'Ah, poor Kathryn. What can we do for her?'

'Not much, I am afraid, except try to prepare her, and plan to keep in touch. But she will manage, will Kathryn. She has backbone, that child.'

'I wish we had had news about Mark Weatherby.'

'Why? What use would news of him be to her now? She has made her bed, poor child, and must learn to lie in it.'

She received a note that night from the friend in the north of the county to whom she had written for information. It was not much help, however, since it gave Windover Hall as the last known address for Mark Weatherby. 'Even though his mother is dead, you would have thought he would have let his friends know of his move.' She handed the letter to Janet. 'How very odd. I suppose we must tell the poor child.'

'Of course we must. It's more than odd, you know. I do begin to wonder if some mishap has not befallen the young man.'

'For goodness sake don't suggest that to Kathryn. She has enough anxiety to bear right now.'

'And her husband taking her home by way of Hull.'

'Just so. How I wish our book was finished, and a success.'

'We must work harder; it will be an inducement.'

They travelled back post, by long stages, and if Thomas regretted not being able to spend a day with his friend in Nottingham, he kept quiet about it. He thought Kathryn still hoped to find her mother alive, thought her foolish to do so, but felt he must indulge her foolishness. He had accidentally overheard Lavinia telling her about their failure to get news of Mark Weatherby, seen her face, and drawn his own conclusions. It had been honest of her to tell him about Mark, but sometimes he wished she had not done so.

They reached Hull at last late on a wet October afternoon when wind and rain lashing in from the northeast gave a savage foretaste of winter. One glance at the windows of the house in the High Street told him the whole story. 'I am so sorry, my dear.' He took Kathryn's hand as the carriage steps were let down.

'You mean — ?'

'The house is in mourning. Closed shutters. I knew I could count on my mother to pay every tribute to yours. A sad homecoming for you, but let us hope we are in time for the funeral. Ah, here is my mamma. I was sure she would be on the lookout for us.'

'My dears!' Mrs. Comyn was in deepest black, making Kathryn aware of her own now unsuitable maroon travelling dress. Turning from her son, she embraced Kathryn with the familiar smell of camphor. 'We must get you some mourning, child. Mrs. Paris shall come first thing tomorrow. I warned her to hold herself in readiness. You must not go out until it comes home.'

'But, the funeral?'

'Was today. Mr. Morewood did not feel he could wait longer. I believe he is anxious to get the little boys away as soon as possible.'

'Away?' They were inside the darkly mourning house now and Kathryn looked dazedly about at black-draped pictures.

'I believe he means to take them south, to his sister. I am afraid things are all at sixes

178

and sevens at Windover Hall.' She exchanged a significant look with her son.

'I'll ride up tomorrow,' he told her.

'I think you should.'

'But I must go too,' protested Kathryn. 'The little boys . . . Sally . . . the servants. And —' Hesitating. 'The grave?'

'Impossible,' said Mrs. Comyn. 'I told you, child, you cannot stir out of the house until you are suitably clad. Matters have been strangely enough handled up at the Hall without your making an exhibition of yourself.'

'I have no doubt I shall have to go up many times before things are settled,' Thomas told her. 'I promise that you shall come the next time.'

'But — if he takes the little boys away? They are my brothers.'

'Half-brothers,' corrected Mrs. Comyn. 'Dear child, think a little. I know it is all enormously sad, but this is your home now, we are your family, and we do have to recognise that Mr. Morewood is not the most eligible of connections.'

'Sold? Windover Hall is to be sold?' Kathryn could not believe the news her husband brought back.

'You had not expected it? I am so very sorry; perhaps I should have warned you, but I thought you must understand that it would be inevitable, in all the unfortunate circumstances. At least the sale should clear Mr. Morewood's debts and make it possible for him to settle in a smaller way in the south. He means to be near his sister, he tells me, for the little boys' sake; they are good friends with her children already. You must see the sense of it, Kathryn. And we will keep in touch, of course. Something at Christmas . . . The boys to visit when they are older . . . They are your half-brothers, after all, your mother's sons.'

'My mother —' She had been wondering how to ask the question. 'Was there anything? A letter? A message?'

'I'm sorry.' He had made up his mind to spare her the painful details of her mother's death. 'It was so sudden, you see. She hardly had time to suffer, Kathryn. You must comfort yourself with that. No time for messages either. Just remember how much she loved you.'

'Did she?' asked Kathryn thoughtfully. 'Do you really think so?' And then, wishing he had volunteered the information. 'Did she leave a will?'

'I am afraid not. Mr. Renshaw sends his apologies, says he tried to persuade her, never succeeded. An awkward enough business at the best of times, and I am afraid Mr. Morewood being the man he is does not make it easier. We tried, both Mr. Renshaw and I, to make him see reason. No use, I am afraid; he sticks to the letter of the law. You must not mind it, my dear, that you come to me empty handed.'

'It's outrageous! You mean, not even her jewels, the family jewels? She always said I should have them.' How odd to find herself minding so much about mere things.

'He says they should go to the boys' wives.'

'Looking ahead,' said Kathryn dryly. She was doing the same thing. Empty handed. She imagined Mrs. Comyn's reaction. 'I'll make it up to you,' she said. 'I promise you.'

'But you do, Kathryn.' He really meant it, she thought, and wondered if she deserved it.

She felt the difference in Mrs. Comyn almost at once. There was nothing overt, nothing to put one's finger on, but she felt herself subtly devalued in a way that it was hard to analyse, and impossible to deal with. She had expected, when she returned from her wedding tour, to take over the reins of the household, but this simply did not happen, and every day she let go by without protesting made it more difficult to do so. Her offers of help were gently and irrevocably put aside, and she recognised, too late, that it had been a mistake to make them. She should have stood on her rights, but how could she? What were her rights?

She felt a gradual dwindling of respect from the servants, and could hardly blame them. Mrs. Moss went every morning to Mrs. Comyn's rooms to take her orders for the day. There was never any question of which Mrs. Comyn.

Thomas had been very busy since they got back, and, she thought, preoccupied. She wondered if Mr. Robertson had perhaps taken some kind of advantage in their absence, and decided that whatever she did she would not trouble her husband with her problems. He was frankly relieved that their state of deep mourning meant an absolute minimum of wedding visits, and after one or two takings of tea with her mother-in-law's friends, Kathryn was grateful too. If there was any conversation in Hull, she was yet to find it. She began to fear that like so much in this thriving, bustling town, talk was a male prerogative. Thomas went to Cresswell's Coffee Rooms every day to read the London papers, and was out two evenings a week. Saturday night he always spent with a group of friends at the George Club, a habit of which his mother bitterly disapproved. There was card playing, betting, and even, horror of horrors, a cockpit at the George Inn in Blackfriargate, but Thomas patiently explained that it was the friendly meeting over dinner that he went for. Their neighbour, Sir Henry Etherington, the town's great man, often came in; the evening was an essential part of the business life of the town. Mrs. Comyn was never quite convinced, and even Kathryn wondered a little, when her husband came home late, smelling of spirits and rather inefficiently amorous.

Mrs. Comyn approved of Thomas's Thursday evenings, and Kathryn envied them. They were spent at a discussion group in the street romantically named the Land of Green Ginger, where he and his friends debated such topics as whether a man in his natural untaught state, or a man who has acquired learning, possesses the greater share of content. Kathryn tried to enliven Friday's dull and lenten dinner by getting her husband to describe the discussion, in the hope of reviving it among themselves, but it was no use. Abstract ideas, in so far as she recognised them, were anathema to Mrs. Comyn. She soon had the conversation back where she liked it: the servants, the weather, and the price of the fish they were eating.

'Thomas?' Kathryn still found it hard to use his name, but knew he liked it.

'Yes, my dear?' She had found him in their bedroom, when she knew he would be ready dressed for his Saturday night at the George, always a happy time with him.

'Would you mind very much if I had my writing desk put up in your dressing room? And maybe a shelf for my books?' She had been deeply thankful that she and Sally had packed up all her possessions for shipment by wagon from Windover Hall so that at least her step-father had not got his greedy hands on them, but when they had reached Hull at last there had been nowhere private to put them. Mrs. Comyn might sleep in the garden wing, but once she had breakfasted she came over and spent the rest of the day, sociably, as she called it, in the front parlour with Kathryn. Her favourite, high-backed chair was there, with a commanding view of the High Street outside. The snug little sitting room Thomas had made for her in her own room looked out over the garden, a fatal drawback. A light sleeper and early riser, she was always established in the parlour when Kathryn joined her, ready for an audience to her comments on everyone who passed by and most particularly on callers at the bank. Kathryn, listening to her ideas about what business had brought Mr. Bell, the bookseller, or Mr. Dawson, the apothecary from Silver Street, to the bank, could only hope that she was the only person who knew of the close interest her mother-in-law took in her son's affairs. It was a hope soon quenched when she heard Mrs. Comyn describing the morning's callers to her two best friends, the Misses Evangeline and Patience Harris. These were two maiden ladies, daughters of a curate at Hessle, who had died leaving them in such straitened circumstances that they were glad, Kathryn thought, to earn their fortnightly cup of tea by listening avidly to the morsels of gossip their hostess saved for them.

She did not feel she could speak of this to Thomas, though she did sometimes find herself wondering whether he had not had it in mind when he made that comfortable little sitting room for his mother at the back of the house. If he had, his trouble had been for nothing, and it was, simply, maddening to her that Mrs. Comyn had that quiet room and never used it, whereas her own attempts at reading or writing were incessantly interrupted by her mother-in-law who looked on reading in the morning as sinful and writing as only marginally less so.

'In my dressing room?' As always, Thomas gave her request due consideration. 'But, why, my dear?' He reached into the press for his gold-headed cane. 'Why hide yourself away?

185

Surely the parlour would be more suitable, more accessible for the servants when they have any problem?'

'But they don't come to me,' said Kathryn.

'Oh.' Had he been trying not to notice?

'Yes — Well . . . Maybe, soon, you will have other interests to occupy you.' He flushed crimson, and she was glad that this was as near as he would get to speaking of everyone's silent, pressing hope that she would become pregnant. 'But in the mean time —' He moved over to open the dressing room door. 'Your desk by the window there? And a shelf for your books beside it? I really do not see why not, Kathryn. I shall like to think of you racking your pretty little head there while I am away at work. What were you thinking of doing, exactly?'

'There is so much I don't know. So much to learn. We — I had planned to study European history this year, and to read some Tacitus —'

'You read Latin?' Now she had surprised him.

'A little.'

'Best not tell my mother.' His smile was complicit. 'But I'll remember when I am stuck on a quotation in a letter from one of my more learned friends. I never could come to terms with all that grammar.'

186

It gave her the opening she had hoped for. 'There's something else I would so much like to do,' she told him. 'About your letters. I could not help hearing the other day, when Mr. Robertson was grumbling about the amount of time the clerks have to spend taking copies of your letters to Mr. Bradshaw and Mr. Brierley about the passenger canal boats. I would dearly like to copy those for you if you would let me.'

'You?' It was an entirely novel thought to him.

'Aunt Lavinia complimented me on my hand,' she reminded him. 'And I have all the time in the world, whereas those poor clerks in the counting house seem always to be in a hurry. I truly think they are more likely to make mistakes than I am.' Unspoken between them was the knowledge that Robertson disliked and disapproved of the passenger boat project. It was inevitable that he made it difficult for the clerks to spend as much time. on it as was needed.

'Would you really like to do it?' Doubtfully. 'It seems dull enough work for a young lady.'

'I would love to do it!' Her tone carried complete conviction. 'I feel so useless as it is. Doing that, I would feel I was really helping you, sharing something with you.'

'Then we'll give it a try! I'll give the orders

for your desk and shelves in the morning, and Kathryn . . .'

'Yes?'

'Best let me explain it to my mother.'

'Oh, yes,' she said fervently.

She thought he must have handled his mother brilliantly, but then he had had a good deal of practice at this. Mrs. Comyn made it clear that she thought the whole project an absurd one, of which no good would come, but Kathryn found herself free to spend her mornings peacefully in the dressing room, dividing her time between the studies she had planned with Mark Weatherby and the increasing pile of letters to copy for Thomas. He was delighted with her, and by spring time, he was simply giving her the gist of the letters and relying on her to produce both original and copies for his approval. 'Which is more than I would trust either of those young men to do,' he told her, one mild April morning. 'And what is more, I hear you are taking over the garden too.'

'If you don't mind?'

'Mind? I should rather think not. It is something for which mother and I have never had any genius, and of course the gardeners know it. They seem to have a great respect for you.' A note of surprise.

She did not tell him that she had run the gardens as well as the rest of Windover Hall since she was fourteen. The less they spoke about Windover the better. He never had taken her back, and she had been, quite simply, outraged when he had broken it to her that all the servants there had been let go with a week's wages. He might not have felt them his responsibility but they were most certainly hers. It had brought on their first quarrel, and Thomas had sulked and slept in his dressing room for a week. And the worst of it was that she was not quite sure whether she was glad or sorry when he had decided, with nothing further said, simply to come back to her bed as if nothing had happened.

12

When she thought about Hull, many years later, it was the smells Kathryn remembered first: whale oil, and soap, and tar, and the strange, sweet smell of the sugar-boiling house in Wincolmlee when the wind was from that direction. She made pot pourri from the old-fashioned roses in the garden, and lavender bags from the newly trimmed lavender hedges, but still the house stank of one thing or another, depending on the prevailing wind. Thomas and his mother genuinely did not notice this, she realised, and did her best to hide her own discomfort. But she was not well that spring of 1791, a most unusual state of affairs with her.

Her mother-in-law was the first to notice her failing appetite, and inevitably drew the wrong conclusion. But when a series of probing questions established that she was not, as she delicately put it, 'increasing', she launched into attack. Hull was no place for fine lady airs and graces. She had expected that no good would come of all this studying, and she was being proved right. 'What is that you are reading now, child?' She had found Kathryn at her desk in the dressing room, and loomed large in the doorway, making escape from her questions impossible.

'It's Mr. Burke on the French Revolution. I promised Thomas I would read it and give him the main heads before Thursday, when they are to discuss the situation in France at the club.'

'Most unsuitable. I shall tell Thomas so. And I suppose those are some of the business letters you copy for him? Not at all the occupation for a young lady. Miss Evangeline was asking me about it just the other day. Mr. Robertson is a connection of theirs, and we all know how he feels about your intrusions into the counting house.' Everyone in Hull seemed to be related to everyone else. 'And that reminds me,' her mother-in-law went on. 'I had meant to say a word about your conduct when the Miss Harrises took tea the other day. It is not the part of a well-bred young lady to take up an older one as you did Miss Evangeline.'

Kathryn flushed crimson. 'She said Mr. Wilberforce was a fool for introducing his bill about the slave trade. She practically said slavery was ordained by God. I'm sorry if you did not like the way I spoke to her, but I think she should have remembered that apart from being a great philanthropist, Mr. Wilberforce is an old friend of my family's.'

'Maybe the less we say about your family, the better. I have had it in mind to suggest to you, Kathryn, that you should not always be talking about the way things were done at Windover Hall. Why, what in the world is the matter?' Kathryn had broken into a passion of tears.

They were the first she had shed in public since she received the news of her mother's death, and once she had started she could not stop. Mrs. Comyn passed from anger, to rage, to fright, and ended by sending post haste for Mr. Dawson, the apothecary.

He arrived to find Kathryn lying on the big bed still crying, but quietly now, hopelessly. Beth was sitting beside her, holding her hand and offering smelling salts. Mrs. Comyn, who had greeted him downstairs with the news that her difficult daughter-in-law was in helpless hysterics, but not, unfortunately, in the family way, loomed in the doorway.

Mr. Dawson was a member of the Thursday Club and a family man. His own daughters were not much younger than Kathryn and were still away at school, learning to be ladies. He thought of their lives, and what gossip had told him of Kathryn's, and felt immensely sorry for her. 'Well, now.' He smiled down at the red-eyed gasping figure on the bed, and picked up her wrist to feel her pulse. 'Here's a pretty kettle of fish! And what I would prescribe first and foremost for you, Mrs. Comyn, is a breath of fresh air. Will you do me the honour of taking a turn in your garden with me? Your husband tells me you have done great things there. He boasts of you, I should tell you, in a quiet way, at our Thursday meetings.' He addressed it to Kathryn but meant it for her mother-in-law. 'The pulse is no worse than one should expect,' he told the older lady now. 'And no sign of fever. I shall expect you in the garden in five minutes, young lady. The air will do you more good than anything else I can prescribe.'

He spent the five minutes downstairs with Mrs. Comyn, asking a few gently probing questions about the family's regimen. By the time Kathryn joined them, hair tidy and face washed, he had a pretty good idea of what was the matter.

'That's better.' He smiled down at her, took her arm and guided her down the flagged walk between two neatly clipped lavender hedges. 'This is your territory, is it not, and it does you credit. But is walking here all the exercise you get?'

'Most of the time.' She managed a wavering smile for his compliment. 'Thomas takes me to walk on the Garrison Side across the river on Sunday afternoons if it is fine, but you know what it is like.'

'More talk than walk,' he took her point. 'Do you not ride, Mrs. Comyn?'

'Oh, yes! I used to ride every day at Windover —' she stopped, flushed crimson then turned very white.

'What is it?'

'Please,' she held out an impulsive hand, 'don't tell Mrs. Comyn I said that. She thinks I talk too much about Windover Hall.'

'I shall tell her nothing of what we have discussed,' he said robustly. 'Why do you think I brought you out here? But I shall tell her, and that hard-working husband of yours, that what I prescribe for you is fresh air and exercise. Has young Thomas taken you to that house of his at Hessle yet?'

'No. He's been so busy . . .'

'I shall tell him it is time you both had a holiday.' There was no need for him to specify what it would be a holiday from. 'I'll have a word with him at the club; no need to make a performance of it. And in the mean time you are to spend an hour a day walking in the garden, Mrs. Comyn.'

'Like a prisoner at exercise?' She caught her

breath. 'Forget I said that, Mr. Dawson. And, please —'

'Yes?' He was immensely sorry for her now.

'Don't let Mrs. Comyn decide I ought not to be copying my husband's letters for him.'

'I promise you I won't. I just hope that husband of yours knows what a lucky fellow he is, Mrs. Comyn. Now, I shall leave you here beginning your programme of exercise and have a quick word with your mother-in-law as I go. You may count on me.'

'Thank you.' She turned and began to walk away from him down the straight path that led to the far wall of the garden and the bristling masts and river sounds beyond. Downstream, the bells of Holy Trinity struck the hour.

When she came in, an hour later, she was surprised to find the younger of Mr. Robertson's two clerks hovering in the side entrance of the counting house. 'Mrs. Comyn.' He held out a tight little bunch of violets. 'We were all so very sorry to hear you are not quite the thing. Please — I had an errand to do in the town. I thought you might like these.'

'Oh, I do.' She took them, smiling at him warmly, with a shine of tears in her eyes. 'I do thank your Mr. Turner, they are just what I needed to cheer me up.'

'I'm glad.' He was blushing. 'And, Mrs. Comyn, please remember that if there is ever anything, anything in the world I can do for you, it will make me the happiest of men.'

'Mr. Turner —' Robertson's voice from the counting house made him vanish like a guilty thing, and Kathryn turned in at the family's entrance to the house wondering how many prying domestic eyes had witnessed the little encounter. But it was good to have a friend.

'You should have told me you were not feeling quite the thing.' Thomas had reserved the reproach for the privacy of their bedroom. 'I met Dawson outside Trinity House and he gave me a rare scold about you. Thinks we've been neglecting you among us. I am afraid that my mother was not best pleased about that.'

'Oh, why did you tell her?' She had pleaded headache and gone to bed early, hoping to postpone this conversation at least until the morning.

'You know I tell her everything.' He climbed into bed beside her, reached to pull up her nightgown, plunged ruthlessly into her. 'Now you will feel better.' He turned away, and slept instantly.

Next morning he remarked on what a pity it was there was no one for her to ride with.

'But I shall take you out to Hessle the first weekend I can spare the time. You will like it out there, I am sure. And in the meanwhile I have promised Dawson we will not neglect our Sunday walks on the Garrison Side. You enjoy those do you not? Next winter will be better for you; we will be out of mourning and will go to all the assemblies, you and I, and dance away with the best of them as we did in Scarborough. What a long time ago that seems.'

'Yes.' Listlessly. It seemed a lifetime ago to her.

'Besides, everything may be different next winter. My mother says it often takes a little while —' He stammered into silence at sight of her face.

'What takes a little while?' She asked it ruthlessly, knowing he would not be able to find words for his hopes. 'I must go and take my walk.'

She soon learned just how many times she could pace the garden in her statutory hour, and got almost used to the feeling of eyes upon her from the blind windows of the house. She had begun by counting the paces, but, soon tiring of this, took to telling herself stories, as she had done long ago, as a child, on the rare occasions when she could not sleep. She had always been her own heroine and the stories had stopped when she had found Mark. She had not needed them any more. Now, she did.

One of Lavinia Pennam's rare letters arrived at the beginning of May, and, as always, gave a new and more positive turn to Kathryn's thoughts. Lavinia wrote about the failure of Mr. Wilberforce's bill for the abolition of slavery and the shift in liberal opinion about events in France. Like Kathryn, she had been reading Mr. Burke's *Reflections on the French Revolution* and said she found herself reluctantly in agreement with him about the dangerous tendencies now manifesting themselves on the other side of the Channel. 'Janet and I were shocked when Mr. Fox defended the French revolutionaries in the House,' she wrote. And are trying to forget our disappointment in a great burst of work on dear Sir Cradock. I cannot tell you how we miss our amanuensis.'

For a few hopeful moments after reading this, Kathryn imagined suggesting to her husband that nothing would do her more good than a visit to the two ladies in Ross-on-Wye. But he was deeply embroiled in the formation of his Company for the Construction and Management of Passenger-Carrying Canal Boats, and at the same time in the negotiations for the founding of a new Hull Commercial Bank in Whitefriargate. There was no way he would be able to go with her and not the slightest hope that he would let her go alone. Useless to ask what was sure to be refused.

They rode out to Hessle together on a fine Friday in late May and Kathryn's spirits lifted as they passed the town graveyard and reached the open country at last, and the wide view of the Humber. One of the many things that had disconcerted her about Kingston-upon-Hull was that, despite its name, one was so little aware of the rivers that enclosed it. Because its position in the corner of the two rivers was so tight, the houses were inevitably built hugger-mugger close together and it was rarely that one got an unimpeded view of either Hull or Humber.

Now she took a deep breath of salt-smelling air and turned, smiling to Thomas. 'Oh, what a holiday,' she said impulsively. 'Two whole days of freedom.'

'Freedom? Kathryn, what can you mean?'

'Nothing.' She had regretted her words the moment they were spoken. 'Just that it's good to get out of the town and hear the larks sing again.'

'Larks?'

'Up there.' Pointing. She always forgot what a town boyhood he had had. 'Shall we have a gallop?' Eagerly.

'Not yet, Kathryn. We are hardly out of

sight of the town.'

'We used to gallop on the sands at Scarborough. In full view of the town.'

'That was Scarborough.' They were silent for a while.

His house stood by itself, close to the river, upstream from Hessle. It was solidly built of brick and tile and surrounded by pear trees in full if straggling blossom. 'Oh, how pretty,' she exclaimed.

'Sadly neglected, I am afraid. But I am glad to see that Ben has scythed the grass for us.' She had hoped for a kind of picnic existence in the little house but learned that he always sent a couple of servants in advance to help the caretaker make all ready for him. He was a man who liked his comforts, her husband.

But the ride had given her an appetite, and she was glad enough to sit down to the meal of his favourite steak with batter pudding and port wine that awaited them. Afterwards, she was eager to go out and explore while the light lasted. 'Yes,' he agreed, 'but fetch a shawl, my dear. It will be cool by the river. We don't want you catching cold to add to your other troubles.'

'Troubles?'

'This nervous affliction of yours. That's right.' He draped the shawl carefully round her shoulders. 'This is the shortest way to the river.' He looked back at the house, judged that they were out of earshot. 'I have been wanting a quiet word with you, Kathryn. My mother is a little anxious about you. About us.'

'Is she?'

'I'm afraid so. It is affecting her appetite, I am sorry to say, and her sleep.'

'I'm sorry.' Kathryn had a vision of her mother-in-law, only the day before, treating her friends, the Miss Harrises, to 'a little supper' of potted lobster and sweetbreads, followed by jelly and macaroons in brandy. Easy enough to pick at one's dinner if one were sure of a supper like this later on. 'My mother always found that if she ate anything late at night she did not sleep very well,' she ventured.

'We are not talking about your mother, Kathryn, but mine. And that is another thing that is troubling her a little, I am afraid. She feels you, always, comparing our house and our habits with Windover Hall. Well! Even you, Kathryn, besotted as you are on that place, must see, when you think about it, that it is hardly the thing to be doing that. I am sure, to a sensible girl like you, just a hint will be enough, but I am afraid it is more than time that I gave it you. I thought it would be easier for us both if we came out here, where we can be private.'

'You manage to be private with your mother at home.'

'She is my mother.'

'And I am your wife.'

'And my Cousin George has just engaged himself to a young lady in Beverley.'

They had reached the river and she looked unseeing at the sloping gravel beach, washed now by the rising tide, as she faced him and took it in. 'And will marry her forthwith and get an heir for Comyn's Bank. I'm sorry I am a disappointment to you, Thomas.' She put just the slightest emphasis on the 'you'.

'Your mother had sons.'

'I thought we were not talking about my mother. Your mother had only one son.' And then: 'Don't answer that. It's disgusting. I'm ashamed. You are making me behave like yourselves, you and your mother, and I won't. Leave me alone, Thomas. Give me time.' There was something more she wanted to say, but how could she? Give me pleasure, every instinct in her cried out, and I'll give you your heir. Useless. Hopeless.

More than ever that night, she felt herself a thing, to be used for a purpose, not a person at all. She woke late, jaded and unrefreshed, to find that Thomas was already up and out.

'He's gone fishing,' Beth told her, bringing

chocolate and rolls. 'They say he always does in the mornings when he's here. Fish for dinner, if you are lucky.' She was trying to make a joke of it, but it was not one Kathryn felt inclined to share. She had not so much hoped as expected that Thomas would take her for a long ride this morning. Had actually been looking forward to it.

She crumbled her roll, drank a little chocolate, came to a decision. 'Tell Ben to saddle up for me,' she told Beth. 'I can't very well walk in the garden here; it's too overgrown, but a ride is just what I need.'

'By yourself?' Doubtfully.

'I always did at home. Oh dear!' Ruefully. 'Beth, am I always saying that?'

'No, ma'am. Honest you don't. Just from time to time, and who can blame you?'

She rode away from the river, for fear of coming on Thomas at his fishing, and found the flat, drained country dull enough, but saw swans nesting in a ditch and a heron flap slowly over towards the Humber. And all the time she was thinking of the knowledge Beth had betrayed of her situation. Did they talk in the servants' hall about how she pined for home? Home. It was gone. It did not exist any more. The new people had moved in to Windover Hall before Christmas, and Thomas, who had gone up to Scarborough to see Mr. Renshaw on business, had told her, casually, that they were said to be doing great things in the garden. 'Renshaw says you wouldn't know the old place.'

Windover was gone. Her garden was gone, and the shrubbery on the cliff. And she was caught. Trapped. She had done it to herself, with her eyes open, and there was no escape. The ladies at Ross might say they missed their amanuensis, but that did not mean they would welcome her as a runaway wife. 'I can't bear it,' she told her horse's ears. And then: 'I have to.' And then: 'Talking to oneself is a first sign of madness.'

A light drizzle had begun to fall and she turned and rode slowly back to the little house that was not home.

Thomas, returning empty-handed from his morning by the river had been far from pleased to find she had ridden out without him, and greeted her with the sullen look she had come to know so well. 'I had meant to take you riding after dinner,' he told her reproachfully over the inevitable steak.

'What a pity you did not leave a message to tell me so. I would most certainly have waited. But the servants said you usually fish all day.'

'And so I shall. We will be riding to church in Hessle tomorrow morning, naturally. I just hope no one from there saw you out alone this morning. I am afraid it would be bound to get back to the Miss Harrises, who keep up their connection with Hessle most assiduously. Indeed, they sometimes come out to church there, if —'

'They can find someone to bring them in their carriage.' Kathryn finished his sentence for him. 'May we expect to see them there with your mother tomorrow, Thomas?'

'I suppose it is possible. She did say something about the weather . . . If it were to be fine . . . A breath of country air . . .'

'And a chance to make sure that her daughter-in-law is behaving herself!'

'Kathryn!'

'And then she will come back with us for a surprise dinner, which the servants are probably busy preparing already, having been given their orders before we even left Hull. A surprise to no one but me, who thought, poor fool, that this was a country weekend planned for my pleasure.'

'Why, so it is. Mr. Dawson said —'

'I doubt he advised you to bring your mother too, Thomas. Well . . .' She folded the well-starched table napkin that had been part of the unwelcome formality of life in Thomas's 'cottage'. 'If we are expecting your mother for dinner tomorrow, I had best make sure that the house is fit to receive her. If you will excuse me, I will leave you to your wine.'

A surprise visit to the kitchen confirmed her guess. The preparations there told their own tale, and it hardly needed the hunted look old Betty gave her, caught stirring the sauce for one of the rich confections everyone knew Kathryn disliked and Mrs. Comyn loved.

'It's so we won't have to work on Sunday, ma'am,' Betty answered Kathryn's questioning look. 'You know the mistress don't approve of that.'

'So, will you be able to come to church with us, Betty?'

'Oh, no, ma'am. You know that is quite out of the question.'

13

Thomas had gone back to the river. Kathryn picked up the *Estimate of the Religion of the Fashionable World* that everyone said was by Hannah More. She had expected to enjoy its scathing attack on practice without principle, but today Mrs. More's Johnsonian rhetoric could not hold her. She put the book down, prowled the house looking for something else to read, something readable, a novel? But of course there was nothing.

At least the rain had stopped. She picked up her shawl and went out into the shaggy garden. The pear trees must be pruned in the autumn, then perhaps they would bear next year. She shivered, and pulled the shawl more tightly round her shoulders. Could she bear next year? Or the year after? Or the one after that? With Thomas. And his mother. And, if they got their wish, with Thomas's children. She would not be allowed to bring them up. She saw it all with the clarity of nightmare: little Thomas being spoiled by his grandmother; running to her wing of the house, to be indulged. Lip service. Practice without principle. Church on Sundays, but not for the servants. No real, loving goodness anywhere. And tomorrow she must go to Hessle Church, show pleased surprise at sight of her mother-in-law, welcome her back to the dinner that was being prepared now in the hot little kitchen.

'I can't bear it.' Talking to herself again. She could see Thomas now, standing on the river bank, shoulders hunched, concentrated on the line that drifted upstream with the tide. The set of his shoulders told her that he was sulking still, probably would go on all day, then turn to her in bed as if nothing had happened. 'I can't bear it.' She said it again as she turned on to a narrow disused path that should take her back to the river upstream from Thomas.

She was hurrying, almost running. Why? A bramble caught her skirts and she pulled against it, felt the light cloth tear, knew it did not matter. Nothing mattered. She was beyond that.

And here was a turn in the path that led through alder and willow to a little secluded beach of fine gravel. It was as if she had known it would be there. This was all planned, determined, settled in advance. She dropped the cashmere shawl on the stones. Why waste good cashmere? Nothing else to do. Nothing else to think. She was wading already into the water, feeling it lap around her ankles, begin to pull a little as she got in deeper. Icy cold, and a smell of salt in the air from the rising tide. Not long now, and all of it over: the misery past, present, and, worst of all, to come.

'Kathryn!' Thomas's shout made her stumble, nearly fall, but instinct steadied her, fighting the instinct to die. 'Kathryn, what are you doing? Kathryn, come back!'

Back? The water was round her thighs now, and the going harder. All over so soon. But Thomas's voice, desperate now: 'Kathryn, I can't swim!'

She turned back, slowly, hypnotised, mesmerised by his admitted helplessness. Would he have tried to save her? Drowned too? She would never know, but she doubted it.

He held out his cold hand for her icy one. 'Kathryn! What is it? What possessed you? Why?'

'I couldn't bear it,' she told him simply. 'Now, I suppose I have to.'

'We'll say you fell in. Slipped from the bank.' The crisis over, he was his practical self again.

'And you rescued me? Gallant Thomas.' It was hard to come to terms with being alive. 'I think I want to go to bed,' she said. 'By myself, Thomas.'

After that, everything was different. Thomas spent the night in the guest bedroom kept ready for his friends, and Kathryn slept for twelve hours. She neither knew nor cared whether the servants had accepted her husband's story that she had slipped and fallen into the river. It did not seem to her to matter very much. Nothing mattered. She was alive and did not want to be. Or did she? Could one help it?

Waking after that immense, refreshing sleep she felt real hunger for the first time in weeks and demanded an egg for her breakfast.

Thomas came in with his hands full of wild iris and found her eating it. 'That's good. That will do you good. Look! I picked these for you; I know how much you like flowers.'

'Thank you. Put them in some water for me, Beth?' She knew they would wilt, but was touched by the gesture. 'You got wet!'

'Nothing to what I did yesterday.' He was enjoying having rescued her. 'How do you feel this morning, my dear, after your fright? Will you be well enough for church? We should give thanks, I think, if you feel strong enough.

My mother does not come, by the way. There was a message.' His betraying colour was high and she did not ask for details.

'The ride is just what I need. Of course I shall come.' She rose from the table. 'I'll be ready in five minutes.'

'You are always so prompt. It's a great virtue in a young lady.'

'Compliments, Thomas?' But she smiled at him more spontaneously than she had for a long time, aware that something basic had changed between them.

She thought this again as they rode down the lane between frothing hedges of hawthorn blossom and Thomas reined in for a moment to ask: 'Is that a lark, my dear?'

And she was sure of it when, the service over, and the congregation out again in the sunshine, they were approached by the Miss Harrises. 'We were so very sorry to hear of your poor mother's indisposition, Mr. Comyn. Such a pity, this fine morning. I trust it is nothing serious.' This was Miss Evangeline, always the leader.

'I do not think so. Just a touch of fatigue,' Thomas told her. 'We are quite ashamed, my wife and I, that we have let her overexert herself so, running the house for us. We are going to change all that now, are we not, Kathryn?'

'I shall do my best.' Kathryn concealed her astonishment.

'So, no more time for lonely rides by the river, I hope,' said Miss Patience archly. 'A little bird told us you were seen out all by yourself yesterday, dear child. Surely not the wisest thing in these dangerous, revolutionary times.'

'Dangerous?' asked Thomas. 'Dear Miss Patience, you surely do not expect a boatload of French *sansculottes* to come upriver for the express purpose of molesting Mrs. Comyn in her own garden?'

'Mrs. Comyn?' Honestly surprised. 'You mean something really did happen to her? No wonder she could not bring us to church.'

'I believe you quite forget, Miss Patience, that there are two Mrs. Comyns now.' His smile was sweet, his tone icy, and Kathryn found herself thinking that he must be a formidable business opponent.

He had certainly reduced Miss Patience to an apologetic incoherence from which her sister rescued her. 'But it is a dangerous world, just the same. What's this I hear of your falling into the river, child?'

'And my husband gallantly fishing me out?' Kathryn smiled at the older woman. 'Thomas has told me that news travels fast in these parts, and I can see that it is no more than the truth. Servants' talk, I suppose. And that

212

reminds me that we should be on our way, Thomas, or the delicious meal they have prepared for your mother will be quite spoiled. Do give her our love, Miss Harris, if you should chance to call this afternoon, and tell her we undertake not to be late home tonight. Oh — and that we are none the worse for our wetting, of course, and her son quite the hero.'

Kathryn did not expect that Mrs. Comyn would yield up control of the household without a struggle, and she was right. From time to time she felt herself actually sorry for her formidable mother-in-law in the tussle that followed between her and her son. She herself did her best to keep out of it, but of course it was impossible to do so entirely. The servants inevitably made the most of it, appealing from one Mrs. Comyn to the other, but Kathryn had been dealing with servants since she was fourteen and stood no nonsense now that she had Thomas behind her. And she had more sense than to make any drastic immediate changes in the household routine. She would make them, but slowly and carefully.

Instead of walking in the garden, now, she went to the market, something Mrs. Comyn had tended to delegate to Mrs. Moss, who bitterly resented the innovation. Kathryn began to understand why when the household expenses fell sharply and she realised that the figures presented formally to her mother-in-law at the end of each week had borne little or no relationship to the actual spending.

'They were the purest moonshine,' she told Thomas in the weekly accounting that now took place ceremonially in his study. 'Look at the figure for candles! At this time of year. We don't burn the half of that. And as for the consumption in the servants' hall! I think we must be entertaining half the domestic population of Hull. And, another thing, which I mind more. I am afraid Mrs. Moss has been giving sweeteners, and taking them too.'

'Sweeteners?'

'Well, bribes, if you want to call a spade a spade.'

'Which I do. It's one of the things I most respect in you, Kathryn. That you do, too. So, what shall we do about it?'

'I think she must go, but not at once. I don't want to take too much upon myself too fast. Still less to seem to be criticising the way your mother managed. You can't blame her. I don't suppose she had ever really run a house. I checked back through the books, and Mrs. Moss was clever enough to keep her lying figures more or less consistent. Besides,' smiling at him, 'I have the very strongest feeling that it happens everywhere in Hull, so if your mother should have been puzzled by what she thought a high figure, and compared notes with a friend . . .'

'Hers would have been high too.' He took her point. 'So, what do you suggest?'

'That we go on as we are for the time being. Mrs. Moss is disliking it very much. She misses her trips to the market quite as much as I enjoy mine. I think we can rely on her to get in a rage and give in her notice sooner or later.'

'And what then? Have you a plan for that too?'

'Well, a little bit of one.' Colouring. 'Beth heard from her cousin Sally the other day.' She paused. 'Do you remember Sally? No, why should you? She was my right hand, my prop and stay at Windover.'

'A little, brisk woman with a smile?'

'That's Sally. I never could understand why she did not come to me when my step-father let all the servants go in that monstrous way after mother died. I minded dreadfully at the time.'

'I'm sorry.' He was remembering how hard she had taken the news, and how little notice he had taken. 'So, where is she now?'

'The most comic thing, or at least, I suppose not really for Sally, though she can cope with anything, I think. But she went as cook house-keeper to a widowed clergyman somewhere on the other side of York. And he has asked her to marry him.'

'Good gracious!' Thomas was remembering Sally more clearly now. 'Most unsuitable,' he said. 'And most unfortunate. Otherwise I was thinking we might ask her to come here.' And then: 'What is it? Why do you look like that?'

'You cannot be imagining she accepted him?'

'A chance like that? But, of course. She'd be a fool not to.'

'Then she is a fool. You think marriage is all about money, and . . .' she was actually stammering a little 'and convenience, don't you, Thomas? Well, it's not, not always. Sally had the wits to see that, even if —' She stopped, turned scarlet. 'She is still working for him, but she says it is awkward, she is looking out for another post. She's a wonderful cook, is Sally. A wonderful person.'

In the end, it was the elder Mrs. Comyn who precipitated the inevitable domestic explosion. She had spent more time in her own wing of the house since the changeover, explaining to anyone who cared to listen that she could not bear to see the ramshackle way things went on these days. And she was giving more and more Saturday night entertainments 'to a few dear friends' and ordering elaborate 'little' suppers from the main kitchen.

Kathryn was always invited to these parties, but it was an unspoken if well understood thing between the two ladies that she never went. In fact, it suited her beautifully. Thomas dined at the George on Saturdays and spent the evening there. She was able to have the kind of light, early meal that suited her and get on with her work for him, which had suffered when she took over the housekeeping and had to master Mrs. Moss's sibylline books.

But Mrs. Moss had her own Saturday habits, and did not mean to change them for anyone. As Kathryn had deduced, the entertainment at Comyn's had always been lavish and Saturday night was known as their night in the network of Hull's belowstairs. At first, she had managed well enough, sending over to Mrs. Comyn's wing the by-products of her own Saturday evenings, but these were becoming increasingly more difficult to supply, with Kathryn's firm hand on the marketing.

This fine July Saturday, the older Mrs. Comyn's message, sent across by her maid, brought Mrs. Moss to Kathryn in a towering rage. Smoked oysters and fricassee seemed to be the burden of her tirade, with 'short notice' and 'some people' as variations on the theme. 'Special party for the new preacher indeed!' She had wound herself up to an outraged conclusion. 'Wasn't sure he would come! Of course he'll come to Comyn's, long-jawed, long-winded hungry fellow like him.'

'Let me understand you, Mrs. Moss,' said Kathryn quietly, putting down her pen. 'What new preacher are we talking about?' There had been no mention of anything out of the ordinary when Mrs. Comyn had issued her usual casual invitation to 'meet my friends to-morrow evening'.

'The hell-fire young man who has taken over the disused meeting house in Fish Lane,' explained Mrs. Moss. 'Preaches damnation and lives in one room behind the shop, if you take my meaning. I reckon he could eat a horse, let alone my smoked oysters.'

'Yes,' said Kathryn gently. 'Your smoked oysters, Mrs. Moss. I seem to remember buying a barrel just the other day. I never eat them, and surely they can hardly be finished already. And yesterday's veal would make one of your delicious fricassees, I am sure. If Mrs. Comyn is entertaining a man of God, we must see to it that Comyn's does itself justice. I know I can count on you.' She smiled and picked up her pen. 'I may even drop in for a few minutes, to meet this formidable new preacher. I know I shall not be disappointed in your provision.' She had Mrs. Moss in a cleft stick, and they both knew it. If last week's oysters and yesterday's veal had indeed been finished in the servants' hall, Mrs. Moss had the choice of admitting it, or replacing them at her own expense.

Mrs. Moss saw things less clearly, lost her temper and gave in her notice. Kathryn accepted it gravely, and was only mildly disconcerted when Mrs. Moss announced that she was leaving not next week or next month but now, this minute. 'If you do that,' Kathryn told her, 'you must see that it will not be possible for me to give you a reference.'

'I do not need one. I have friends, Mrs. Comyn, which is more than can be said for some.' She flounced off to her packing, and Kathryn seriously wondered if she should insist on overseeing this. But she thought the woman had feathered her nest well enough financially not to bother with the small pickings she might be able to put into her box.

When Mrs. Moss had gone, she descended upon the servants' hall and found the rest of her staff in a nervous huddle. 'I am glad you are all here.' She greeted them gravely. 'I am sure you are going to stand by me in this crisis. Mrs. Comyn has a gentleman coming to sup with her. I beg your pardon, Piers?' to the butler, who had snorted.

'I beg yours, ma'am,' said Piers. 'But that Mr. Jones is no gentleman.'

'All the more reason why we should treat him as one, Piers. Being, as he seems to be, a man of God.'

'Seems is right, ma'am. I could tell you a tale or two —'

'Pray don't,' she interrupted him gently but firmly, and proceeded to a rigorous examination of pantries and larder, concluding with: 'Well, I can see I shall have to try my hand at one of these modish Indian curries for Mrs. Comyn and her guests. I have been longing to do so, and you will all help me, I know.'

'Of course we will, ma'am,' said Piers, and she knew her battle as good as won.

She made a point of being asleep when Thomas came cheerfully home from the club, so there was no chance to tell him of Mrs. Moss's departure until Sunday morning. And then she found him preoccupied. 'She's actually gone? Well, that's a relief . . . so long as you are sure you can manage, and that your Sally will come. I know I can count on you. My mother had Mr. Jones to supper, you say? I've heard some odd reports of that young man.'

'She seems to think the world of him.' It had made Kathryn just faintly anxious to see how her mother-in-law and the Miss Harrises hung on the young man's ranting ungrammatical words.

'One of her enthusiasms? It will pass soon enough. Are you nearly ready, Kathryn? I would like to get to church early this morning. There were some very disturbing rumours going about at the club last night.'

'Rumours?' He was tying his neat cravat and she met his anxious eyes in the glass as she stood behind him.

'You remember I told you we had decided, after some discussion, that we would not be celebrating Bastille Day this year at the club?'

'Yes, I was sorry.'

'I know. But it looks as if we were well advised. Dr. Priestley and his friends held a celebratory dinner as usual at Birmingham, and he has had his house burned down by the mob for his pains.'

'What? The man of letters? His library?'

'I am afraid so. By a mob screaming for "King and Country".'

'I hope Government disowns them.'

'I expect it will, but the damage is done. I expect bad news from London in the morning.'

'It will affect your plans?'

'Anything like this is bad for business. It shakes confidence, you see. And then there's this talk of a possible war with Russia. Madness! Just think what that would do to trade, here in Hull.'

'Yes. But, poor Dr. Priestley! No one was hurt, I hope.'

'Not that we have heard. There will probably be more news this morning.' He picked up his hat. 'Are you ready, Kathryn? Then let us go. My mother does not come this morning, I believe.'

'No. I rather think she means to go and hear Mr. Jones in the new chapel.'

'Does she?' She could see he did not like it, and no more did she. She had taken one of her rare dislikes to Mr. Jones, a sallow young man in a rusty black coat who had managed at the same time to eat an enormous meal, fawn on Mrs. Comyn, and threaten his little audience of women with the pangs of hell if they did not listen to him. The other three seemed to enjoy it, but Kathryn had been sickened by it all. She suddenly realised why.

'I cannot like that young man,' she told Thomas as he wrapped her shawl round her shoulders. 'He reminds me of Mr. Morewood.'

14

The invitation to George Comyn's wedding arrived a few days later. 'Not much notice.' Thomas handed it to his mother.

'You won't go.' It sounded more like a command than a question.

'Surely we ought to; your only cousin?' Kathryn could not help minding the way Thomas turned first to his mother. 'George came to our wedding,' she reminded her husband. 'And I should dearly like to see Beverley.'

'This is a family duty, not a party of pleasure,' said Thomas quellingly. His face had taken on the sullen look again, and the fingers of his left hand were beating a nervous tattoo on the table. 'You think it would be better not?' He turned back to his mother.

'Much better,' she said, and that seemed to be that.

Kathryn tried again, later, in the seclusion of their bedroom. 'Are you sure we should not go to George's wedding, Thomas? I liked what I saw of Cousin George, and it does seem like a family duty to me.'

'Duty?' He turned on her, suddenly, savagely. 'What do you know about duty?' For an incredible moment, she thought he would strike her, his hands were clenched as for a blow. Then: 'Leave my family alone,' he told her, and retired to his dressing room.

It was the beginning of such a long withdrawal on Thomas's part, that Kathryn grew seriously anxious about him. But then, everything was awry that summer. The King and Country riots had not been confined to Birmingham, and at the same time Revolutionary and Constitutional Societies were springing up all over the country, which was increasingly and dangerously divided over events in France. It was all bad for business and Thomas's correspondents wrote expressing what Kathryn thought well-founded doubts about the wisdom of trying to float his canal company at such a time of national uncertainty.

This made Thomas gloomier than ever, but he warmed to Kathryn a little when she helped him marshal his arguments in defence of his scheme, though rather against her own better judgment. When she went to the counting house for supplies of paper or pens, she thought Mr. Robertson looked sour, and Mr.

Turner anxious. The other clerk had left to set up in business for himself and there seemed to be some delay in replacing him. 'Robertson's not the easiest man in the world to suit,' Thomas explained. 'Will you mind, my dear, doing some of the general copying for me as well as the work for the canal company?'

'Of course not. You know I enjoy it.'

Thomas received a letter from John Brierley in Nottingham towards the end of July. 'I hope this is his final answer, committing himself to the company.' He opened it eagerly, but his face fell as he read. 'Still more doubts; there's no satisfying the fellow. Oh —' Brightening. 'He has to come to York on business; suggests I meet him there. Talk things over. His wife and daughter are to accompany him. It is the Musical Festival at York. Mrs. Jordan is to be acting with Wilkinson's company at the Theatre Royal and they quite long to see her. Have you ever been to the theatre, Kathryn?'

'No. Oh, Thomas!' And then, looking down at her sober dress: 'But I am in mourning still.'

'Need they know that in York? It's a long time, now. Would you very much mind coming? It would be the greatest possible help to me. I remember how I wished, when we were in Nottingham, that I had been able to arrange for you to meet Brierley, tell him how much you had enjoyed sailing the canal. If you could get his womenfolk to share your enthusiasm . . .'

'I would be happy to try,' said Kathryn. 'I've always wanted to go to York. And to the theatre . . . Mrs. Jordan! They say she is beyond anything great. But, Thomas, what will your mother say?'

'We shall simply tell her that you are accompanying me on a business trip. No need to mention that you are packing colours. We won't go to the Balls of course; that would not be at all the thing, but quietly, to the theatre in a small party with business friends, I can see no objection. We just won't speak about it. There was a little talk about Mrs. Jordan when she first acted here in Hull . . . Least said soonest mended after all. I'll write Brierley today. And the hotel in York, the town is bound to be as full as it can hold, but I always stay at the Black Swan. They will fit us in, I am sure. It will be quite a little holiday for you, Kathryn, just what you need, so hard as you have been working.'

The scheme, as he put it to his mother, sounded impeccable. A business conference, and Kathryn needed to keep Mrs. and Miss Brierley out of the men's way while they held their discussions. 'And you will be able to do some useful shopping against the winter.' He turned to Kathryn. 'York is quite a metropolis, you know.'

'I do look forward to it,' said Kathryn with perfect truth.

After a discussion with his mother, Thomas decided that they would use their own carriage for the trip to York, rather than taking Mr. Umbler's diligence. 'That way I shall have time for a good look at the new canal from the Humber to Market Weighton,' he told Kathryn. 'You must remember seeing the other end of it when we sailed up the Humber last year. We'll dine at Market Weighton and be in York comfortably in time to take tea with the Brierleys. We will send back the carriage of course. My mother feels she will need it, and really the streets of York are so narrow, one is better on foot, or in a chair. You won't mind?'

'Of course not. But do you not think we should stop in Beverley to pay a call of congratulation on Cousin George and his bride?'

'No, Kathryn, I do not.' And then, aware that he had spoken too sharply. 'I shall need all my time at Market Weighton.'

Kathryn was disappointed, but still enjoyed every minute of that day's drive to York. They had not left Hull since their ill-fated trip to the house at Hessle, and as the weather had grown warmer she had found town life and town smells increasingly oppressive. Now, she took deep breaths of clear air when they stopped at the top of the hill between Beverley and Market Weighton to look at the wide view that encompassed the Humber, with the mouths of the Trent, Derwent, Don, and Aire all opening into it. 'If only one could get a bird's eye view of all the country like this, our canal plans would be easier,' Thomas told her as he named the rivers for her.

'I suppose you could ask one of those balloon enthusiasts to draw a map for you,' she suggested. 'That would give a really useful purpose to their rash flights.'

'Or I could go up myself!' Eagerly. 'That's a brilliant notion, Kathryn. I'll most certainly think about it.'

They stayed longer than they had planned at Market Weighton, where Kathryn enjoyed listening to Thomas's quick, acute questions about the canal terminus quite as much as he did the heavy dinner at the Post House.

When they reached York at last it was to learn that the Brierleys had already left for the Theatre Royal. 'Mrs. Jordan plays Hippolyta and Miss Hoyden tonight.' Thomas was reading the note John Brierley had left. 'In *A Trip to Scarborough*. They did not feel they could miss it. He hopes we will join them, but I am afraid it is really too late. I'm sorry.' Recognising her disappointment. 'But, arriving late we might find ourselves a little too much in the public eye. I will see you settled and join them for the after-piece. It would not be at all the thing for you to do that.' He said it firmly, forestalling her plea.

But in fact the long day had left her glad enough to settle down to the luxury of a bed to herself, if only for a while. And in the morning, Thomas had a tale of disappointment to tell.

'I don't know what has got into Mrs. Jordan,' he said over a luxurious breakfast in their sitting room. 'Says she's not well; says the good people of York do not appreciate her genius. Gives herself the airs of a princess already. Of course it's not liked.'

'A princess! What do you mean?'

'Oh.' He flushed up to the edge of his nightcap. 'You don't know; how should you?' He thought about it. 'But the Brierley ladies do, no question of that. What's to do? Kathryn, will you promise not to say a word to my mother?'

'Well, of course.'

'Actresses are different. Well, no, it's not exactly that . . .' He pushed back the nightcap to run an anxious hand through dishevelled fair hair. 'The thing is . . . Kathryn, you must know that there is a kind of woman of whom we never speak.'

'Why, yes, of course. My step-father —' She stopped, recognising his appalled embarrassment.

'Yes, quite so. I am glad you understand so much, though sorry . . .'

'Yes.' Impatiently. 'Do try to explain, Thomas.'

'Well, then, actresses — some of them — are a special case. Seem to be. Some of them are almost ladies — behave like ladies at least. No one has ever said a word against Mrs. Siddons. Or Mrs. Inchbald. But I am afraid some of them . . . Some of them are no better than they should be. And yet go on mixing in society. In the very highest society. Of men . . . The thing is — why Mrs. Jordan is giving herself such airs —' He paused again.

'I thought in private life she was really Mrs. Ford,' she prompted him.

'Ah, you do know that. Well, the thing is, though she has been calling herself Mrs. Ford, and mind you Ford is here in York with her, and there are children. But —'

'They are not married?'

'That's it.' He was grateful to her. 'And now, she is after higher game.'

'You said: princess?'

'Well: duchess. It's the young Duke of Clarence . . .'

'The sailor prince?'

'That's the one. Though why he wasn't cashiered — or whatever they do in the navy — when he sailed home from Canada against orders! But royalty, you know . . . It has to have ended any hopes of a career in the navy. The Admiralty won't forget, even if the King his father forgives him. So there he is, at a loose end in town, and . . .'

'He met Mrs. Jordan?'

'Just so. The gossips say he has offered her a settlement. Can't marry her of course. Not the slightest question of that. Brierley was saying last night that he thought if Ford were to offer her marriage she'd take him, even now, because of their children — devoted to her children, they say she is. One of them not his, mind you. Can't blame him for hesitating.'

'Oh, the poor thing.'

'A fallen woman, Kathryn. And giving herself the airs of a prima donna. Brierley tells me she insisted on opening in *The Country Girl*, which is not at all the kind of play of which the starchy ladies of York would approve. And when she was coolly received in that, she took against the place and has barely exerted herself all week. Last night was her benefit, but the house was thin because of the way she has been carrying on. Do you know, Brierley said, when she made her first appearance as Hippolyta and got only lukewarm applause, she turned her back on the audience. Imagine that! By the time I got there, the evening had gone from bad to worse, and even her Hoyden failed to please. I am really glad you were not there, Kathryn; it would have made a sad enough introduction to the theatre for you. We must just hope that she thinks things over and realises what a mistake it is for an actress to alienate her audience. A fortunate thing today is Sunday and there will be time for her to think again. It's to be *The Spoiled Child* and *Know Your Own Mind* tomorrow, and Little Pickle is known for one of her great parts. But what am I doing, keeping you talking! I told Brierley we would meet them in good time to walk to the Minster for the service.'

The Brierleys were a surprise. Thomas had told Kathryn that they had moved from London to Nottingham a few years before, but this had not prepared her for something cosmopolitan about them. And they were all of them older than she had expected. John Brierley had white hair in almost shocking contrast to the brilliant blue eyes his daughter Jane had inherited along with her mother's brown skin. But Jane Brierley had not inherited her mother's now fading good looks. She was tall and strongly built like her father, with a touch of red in her hair that she must have got from him, and a high-boned, formidable face. And she was visibly in a very bad temper, simmering a little, an explosion waiting to happen.

They made an awkward enough group, Kathryn thought, as they set off for the Minster. The two men, of course, walked ahead, already deep in talk, the three women following as best they could through the crowded, narrow lanes.

'Oh, these husbands of ours.' Mrs. Brierley had taken Kathryn's arm in a surprisingly firm grip for so small a woman. 'We must bear with them, I suppose, though whether they should be talking business on the Sabbath day —'

'Sunday, mother,' said her daughter impatiently. 'And you know what father and I think of all this Sabbatarian nonsense. I suppose you came yesterday because you do not approve of travel on Sunday?' She fired the sudden question at Kathryn.

'My mother-in-law most certainly does not.'

'And you take her opinions for holy writ?'

'I did not say that.'

'Why, no more you did.' She fell behind for a moment under pressure from the crowd, then caught up. 'So you are not entirely the mouse of virtue that you look.'

'Good gracious, do I?' Kathryn could not help laughing, but then remembered Hessle and the cold waters of the Humber. 'No, I am afraid I am not,' she said. Suicide was a great sin, and she had almost committed it. Why did it suddenly come over her, now; as they entered the high doors of York Minster? Despair. The sin against the Holy Ghost. But Thomas was speaking to her, directing her into a pew. She knelt and prayed, knowing that she was saying nothing.

After dinner, John Brierley proposed a turn in the Long Walk by the river. 'You will wish to rest, I know,' to his wife. 'But Jane can fetch you your water from the Lady Well. I am sure you are a good walker, Mrs. Comyn, like my daughter.'

The two men were soon in the lead again, deep in talk of levels and gradients, and Kathryn, following with Jane Brierley, through the well-dressed crowd that strolled under the elms by the river, tried to adjust her pace to her companion's longer step and said: 'Is it your first visit to York, Miss Brierley?'

'Gracious, no. I was at boarding school here, and very dreary it was. And the weather is fine, is it not? And the view of the river delightful? And the sermon was most improving!'

'No it was not. You know perfectly well that it was a dead bore. And since you have covered all the usual conversational openings, maybe you would come down to cases and tell me why you were in such a temper when we first met.'

'You noticed?' Surprised.

'Of course I noticed. You were simmering like a tea kettle.'

'Sounds unattractive. You really are not the mouse you look, are you? I'm sorry if I seemed cross. That was rude of me. It's not your fault —'

'That you have to waste your Sunday keeping me amused while the men talk business? Tell me; what is it you would rather be doing?'

'Reading. I found a book in the Circulating Library here that I have been longing to read; *Thoughts on the Education of Daughters*. Do you know it? It is by a woman named Wollstonecraft. I heard about it before we left London and have been wanting to get it, but my father,' with a darkling look at the two earnestly talking men, 'does not approve of money spent on books. He will pay my milliner and my mantua maker to dress me up for the marriage market, but when I try to improve my mind he says it will only spoil my chances. Chances! Look at me.' And while Kathryn was still desperately searching for something, anything to say, she went angrily on: 'I sometimes wonder if our move to Nottingham was not really because father was afraid I was going to turn bluestocking. If it was, we have all paid for it. I really think it is killing my mother. She was happy in our little house in Clapham. Not London really; we had a garden and a few fruit trees and a view across the common. Nottingham is horrible. Well, you have been there. You know.'

'Hull's not much better. Not that that is any comfort. Your father seems such a kind man.'

'Oh, he is. He will give me everything except what I want. I am twenty-three. How old are you?'

'Eighteen.' It was an apology.

'And married. For love?'

'No.'

'But you are happy.'

'No.'

'Oh.' It silenced her for a moment. Then: 'Forgive me. I had no right —'

'Of course not. But I think I would like to talk about it. I never had a female friend, except Sally.'

'Sally?'

'My maid. She's a good friend. Our house-keeper now. But it's not the same. One can believe as much as one likes in the equality of man, in all being sisters, but it doesn't really work, does it?'

'It will, I am sure. It's a question of education, I think. You must read Miss Wollstonecraft's book; it's fascinating, so far as I have got. Does your husband let you buy books?'

'Oh, yes. He's very good. I ought not . . .' But they had reached the Lady Well and the two men were waiting for them.

'How do you like the Brierley ladies?' asked Thomas that night.

'Very much, what I have seen of them.' Kathryn felt a traitor as she remembered her talk with Jane Brierley. 'But poor Mrs. Brierley does not look well. Her daughter seems worried about her.'

'So is her husband. Nottingham does not seem to suit her, but what can he do? He has committed himself to the business there.'

'I see. And how is your business going? Have you converted him yet?'

'Not quite, but I am hopeful. Did you tell Jane Brierley about the canal boats?'

'Not yet. I'm sorry —'

'No hurry. Better if it comes casually into

the talk. And maybe best when her mother is there too. John Brierley thinks very highly of his wife's judgment.'

'More so than of his daughter's?'

'He did say something made me wonder. Naturally, he wishes she had been a boy.'

'Naturally.' But as usual he missed her note of irony.

Monday brought disappointment. Mrs. Jordan had refused to act another night at York and had gone off to sulk at Castle Howard. 'Poor Mr. Wilkinson is at his wits' end,' Thomas reported. 'The theatre will be dark tonight, but I hear that Wilkinson has been to and fro to the Mansion House all day, where John Kemble himself is staying with Mr. Wilson, the Lord Mayor. He and Wilkinson are old friends. It will be a rare stroke of luck if Kemble agrees to act instead of Mrs. Jordan. Why, not even my mother could object to our going to see him in one of Shakespeare's plays. I saw him as Coriolanus at Drury Lane the year I went to London on business,' he told them. 'And I thought him grand beyond belief. But you must have seen him many times.' He turned to John Brierley.

'No, never. We left London before he took over as manager at Drury Lane. But of course we have seen his brilliant sister, Mrs. Siddons, many times, have we not, my dear?'

'Yes, a pity she does not chance to be in town to make your pleasure complete. She is truly magnificent. And quite the lady with it, received in the best society.'

'A very different kettle of fish from the Jordan,' said her husband, and received a warning look from his wife. 'Oh, I look on Jane as quite a woman grown these days.'

'Thank you, papa,' said his daughter, rather dryly, Kathryn thought. 'So you have decided that it will be safe for Mrs. Comyn and me to go shopping on our own tomorrow, since poor mamma does not feel up to it?'

'If Comyn does not object, I see no reason why you should not. A married lady after all . . . What do you think, my dear?' to his wife.

'If Mrs. Comyn would be so good . . .' A little doubtfully.

'I would be delighted,' said Kathryn. 'I have a great deal of shopping to do which I know my husband would find a sad bore, so if Miss Brierley will really give me the pleasure of her company —'

'You undertake to keep me out of mischief,' said Jane Brierley with a first smile that transformed her angular face.

The two girls spent a happy morning up and down the narrow lanes of York and Kathryn found herself infinitely grateful for her companion's knowledge of the town and its shops, and for her quick, clear-headed advice when she found herself undecided. 'You should think what you want, not what your mother-in-law does,' said Jane Brierley when Kathryn was hesitating between a plain and a fancy chintz. 'Is she such a tartar?'

'Well — yes.' Reluctantly.

'And does not wish to surrender her son. But you are winning, I think.'

'Not winning.' Kathryn disliked the word. 'And — I must not talk about my husband.'

It got her a quick look of respect. 'You are quite right, and I apologise. And now, since we have finished our domestic duties, let me introduce you to York's bookshops. It's one of the few towns outside London where one can buy books as well as borrowing them.'

They returned in great charity with each other, to find that Kemble had finally agreed to act Othello that night. 'They have been rehearsing all afternoon,' Thomas told Kathryn. 'I am only sorry it is not a more agreeable play for your first one, but he is supposed to be great in the part.'

'It's a horrid play,' said Kathryn. 'Desdemona is such a silly girl.'

240

15

That evening at the Theatre Royal in York was a milestone in Kathryn's life. She had read a great deal of Shakespeare with Mark Weatherby and he had told her about his own love of the theatre, but the reality of it was overwhelming. And, happily surprised, she recognised that her husband felt the same. She sensed his excitement as they entered the theatre, found herself sharing the thrill of it as she looked round the crowded, brilliantly lighted auditorium. The only place of this size she had been in before was a church. She reached out, hardly aware she was doing it, and took Thomas's hand. 'Thank you for bringing me,' she said.

'Just you wait.' The curtains were parting.

She had not known what to expect, so had expected nothing. Now she was enthralled, spellbound, lost in a whole new world. At last, returning his drenched handkerchief to Thomas, she said. 'Thank you, Thomas.'

'Do you want to stay for the after-piece?'

'I don't think so, do you? I'd like to go home and think about it.' Othello's resonant lines, so deliberately spoken by John Kemble, were echoing in her head. 'He's tremendous,' she said.

'And such a presence.' Thomas turned to tell the Brierleys they meant to leave. 'They think they will stay. You and Miss Brierley have your plans made for the morning?'

'Yes.' She was still in a daze as he took her arm to guide her through the happily murmuring crowd. It was something she was never to forget, that sound of an audience totally carried away by what it had seen. Many other people had also decided to leave before the farce and the small square outside the theatre was full of groups of people enthusiastically comparing notes in the warm summer night.

'Shall we walk home, rather than wait for a chair?' asked Thomas. 'Would you mind that?'

'I should love it.' He took her arm and a strange little thrill ran through her.

Back in their rooms, she thanked him again. 'It was so sad,' she said. 'And so wonderful.'

'And you're beautiful, Kathryn. I love you.'

He had never said it before. She looked at him for a long moment, wide-eyed, wishing she could echo his words, knowing she could not. But he was pulling the light pelisse from her shoulders, fumbling at the fastening of her dress. They fell into the wide bed together, and for the first time she felt pleasure as her body answered to his. But, much later, she dreamed of Mark Weatherby.

They saw Kemble act Hamlet the next night, and stayed an extra day to see his Macbeth on Thursday. But Mrs. Brierley was increasingly unwell and her husband felt bound to take her home on the Thursday morning, having come to a final agreement with Thomas that Kathryn suspected of not being quite satisfactory to either of them. Because of Mrs. Brierley's illness, Kathryn had seen less of her daughter than she had hoped, but she felt that she had made a friend, and they parted with faithful promises of regular correspondence. Kathryn had managed to say her piece about the comfort of canal boats, which had got her a rather watery agreement from Mrs. Brierley and a look of wicked complicity from her daughter. They were to travel home by Umbler's diligence, which left so conveniently from the Black Swan, and were up betimes for its nine o'clock start.

'But — your mourning?' Thomas looked at her across the loaded breakfast table.

'I'm sorry, Thomas.' She looked down at her pale muslin. 'I thought about putting it on again and did not feel I could. It would be acting a lie, do you see? Do you mind very much?'

'It's my mother I am thinking about.'

'I know.' They also both knew that there was not time for her to change her dress. 'Besides, we are surely going to tell your mother that we went to see Mr. Kemble. You said yourself that she could not help but approve of him.'

'So I did.' He sounded less sure of himself now, and she could not help feeling sorry for him.

'After all.' She poured him more chocolate and returned to the attack. 'We do mean to go to see Mr. Wilkinson's company when they come to Hull this winter, do we not?' It had, of course, been impossible the previous winter because of her deep mourning, but she had been aware at the time that Mrs. Comyn had been as glad about this as her son was sorry.

'Indeed we do. Very well. I believe you are right after all, my dear, as you so often are. Best get that argument over with.' She felt him mentally squaring his shoulders for the battle with his mother and was sorry for him again. But it was a battle that must be fought. And if they could win it now, it would be easier, when the actors reached town in November, to establish that they were going to invite Mr. Wilkinson and the élite of his company to dine with them as many of the leading citizens of the town had done last year. After all, if John Kemble stayed with the Mayor of York, there was no reason why a Hull banker should not invite his friend Tate Wilkinson to dine. Her mother-in-law would oppose it bitterly, she knew, but she meant to win. And, thinking this, she thought that meeting Jane Brierley had done her good.

The coach reached the White Horse Inn in Hull Market Place punctually at four o'clock, and she and Thomas walked home arm in arm, leaving their baggage to be collected by a servant. 'You seem to have shopped to some purpose.' Thomas looked at the results piled high on the flagstones.

'I enjoyed it. I enjoyed it all so much. I do thank you, Thomas.' She smiled up at him and he thought that it was well worth the expected scolding from his mother.

But this proved worse than either of them had imagined. Kathryn had been aware of surreptitious glances at her dress from the neighbours as she and Thomas walked home down the High Street, but she was still taken aback by the look of outrage she got from Mrs. Comyn.

'I expected you yesterday,' was all her greeting to her son.

'I'm sorry, mother. I sent a message.'

'Yes. And confessed what kept you. The theatre. The devil's playground. And you have encouraged your wife to forget her natural duties and go with you. Consorting with strumpets!'

'Well, not exactly consorting, mother.' Thomas took her arm and urged her into the parlour, aware of the listening ears of servants lined up to greet them. 'We did indeed have the good fortune to see John Kemble as Othello, Hamlet and Macbeth. Three of Shakespeare's most brilliant creations. And brilliantly performed. Were they not, Kathryn?'

Kathryn had not expected the appeal, but rose to it as best she could. 'It was extraordinary,' she told her mother-in-law. 'A real experience. It has done me so much good; I feel as if life was different, somehow; that there are possibilities I had not understood.'

'The devil's possibilities,' said Mrs. Comyn. 'I had not expected it of you, Kathryn, but I suppose I should have, all things considered. It is all of a piece! You have seen fit to abandon your mourning, I see. Your mother is forgotten so soon? I suppose I should let that be a warning to me. My health has been good while you have been away, I am happy to tell you, since you do not choose to ask.'

'You have not given us the opportunity, mother,' said Thomas, rebellious for once. 'But of course we are delighted to hear it. I trust your friends have been faithful visitors while you have been alone.'

'Oh, yes, they have taken pity on my solitude. Mr. Jones has been the greatest possible comfort to me; he has come to pray with me every evening. I cannot begin to tell you how shocked he was when I told him the reason for your delayed return. To stay to see an actor perform! One of Satan's children. He wants a word with you about this, Thomas. He expects to see you both at our evening prayers tonight. He has been scandalised that we do not hold family prayers here in Hull. It seemed the ideal opportunity to make a beginning.'

'Where?'

'In the dining room, naturally.' But now she had the grace to sound just faintly uncertain.

'Without consulting me?'

'You were in York, enjoying yourself with your friends.'

'It is my house, mother. Did you invite the servants to join you for prayers, or order them to?'

'Naturally, I told them to.'

'And naturally they obeyed. It will not do, mother. I'm sorry. If you wish to hold prayers in your own wing of the house, that is entirely your own affair, and if any of the servants wish to attend them, I am sure Kathryn will make it possible for them to do so. Will you not, my dear?' He turned to Kathryn, who had been listening awestruck to this unprecedented confrontation.

'Indeed I will. I will have a word with Sally directly.' And she escaped before the next round of the engagement.

'I didn't think there was anything I could do about it,' Sally told her. 'But I can tell you I'll be glad not to have that young man preaching hell fire and damnation in our dining room. Prayers! I'll give him prayers. Curses is nearer the mark. Death and destruction for anyone who doesn't see things just his way. And no hope of salvation unless you are "saved" as he calls it, and I couldn't just make out how that worked. Oh, and one other thing, Miss Kathryn — ma'am, I should say. I think Mr. Robertson is quite taken with Mr. Jones's teachings.'

'Oh dear, is he?'

'I told mother I was not prepared to go and be prayed at.' Thomas joined Kathryn looking ruffled. 'The meeting is to be in her sitting room from now on, but I said I would see Mr. Jones for a few minutes after it today.

I am sure you would rather not be present.'

'I should just about think not. But stand no nonsense, Thomas.'

'I do not intend to. Holy Trinity and its ways, Mr. Clark and Mr. Milner's sermons have been good enough for me, and I for them, I hope, all my life, and I do not mean to be changing now, whatever my mother and this hell-fire preacher of hers may say.'

It was the beginning of a deep and serious division in the family, which mirrored a similar one in the town as a whole. Mrs. Comyn kept more and more to her own wing of the house, where Mr. Jones was a constant visitor. Some of the servants went on attending the daily prayers there, others did not, and the same division appeared in the counting house. Mr. Robertson made a point of attending, Mr. Turner made just as much of a one of staying away. It was a comfort to Kathryn, who could collect her supplies of paper and pens when she knew Robertson would not be there with his disapproving looks.

Everything was different now that she was out of mourning. Thomas had subscribed for the twelve full assemblies and eight subscription concerts to be held in the modest Assembly Rooms in Dagger Lane, and promised to take her also to the fortnightly card assemblies when he could. 'I know you do not like cards much better than I do, my dear, but it remains a way to meet one's friends, and from time to time there may be a little informal dancing, which we will both enjoy.'

'Your mother and Mr. Jones will not approve.'

'I fear not. But I have done my best to explain to her that it is part of a banker's business — and therefore his wife's — to mix in society. I hope you have a fine new gown to dazzle us at the opening assembly of the season.'

'Not precisely new. I have so much of my bridal finery quite unworn because of poor mamma's death. Beth and I have been busy making a few alterations and flatter ourselves that I will be quite up to the mark. Your mother must surely approve of that.'

'Is she grumbling at you, Kathryn?'

'Well, I am afraid she thinks I would be better occupied making pen wipers for her charity bag than writing your letters and refurbishing my ball gown with poppy-coloured ribbons.'

'I look forward to seeing you in it. And as to the letters; I truly do not know what I would do without you. Robertson finds fault with every candidate who presents himself for our vacancy. I sometimes think there is no pleasing the man.'

'I do wonder if you should not make him a partner.'

'Make him a partner! I'd rather get rid of him altogether if he goes on opposing me in all my plans. And treating me as if I was still merely a schoolboy on his promotion. He had the impudence to suggest, just the other day, that rather than hiring another clerk we should invite my Cousin George to join the bank. It made me a wonder a little . . . I think I must make time to ride over to Beverley and call on Cousin George. I have not done so since his marriage, and should have. But I am keeping you from your sewing. I expect you to be the belle of the ball tonight, your first formal appearance in Hull society. And of course everyone will be there.'

Mrs. Comyn made them late by fighting a last rearguard action over Kathryn's poppy-coloured ribbons, and the Rooms were already crowded when they entered them. Thomas had been right; everyone was there for this opening ball of the season and Kathryn was pleased and surprised to find she had so many friends. The Rooms might not compare with Scarborough's elegance, but when she remembered the cool welcome she had received on her first appearance there, she could not help thinking there was something to be said for Hull.

Thomas was surprised too. He had meant

to put heart into his little wife when he told her she would be the belle of the ball. It was a shade disconcerting to find that, in fact, she was. Naturally, all his business friends and acquaintances felt they must do their duty by his bride, but that did not explain the crowd of younger men who were soon surrounding her with pleas for dances, including, he saw without enthusiasm, several young officers from the recently enlarged garrison at the citadel. He had promised Kathryn the first two dances, 'to make sure you do not find yourself without a partner,' but was disconcerted to find, when he returned from a round of greeting his friends and their wives, that she had entirely filled her programme for the evening. 'You did not save the supper dance for me?'

'You did not ask me to.' They were taking their places in the first set. 'Everyone is being extra kind,' Kathryn went on, 'because of my having been in mourning all last winter.'

But it was not just that, he realised, as the top couple led off. It was not just the poppy-coloured ribbons either, though he flattered himself that his wife was the most stylishly dressed woman in the room. There was something about his Kathryn tonight — he watched Sir Henry Etherington smile as he took her hand — something disturbing. She was coming back to him now, a ship in full sail, her hand held out. He took it, and remembered she had never said she loved him. Why did he suddenly remember John Kemble playing Othello? 'It is the cause, it is the cause, my soul . . .' He tripped over his wife's feet, apologised and concentrated almost desperately on the dance.

16

Tate Wilkinson and his company opened at the Theatre Royal in Finkle Street on November 1st. Mr. Cherry might not be as great as John Kemble, nor Mrs. Taylor as Mrs. Siddons, but *She Stoops to Conquer* was Kathryn's first comedy, and she enjoyed every minute of it, happily aware of Thomas at her side, laughing as heartily as she did. But the house was not quite so full as usual, he told her; various regulars were absent. 'Mr. Jones's influence is beginning to show, I am afraid.'

'Then we must most certainly make a point of inviting Mr. Wilkinson to dinner.'

'Yes.' Doubtfully. And then: 'I believe you are right. There is little enough harmless entertainment here in Hull; we must not lose our theatre for lack of support. I will call on Mr. Wilkinson tomorrow and extend the invitation. Will you tell my mother, or shall I?'

'It would come best from you.' If Kathryn secretly hoped the invitation might lead to Mrs. Comyn's taking her disapproving presence elsewhere as she frequently threatened to do, she was disappointed. Mrs. Comyn stayed, and fulminated. And Kathryn was sad to find the evening with Mr. Wilkinson and his leading actors disappointing. Mr. Wilkinson was a friendly, talkative little man, and for a while she was happy to listen to his theatrical anecdotes, but he seemed to think only of himself, blandly ignoring her attempts to steer the conversation to more general topics, to politics, the state of things in France, or travel.

But if she found their conversation dullish, the actors' performances were the bright note in that long winter. She thought she would never get used to the fog that crept in from the sea to pick up the dirt and smell of Hull's thriving trade. Thomas did not notice the fog, but then Thomas was immensely busy and cheerful that winter. Things seemed to have settled down between him and Robertson; a new clerk had been hired and there had been no more talk of Cousin George. 'The canal business is booming,' he told her in bed one cold December night. 'Do you know that a £40 share in the Fazeley and Birmingham Canal sold at auction for £1,080 the other day? Just you wait till we float the shares in Comyn's Passenger Barges! Do you fancy yourself as Lady Comyn, my dear?'

'Thomas, you frighten me! Don't count your chickens so soon, it makes me nervous.'

'You nervous! Nonsense. Or — is there something you are trying to tell me, Kathryn?'

'I am afraid not.' She felt his disappointment and tried not to let her own irritation show, but she was getting very tired of Mrs. Comyn's speculative glances and probing questions about the state of her health. Of course she was sorry that she was taking so long to produce an heir for Comyn's Bank, but she hated being watched and questioned at every turn. 'Oh, Thomas, do leave me alone!' It came out more impatiently than she had intended as she pushed his hand away from her shoulder. 'You make me feel like some kind of prize animal.'

'George's wife Anne is expecting. My mother heard today.'

'And lost no time in telling you.'

'She thinks you are working too hard. That I am asking too much of you. And Robertson says that now we have Peters as well as Turner there is no reason why all my copying should not be done in the counting house. I shall miss your help, Kathryn, you know I will.' He sensed her furious reaction.

'You have settled it all between you? Discussing me behind my back! And not only with your mother. With Robertson! And what does Mr. Jones think about it? That

I am barren as a punishment for my sinful ways? My theatre-going! Is that what he says?' And then, alerted by a change in the quality of his silence. 'I really believe it is. And your mother told you. And you let her do so. I wish I was dead. Then you could marry again . . .' She was crying now, tears of rage.

'Don't, Kathryn. Please don't.' They were both remembering that day by the river at Hessle. 'I'm sorry. You're right. Perhaps I should not have let her talk about you. But she is my mother, Kathryn. She cares about me.'

'And I don't?' She was aware of a gulf opening before her. Was he going to ask her if she loved him? And if he did, what could she say?

It was almost a relief when he did the other thing. She did not resist now, but neither did she enjoy it. Did he? She was less and less sure.

Kathryn missed writing Thomas's letters, and it worried her that she was now so totally out of touch with his business life. She felt the change too as a small but important defeat in the undeclared war that she seemed always to be waging with Mrs. Comyn and Mr. Jones. They prayed for her, she knew, every night. And when the news came in the middle of

January, that the Pantheon Theatre in London had burned down, they described it as a direct intervention of providence. 'The King's Opera House, they called it,' said Mrs. Comyn. 'From the King's Theatre that burned down three years ago. A lot of Italians singing about most unsuitable subjects. They should have been warned by that first fire. The Pantheon has always been a den of wickedness: balls and masquerades and every kind of folly, but Mr. Jones thinks the theatre — and most particularly the opera — even more dangerous to public morals.'

'You don't think the public need some harmless entertainment, mother?' Thomas came to his wife's defence. 'Goodness knows, there is little enough to do these long winter evenings in Hull.'

'What about this new Society for Literary Information you are so occupied with setting up? A very much more suitable project.'

'But is it not to be for gentlemen only?' asked Kathryn. She had been bitterly disappointed when Thomas broke this to her, and was consoling herself with French lessons from an émigré priest.

'Mr. Jones says a woman's place is at her own domestic hearth.' Mrs. Comyn had a habit of quoting Mr. Jones as if his remarks had divine authority, and it ended the discussion.

It was unlucky for Tate Wilkinson and his company that when they put on a spectacular production of *The Siege of Belgrade* a few days later they overdid their use of gunpowder and smoke and caused a panic in the house. This meant more talk of divine judgment from the anti-theatre party, and Kathryn was almost relieved when the season ended without further disaster at the beginning of February, and the company returned to their base in York.

The day after they left, Mr. Jones found Thomas standing at his study window looking out at his wife, who was taking her daily walk up and down the garden.

'One of the fairest of Eve's daughters.' Jones smiled his unctuous smile, as if delivering a blessing. 'If only all be right within . . .' And then, before Thomas could protest: 'Beware of pride, Mr. Comyn, by that sin fell the angels. See how she walks like a peacock about your alleys. No wonder if she is the toast of the young blades on the Garrison side. And a little bird told me that the French gentleman who is giving her lessons quite boasts of his adoration for her. Have you not wondered, Mr. Comyn, why the Lord has not chosen to bless your union? Sinful thoughts, Mr. Comyn,' shaking a reproachful finger at him. 'The Lord listens to them just as closely as

He does to your words. Your mother is anxious about you, Thomas. Rightly so, I begin to fear.'

'My mother? About me?'

'You dined with your Cousin George last week. And did not choose to tell her. We have been praying for you most earnestly, Thomas. She has told me the whole sad tale. How she found you, two innocent boys. As she thought. Gross. Horrible. Not to be described. How can she feel you have truly repented, even after all these years, if you sneak away to dine with him in secret? There: your wife is coming in. You would not wish her to know about this old sin of yours, I am sure. We shall expect you at our prayer meetings, Thomas.'

It worried Kathryn more than she liked to admit even to herself when Thomas started attending his mother's prayer meetings. With the actors gone, the days dragged, and she missed her letter-writing for Thomas more than ever, missed him a little too. He was out a good deal in the evenings that winter, busy with the setting up of the new Literary Society, and when he was at home he always had work to do.

'What are you so busy with?' She looked up from her needlework to ask it one wet March night.

'Just some figures young Peters got together for me about the subscriptions to the canal scheme. I don't quite seem to make sense of them.' He ran a hand through his fair hair and she wondered if it was thinning just a little.

'May I look? You know how I enjoy sums.' She held out her hand for the closely written paper, was amazed when he held on to it, flushing.

'No, really, Kathryn; it would not be at all the thing. You must understand, once and for all, that women and business do not mix. It is not good for you; and it is not at all good for the business.'

'What in the world do you mean?'

'I am sorry to say that Robertson had to complain to me the other day about Turner's work. He said he had hesitated to do so for a long time, but felt he must speak. He did not like, I could see, to tell me to my face that I should have had more sense than to let you be running in and out of the counting house to get paper and pens whenever the whim took you. One can hardly blame young Turner, Robertson says, when you are quite the little queen of Hull.'

'Mr. Robertson called me that?'

'He says you are the toast of the citadel. They drink to you under that title. I asked him not to tell my mother.'

'You wasted your breath.' She was getting angrier by the minute. 'What else had Mr. Robertson to say?'

'He asked me to speak to Turner. Warn him that if he does not pay more attention to his work, stop looking out the window for you, he will have to find himself another position. I have watched him, Kathryn, since Robertson spoke of it. He ogles you! It's worse than the young officers, and lord knows they are bad enough. I was thinking only the other night what a fortunate thing it is that my mother does not attend the assemblies.'

'Tell me something, Thomas.' Her voice was dangerously quiet. 'How long is it since you had this interesting conversation with Mr. Robertson, and what did you say to him at the time?'

'Thanked him, of course. It was a little while ago; I have been wondering just what to say.'

'And watching? Turner? And me?'

'Kathryn, I have seen nothing —'

'There was nothing to see. And what does your mother say about this great scandal?'

'That it was only to be expected —' He broke off, aware of the fatal nature of the admission.

'From a daughter-in-law who wears poppy-coloured ribbons.' She had dropped her work and was looking at him across the great gulf that had opened between them. He had not defended her; he had gone straight to his mother. Worse than that. He had been ready to believe Robertson's hints. And what in the world could she do about it? She was helpless, trapped. 'What can I do?' She was asking herself, not him.

'Keep away from the counting house.' Thomas returned to his figures.

She did not want to see them now. What did she want? What was there to hope for? And yet, on the surface, nothing seemed to have changed. She and Thomas went on, apparently, just as before. Nothing happened to Turner, which was some comfort. She got through her days as best she could, and resigned herself to a night-time pattern of Tuesdays, Thursdays and Saturdays, with Saturday the worst, because Thomas came home drunkish and crossish from his dinner at the George. And nothing came of it.

That was the wettest summer for years. Looking out of the streaming window at her garden where nothing thrived, Kathryn thought that the harvest was bound to fail. 'It will be a bad winter, I am afraid,' she said to Thomas. 'Will it affect your plans for the canal company?'

'Mr. Jones says it is God's punishment for

the country's wickedness.' Thomas now quoted Mr. Jones more often than Kathryn liked. 'As to the canal company, no, of course not. What a nonsensical idea. Just like a woman. All this talk of strikes and disaffection is nothing but propaganda spread by French agents. The country is sound at heart; sound as a bell. And as for those madmen in France, they are too busy killing each other to threaten the rest of us. Brunswick and his army will soon have them on their knees to the king and queen they have imprisoned.'

'I expect you are right.' Kathryn did not agree, but had given up arguing. She was dreaming of Mark Weatherby again. It seemed a hundred, not just three years since he had brought the news of the sack of the Bastille and they had fallen into each other's arms. Like so many other liberal-minded people in England, she simply did not know what to think as she watched the French revolution she had greeted with such enthusiasm tear itself to pieces. And it was quite simply maddening that she did not have direct access to the papers, but had to make do with the bits of news Thomas brought home from the coffee house where he read them.

'That rabble of a French army have actually given a check to the allies,' he told her one morning of late September. 'Some very minor affair at a place called Valmy; means nothing of course. The allies will be in Paris before Christmas, mark my words, and then we shall see justice done for the horrors those madmen are committing.'

'All those innocent people killed!' Kathryn had had a letter from Jane Brierley describing the flood of desperate French refugees who were pouring into London.

'What else does Miss Brierley say?' asked Thomas eagerly. Mrs. Brierley had died that summer and her husband had gone back to London to be near his family. 'Is there no message for me?'

'She says her father blames himself for not taking more notice of her mother's illness while she was alive. I do not think he is capable of thinking about business.'

'That's all very fine.' Angrily. 'But where does it leave me? There are decisions to be taken; plans to be made. Just imagine, if by any chance it should come to war with France, which heaven forbid, but just think, Kathryn, what a fortune my canal company might make with people afraid to travel or send goods by sea, for fear of capture? Bradshaw thinks, and I agree with him, that we should bend every nerve to get the company floated this winter.'

'Are you really sure?' Kathryn had been hoping for the chance to say this. 'The country is in a very strange state, with the price of bread so high. And didn't you say something the other day about strikes in Birmingham and Manchester?'

'A lot of alarmist nonsense. I blame the press who enjoy frightening their readers, think it sells copies. A few madmen choose to form themselves into childish revolutionary societies and they write as if the country was on the verge of ruin. The Royal Proclamation against Sedition will put paid to all that, I promise you. A touch of firm government, that's all we need. And to keep out of the war, of course. I am sure we can count on Mr. Pitt for that. Let the Continent settle its own affairs; we are very well as we are. Business is a little slack just now, it's true, but it will soon pick up. While France is embroiled with Austria and Prussia, and Russia with Poland, we will have a free hand in the rest of the world, and trust our British merchants to make the most of that! Young Peters was congratulating me just the other day on our prospects. That's a promising young fellow who means to go far; he's worth ten of Turner. Robertson and I are seriously thinking of getting rid of that young man.' She was aware of his quick sideways glance as he said this and made herself take no notice. To defend Turner could do him nothing but harm.

Mr. Wilkinson's company arrived as usual at the end of October and were dined more lavishly than ever by the city fathers. Kathryn thought they were glad of the distraction for the increasingly restless public. But she was not much surprised when Thomas announced that they would not entertain the actors this year. 'My mother dislikes it so much that I really think it better not to. Mr. Jones is convinced that the death of Cousin George's son is the direct judgment of God.'

'The death?' Horrified. 'The baby died? I did not know. When?'

'Poor little thing.' Perfunctory. 'Back in August. Found dead in his cradle. My mother thought it best not to distress you with the news.'

'But I should have written! What will Cousin Anne think?'

'You have never met her. What should she think?'

'That I am quite heartless. But at least I am not glad, like you and your mother. You two Christians!'

'Kathryn!' For a moment she thought he would strike her, but he merely sank into one of the long, sullen silences that made no difference to his regular night-time attentions.

The news of the French victory at Jemappes

and advance into Belgium startled him back into speech. 'It's a direct threat to Holland and we are bound by treaty to defend them,' he told her. 'We must, too. Amsterdam is a vital banking centre; crucial to the Baltic trade. I don't like the feel of things at all. But Pitt will see us through; I'm sure of it. The country is behind him to a man. There will be no more revolutionary talk here now.'

Tate Wilkinson had advertised positively his final appearance as Shylock in *The Merchant of Venice* for December 7th, and the audience was buzzing with news as it poured into the theatre. Antwerp had fallen to the French, and Pitt had called out two thirds of the militia and summoned Parliament to meet on December 13th. Patriotic fervour ran high, and the audience insisted on singing 'God Save the King' both before and after the performance. But Thomas and Kathryn were quarrelling again. Thomas was delighted with Wilkinson's ranting, villainous Jew, but Kathryn had always hated the play and said so. Thomas simmered all the way home, turned on her at last in the privacy of the bedroom. 'You care nothing about me.' He kept his furious voice low, remembering the servants. 'You never have. You never stop to think how I work and toil to support you; how I fight off the competition of men quite as devious as that Shylock! They ought to be banned from trading, as well as from public life. They are behind it all, you know! Peters was saying so, just the other day, and I am sure he is right.'

'You cannot be serious? Think of Mr. Lyon down the road. You know everyone entrusts their valuables to him when they go away.'

'A very clever man. But I could tell you a thing or two about him! It's all a cover, don't you see, for his devious goings on. And of course they are at the bottom of all the bloodshed and mayhem in France. They mean to take over the world one day, you mark my words. But they won't get Comyn's Bank; Robertson and I are seeing to that.'

'What do you mean?'

'Nothing that concerns you. Business is not for the ladies. Your duty to Comyn's is quite other, as you well know. And you have failed in it. I have been thinking about this, all the time, for a long time. Mr. Jones is right, I can see. It is the sin in you that prevents it, and that sin must be chastised.' He turned to the closet and brought out a riding whip, small and neat and deadly. 'Take off your clothes.' He went to the door, opened it and listened. 'They are all in bed in their own part of the house now. Take off your clothes, Kathryn.'

17

Horrible. She fought him, but he was too strong for her. Most horrible of all was his silence, and the way he avoided striking her where it would show. And then, there was worse. He fell on her as she lay bleeding, trying not to cry, and took her savagely. And she found herself responding to the violence, and loathed both herself and him.

They never spoke of that night, moving through the muted festivities of Christmas and the New Year as much as possible as if it had not happened. Mr. Jones did not approve of Christmas frivolities, and Kathryn's only present that year was a copy of Mr. Paine's *Rights of Man*, sent her by Jane Brierley, which luckily arrived when Thomas was not at home. Knowing that the author had had to flee the country after its publication, she made it a cloth cover, hoping it would look like a Bible, and was reading it one bleak January evening in the comfortable knowledge that Thomas, Robertson and Peters were all at prayers in

Mrs. Comyn's wing, when there was a quiet knock on the parlour door.

'Yes?' She expected Sally, was surprised to see Turner, who had been avoiding her as carefully as she did him.

'Mrs. Comyn, I must speak to you. They are all at prayers, safe for the next hour. May I?' He came in, shut the door behind him. 'It's about the bank.' He got straight to the point. 'I'm worried to death about it. Something is going on that I don't understand. No more does Mr. Comyn, I think. Well — he's so busy with his canal scheme, I don't think he pays enough attention to Robertson and Peters. They are hand in glove you know. I've seen them out in the town together. I don't like it at all, Mrs. Comyn. They are clever men.'

And Thomas was not. No need to say it. 'But what can I do?'

'Speak to your husband. Make him pay attention.'

'I did try, back last spring. He was puzzled by some figures.'

'I'm glad to hear it.'

'But he took no notice . . .'

'I see.' He obviously did. 'You could try again? I truly think you should, Mrs. Comyn.'

'But I can't mention you.' Nor could she tell him the other reasons why it was so difficult.

'I'm afraid not.' So much they did not need to say.

'Then I'll have to wait for an opening.'

'Don't leave it too long. I'm afraid . . . If it were not . . . I have seriously thought of leaving Comyn's Bank. Any crisis . . . Any failure of confidence in the city . . . Mrs. Comyn, I don't like to think what might happen.' He had been standing all this time, turning his round hat over and over in his hands, his eyes on the turkey carpet. Now he raised them to meet hers directly. 'I only stay for your sake.'

'Oh!' What could she say? 'I do thank you, but —'

'I'd die to serve you. Let me say it this once. And now, I must go. I've said too much. But, Mrs. Comyn —'

'Mr. Turner,' she interrupted him. 'I do thank you from the bottom of my heart, but, please, you must go.'

'I'm sorry.' And then, defiantly: 'But I'm glad I've said it. God bless and keep you. And, do, please, speak to your husband.'

'I promise you I will, just as soon as the chance comes.'

But would Thomas listen? He found her sitting there when he emerged from his mother's wing in the little glow of self-satisfaction the prayer meetings induced in him. 'What, doing nothing?' His tone just failed to be jocular. 'You know the saying about the devil and idle hands, my dear. I should be sorry to think that our prayers had been wasted.'

'You have been praying for me?'

'We always pray for you. Mr. Jones was particularly eloquent today. Shall I tell you what he said?'

'I would rather you did not.'

'It was very moving, Kathryn.' Reproach-fully.

'I am sure it was. I will remember to pray for Mr. Jones tonight . . . Did he pray for Cousin Anne too?'

'Cousin Anne? What is she to the purpose?'

'I expect she and Cousin George want a child just as badly as you do, if not worse, poor things, after losing the baby.' She regretted the words as she spoke them. Inevitably they made him angry and any chance of turning the conversation to Comyn's Bank was gone for the moment. She rather hoped for another opening when she and Thomas went to see Tate Wilkinson in Mr. Addison's *Cato* a few nights later, since the theatre remained the strongest bond in their strained relationship. But once again, as with his Shylock, she found herself out of sympathy with Tate Wilkinson's portrayal of the tragic hero who killed him-self rather than surrender to tyranny. 'It's all rant, all fustian.' Turning to Thomas she saw that he was shrugging himself into his coat, ready to leave. 'You don't mean to stay for *Fortunatus?* It's supposed to have some of Mr. Wilkinson's most striking effects.'

'Nothing but a vulgar pantomime. No. I promised mother we would be home early. They are praying for the King of France to-night; it will be a long session and she is bound to be exhausted. I promised I would not be too late home.' He picked up her pelisse and wrapped it round her shoulders, taking compliance for granted. 'Those rascally French will never be so blind to world opinion as to condemn, still less guillotine King Louis,' he went on as they threaded their way through the crowd. 'But it must be a terrible time for him, just the same. He needs all our prayers.'

'If they did murder him,' she seized the opening, 'it would be a terrible blow to public confidence would it not?'

'It certainly would, but I told you, my dear, it is not going to happen.'

'But, just for the sake of argument, if it did. Would Comyn's Bank be in a position to last out a public panic? I mean, suppose everyone were to ask for their money at once?'

'I'll suppose no such thing.' Angrily. 'Comyn's is the oldest bank in Hull. Solid as a rock. Everyone knows that.' He was bowing

274

and smiling his way through the crowd as he spoke. 'And I must tell you, I hope for the last time, Kathryn, that this is no subject for the ladies. Ah,' relieved. 'Here is your chair.' He helped her in. 'I shall walk. The air will do me good.'

Bounced home through the quiet streets, she could only hope that her question might stay with him until the morning, that he might be moved to enquire a little into the state of affairs at the bank. And, of course, at the same time, she, too, would remember the unhappy King and Queen of France in her prayers.

They were wasted. The public was still reeling from the news of the summary trial and execution of Louis XVI when the French capped it by declaring war on England.

'It has united the country as nothing else could have.' Thomas insisted on looking on the bright side. 'We are all patriots now. Pitt will get his men and his money.'

'Has it meant a great fall on 'Change?' Kathryn ventured the question.

'Well, of course. Bound to have. Everyone is looking to his affairs; it's human nature. But the public will soon see that the result of this war is a foregone conclusion. What is the French army but a parcel of undisciplined ragamuffins?'

'They seem to have managed to give a good

enough account of themselves this winter.'

'A flash in the pan; nothing but a flash in the pan. They say the Duke of York himself is taking our gallant soldiers to the Low Countries. Then those frogs will see some action. And business will be brisk here in Hull, too, with the fleet to be got up to strength in a hurry. I expect all the ship builders in town on my doorstep in the morning, asking for loans to start work. The Press Gang will be out in the streets any minute now. We must see to it that the menservants never go out without their protections in their pockets. They are an idle enough set of rascals, but I would be sorry to lose any of them just the same.'

Kathryn felt the tension in the town streets when she went to market. The whalers were hard at work preparing for the spring's arduous voyage and there had already been scuffles between protected men and the Press Gang. Prices in the market were high and tempers short, and Kathryn found herself enjoying the daily shopping trip less than she used to. She sometimes thought she was watched; told herself she was imagining things, but confined her walks more and more to her own garden and the stretch of quay outside. She had taken to slipping out of the gate in their wall to watch the organised bustle of loading and unloading, and she had made a friend this way. Sir Henry Etherington, the town's great man, lived a little way down the quay, and he too liked to take his daily walk there. She had heard him from time to time cursing the longshoremen when the goods they were unloading impeded his walk; and had noticed with amusement that they now set the arms of the weathercock when they were busy, so that he stayed indoors thinking the wind unhealthily in the east. But she found him out walking among the bales and kegs one fine March morning, and they exchanged their usual friendly comments about the state of the weather and the state of the world. This was usually the limit of their exchanges, each tacitly aware of a spouse at home. Like the Comyns, the Etheringtons were childless, but they were in their fifties. Kathryn thought Lady Etherington a shrew, but she was fond of the ugly, old-fashioned, plainspoken baronet.

Today he lingered, apparently watching a schooner threading the crowded river mouth on its way up to the New Dock.

'It's true, what they say,' he took her arm and led her down to a quiet spot at the edge of the quay. 'As bad to get up the Hull to the New Dock as to come all the way from Petersburg.' He looked round as a group of sailors burst into a rollicking shanty. 'A word to the wise for your husband, Mrs. Comyn. Tell him to batten down his bank's hatches. My wife is a little anxious about how things are going at Pease and Harrison's, and when troubles come, you know, they don't come singly.' He took off his hat in farewell, revealing his old-fashioned pigtail. 'To your husband only, Mrs. Comyn.'

'Of course. And I do thank you, Sir Henry. My regards to Lady Etherington.'

'And mine to Mr. Comyn.' It was a formula, never in the usual way passed on. But today was different. Sir Henry's wife was sister to Mrs. John Thornton, wife of one of Pease and Harrison's London agents. If she was anxious, there was cause. Kathryn went straight back across the garden and sent a maid over to the bank with a note asking her husband to come and speak to her as soon as he could.

'What is it now?' He had not been pleased at the unprecedented summons, and showed it.

'I was talking to Sir Henry on the quay.' She repeated the message, only to have Thomas fly into one of his increasingly frequent rages.

'Gossiping on the quay! Devil's work! No good ever came of that.' Thomas had never been invited into Sir Henry's grand baronial hall. 'Female gossip and tattle. Or, maybe worse, maybe a devil's snare set by Sir Henry in the hopes that I'll make a public fool of myself. That's it! And he knew who would be the first dupe to fall into his schemes.'

'But, Thomas!' It was not the first time she had feared, if not for his reason, at least for his rationality. 'Do, please, believe me, it was a friendly warning, no more. I'm sure he wants to help.'

'Friendly —' He used a word that shocked her and slammed his way back across the yard to the bank.

When a panic run on Pease and Harrison's forced it to close its doors and suspend payments a few days later, Kathryn did not say, 'I told you so.' She did her best to say nothing, but the look on Thomas's face frightened her. And it was impossible, sitting in her salon, not to be aware of the stream of callers at their own bank across the yard. In her desperate anxiety for Thomas, for all of them, including the people who had thought their money safe in Comyn's Bank, she went to old Mrs. Comyn to ask her to urge her son to seek help before it was too late. The old lady heard her out in grim silence, then spoke.

'As I thought. You married my son for his money and now you are afraid he will lose it. But I tell you, woman, the number of hairs on my son's head are counted and there is an angel looking after each one of them. He will be one of God's saints, when you are sunk to the bottom of the bottomless pit.'

'Yes, but Mrs. Comyn,' Kathryn was desperate now, 'the Lord may look after Thomas, he's a good man, or means to be, but what about all those poor people who have their little savings, their safety for old age, invested in Comyn's Bank.'

'The Lord has His wings spread out under Comyn's Bank,' said Mrs. Comyn.

All next day, Kathryn listened to the tread of feet going and coming from the bank, and could not bear to look at the anxious faces. At the market, she thought people looked at her strangely, some with ill-concealed sympathy, some with what almost seemed like hate. She decided to send Sally next day, and thought herself a coward.

Thomas came home late from the bank that night and said he did not want any supper. He had not gone to prayers in his mother's room either, which worried Kathryn still more.

'Let me make you a posset, Thomas.' She tapped on the door of his study. 'Please. You must have something.'

'I am in the hands of the Lord, Kathryn. He who does the ravens feed will care for me.

Now, if you ever even understood what it might be to love me, leave me in peace, wife. I must have quiet. I must think. Get you to bed, Desdemona.'

'Thomas!' She was terrified. For him, for herself, for them all.

'It's the Lord's will,' he told her. 'The punishment for sin. Get you to bed, woman, before I do something I shall regret.'

It was late. The lights in the servants' quarters were all out. Should she wake Sally? Wake his mother? But what help could they give him? Give her? He asked for quiet; he must have it. 'Good night, dear Thomas. Sleep well. Things will seem better in the morning.' She hoped she had not understood the savage grunt he gave as she closed the study door behind her.

She went to bed, but not to sleep. When Thomas came up, she would pretend sleep. She was not just frightened, she was terrified. Sleep had not saved Desdemona. Should she rouse Sally? Beth? Ask to spend the night with Mrs. Comyn? But how could she, just because Thomas had talked a little wildly? She had told no one when he beat her, that time before Christmas, why should they believe that she had real cause for fear?

The night was quiet now, the sounds from

the river stilled at last in the wet, moonless night. It must be long past midnight and still Thomas did not come up. He would make himself really ill if he got no sleep, and to-morrow must be faced. She would make him the posset she had offered, persuade him to take it. She had relit her candle and was reaching reluctantly for her dressing gown when the unmistakable sound of a shot from down-stairs stopped her breath for a moment. Thomas's study? She thought so. And no one else would hear it. Rouse the servants in their wing? Not yet. Every instinct was against it. First she must find out what had happened down there in the study.

The old house was still again as she crept down the stairs, her candle making strange shadows on the dark panelling. The study door was shut, as usual. She tapped on it; no answer. Had she expected one? She pushed it open, gasped, blew out the candle and put it down. No help for Thomas, no hope now. The one shot had finished him, the weapon lay where it had dropped from his hand. His blood had soaked the papers on his desk and made a darker stain on the turkey carpet. Oh, poor Thomas.

And poor Mrs. Comyn. Her mind was rac-ing. Suicide was an unforgivable sin. How would his mother bear it? And then, there was

Comyn's Bank. If there had been a run on it already, Thomas's death by his own hand would finish it. An accident! It had to have been an accident. That way there might be a chance of saving something from the wreck. But how? She must have help. Who?

Nobody. She found she had sat down in the big chair facing the one from which Thomas had fallen. The lamp was burning low. In a minute she must mend it. But first she must work out what to do. The grandfather clock struck one, reminding her of time inexorably passing. What could have happened here? She and Thomas must have been together. She must be the witness to the 'accident'. They had been talking late about the crisis at the bank. He had been cleaning his sporting guns while they talked. Was this likely? Not very. But possible. And what had made his hand slip? Something she said? Suddenly, coldly, she realised that if she told this story, she risked being charged with her husband's murder.

And in the same breath she thought of a possible ally. Sir Henry Etherington was a magistrate; it would be entirely logical to send to him for help. And, better than that, he was a man who loved Hull; he would see, as she had, what havoc this suicide of a leading banker might wreak in the town. If she could present him with a convincing enough case for accident, he would be glad to accept it, would back her up for the town's sake. She looked down at her night clothes. If she had been talking late with Thomas she would have been dressed. Slowly, shivering, she mended the lamp, relit her candle and made herself go upstairs, dress again, make up her bed as if it had not been slept in. One last look round the room; she picked up the candle.

She could not use it. It must be beside her bed as usual, witness that she had not been upstairs. She took a deep breath, blew it out and stood for a moment getting her bearings in the heavy darkness. Then, very slowly, very carefully, she began to feel her way downstairs, back to the study and the horror that awaited her there.

When the clock struck two, she thought she had done all she could. Thomas's cleaning materials were on the desk now, among the bloodstained papers, blood on them too, and some on her gown. She thought she knew what she was going to say, to the servants, to Sir Henry when he came, as she prayed that he would. No more time to lose. Every moment that passed made her story of late night talk less probable. She walked deliberately across the room to the bell that rang in the servants quarters and pulled it again and again.

★ ★ ★

Half an hour later she and Sir Henry were alone in the room that smelled of Thomas's blood. He had come even more swiftly than she had hoped and had taken command of the hysterical servants, sending one for the doctor, another for the constable, and Sally to break the news as gently as possible to Mrs. Comyn, who was bound to be roused by the commotion. Now he was looking quickly and efficiently through the papers on Thomas's desk, ignoring the blood on them. 'You did not think to look at these, Mrs. Comyn?'

'No.' She was sitting in the chair where she had sat before and was suddenly overwhelmed by her own stupidity.

'I thought not. Just as well as it happens. It is better that I burn this, but take a look at it first, Mrs. Comyn. It would never stand in law, but it would cause infinite trouble. Your husband was out of his mind, I take it. I had wondered . . .'

'I'm afraid so.' She was looking with horror at the rambling document in which Thomas had tried to revoke his previous will in her favour. He had given his reasons, accusing her of every sin in the canon. She raised burning eyes to Sir Henry's. 'It makes me ashamed to read it. Poor Thomas.'

'Yes. A fortunate thing he was too much

the man of business to destroy the original will.' He picked it up. 'You know its terms?'

'No.'

'Drawn up by your man of business in Scarborough. Before your marriage, I take it. He knows his job, I'm glad to say. Absolute control of the bank to you for a year after your husband's death.'

'Absolute?' She could not believe it. And then: 'For a year?'

'It's customary,' he told her. 'With advisers, of course. And often just nine months, but your Mr. Renshaw is clearly a cautious man.' He put the will down. 'This gives us just what you need. You will close the bank tomorrow, Mrs. Comyn, in mourning for your husband. No one can object to that, and it gives us what we so vitally need: time. But here they come. If I were you, Mrs. Comyn, I think I would break down as soon as the first formalities are over. Go to bed. Try to get some sleep. I will call in the morning.'

'I do thank you, Sir Henry.' The door opened and Mr. Dawson came bustling in, so shocked to find her still in the room with her husband's body that breaking down into hysterics was no problem at all.

18

For a few minutes, Kathryn refused to move from the big chair into which she had sunk, shaking and sobbing. No need to pretend, but she desperately needed time to think. And to hear what Sir Henry said to Mr. Dawson. He was relaying the story she had told him with complete conviction, and it sounded better than she had feared. Heartless to be thinking like this, so coldly, but there was no time for anything else; not if the bank was to be saved. The bank. That was it. Her eyes turned to the big key to its one door, always ceremonially delivered to Thomas last thing at night. It was the only key. She thought it was the only key. Thomas opened up, first thing in the morning, when the clerks arrived.

'What a tragedy.' Dawson had finished examining Thomas's body, bent to cover the shattered face with his handkerchief. 'You should go to bed, Mrs. Comyn; there is nothing more to be done here tonight.' He helped her gently to her feet.

'It was the bank — Something I said about the bank distracted him.' She repeated what she had told Sir Henry. 'He was so worried . . .' And then, a convincing gasp. 'The bank! The key! The clerks will be coming in the morning. Thomas always lets them in. They mustn't — Please —' She swayed a little as she stood between the two men, and that was easy enough to do too. 'The bank's books. I must have the books. They are my responsibility now. Sir Henry says the bank must stay closed tomorrow,' she told the apothecary. 'Of course it must. But I must have the books.'

Mr. Dawson demurred at first. He did not much like the idea of unlocking the bank in the middle of the night, but he also wanted to get back to his bed, and he had never liked hysterical women. In fact he was a little surprised at young Mrs. Comyn whom he had always looked on as a woman of sense, but a hint from Sir Henry explained everything. While Kathryn sobbed noisily into her handkerchief, Sir Henry quietly explained the terms of the will.

'A year, hey? Playing it safe enough. And you think —'

'Well, I did wonder,' said Sir Henry, with truth.

Half an hour later, Kathryn was safe in the

big curtained bed with a newly replenished lamp and the books of Comyn's Bank. No time tonight for sleep. As he left, Sir Henry had remarked casually, that it was Thursday morning now. 'I think the bank should reopen on Monday, do not you, Mrs. Comyn?' He had also managed to tell her, without actually saying it, that he would help her with every means in his power except money. An elliptic phrase, here and there, had conveyed this with almost brutal clarity, and she was grateful. She would waste no hopes on him. But it meant, more than ever, that there was no time to be lost.

She had not seen the bank's books since Peters came, but the fact that she had known them well before was a great help now. It was just daylight, and she had blown out the lamp and moved over to her own little writing desk in Thomas's dressing room before she understood what had been happening. Soon after Peters had been taken on, the bank had begun to deal with a new company in London as well as with its official agents there, Messrs. Goldfern of the Strand. Under various pretexts large drafts had been drawn on Comyn's by Price, Jones and Price of Clerkenwell, and, look how she would, Kathryn could find no evidence of their repayment. No wonder Comyn's resources had been low when the run began; no wonder poor Thomas had been in despair. If the bank had opened this morning, and the run continued, as it was bound to do, it would have been forced to suspend payments as Pease and Harrison's had.

Of course. She ran a tired hand through her hair. That was why Sir Henry could not help with money. He had probably already done all he could for Pease and Harrison. Which meant, she faced it, that no one in Hull would be able to spare the cash to save Comyn's. That cupboard was already bare.

Go to York? No, London. When she used to write Thomas's letters for him she had liked the feel of Messrs. Goldfern. There had been something about their business letters: something human. She would go to them for help. It was early still, but the maids would be up, the terrible tale being told in the kitchen. Belatedly, she wondered how old Mrs. Comyn had taken the news, but there was simply not time for her yet. She took a deep breath and rang her bell.

'You've not been to bed!' Beth was shocked at sight of the bloodstained dress Kathryn had forgotten.

'Oh! I must change. There will be time for that — and for sleep — later. First, tell Sam coachman I want the coach ready as soon as possible. I'm travelling to London, fast. Have him send a man to see if we can get put across the Humber to Barton this morning, quicker that way. I'll pay anything, say. And I'll need an armed man for the journey. And you, Beth, of course. But, tell me, how is Mrs. Comyn?'

'Bad. Mr. Jones is with her now.'

'He's early. I'm glad. He will take care of her. No, don't bother looking for my blacks.' Beth had moved over to the big clothes press. 'I can do that. I want those orders given at once. As quick as possible, tell Sam coachman. I must get to London and back by Sunday night.'

'Can you?'

'I must.'

Beth's shocked look at her dress had been a warning, and she quickly put on the black she had worn for her mother. It was not exactly widow's weeds, but it would serve. Would she ever have time to mourn poor Thomas?

She was just ready when Beth knocked to say that Mr. Jones wished to see her.

It had to be done. 'I'll be down in a few minutes, tell him. And coffee and rolls in the breakfast room, please. At once. For two.'

This got her a look she did not quite understand, but the whole household was obviously in turmoil. She adjusted her black veil and went down to face Mr. Jones's sympathy.

If sympathy was the word, which clearly it was not. He blamed her for Thomas's death. She would have to get used to this, but today there was no time.

'I'm sorry.' She would not let him pray with her. 'I have been up all night, Mr. Jones, and must leave for London as soon as possible. Will you join me for breakfast?'

'Breakfast? London?' He gobbled with surprise. 'But you are in mourning, Mrs. Comyn, must I remind you of that?'

'No need, Mr. Jones. But I can mourn while I work.'

'Travelling! Work? How am I to believe my ears?'

'Please try to. If you do not feel able to join me at breakfast, Mr. Jones, perhaps you would be so good as to give my deepest sympathy to Mrs. Comyn and tell her I am doing my best to save her son's bank for its customers.' She swept past him with a rustle of black bombazine and had managed half a roll and a cup of coffee, when a heavy banging on the house door heralded Mr. Robertson, who had heard the news and arrived early.

'The books are gone!' He had forgotten everything else in shock at the discovery.

'We should condole with each other first,

I think, Mr. Robertson.' She rose to face him. 'Over the death of a good man. And, then, I would very much like to know how you found out the books are gone from the bank, since I took the precaution of removing the only key last night.'

'Oh!' It stopped him for a moment. Then, smiling a little: 'A polite fiction, Mrs. Comyn. Of course Mr. Comyn knew I had my own key in case of emergencies.' Then, belatedly: 'Poor Mr. Comyn.'

'I dislike to contradict you, Mr. Robertson, but that has never been my understanding. At least you locked the bank behind you, I trust, before you came over here.'

'Of course. It is nowhere near opening time yet.'

'We are not opening today.'

'Not opening?' He thought about it. 'Out of respect, you mean. Just as well, I suppose. So — if I may have the books, Mrs. Comyn? Peters and I can see that everything is ready for Mr. George.'

'You are ill informed for once, Mr. Robertson. The bank is my responsibility for the next twelve months.'

'Yours?' His tone blended astonishment, outrage — and fear? 'But he said — He told us —' He stopped, swallowing the end of the sentence.

'What did my husband tell you, Mr. Robertson?'

'Nothing. I don't know what I am saying. Forgive me, Mrs. Comyn, it's the shock.'

'Yes.' She almost felt sorry for him. 'We must talk, Mr. Robertson. I am glad you are come. Sit down; let me give you a cup of coffee.' She poured and passed it to him. 'I have been working on the books all night. I know just what you have been doing.' She raised a hand to silence his protest. 'We won't discuss it, if you please. Nor do I mean to say anything about it, if you undertake to make good your defalcations. The bank cannot stand another scandal. I am going to London today, to see if I can persuade Goldfern's to see us through the immediate crisis. I'll need your promise, in writing, for them, but you have my word that it will go no further.'

Coffee spilled into his saucer. 'But, Peters?'

'He's your affair. And I will leave you, when you have made restitution, to choose your own time, and your own pretext, for leaving the bank. And taking Peters with you. And now —' She held out her hand. 'I'll have that key, Mr. Robertson.'

When he had gone, she tried to make herself eat and drink some more, but could not. The coffee tasted disgusting, she could not swallow the rest of the roll. There would be time for food, and for sleep, on the way to London. She found Beth packing her carpet bag and told her to put the bank books on top.

'But, madam —' Beth had been screwing up her courage. 'Did you ought to go? It's a terrible long journey to London, Sam says. We won't get there till the small hours. If then. And you in your condition —' She paused.

'My — what in the world do you mean, Beth?'

'Don't say you didn't know? But, miss — ma'am — you must! It's over two months, and nothing for the wash —' She put a hand to her mouth. 'I've not said a word to a soul — nosy lot of bitches — but I made certain *you* knew —'

'Dear God!' Now, at last, it all fell into place and she did. 'Oh, Beth, he'd have been so pleased.'

'There's others won't,' said Beth darkly. 'That's why, don't you see, ma'am, you've got to take care of yourself.'

'But I've got to go to London. And you are going to take care of me, Beth. And — not a word to a single soul till I give you leave.'

'You don't need to say that.' Reproachfully.

'No, I don't, do I!' She laughed and gave the girl a quick hug. 'My goodness.' Possibilities were opening up before her. 'I believe that's what they meant last night.' She wished now that she had contrived to see poor Thomas's will, but was sure that it must provide for her to keep control of the bank as mother of the heir. She smiled at Beth. 'I suppose it might be a girl.'

'Never,' said Beth.

She was a tower of strength through a journey that was just as exhausting as Sam the coachman had warned. Most cheering of all was her stalwart attitude towards childbearing. The eldest of ten herself, she had watched her busy mother work her way up and pretty well through one birth after another. 'It's only the gentry ladies seem to find it hard,' she explained to Kathryn.

'Then I won't behave like one.'

'You won't find it easy.'

'I'll manage.' Kathryn had not enjoyed the parting with a horror-struck mother-in-law who thought she ought to be in a darkened room and floods of tears. But she was mistress of the house in the High Street now, and everyone knew it.

Kathryn slept a good deal on the journey, and woke to find Beth's supporting arm around her. They made good time, but London was waking to Friday morning when they rattled over paving stones at last. Extraordinary to be here for the first time, and find herself too preoccupied with her mission to have more than a glance for the sights and sounds of the great city. She knew so little about the Goldferns. Did they, or did one of them, live over the bank in the Strand? Or would she have to wait until it opened? How would she wait? In the carriage? But London's streets were crowded with traffic, the horses were exhausted and so must Sam be though he would not admit it.

It was an immense relief when Sam pulled his horses to a halt outside what was obviously a family house, with the bank premises occupying the ground floor. A maid was scrubbing the steps of the house entrance and Sam returned to the carriage after a quick word with her. 'Mr. and Mrs. Aaron Goldfern live here. They are at breakfast.'

'Thank God. Send in my name, Sam, my apologies. Say it's urgent.'

'You're the one used to write to us?' Aaron Goldfern was much younger than she had expected. 'My father always enjoyed your letters. He'll be delighted to meet you, Mrs. Comyn, however sad the circumstances.' He looked at his watch. 'He is always here for opening time, so perhaps you would like to rest for half an hour, drink some tea with Mrs. Goldfern, then tell your story, put your case, once to both of us.' He pulled a bell. 'Tell Mrs. Goldfern we will be with her directly.'

There was something immensely reassuring about the sight of young Mrs. Goldfern breakfasting with her children, a sturdy pair of boys whose age Kathryn found it hard to guess.

'You poor thing!' She came forward, friendly hand outstretched. 'My husband said he was afraid it must be bad news, but this is worse than anything. But, sit down, eat something, you must be worn out. You'll take coffee?' Her hand was hovering over the silver pot, but she was quick to sense Kathryn's reaction. 'No? Tea maybe? I often prefer it.' A sparkling glance from large dark eyes suggested that she had recognised Kathryn's condition, and she pressed dry toast on her as if it were the most natural thing in the world. 'Don't try to talk,' she advised. 'Rest a little, you've had a long night.'

'Thank you.' Kathryn felt a sheen of tears in her eyes, and felt that this was noticed too, while Mrs. Goldfern engaged her husband and children in lively talk that left her free to do her best by the tea and toast that she needed so badly and did not want at all.

'There's grandpa now.' Mrs. Goldfern had been the first to hear the carriage. 'Very well, boys, you may go down and greet him, but don't waste his time. He has a visitor, tell him.'

And then, to Kathryn; 'Better now, my dear?'

'Much. I do thank you.'

'For nothing, child. How old are you, for goodness sake?'

'Almost twenty.'

'A great age.' Mr. Goldfern was on his feet. 'I think my father will be in his study by now, Mrs. Comyn.'

'Don't let him shout at her, Aaron. And bring her back to me when you are finished. I want to show her London.'

'I doubt there will be time,' said her husband. 'This way, Mrs. Comyn.'

If the son had been younger, the father was older than Kathryn had expected. Frail and white-haired, he was already shrinking a little with age and looked as if he could not say bo to a goose, until you saw his eyes.

'Mrs. Comyn.' He came forward to take her hand in a firm clasp. 'I cannot tell you how delighted I am to meet you at last.'

'Why, thank you!'

'Aaron here used to tease me about your letters,' he told her. 'He said I looked forward to them like a lover. And now you are come to us for help, which I only hope we can give.' He had placed a chair for her across his big desk, waved his son to sit beside him. 'Your husband is dead, my son tells me. I am so very sorry. But that is not all?'

'By no means.' She plunged into her story, aware of his keen eyes fixed on her face. She described her anxieties about the bank, and Turner's warning. 'Thomas was obsessed with his canal scheme.' She tried to excuse his blindness to what was going on.

'I know. And a good scheme it was too.' Kindly. 'If it had not been for the war with France. But go on, Mrs. Comyn. Forgive me for interrupting you.'

She had come to the night of Thomas's death and was finding it appallingly difficult. It had been one thing to tell a lying tale to Sir Henry Etherington, this was something else again.

'Stop a moment, Mrs. Comyn.' The thin white hand was raised in warning. 'If we are to help you, my son and I, we must have the whole truth, and nothing else.' His smiled warmed her heart. 'You're a hopeless liar, child. If you managed to deceive those block-heads in Hull, it's a miracle. No,' smiling again. 'They're not expecting a woman to think, so why should they notice when she did. We Goldferns listen to our women, and we are listening to you. Between these walls, Mrs. Comyn. It goes no further. I speak for us both. Aaron?'

'Yes, father.'

She was silent for a moment, looking from

one to the other. Then, 'Yes,' she said. 'I'll tell you.'

She had not known what a relief it would be, but would not let herself cry.

'You did well,' said Goldfern senior at last. 'You were quite right, of course. There would have been no saving Comyn's if the true facts had come out. As it is . . . What do you think, my boy?'

'It's bad. More than we could handle on our own.' Aaron had the books in front of him. 'And this promise,' he tapped the paper Robertson had signed, 'may not be worth much. I've heard little good of Price, Jones and Price. Keeping themselves afloat in these hard times may be as much as they can manage. But you were entirely right, Mrs. Comyn, not to make a public issue of it with this man Robertson. That could only have been disastrous. But I'm afraid —'

'No.' His father interrupted him. 'Don't be afraid. Nor you, Mrs. Comyn. You can see that Aaron is our man of business, but I am the senior partner. And I owe a debt to Comyn's Bank.'

'A debt?' His son took the astonished words out of Kathryn's mouth.

'A debt of honour. You never met old Comyn, did you?' To Kathryn.

'No.'

'He was a careful man, and a good banker. And he took a great risk on me many years ago, when he was still feeling his way as a banker. I arrived in Hull penniless, starving, off a sloop from Danzig. My family were all dead, slaughtered, a pogrom — You know about those?' And when she nodded, wordless, he went on. 'The ship's captain took all my money, promised he was going to London, dropped me on the quay at Hull like a bit of worthless goods — which was pretty well what I was. Old Comyn — but he was young Comyn then — found me there, took me in. The good Samaritan.' He rose. 'No time to lose if you are to be back by Sunday night. I'll go to the Bank of England, Aaron. You talk to our other friends in the City. And my daughter will put you to bed, Mrs. Comyn. You have done your part.' And then, with a very kind look. 'Don't be too hopeful, child. It is not going to be easy.'

19

Kathryn slept all day in the quietly luxurious room at the back of the house overlooking the Thames. River sounds reminded her of Hull when she woke, hungry, in the twilight. Beth was there, with a tray. 'Mrs. Goldfern says you're to stay where you are. She seems to know about you — I swear I didn't tell her.'

'I know. Are the gentlemen back?'

'Just come. No news yet, I'm afraid. They've a meeting in the City in the morning. Mrs. Goldfern says she'll come and tell you about it when you've had your supper. No need to give up hope, she says, but it looks like travelling on Sunday, and what in the world will Mrs. Comyn say about that?'

'Oh, Beth, if that were the worst of our worries!'

She had eaten all the soup and most of the cold chicken, and drunk the glass of delicious wine when Mrs. Goldfern tapped on the door. 'That's good.' Her eye swept the tray. 'They are eating like horses in the dining room. It's been a long day's talking, and nothing settled, but you are most absolutely not to despair. There is to be a meeting in the morning: all the Directors of the Bank of England who are in London, and some other senior men in the City. They will put their proposals for saving Comyn's to them. They would like to tell you about them, if you feel well enough to join us for tea?'

'I'll be down directly.'

'No hurry; they are still at their wine.' She paused in the doorway. 'I think I should tell you, my dear, that this is the first time since I have known him that my father-in-law has consented to do any kind of work on a Saturday. It's our Sabbath, you know, and though he is officially a member of your Church of England he has always managed not to work on the Sabbath. He's a good man, my father-in-law.'

Kathryn tried to thank Mr. Goldfern senior when she joined them in the drawing room, but he would not let her. 'Too soon for that. We've a hard fight before us in the morning, and, besides, you may not like what my son and I are suggesting for Comyn's.'

'Oh?' She took the cup Mrs. Goldfern offered. 'I wish I could come to the meeting with you.'

'I am sure you do, and we did consider it, but you will have the sense to see what a mistake it would be. These are a set of hard-headed British business men who keep their wives in the same kind of innocent luxury as they do their horses. The idea of a woman — and a very young woman at that — involved in the running of a bank would shock them almost out of their senses.' Smiling. 'I do hope you had not been planning to run the bank yourself, Mrs. Comyn, if it should be saved.' His smile broadened. 'You had! Think about it a little and I am sure, an intelligent young woman like you, that you will see how totally impossible it would be. Think of one of the more pompous of the Hull city fathers and imagine him having to discuss his financial affairs with you. And then think, if you will, how your husband did his business. In the coffee house. At the club. Yes?'

'Yes. I've been a fool.'

'Nothing of the kind. Just not very realistic. Now, what we are proposing is that we send a man of our own back with you to take over the running of Comyn's. Under your command, of course. We have the very man for you. Not too old, not too young. A bachelor who lives for figures — Oh, and not Jewish either.' With another of his friendly smiles. 'Will you trust us about this, Mrs. Comyn?

You will need another man anyway, for protection on the journey back with so much money as I hope you will be taking. Though entire secrecy is just as important, and we are looking to that.'

It was a blow, and he knew it and gave her a few minutes to take it in, turning to ask his daughter-in-law for more tea. Had she really been imagining herself running Comyn's Bank in person? If nothing else, her condition would make it impossible.

She did not sleep much that night. There was too much to be thought about, to be faced. Suppose the worst. Suppose Comyn's did go bankrupt, what would become of her and the child she was carrying? Would anything be saved from such a wreck? She simply did not know. Nor did she know if Mrs. Comyn had means of her own. The idea of finding herself responsible for the old lady as well as for herself and the baby was daunting beyond belief. Best not think about it.

She had been ordered breakfast in bed and was grateful. The meeting in the City began at nine. 'Did they think it would take long?' she asked Mrs. Goldfern, who had come to drink a cup of tea with her.

'They said the longer it took the better the omen. And my father-in-law left a message for you. He said you must not be worrying yourself about anything. Goldfern's will look after you.'

'Oh, he is good!'

'Yes. Now I must leave you and see to my household. If the news should be good you will want to leave at once, I imagine.'

'Yes indeed. The sooner I am back, if it is good news, the better for everyone. Besides,' with a wry face, 'my mother-in-law disapproves most dreadfully of Sunday travelling. The less of it I have to do the better.'

'Will it be bad? Even if the news should be good?'

'I'm afraid so.'

The long day dragged. A message about noon reported that the meeting had adjourned for refreshment, and urged that Kathryn be ready to leave instantly. 'But the master says you're not to get your hopes too high,' the man warned. 'They are not out of the wood yet by any means.'

'I'd pray if I could,' Kathryn told Mrs. Goldfern. 'But I can't somehow.'

'Praying for money?' Thoughtfully. 'A little vulgar perhaps.'

'It's not just that. Give me something to do, Mrs. Goldfern, please. Mending; sewing; anything.'

They were both hard at work on shirts for the boys when a hansom cab rattled up to the door. 'They are come.' Mrs. Goldfern had hurried to the front window. 'They have brought Mr. Transome. He's carrying a bag. Oh, my dear, I am so happy for you.'

Kathryn found herself being hugged by both Goldferns, incoherently introduced to Mr. Transome, a tall, sober-looking, dark-haired young man, who would not let the bag he was carrying out of his hands.

'You're ready to leave this minute?' said Mr. Goldfern senior. 'Good. We've kept our doings as dark as possible, but we want you well out of town before the rumours of our success get out, as they are bound to do. It would be a pity to lose Comyn's funds to a highwayman, after all our trouble.'

Ten minutes later the bag was under Kathryn's feet and Mr. Transome was leading the way on horseback as the coach pulled out of the stable yard and turned in the wrong direction. 'Transome knows a way will get you out of town unobserved,' Aaron Goldfern had explained. 'He's armed, of course, like your man. God speed you, Mrs. Comyn.'

She hoped her thanks had been adequate. How could they have been? If she got safe to Hull Comyn's Bank would survive. 'Oh, Beth, I think I am going to cry.'

'Do,' said Beth.

Once again she slept a good part of the way,

but this time she was comfortably aware of not being responsible for the party. When they drew up for the change of horses it was Mr. Transome who saw to it that they got the best, and very quietly and well he did it. She was beginning to think Comyn's Bank lucky to get Mr. Transome.

The journey back took longer, because she and Transome had agreed that there would be little chance of getting a boat to cross the Humber for Barton on a Sunday. The church bells were ringing for evening service in Hull as they came in by the Goole Road. Kathryn had been badly shaken passing through Hessle. That mad moment when she waded out into the Humber there, seeking death — could it have had any influence on Thomas? It was a grim thought, she knew, with which she must learn to live, as she must learn to live with his child.

And with his mother. She had hoped to find Mrs. Comyn gone to chapel; it had been the only compensation for arriving at this grossly unsuitable hour on a Sunday, but there the old lady was, standing ramrod stiff in the doorway to greet them.

'The bank is safe.' Kathryn and Mrs. Comyn had never kissed each other if they could help it. 'Goldfern's have come to our rescue.' She introduced Mr. Transome, who had already taken charge of the all-important bag.

'Naturally it is safe. I told you the Lord had it in His keeping. My nephew George is here, come to condole with me. He is convinced, as am I, that this madcap scheme of yours was totally unnecessary. Funds would have been volunteered locally if it had been known they were needed. Sir Henry Etherington as good as told me so, when he paid his visit of condolence.'

'Did he indeed?' There was no answer she could make to this, no way she could refer to that desperate conversation in the small hours of Thursday morning. If Sir Henry had decided to take what credit he could, she was helpless to prevent him.

And here was Cousin George, looming behind his aunt, more handsome than ever, but portentous in the deepest possible mourning. She felt threatened. Absurd. It was just that she was so deathly tired.

Cousin George was saying charming, suitable things, and she was replying in kind. He was there for the reading of the will, which was to be next day, he told her. 'We assumed you would be back from this crazy journey of yours.'

'Not so foolish as all that.' She had taken both keys to the bank with her, now handed one to Mr. Transome. 'You will wish to be rid of your responsibility,' she told him. 'I will arrange for an overnight guard. And you must be my guest for tonight, Mr. Transome.' She felt an instant increase in her mother-in-law's rigidity, and had to be relieved when Transome thanked her civilly but declined. He would put up in an hotel until he could find himself lodgings.

'But you are staying, I trust?' Kathryn turned to Cousin George when Transome had gone across to the bank.

'George is staying with me,' said Mrs. Comyn.

'Which is a relief,' Kathryn told Beth, safe in her room at last. 'But it worries me a little just the same. Am I a fool to feel threatened, Beth?'

'No; sensible. Sally says a lot has been going on while we were away. I think you should send for the doctor, Mrs. Comyn.'

'Mr. Dawson? Why?'

'You're too tired to think. The will is to be read tomorrow. You must tell Mrs. Comyn — and that Mr. George — your good news before then, and, ma'am, you need to make them believe you.'

'You are absolutely right, Beth, and I do thank you. But will Dawson mind being sent for on a Sunday?'

'He's a terrible old gossip; he'll be pleased, really. But if you could bear to, I think you should have a spasm or a fainting fit or something. Then I'll get in a panic and send for him.'

'Oh, Beth, what would I do without you?'

Mr. Dawson was easier to convince than Kathryn had feared, but then she did not know of his conversation with Sir Henry on the night of Thomas's death. He was, in fact, delighted to have his guess confirmed, and prided himself not a little on his own acuteness.

He gave her so much good advice as to how she must take care of herself and her 'precious burden' that she told Beth afterwards she would have been liable to take to her bed for the next seven months if Beth had not told her about her own mother. But she left Mr. Dawson to give her news to her mother-in-law, and let Beth put her to bed, where she slept for twelve hours.

It was just as well, since Monday morning inevitably opened with a crisis at the bank. She had arranged for Transome to arrive well before it was due to open, and when Robertson came for the key soon afterwards she explained the new situation to him. His cold rage would have frightened her if she had not had Paul Transome at her side. But it was quickly over. Robertson was helpless, and knew it, but a quickly stifled reference to 'Mr. George' made Kathryn wonder very much if George might not have had some part in the affair of Price, Jones and Price.

She neither liked nor trusted Mr. Salmon, the lawyer, and it was with a sigh of relief that she heard him announce that the will was indeed the one that Renshaw had drawn up before their marriage. As mother of the heir, she would have control of Comyn's until the child came of age. Childless, she was assured of a comfortable income unless she remarried, when it would stop. And George Comyn would take over the bank. For the moment, he and Sir Henry Etherington were named as advisers, which explained Sir Henry's presence. She rather wished their function had been made a little more clear. But at least the fact of her pregnancy appeared to be generally, if tacitly, acknowledged, and she was grateful to that useful gossip, Mr. Dawson.

Dispensing the inevitable cake and wine, she was aware of all kinds of curious undercurrents in the little group. She had to be condoled with for the loss of her husband and at the same time congratulated on the saving of Comyn's Bank. The run on it had apparently stopped as soon as news of her return from

London had got out. And indeed, looking across the yard now, she could see that last week's stream of customers had diminished to the usual trickle. 'It seems so strange,' she said to Sir Henry when he congratulated her on this. 'If I had just gone to London and come back announcing that I had brought the funds it would have had the same effect.'

'Not necessarily.' With an odd little smile. 'It would depend on how good a liar you are, Mrs. Comyn.'

And just what did he mean by that? She thought she would rather not know, and was glad to turn away to speak to Mr. Jones, who had been brought to the will reading by Mrs. Comyn and made no attempt to conceal his disappointment at not being mentioned. The servants had not been mentioned either, and she lost no time, when the guests had departed, in getting them together and promising them gifts as from her husband. 'I am sure he intended to add a codicil about this,' she explained. 'But people do so dislike writing their wills.' It was odd to think that she still had no need to write one. Thomas's left her with nothing that was really her own, except what she could save from her income, and, more disturbing still, it did nothing to clarify the situation so far as old Mrs. Comyn was concerned. Would she go on living in her wing of the house?

It seemed that she would. She had taken the news of Kathryn's pregnancy oddly. For a moment, Kathryn had wondered if she was going to refuse to believe in it. Then, quite evidently, she had thought again, decided to accept it. Which was a relief, Kathryn supposed, but she still had the curious feeling of being, somehow, unsafe. Perhaps this was just another aspect of pregnancy, which she was finding an up and down sort of business, but Beth promised that she would feel much better in a week or two.

In the mean time, a new regime was gradually establishing itself. Transome had found rooms in the house where Turner lodged, and reported well of affairs at the bank. Robertson and Peters were co-operating, he told her, and he had hopes that if there were no new failure of public confidence in the course of the summer, they might begin to repay the Goldferns' loan by the autumn. He also reported that George Comyn and Sir Henry were taking their duties as advisers lightly enough. 'Which is a relief to me, Mrs. Comyn, because I don't know which of their advice I would like the least.'

'I do hope you are happy here in Hull, Mr. Transome.' She had been wanting to ask him the question.

'Happy?' He thought about it. 'I'm not sure I ever reckoned to be happy, Mrs. Comyn. Happiness is not for the likes of me, born in the gutter and bred by our own exertion. But I can tell you this, I am finding the saving of Comyn's Bank immensely interesting. And I reckon that is better than happiness any day.'

'I'm so glad.' One day she must ask him how he had managed to pull himself up out of the gutter, but not yet.

She had written to the ladies at Ross to tell them of Thomas's death and her expected child, and had even let herself a little wonder whether they might not volunteer to come and be with her at this difficult time, but their answer, when it came at last, was disappointing. Cousin Lavinia wrote, sending all kinds of love from them both but reporting that Janet had not been well. They had sent the manuscript of *The Gest of Sir Cradock* to Mr. Cadell the publishing bookseller, and had received it back, dog-eared, coffee-stained, but apparently unread, with an uncivil note of rejection. 'Janet has taken it hard,' wrote Lavinia. 'I am truly sorry, dear child, not to be able to offer to come to you at this sad time. I do hope you are finding your mother-in-law a comfort and support.'

Comfort and support. Kathryn laughed, because she would rather do that than cry. She had had a loving note from Jane Brierley too, but it contained nothing but bad news. The crisis of confidence that had shaken Comyn's Bank had ruined John Brierley. 'It was that unlucky canal scheme, I am afraid. Father takes it hard. Well, it is hard on a man to have the world to begin all over again. We have moved back to Nottingham and he is looking for work, but the times are bad, as you know. I am hoping to do something in the translating line, but have had no luck so far. In the mean time we are looking for cheaper lodgings and I will let you know when we move.' And then, a scribbled postscript. 'Dear Kathryn, be careful how you write. I am afraid my poor father is very unhappy — and angry.'

Rightly so, Kathryn thought miserably. This was the worst of all. John Brierley had never been so enthusiastic about Thomas's scheme as Thomas himself, had let himself be persuaded into it, she thought, for friendship's sake, and now it had ruined him. After thinking it over she sent for Paul Transome and explained the state of the case to him. 'I do feel my husband was responsible,' she said at last. 'Is there something we could do to help, Mr. Transome?'

'The bank, you mean? I am so very sorry, Mrs. Comyn, but I do not really see how. I have had angry letters, already, from a Mr. Bradshaw in Burton-upon-Trent, also blaming Mr. Comyn for the difficulties in which he finds himself. I have written to him pointing out that business is business. He embarked on the project of his own free will . . . I am afraid the same must apply to your friend's father, though I am deeply sorry to have to say so. But on the other hand —' He had seen and pitied her disappointment. 'If you wished to draw in advance on your next quarter's allowance, Mrs. Comyn, and have me send a draft to this Miss Brierley, from yourself, I could arrange that for you. But it would leave you short, I am afraid. Things have not worked out just as I would have wished. I cannot imagine that Mr. Comyn expected you to meet the expenses of a double household out of the amount allotted you. I have been wondering whether to suggest, either to you or to Mrs. Comyn, that it would be appropriate for the older lady to make some sort of contribution to the household expenses.' He let the suggestion hang, then added: 'She is a rich woman in her own right, did you know that?'

'No. I did wonder. But I can't ask her, Mr. Transome.'

'No. I rather thought you would feel that. Shall I?'

'I don't think it would do any good. In fact, it might even make matters worse.'

'They're not good? I was afraid . . . I am sorry. I wish the good Lord would send His chariot to carry off that Mr. Jones.'

'Oh, so do I.' She could not help laughing, and it did her good.

20

Kathryn missed Thomas in all kinds of unexpected ways, and hardly admitted even to herself that most of them were pleasant. Once again she found herself cloistered by her mourning. If she went out, she was aware of disapproving glances. She could not go to market; if she walked on the quay she thought Sir Henry Etherington looked at her oddly. And it rankled in her that no one, no one at all, ever thanked her for what she had done for Comyn's Bank, and therefore for the town. On the contrary, she got the impression, particularly from Mrs. Comyn's friends the Misses Harris, that her trip to London had been a most unsuitable adventure for a new widow, while Mrs. Comyn persisted in her conviction that 'the good Lord' would have saved the bank anyway.

It rained all May that year, and if it had not been for Beth, Kathryn might well have taken to her bed, but Beth would have none of this. 'Mother always said fresh air and exercise did her good, if she could just find time for them. The sun's out at last, ma'am, and you should be out in it.' She reached down a glum black bonnet from the shelf.

'I wish I was at home — Windover, I mean. Able to run out into the garden.' She tied bonnet strings reluctantly. 'Beth, how is your mother? What do you hear from her?' She was suddenly ashamed not to have asked the question before.

'Nothing, ma'am. How could I? We can't neither of us write, you see. Nor read.'

'Oh, Beth, I am so sorry.' Horror stricken. 'Shall I write and ask Mr. Tench about her? I'd like news of Windover too.'

'Oh, if you only would, ma'am. And, ma'am — ' Hesitating.

'Yes.'

'Would you — could you teach me to read, do you think, or would I be too stupid?'

'Of course not. Indeed I will, Beth, it will be a pleasure — and a change from this eternal French. Monsieur Japrisot does ogle one so.'

'He likes to be called Father,' said Beth.

'I know, but I won't. There's nothing fatherly about him. And that reminds me; Mrs. Comyn said something about my lessons with him the other day. It annoyed me at the time, but I think maybe you should join me in them? Would you mind, Beth?'

'I'd love to,' said Beth. 'And, if I may say so, ma'am, I think it's a good idea. It's not just old Mrs. Comyn talking. He's a proper fool, that Japrisot. Bunches of roses — as if you haven't plenty of your own — and talking about you all over town.'

Mr. Tench's letter brought bad news. After a long series of rolling sentences of condolence for Kathryn, he turned briskly to the subject of Beth's parents. Her father had been turned away without a character by the new owner of Windover Hall and had lost his cottage as a result. 'They have left the village, the whole pack of them,' wrote Mr. Tench. 'No great loss.'

'Oh, Beth.' Kathryn had stopped reading aloud. 'I'm so sorry. He doesn't say where they are gone.'

'He would neither know nor care,' said Beth. 'But they will have gone to York; father has a brother there will help them. I hope.'

'So do I!' They both knew how slender were the chances of a farm labourer without a character finding work in York.

'Do you know your uncle's direction in York?'

'How should I? You mustn't mind it so, ma'am. It's not good for you.'

'But it's my fault, Beth. If I hadn't brought

322

you away with me you'd not have lost touch with them.'

'But I wanted to come. Besides — I had to. They couldn't keep me, not with bread going up and farm wages going down. They'll be all right, ma'am. Mother's a wonderful manager. I just do hope she's not expecting again.'

'Mrs. Comyn would say the Lord will look after her.'

'I sometimes think it's better to look after oneself,' said Beth.

There was a sudden cold spell at the beginning of June and Kathryn was in her room looking for a warm pelisse for her daily walk in the garden, when Beth appeared looking both frightened and angry. 'Mr. Turner spoke to me in the yard, ma'am. He wants a word with you, on the quiet. He's overheard something — I won't believe it! You won't either, not if you don't hear it yourself.'

'As bad as that?' Kathryn put a protective hand on the bulge she was beginning to notice. 'But how, Beth?' Her every movement was overlooked by hostile eyes from Mrs. Comyn's wing.

'If you'll walk on the quay this morning. Sir Henry is in town, Turner says. He'll meet you there, "by accident".'

'Good.' Her hands shook as she wrapped

the pelisse round her shoulders. Horrible to have to make assignations in her own household. What was happening to her?

Turner had picked his moment well. The staithe below the Comyn house was empty, all the longshoremen gathered to work on a ship moored further downstream. 'Mrs. Comyn.' He joined her almost at once. 'You must believe what I am going to tell you.'

'I probably will,' she said.

'I dropped into the George last night. I don't usually go there — it's a bit above my touch, but it was such a cold night I thought I'd have a toddy to warm me on my way home. I was sitting in a corner reading my paper, when I heard voices through the partition. Mr. George it was, I'd know his voice anywhere. "If it's a girl, there's no problem," he said. "Pension her off, send the pair of them down to the old ladies in Wales, and leave me alone to get rid of Transome. If it's a boy, we'll have to act fast. You're sure you can do it?"

' "Of course I can, so long as I am sent for." That was another voice. I couldn't believe it for a minute. "Which I shall be. I'll get the maid out of the way; easy enough; an errand. Then give madam something to make her delirious. Mrs. Comyn and Jones as witnesses; when she comes to herself she'll be safe in the lunatic asylum. I'm on the board there.

It's a lot easier to get into those places than out again."

' "And the right place for her," said Mr. George. "A murderess . . ." ' Turner's eyes met hers wretchedly: 'Forgive me, Mrs. Comyn, but you had to know.'

'Yes.' Her hand was at her waist again. 'Mr. Dawson?'

'I'm afraid so. And I'm afraid he believed what he was saying. Don't forget that, Mrs. Comyn. And don't forget either that I will do anything in my power to help you.'

'I am sure of it. But — Mr. Transome? Would he help, do you think?'

'What could he do? Besides, he's a figures man, if you take my meaning. I don't reckon he knows much about people. You're shivering, Mrs. Comyn.'

'Not with cold.' But it was high time they parted. 'I do thank you, Mr. Turner.'

'Just so long as you believe me.'

'I'm afraid I do.'

She found Beth awaiting her anxiously in the bedroom, the one place in the big house where they could be sure no one was listening.

'You believe him?' Beth asked.

'Oh, yes, I believe him. I think I've been frightened ever since we got back from London. But, Mr. Dawson — I'd not have thought he — Beth, what am I going to do?'

'What are we going to do?' Beth corrected her.

'Thank you! Beth —' She had to ask it. 'You don't believe it, do you? That I killed him?'

'Course not. Though mind you I'm not sure I'd have blamed you if you had, the way he treated you. But that's not the point, is it? The thing is, there has been enough slanderous talk in the town so I think you'd have a hard time getting out of the trap they are setting for you. You're the stranger, see, the incomer; they'll close ranks against you. And Mrs. Comyn will have the bringing up of your son.'

It had been her nightmare all along. 'Get away, you think? Cut and run for it now?'

'Well, you certainly can't wait to see if it's a boy or girl,' said practical Beth. 'What about the ladies in Ross, ma'am? Would they have you?'

'I'm sure they would, but would I be let go?' Imagine telling this story. No one would believe her. Not even Mr. Renshaw. Telling it would merely convince people that she was indeed mad. Worse still, if she did try to go, might they not trump up an accusation of murder? That would hold her until the child was born, and then, if it was a boy . . . Her mind scurried frantically among grim possibilities. 'Beth, you'll really come?'

'Course I'll come.'

'Then we'll go to York first. We'll be dead poor, you know; have to earn our living.'

'I do,' said Beth cheerfully.

'Bless you! When we get to York, I'll go to Mr. Wilkinson. We can't stay in York of course, just long enough to lay a false trail and find your family. Then I think it has to be London; much the best place to vanish in. And I am sure Mr. Wilkinson will give me introductions to friends there who'll help me find work.'

'As an actress?' Shocked.

'As anything!'

'But how are we going to get away?'

'I'm trying to think. Which of the servants can we trust?'

'Sam coachman,' said Beth instantly.

'I was thinking that. So — I'll take a fancy for a few days at Hessle. Sam will take us to York instead.'

'It would cost him his job,' objected Beth. 'He's a family man, Sam.'

'Oh! You're right. We can't do that. I know! I'll decide I must go to York to buy baby linen. Sam takes us there; I send him back; you know Mrs. Comyn doesn't like to be without the coach. I'll name a day for him to fetch us. When he comes, we won't be there.'

'It will be a nine days' wonder.'

'It will be that, for certain. But can you see

a better way, Beth?' How strange it was to feel their relationship changing, moment by moment, from mistress and servant to fellow conspirators.

'Honest, I can't,' admitted Beth.

'And that way,' Kathryn was beginning to like the idea, 'I will have a reason for drawing considerable funds from the bank. Nothing but the best for the heir to Comyn's.'

'Will you say anything to Mr. Turner?'

'I think, best not, don't you? And, Beth, I am afraid the same is true of Sally. What they don't know can't hurt them.'

'I hope,' said Beth. 'You just can't tell with Mrs. Comyn, can you? Will we go to those kind Goldferns in London?'

'Beth, I don't think I dare. Not till the baby's safely born. I've kept thinking about it, and I don't believe I can risk it.' She had told the Goldferns the true story of Thomas's death, and they had believed her, but to come on them with a still more unlikely tale . . . She could imagine George Comyn arriving to fetch her; using that charm of his; talking of hysterical females. And taking her 'home' to Hull. He had deceived her for long enough — it weighed on her mind that she had rather liked George — why should the Goldferns be proof against his wiles? 'I rather wish now that I hadn't drawn my next quarter's allowance to send to poor Jane Brierley,' she went on, 'but never mind, with what I take out for baby clothes, and my savings, I am sure we'll manage until the baby is born and the last quarter is due. That will be the time to tell everyone. And in the mean time you and I are going to work for our living, Beth. I've always wanted to.'

'And I always have,' said Beth.

Inevitably, Mrs. Comyn made a thousand objections to Kathryn's trip when she announced it, but on the surface, Kathryn's power in the house was absolute. She listened to all the objections her mother-in-law had to make and then said, simply: 'I am sorry, ma'am. I intend to go.'

'Wholly unsuitable! I dread to think what Mr. Jones will say.'

'Then I beg you will not tell him until I am gone. I find argument very unpleasant these days and would be glad to be spared his strictures.'

She was not, of course, but she listened to them quietly enough, telling herself that it was for the last time.

Everything was for the last time. It was very strange. She had not been happy in Hull, but she had grown used to the place. She would miss her garden, she thought, and the busy sounds of the river. Not much else. How very sad.

But there was little time for thoughts like these. She and Beth were busy packing all her most valuable possessions into the largest portmanteaus they dared take without arousing comment. They were taking two extra ones, full of winter clothes, which Beth would carry down and stow in the coach herself, explaining that they were empty, to hold the baby things on the way back. Kathryn was wishing she had her mother's jewellery to sell. The small pieces Thomas had given her would not go far to keep the wolf from the door. She sometimes wondered if she was mad, then reminded herself that this was just what it was all about. Confined in the insane asylum, she knew, she might soon be mad indeed, from the sheer horror of the conditions. Thomas had gone there once and told her about it, white-faced. And, besides, there was the baby to think of.

The whole household was on the doorstep to see them go, and Kathryn kissed Mrs. Comyn and felt like Judas. Mrs. Comyn held her hand for a moment. 'One thing comforts me,' she said. 'I have had enquiries made and am glad to tell you that Mr. Wilkinson and his band of ruffians left York for Leeds a little while ago. So there is one temptation you will be spared, thank God.'

'Goodbye.' Kathryn stepped into the coach. Gone to Leeds. The words echoed dully in her brain and she hardly noticed that she was driving down the High Street for the last time. She hoped it was the last time. Don't think like that; defeatist thoughts. Nor must she let Beth see what a blow the news had been. There was something both touching and heartening about Beth's confidence in her own ability to look after them both.

She had booked a room in the Black Swan where she had stayed before, with Thomas, a million years ago it seemed. When they arrived, late on Monday afternoon, she told Sam to come for them on Friday.

But Beth had not been quick enough to prevent him from picking up one of the supposedly empty bags. 'Ma'am —' He stood there twisting his cap in his hands. 'What's happening? What are you doing?'

'Don't ask me, Sam. Know nothing. Say nothing. Please?' She thought of tipping him, reached out and clasped his hand instead. 'Come on Friday, Sam, and — I'm sorry.'

'You can count on me. And God keep you, ma'am. And you, too, Beth.' He replaced his cap firmly on his head, touched it in salute to them both, turned on his heel and returned to the coach.

They looked at each other in silence for a

moment, feeling immensely forlorn, then Kathryn squared her shoulders. 'Here we are,' she said. 'Let's go upstairs.'

'But what are we going to do?' Alone in the luxurious room Kathryn had felt she must reserve, though the expense frightened her, Beth turned to her near tears. 'Suppose he talks?'

'He won't,' said Kathryn. 'But I had decided already that we must leave for Leeds in the morning. I'll make the arrangements while you go and see if you can find your family. Thank goodness for these light evenings. If you find them, give them this, Beth.' She handed over a banknote. 'I wish I could make it more. And find someone to write down their direction for you, so that at least you can keep in touch. I do hope you find them.'

'Oh, I shall, ma'am, I remember the way to uncle's well enough. And I do thank you. But will you be all right on your own?'

'Of course I will.' It was luxury to find herself alone, unwatched, in the impersonal shelter of this comfortable hotel. But the manager was not pleased when she told him that they had to leave in the morning. 'The room was booked for four nights,' he protested.

'Anyone can see your fine hotel is as full as it can hold,' she told him. 'You'll have no trouble letting it again.' She was using her mother's voice, she noticed with amusement, the voice of the aristocrat, and it worked. He retired, grumbling, into his office and she put on her bonnet and went out to make discreet enquiries about coaches to Leeds. From now on, they would travel by public conveyance for reasons of economy as well as secrecy.

She knew that Mr. Palmer's mail coach came on from Hull, which put it out of the reckoning, even if it had not left in the middle of the night. She actually found herself thinking nostalgically of Thomas's passenger boats as she booked their places for a slow roundabout journey that would take them most of the next day for what the mail coach did in four hours.

But Beth came home triumphant, having found her family living a few doors away from her uncle's house. Her father had got work as a market porter, two brothers and one sister had died of the fever soon after reaching York, and her mother was not pregnant. 'She begins to think she's past it.' Beth had produced all this information on the same note. She had been crying, Kathryn could see, but she could see too that for so poor a family the loss of three mouths to feed was not an unmixed disaster. 'The others is better, ma'am,' said Beth. 'And mother sends her best regards and thanks.' She handed over a filthy scrap of paper. 'And that's their direction.'

They found lodgings not far from the Theatre Royal in Leeds, and tired though she was from a long day's jolting over dreadful roads made worse by the rain, Kathryn sent a note round to the theatre at once asking Mr. Wilkinson to call on her. She then spent a sleepless night wondering what in the world she would say to him. She was beginning to wonder if she had been mad to embark on this venture. But what else could she have done?

To her relief, Mr. Wilkinson arrived promptly next morning, and she soon realised that she owed the early visit to his curiosity. She knew him for an inveterate gossip, and must contrive to tell him as little as possible, while enlisting his help. Luckily, he had his own tale to tell. Audiences were poor, he told her, because of the war. Even his friend Mrs. Inchbald's play *Every One Has His Fault* was drawing merely moderate houses. 'Shall I give you passes for tonight?' And then, aware of her mourning at last: 'But, Mrs. Comyn, you are alone? What in the world?'

Strange and rather reassuring to find that the events that had changed her life had not even been reported at York or Leeds. She told him as briefly and simply as possible about Thomas's 'accidental' death and referred briefly to the trouble at the bank. 'All over now, I am glad to say.' In answer to his horrified exclamation.

'But, Mr. Wilkinson,' she came straight to the heart of the matter, 'I am sorry to tell you that I find I cannot live with old Mrs. Comyn.'

'That old dragon. You do not at all surprise me, ma'am. But what are you going to do?'

'You will think me very bold, but I am going to London to seek my fortune.'

'By yourself?' Appalled.

'My maid comes too.' She had noticed him eyeing Beth with some interest and it struck her what a handsome girl she had grown to be. 'I was hoping, Mr. Wilkinson, that you would feel able to give me introductions to some of your many friends in London. I am afraid I know no one there.'

'Introductions? What precisely had you in mind, Mrs. Comyn? And, only consider, your mourning —' He was obviously horrified at the whole thing.

'I may be in mourning, Mr. Wilkinson, but I must live. Besides, I want to work!' It was true; she needed to work, to occupy herself, to become a different kind of person. 'The thing is,' she went on, 'that I don't know what I am fit for. I would dearly like to do anything connected with the theatre, or —' she was aware that he was not enthusiastic — 'I write a good hand, understand French: copying, translating maybe?'

'My dear lady, can I not persuade you to think again? The times are hard . . . Theatres badly hit . . . Mrs. Comyn is a dragon, we agree, but surely the place for you is your husband's — your late husband's house. Or,' on a suddenly hopeful note, 'your own family? Is there not a step-father somewhere?'

'I would rather die than turn to him. And, believe me, Mr. Wilkinson, I find life in Hull equally impossible. I was wondering . . . your friend, Mrs. Inchbald? Surely she must know a great deal about how one can go on in London? And Mrs. Siddons, perhaps? If you do not think it asking too much.' This was all being infinitely worse than she had imagined.

But he greeted this suggestion with relief. 'Yes, of course. Mrs. Inchbald and Mrs. Siddons. A capital notion. I'll write them both notes this very day. They will know what is best for you, I am sure. And dear lady, let me persuade you to come and see our play tonight. Strangers here in town. Why not?'

The temptation was overwhelming. Beth had never seen a play and she could sense her eagerness. Besides: 'Thank you, Mr. Wilkinson, we would like that, and perhaps we could pick up your notes for the two ladies at the same time? I would very much like to leave for London in the morning.' All the time, she was aware of the days ticking away towards Friday, when their flight must be discovered.

21

They beguiled the exhausting journey to London by comparing delighted notes about Mrs. Inchbald's comedy. 'I see now,' said Beth as they bolted down a disgusting and expensive dinner at Nottingham, 'why you want to find work in the theatre. Oh, ma' am, do you think there might be something I could do?'

'No reason why not. Thomas always said he thought there was as much luck as anything in the way actors got started. And, do you know, I thought Mr. Wilkinson quite had an eye for you yesterday.'

'He did, didn't he?' said Beth cheerfully, and Kathryn thought once again how things were changing between them. 'Beth,' she said. 'It's time you stopped calling me "ma'am" We're companions now, not mistress and servant.'

'Oh, ma'am, I couldn't.' But Beth's eyes sparkled.

'I think you could, if you put your mind to it.'

'Well,' doubtfully, 'if you wish it, I'll try. But don't you think we'll do better to go on acting as mistress and maid? It looks more respectable somehow. Besides, look at our clothes.' She rose at the summons to return to the coach. 'And after all, Miss Kathryn, you're paying our way.'

'While I can.'

They reached London on the third day, too tired almost to think, and Kathryn decided they had best spend that night at least at the Black Swan in Holborn, where the coach stopped. They would start to plan, and to economise, in the morning.

But in the morning Beth made Kathryn stay in bed. 'You're worn out, and no wonder, two nights sitting up in that dreadful coach. You'll rest today or we might lose this baby, and you don't want that, do you?'

'No, Beth, I don't.' How strange it was. She was absolutely certain, in her heart, that this child stemmed from that horrible night when Thomas had beaten her. How could she want it? But she did. Thomas's son. She would bring him up to be a happier, and therefore a better man than his father. That was what this was all about, after all. 'Yes, I would be glad of the rest. Beth, if I wrote notes to Mrs. Siddons and Mrs. Inchbald, could you get them delivered for me, do you think?'

'I'll take them myself if it's not too far. I'm longing to see something more of London. I walked about a bit last time we were here, you know. Mrs. Goldfern gave me leave. And a map. She said I would come to no harm, and I didn't.'

She sounded almost disappointed, Kathryn thought, as she let herself be propped up in bed to write the notes. 'Can you walk as far as Great Marlborough Street? Mrs. Inchbald's house is nearer, but that is where Mrs. Siddons lives.'

'I'm sure I can,' said country-born Beth. 'I shall like it. And it will save both time and postage.'

But she returned with daunting news. Both the ladies' houses were shut up for the summer. 'I should have thought of that,' mourned Kathryn, 'and asked Mr. Wilkinson for letters to the managers of the theatres. They must be here.' It was a dispiriting thought that Tate Wilkinson must have known the two actresses would probably be out on summer tour and had not chosen to warn her of this. 'Oh, Beth, what are we going to do?'

'Have a good night's sleep and think again in the morning,' said Beth stoutly. 'It will be all right, Miss Kathryn, I'm sure it will.'

'Do you realise that it is Friday? They'll

340

know now at Comyn's.'

'I've been thinking about that all day,' Beth admitted. 'What do you think they'll do?'

'I don't know. I wish now I'd left a note for Sam to take back with him, but it was all such a muddle, such a rush. I sent one off this afternoon while you were out, to Mrs. Comyn, just saying I had decided to leave and would let her know my direction when I was settled. It caught the night mail to York; Mrs. Comyn will get it on Monday; I doubt if she'll have done anything before that.'

'No.' Doubtfully. 'You don't think she'll put the Bow Street Runners on us?'

'Of course not.' Kathryn wished she was as sure of this as she made herself sound. 'I wrote to the ladies in Ross, too.' Turning to a more cheerful subject. 'Very much the same thing. The last thing I want is for them to be worrying about me, if Mrs. Comyn should write them. I really will write them when we are settled. First thing tomorrow morning we are going to get out and find ourselves a nice clean attic room.' She had been doing her best to conceal from Beth how alarmingly life in hotels had been running away with her money. She had never paid her own board before and everything seemed to cost more than she expected. 'It is a blow about both ladies being out of town,' she admitted. 'I had thought they would advise us about where we should look for lodgings.'

'Mother said to be careful,' said Beth. 'Terrible things happen to girls on their own in London, she told me. She said not to look for lodgings in the theatre district, nohow, or we might find ourselves where we didn't want to be. Mother's no fool. Do you think, maybe, somewhere down by the river, near where we stayed with the Goldferns? I liked it there.'

'So did I, but suppose we were to run into them? Or, worse still, George Comyn, coming to them to enquire for me. I think he's bound to do that. And I'm afraid of him, Beth.' It was a relief to admit it. 'I think we had better go further out of town, rather than nearer in. We can always move back when we have found work.' She spoke more confidently than she felt and suspected that Beth was aware of this.

But next morning was brilliantly fine, and they both felt a sense of adventure as they set out through the crowded, noisy streets to look for their new home. It took them most of an exhausting morning, but neither of them minded asking help from strangers, and most of the time their own good manners ensured them a civil reply. In the end, a woman selling hot pies in the Gray's Inn Road suggested they try the district round Red Lion Square.

'There's new building there, see, and young couples setting up house; you might find someone glad to let you have a bit of their attic.'

'I like this.' Kathryn's feet were sore by the time they reached the still unfinished square, and her back ached, but she liked the look of the new houses and the sweet scent of hay from the fields beyond. 'Oh, Beth, I do hope we find something here.'

'I think we should sit down for a bit first.' Beth had given her a sharp look. 'There's a little eating house over there looks respectable enough. I could do with something, couldn't you? And we could ask there about rooms. Come on, Miss Kathryn.' She led the way firmly through the low entrance and into a room full of large men and smelling of chops and cabbage.

Their polite good-days got them a few responses and more sharp looks, but a kind of shuffling movement at one of the trestle tables made room for them and they were soon eating away like the rest. The food was remarkably good and so was the porter Beth had suggested. Beth seemed to have taken over and Kathryn, tireder all of a sudden than she liked to admit, could only be grateful. When they were ready to go she asked the stalwart land-lady whether she knew of lodgings to let anywhere. 'We are looking for something very simple, my friend and I.'

'Sorry, miss, not a thing.' The woman was too busy to care.

But an elderly red-faced man in a fustian jacket leaned forward from the far side of the table. 'Try the New Road, north of the square,' he suggested. 'The houses are still going up there; you might find someone having a hard time paying the full price.'

'What do we do?' asked Kathryn doubtfully as they crossed the dusty centre of what would be the square when it was finished. 'Ring at doorbells? It seems a chancy business.'

'It's all a chancy business,' said Beth robustly. 'You're tired, Miss Kathryn, that's what it is. We'll try down here and then it's time we went home. Tomorrow is another day.'

A very expensive one in the Black Swan, thought Kathryn dismally. Then, 'Oh, look,' she said. 'Someone is moving in!' A shabby handcart stood outside one of the newly finished houses on the muddy road. 'Do we dare, Beth?'

'Course we do. Leave it to me, Miss Kathryn.'

As they approached the house a tall young man in his shirtsleeves came out of the open front door and looked anxiously up and down

344

the street. Seeing them, he hurried forward. 'Excuse me, but do you happen to know where I can find a midwife? Or a doctor?' Sweat was running down the fair face and his short hair looked as if he had been running filthy fingers through it. 'It's my wife.' Breathlessly. 'It's all been too much for her; she's started, she thinks.'

'How early?' asked Beth.

'We're not sure.' More distracted than ever. 'But — she's all alone.'

'I'll go to her,' said Beth. 'Direct him to the eating house, Miss Kathryn; someone there will be bound to know.' She turned and went briskly up the steps.

'Don't worry too much.' Kathryn pointed the way back across the square. 'My friend is the eldest of ten. She'll help your wife, I'm sure. Would you like me to see to the unloading of the rest of your things?' There looked pitifully few of them.

'Oh, if you would. He knows where to put them.' A stout man in a baize apron had emerged from the house and was standing, arms akimbo, listening to the exchange. 'Get on with it, man, do. I'm sure Mrs. Reynolds will feel better when we are settled.'

'So shall I,' said the man truculently. 'When you've settled my account.'

'I told you: tomorrow. I promised you —'

'And I tell you, today, or I dump your traps in the street. She won't like that, your missus.'

'But I gave you my word —' The young man was actually close to tears. 'I must find the doctor for my poor wife.'

'Poor wife is right,' said the man. 'Be poorer before you're done by the look of things. Moving into a great house like this without even the money for the cart. One shilling is all.' He turned to Kathryn. 'One shilling, I tell you, and he says tomorrow. Tomorrow won't buy my wife her supper, nor yet my kids.' He moved over to the barrow and picked up a long case clock, the most handsome thing on it. 'One shilling, cully, or this goes in the gutter.'

'But I haven't got it tonight,' groaned the young man, running distracted hands through his hair. 'I told you; tomorrow!'

'And I told you, today.' He picked up the clock.

'No, stop.' Kathryn could not bear it. She pulled out her purse. 'I am sure you are over-charging,' she told the man. 'Sixpence, and no more argument.

'Oh, God bless you.' The young man turned to hurry away across the square.

Kathryn found Beth in the half-furnished front room of the house where a girl about her own age was sitting on a threadbare sofa.

She was crying a little and gripping Beth's hands in her own and even to Kathryn's inexperienced eye it was obvious that she must be close to her time.

'There you are, Miss Kathryn.' Beth welcomed her with relief. 'Is there a bed in the house could be got ready? And we'll need a fire to boil the kettle. Tell Mr. Reynolds to light one the minute he gets back, would you? I hope he's not long.' Her eyes met Kathryn's.

'I'll see to the bed.'

'I am so sorry,' the girl on the sofa raised heavy eyes to Kathryn's. 'All this trouble . . . The sheets are in the big black portmanteau . . . Ouch!' She closed her eyes again as the pain ripped through her.

Kathryn fled. She had never made a bed in her life before, and the contents of the black portmanteau were heart-rending in their darned scantiness, but the sheets smelled of country air and the big brass bed in the first-floor room looked solid enough.

'All done now.' The man in the baize apron had turned civil once he had been paid. He deposited an awkward-looking bag in the front hall. 'That's the last of it,' he told Kathryn. 'Anything else I can do, mum?'

'If you would light the fire for me, we could all have a cup of tea,' said Kathryn, who had never lit a fire. 'I wish Mr. Reynolds would get back.'

'More hair than wit, that one,' said the man. 'Coals and kindling you'll need before you can have a fire. Give me twopence, and I'll fetch them for you.' He saw her hesitate. 'You can trust me, mum, Jem Barnes's word is his bond. I just don't like being diddled, see. Promises! Tomorrow! I'll get you some bread and milk, too; it looks like a long night ahead to me. First ones is always slow.'

'Oh, thank you, Jem. I would be grateful.' She looked in her sadly depleted purse. 'Will that be enough?'

'And to spare. You've not been in London long, I can see. If I was you I'd try out that sofa in the front room myself. You don't look entirely the thing to me, if you don't mind my saying so.'

'Not at all. Thank you, Jem.' But when he had gone she hurried to rejoin Beth who had got Mrs. Reynolds into the big bed. 'How is she?'

'Doing splendidly.' Beth's cheerful tone was for the girl on the bed. 'Where's the man gone?'

'To fetch coals and kindling. I gave him the money. I hope I've not been a fool. If only Mr. Reynolds would get back. What can I do, Beth?'

'Go and sit down for a bit.' Beth echoed Jem Barnes's advice. 'We've got a long night ahead of us.'

'We're going to stay?'

'I reckon we'll have to. Mrs. Reynolds,' her tone sharpened slightly as she spoke to the sobbing girl on the bed, 'have you such a thing as a cot bed and some spare bedding?'

When Mr. Reynolds returned, alone and distracted, half an hour later, he found the fire lit, the kettle boiling and Jem Barnes just ready to leave. 'The doctor wouldn't come,' he told Kathryn wretchedly. 'And the midwife's out already. She may come later, if she gets back.'

'Then it's a good thing we have arranged to stay,' said Kathryn. 'Jem here is very kindly going to fetch a few things from the Black Swan for us. If you don't mind, that is?'

'Mind! I can't begin to tell you how grateful I am.'

'Then don't try.' Beth had appeared on the stairs. 'Go and talk to your wife, Mr. Reynolds. Try and persuade her to calm down a little. It's not the end of the world, having a baby. To listen to her, you'd think no one ever had before.'

'She's only a child herself,' he protested.

'And you seem to have treated her like one.

It's time you stopped, Mr. Reynolds. Now, go and talk some cheerfulness into her. Of all the ill-managed affairs —' She turned to Kathryn when the two men had gone about their business. 'He got the offer of work in the General Post Office, and the chance of this house and came hustling to London with that child wife almost at her time, and of course, everything has cost him more than he expected. And something about the house I didn't rightly understand. And she chooses to quarrel with the wife of the friend of his they were staying with. So here they are. And here we are. What's the attic like?'

'You really think we should stay?'

'Of course we must stay. How will you get your money back if we don't?' The sums Kathryn had advanced to young Reynolds had mounted up alarmingly in the course of the afternoon. 'He starts work on Monday; everything will be different then,' Beth went on. 'Besides, they need us.'

This was unanswerable. The midwife, when she finally turned up, was so visibly the worse for drink that Beth sent her off with a flea in her ear and delivered the baby herself. Her cheerful common sense and a few quiet doses of gin administered when the husband was not looking had combined to relax Peggy Reynolds into what proved in the end a surprisingly easy delivery. If Reynolds was sorry that he had a daughter not a son for his firstborn, he concealed it valiantly, and by the time they all breakfasted together that fine Sunday morning it was being taken for granted that Kathryn and Beth were to stay on as lodgers. Jem Barnes, who seemed to have become a friend of the family, fetched the rest of their things from the Black Swan for them and put up a couple of cots in the attic.

'It ain't exactly what you are used to.' Beth looked around the room. 'Oh, miss, do you think we should go back?'

'Back!' Horrified. 'Beth, now it is you who are too tired to think straight. And no wonder, up all night as you have been. Of course we are not going back; we are going to make up these beds and you are going to rest a while on one of them. Mrs. Reynolds will need you again soon enough.'

'I'm afraid she will,' said Beth ruefully. 'Of all the spoiled babies. Lucky the child seems stout enough and knows its business. It's more than the mother does. I wish you would go down and ask Mr. Reynolds when he expects to get paid, and how much, Miss Kathryn. We must hire them a maidservant, if you and I aren't to find ourselves doing all the work of the house. Which I do not intend.'

'No.' Laughing. 'That is not precisely how

we planned to earn our living. I'll go and speak to him now, Beth, if you will promise to rest a bit?'

Silas Reynolds was calmer this morning and full of apologies and gratitude. And, yes, he told her, the uncle who had got him the job at the post office would be back from his holiday next morning and would advance the money he needed. 'Then I shall be able to repay the money I owe you, Mrs. Comyn, but your kindness, and your friend's, I shall never forget. If you do not very much mind, we thought we would call the baby Kathryn Elizabeth.' It was the highest compliment he could pay.

22

Kathryn came to love that attic. On a still day, she could hear the bells of St. Paul's, and if she leaned far out of the dormer window she could see the fields and green hills of Hampstead. And she liked the curious sloping ceilings and the little alcove by the chimney breast where Beth had tucked their washstand with its basin and ewer, produced along with the cot beds by Jem Barnes, who had a friend in the pawnbroking line. 'You'd be surprised, mum, what folks is having to pop these days, things being so hard. But maybe I don't need to tell you that.' He left the sentence hopefully hanging, obviously full of curiosity about her and Beth, but got no satisfaction.

He found the household a maid of all work, a timid sniffling Susan of fourteen whom Beth swiftly took in hand and trained. 'That Mrs. Reynolds knows no more about real housework than you do, Miss Kathryn, if you don't mind my saying so.'

'No, she doesn't, does she?' Kathryn was

beginning to wonder a little about Peggy Reynolds. Were they perhaps assisting at a runaway match? She suspected so, thought it would perhaps be better not to ask; just hoped that the young couple were married.

Peggy Reynolds had cheered up a bit when Susan arrived, and with revived spirits her looks returned. The hair that had lain so limp on the pillow turned back into golden curls and the pink and white complexion re-established itself. She was a very pretty girl indeed, and used to being treated as such. Her husband adored her, but he adored the baby too, and Kathryn wondered a little how his wife would take this.

But they all loved that good baby and took it in turns to cherish her. Silas Reynolds's first thought, when he got home at night, was for her; and Susan, an orphanage child, was constantly thinking of pretexts to lean over the makeshift cradle.

'This is all very fine.' Kathryn looked round the attic and admired the stuff curtains Beth had just hung. 'But we have been here a whole week, Beth, and done nothing about finding work.'

'I know,' said Beth. 'But you couldn't exactly say we had been idle, miss.'

'No,' laughing. 'What a week. How surprising it all is! Well, Beth, tomorrow we go to church, and Monday we start looking for work.'

It was not a good moment to do so. The great world was out of town, and London was ticking over gently until the great world returned. They had tacitly agreed to begin with the theatres, but found Covent Garden closed for the summer.

'And Drury Lane is being rebuilt,' said Kathryn. 'Tate Wilkinson warned me of that. The company is working at the Little Theatre in the Haymarket.'

'Is that far away?'

'It can't be, surely; they'd never move far afield.'

'I suppose not. But won't it be closed too, like Covent Garden?'

'They can't all be shut,' said Kathryn desperately. 'I'm sure I've seen notices of plays in the summer. Oh, Beth, what a fool I was not to get more information out of Tate Wilkinson.'

'He wasn't just going out of his way to be helpful,' said Beth. 'I begin to think, Miss Kathryn, that there's a great difference between doing favours and asking them. Mr. Wilkinson was glad enough to come and eat your dinners in the High Street.'

'I'm afraid you're right.' Gloomily. 'Never mind, we're going to manage without his help,

Beth, you see if we don't.'

A barrow boy directed them across Leicester Fields to the Haymarket. The little Haymarket Theatre was quiet, tucked away among the houses, but the huge new King's Theatre on the other side of the broad market place was a hive of activity, with billboards announcing *Inkle and Yarico* and *The Village Lawyer* for that very evening.

But when they found the stage door and asked to see the manager they were rudely repulsed. 'Manager, is it?' said the burly man in the frieze jacket. 'If you don't know enough to know Mr. Colman's snug in the King's Bench, you don't know nothing. And we don't take on extras this late in the season nohow.' He finished with so rude a suggestion as to what they should do with themselves that they turned and fled.

'Hey, you two.' An elderly woman in shabby black had witnessed the rebuff. 'From the country ain't you? I was once meself. Take a bit of advice from an old hand and try your luck somewhere else. The theatre's no place for a couple of young 'uns like you. Not without letters that is; not without help.'

'We've got letters,' Kathryn turned eagerly to this possible ally. 'But the ladies are away. Mrs. Siddons and Mrs. Inchbald,' she explained.

'And very nice too; and will be helpful I've no doubt, but wait till they get back, dearies. You'll get nowhere on your own. Or nowhere you'd want to get. Main theatres is closed in the summer, see, and all the casuals come here. Drury Lane's rebuilding, so that lot are on the loose. The nobs is away touring the country and staying with their gentry friends; it's just us scaff and raff stay around. And scaff and raff for an audience too, I can tell you.'

'What do you do?' asked Beth.

'Me! I'm a dresser. Not to the bigwigs. Everybody's butt, that's me. Ten bob a week — when they pay it! Anything goes wrong with the way they look — it's my blame. All goes right, no thanks. I tell you girls, if you're not Siddons or Jordan you'd best find yourselves something else to do. Breaking stones, or minding brats! I tell you to your faces, you're too pretty, the both of you, and too well spoken, to come to anything but bad here in the theatre. George Colman's in gaol for debt; where's the pay coming from? Don't say I didn't warn you, and if you fancy giving me something for the good advice, I'll not say no.' She smiled, gap-toothed, from one to the other. Then, 'God bless you, miss, for a real lady.' Tucking the penny Kathryn had given her into her immense bosom. Then: 'You really want work?' she said. 'Find a genteel family, with not too many kids, and go as nurse-maids. I tell you, dearies, it's safer.' And she rolled back into the theatre, wheezing with laughter.

'Oh dear,' said Kathryn. They looked at each for a few gloomy minutes.

'You're tired, Miss Kathryn. Should we find somewhere we can sit down and eat a bit?'

'We can't afford it,' said Kathryn bleakly. Then: 'I know. Let's buy a penny roll from a stand and eat it on the way to St. Paul's. That's one place we can sit down without being charged for it and I've always wanted to see it.'

'Why not? We've been ever so good, Miss Kathryn, when you think about it. A whole week in London and not one bit of sight-seeing.'

'I wonder just where the King's Bench is,' said Kathryn thoughtfully as they walked back across Leicester Fields.

'Mr. Colman, you mean? Miss Kathryn, it's true what she said, if he's in gaol for debt, he don't sound like the right employer to me.'

'Yes.' Kathryn had been thinking this too. 'It seems to me that she's right. We must find something to keep us fed through the summer, try again when Mrs. Siddons and Mrs. Inch-bald return in September.'

'But not child-minding,' said Beth. 'Or breaking stones!'

They ate their halfpence worth of bread under a tree in Leicester Fields, but had to move on in a hurry when a noisy group of apprentices spotted them there. They lost their way as a result, and Kathryn was tired again when they reached the top of Ludgate Hill. She stopped to catch her breath and admire Christopher Wren's tremendous church, and a shop on the corner of the churchyard caught her eye.

'Beth, do look! It's Mr. Newbery's shop. I used to love his children's books when I was a girl. *Goody Two Shoes* and *Giles Gingerbread* and *Tom Thumb*. Lovely little books, just the right size for a child, with gilt lettering on their jackets — and all that pleasure for threepence! My mother used to buy them for me when she went to the Assize Balls at York.' She stood there for a moment looking at the handsome classical building. 'How strange that he should sell Dr. James's powders too!' She was reading the inscription under the portico that announced that this was also the warehouse for the famous medicine. 'Beth, I wonder — Let's go in.'

'But, Miss Kathryn —' But she had already pushed open the shop door and Beth could only follow.

'Yes, ma'am?' A black-clad young man came forward to greet them civilly as Kathryn looked round in delight at the room full of books. 'What may I have the pleasure of finding for you?' He spoke to Kathryn, but looked at Beth.

'Oh!' Kathryn was beginning to regret the impulse that had brought her into the shop. Impossible to ask this young clerk for work. 'I was wondering . . . might I speak to your employer perhaps?'

'To Mr. Francis? I'd need to tell him what it was about, ma'am. He's a busy man and only up from the country for a few days.' He was civil still, but a little puzzled. 'Would you be a writing lady, ma'am?'

'Well —' Kathryn took a deep breath. 'I might. The children's books . . . I loved them so . . .'

'They was his uncle's, ma'am; Mr. John Newbery. I never knew him. Mr. Francis is something quite other. He lives at Heathfield in Sussex and keeps his carriage. They do say he'll be a magistrate any day now. I doubt he'd care much for your talk of children's books. I told you, ma'am, he's a busy man.' He began to shepherd them back towards the door.

'Oh, please —' Kathryn put a hand to her side. 'If I could just speak to him for a moment. We do so badly need work.'

It was fatal. 'Work is it?' His tone changed from bland to savage in an instant. 'Want my job, do you? Ten pounds a year and sleep under the counter? I can just see you — And your pretty friend, what will she do, dust the books? Now get along with you, the two of you — What is it now?' Sharply, as Kathryn swayed where she stood.

'My friend is not well.' Beth put an arm round her. 'If she could just sit down for a moment. And a glass of water, perhaps?'

'And the two of you off with half the stock while my back is turned? That's your game, is it? I'm not the fool you take me for.' His voice rose angrily. 'I'll call the watch! You had me fooled for the moment; a couple of drabs —'

'Just a minute, Sanders.' Only Beth had seen the glass door at the back of the shop swing open. 'What is all this, pray? Why are you shouting at the young ladies?' The speaker was a handsome country-looking man in a brown suit and a full wig.

'Young ladies, my —' He stopped. 'They come in pretending to be customers, Mr. Francis, then she makes believe to faint — Just a ploy, see, to get me out of the shop. And then where would your stock have been?'

'She doesn't look well to me,' said Francis

361

Newbery. 'That will do, Sanders. Come into my parlour, ma'am, and I'll find you that glass of water.'

'Oh, thank you.' Kathryn was glad to sink into one of the big chairs in the snug little room behind the shop, while its owner shouted for Patty and some water.

Patty had a country look about her too, and tutted around Kathryn, while Beth loosened her bonnet strings and persuaded her to sip a little of the water.

'I am so very sorry; it's been a long day.' Kathryn looked up to meet Newbery's kindly, quizzical glance. 'We'd hoped to get work at one of the theatres, you see, but they are closed, except for the King's — and the door-man there —'

'I can imagine,' said Francis Newbery dryly. 'Let me introduce myself, ma'am. Francis Newbery, at your service. And I must confess vastly curious as to what brings you two damsels erranting to town. I do hope you will let me help you return to your anxious parents as soon as possible.'

'I'm afraid it's not just like that.' Kathryn and Beth had agreed a shortened version of their story, which had done well enough for Silas Reynolds, but Newbery looked thoughtful. He had sent Patty for refreshments while Kathryn was talking and when he saw the way the two girls tucked into them he looked more thoughtful still.

'I am sure Mrs. Siddons and Mrs. Inchbald would do their best for you, if they were here,' he said at last, 'but I wonder if we could not think of some way I could help you. We are always looking for neat-fingered young ladies to parcel up our powders for the market. I am afraid it does not pay very well — And of course it means standing all day.'

'I'd like that,' said Beth at once. 'Miss Kathryn will tell you I am neat-fingered enough. And there would be company, wouldn't there?'

'Oh, yes.' Smiling. 'I'll take you presently to see the loft where they work, but I rather doubt if it would suit you, Mrs. Comyn, just now.'

'No.' She had been afraid that her condition must be beginning to show. 'Mr. Newbery.' She had eaten a great deal of cold chicken and drunk a glass of wine and felt ready to take on the world. 'I was wondering . . . Why I came into your shop was because of the children's books — your uncle's beautiful little books: *Goody Two Shoes* and *Jack the Giant-Killer* and all the others. I loved them when I was a child. Had you thought of publishing another series? There are always children, and with the new Sunday schools more and more of them are learning to read. I am sure you would find that there was a much greater market now than there was when your uncle printed his. People quite in the middle way of life would buy them for their children, I am sure, if they were as charming little books as your uncle's used to be. And then you could print more, which would make it cheaper, would it not?'

'It's an interesting idea.' He was looking at her with respect now. 'But who would I find to write them for me? My uncle had the most expert help with his, you know. Mr. Goldsmith wrote some of them.'

'The author of *The Vicar of Wakefield*?' Surprised. 'Did he really? No wonder they read so well. I am teaching Beth to read out of *Goody Two Shoes* just now,' she explained. 'But, Mr. Newbery, if you would only let me try . . . I had an old nurse used to tell me the most wonderful stories of the north country. Of trolls and vikings and savage sea monsters. I think if I were to write them, quite simply, you know, they might appeal to the modern taste for the gothic. Parents would like them as well as children.'

'And you think you could do it? I would need to see a sample naturally. And some outlines of more stories. I can see you are business woman enough to understand that I could not embark on such a project unless I was sure of enough titles. Nothing more fatal than to give up half way in such a venture.'

'Of course I understand that.' Eagerly. 'Oh, Mr. Newbery, do please let me try. If I were to bring you a story and three or four sketches at the end of the week! It's just what I would like to be doing right now.'

'You think you can produce all that so soon?' Doubtfully.

'I am sure I can. I know the stories, don't you see? It's merely to write them down.'

He laughed. 'You're a brave woman, Mrs. Comyn, but do by all means try. I am afraid I can make no promises until I have seen what you can do.'

'Of course not. A pig in a poke.'

'Just so. I hope you will write as straightforwardly. And now, I suggest you stay here by the fire while I take Miss Prior to see where she will be working. If you would really like to?'

'Oh, yes!' Beth immensely enjoyed being addressed by her surname.

They both started work next day, and Kathryn soon understood what Francis Newbery had meant when he had called her a brave woman. It was one thing to remember the northern stories as her old nurse had told them to her, quite another to write them down in language that was both striking and easy for a child to understand. At the last minute, Mr. Newbery had called them back and handed her a great armful of paper. 'It's proof sheets,' he had explained. 'One always has paper to spare in a printing house, Mrs. Comyn, and it will save you spending your money on it. And that reminds me; would you by any chance be in need of a small loan against Miss Prior's earnings?'

Kathryn had been at once grateful for the thought and glad to be able to refuse. But the paper was a boon. She had had no idea of how many sheets she would have to spoil before she hit on a style that got anywhere near satisfying her. But by Wednesday evening she had a version of *Grendel the Great Monster* which she read aloud to Peggy Reynolds with satisfactory results. 'But it's ever so frightening,' protested Peggy.

'Children like to be frightened.' But she thought a little about it and chose a more cheerful group of stories for her brief sketches. Her main problem was to get the quiet to work in. Beth now went off bright and early every morning with Silas Reynolds and the household missed her horribly. If the baby hiccuped, or Susan did not know how to cook the dinner, she or Peggy Reynolds came hurrying up the attic stairs to ask for advice. And every time they did, Kathryn had to go back to the beginning and start all over again. Useless to try to explain to them that she did not want to be disturbed. 'You're only writing,' said Peggy Reynolds.

Beth took the finished work to Ludgate Hill with her on the Friday morning and Kathryn walked in, all trepidation, towards noon. She wished she had started earlier when she found Francis Newbery obviously dressed and ready to leave for the country. 'My wife expects me betimes on a Friday,' he explained, 'but sit down, Mrs. Comyn, we have to talk, you and I. You found this more difficult than you expected, did you not?'

'It shows?' Ruefully.

'Well — a little. But a promising beginning.' He took her rapidly and ruthlessly through the little story, showing her all the points where she had failed her own intentions; then turned to the pile of sketches. 'You lost courage a bit when it came to these, did you not? I have to tell you that I find them less promising than your monster Grendel. Could you manage more of the horror, do you think? My children always enjoyed a nice bit of blood and bones.'

'Oh, yes,' said Kathryn. 'Easily. You mean you are going to let me try?'

'I shall be delighted to have you do so. I

shall hope for great things when I return to town in the autumn. Then, I hope, you will have enough material for me so that we can discuss terms seriously. In the mean time I shall tell Sanders that you are to have all the paper you need — your friend can bring it home for you. They are delighted with her in the workroom by the way. And I shall look forward very much to seeing how you have got on in September, when I return.' He made to rise and see her out.

She sat where she was, desperate. 'You would not feel that you could make me some kind of advance payment?'

'It's not just my usual way of doing business.'

'You leave the writer to take all the risk?' She pulled on her gloves. 'Well, I am sad about that, Mr. Newbery. But if you are not prepared to risk your money, I think I would be foolish to risk my time. Would you be so good as to direct me to Paternoster Row, where I believe there are other publishing booksellers to be found?'

'Just a moment, Mrs. Comyn, you take a man up so fast. In the unusual circumstances, I believe I could arrange a small payment in advance.'

She thought she had earned his respect, but it still did not net her anything like the sum she had hoped for. It was going to be short commons all summer if she and Beth were to have anything saved against the baby's birth late in September. But this was absolutely not an argument to be used to Mr. Newbery and she bade him a civil farewell and wished him a happy holiday.

'We'll manage,' said Beth, when she heard the bad news that night. 'After all, Miss Kathryn, here we are, two weeks in town and both brought home our first earnings. Only,' conscience-stricken, 'I'm afraid I spent some of mine.'

'I can see you did. It's a very becoming bonnet, Beth.'

'The other girls is so smart, you see. They called me Country Miss and laughed at me for talking funny.'

'Funny? But you talk beautifully, Beth.'

'I've always tried to do everything the way you do, miss.'

23

July came in with a heatwave. The hay was in from the fields beyond the square, the fruit was withering on the trees, and the attic was stifling. Kathryn could not help envying Beth and Silas Reynolds who left the house in the cool of the morning to walk to Ludgate Hill and Lombard Street respectively. Inevitably they started out together, and Peggy Reynolds was soon showing signs of jealousy. She made constant pretexts to come up to the attic, sit on one of the cot beds, and grumble about Beth. The hot weather had upset Baby Liz and her mother was convinced that Beth ought to stay at home and help look after her.

'Jaunting off to London, hand in glove with my husband, while I have to stay home with a screaming child. And as for that gaudy new bonnet! I never saw such airs!'

'But we have to work, Beth and I,' said Kathryn mildly. 'I should be writing now, or we will not be able to pay our rent on Saturday.'

'That pittance! I told Reynolds he didn't know what he was doing.'

'He is allowing for what I was able to lend him the day you moved in.' Kathryn would not let this pass. 'We will pay more when that has been covered. If we decide to stay.'

'Stay? Of course you will stay. Have you any idea how lucky you were to find this snug attic and all the comfort and service we give you? You two girls might be on the streets by now if we had not taken you in. I never heard such nonsense. Naturally you will stay.'

'We won't be able to afford it, if you do not leave me to get on with my work,' said Kathryn.

'Work! Writing!' She flounced out of the room, leaving Kathryn to wonder more than ever whether they should not consider moving. But where to? There was truth in what Peggy Reynolds had said. More and more, as she lived there, was she aware of London as a dangerous place, a place where anything could happen.

But Beth loved it. She no longer came home with tales of being teased at work. On the contrary, she often did not come back until long after they had had their tea, when she would arrive flushed and cheerful from an outing with the other girls. She even went to the theatre a couple of times, spending the night with a friend. Kathryn worried about her a little and wished she felt well enough to go too, when Beth went to see Kemble act Richard III for his wife's benefit. But she was very large now and it was all she could do to make herself take the daily walk in the fields to the north of the square that Beth urged.

'Don't you fret about me.' Beth was tying the strings of another fetching new bonnet ready for church. 'I can take care of myself. We know what we are doing, the girls and I.'

'But how do you manage?' Kathryn worried that Beth seemed able to go on these outings to the Spring Gardens across the river at Vauxhall, or the play, and still contribute her regular share to their savings.

'We let the fellows pay, of course.' Laughing. 'Oh, don't look so shocked, Miss Kathryn. There's no harm in it; not in a gang of us like we are. We see they toe the line; anything over and it's a forfeit. How do you think I got this bonnet?' Giggling.

'I was wondering,' Kathryn admitted, more anxious than ever.

'It was that Sanders! He pinched me — well I won't tell you just where he pinched me, but they all saw, and that was a forfeit all right! Oh, he can afford it, can Jim Sanders. Saving to start his own printing house he is and always on the scrape this way and that for money. If I was Mr. Newbery I'd have a closer eye to him, I reckon, but mind you don't say I said so, Miss Kathryn. And you have to admit it's a becoming bonnet.' She stood on tiptoe to admire her reflection in the tiny sliver of a looking glass she had brought home the week before.

'It certainly is. You look different somehow, Beth.'

'It's town bronze.' She adjusted her neckerchief lovingly and Kathryn saw that it was new too. 'It's easy when you get the knack of it, but the others do say I've got it more than most. It's a way of thinking of yourself, see, that makes them mind you.'

'Them?'

'The fellows. Time for church if we're not to hurry.' She blew herself a kiss in the glass and turned to give a loving tweak to Kathryn's black ribbons. 'I'll show you how when young master's born and you come out of this everlasting mourning. Is he kicking again?' With a quick look of sympathy.

'Like anything. I don't mind it so much in the daytime; it seems friendly, but I do wish he would sleep at night.' Tired all the time, and hungry on their frugal diet, she was finding it more and more difficult to concentrate on her writing in the stuffy little attic.

'They are quarrelling again,' said Beth as they crossed the square towards the church. 'Did you hear?'

'Yes. I do wish they wouldn't. I'm sure it is bad for Baby Liz.'

'Bad for all of us. I know how much of your time she wastes coming up to grumble at you, and he's not much better. Gripe, gripe, gripe all the way to town. I'm glad to see the last of him when we get to the shop. I'll tell you one thing, Miss Kathryn, you don't see me marrying if I can think of a better way of earning my living. It's grief every inch of the way for us women, ask me. Well, look at you and Mr. Comyn, if you don't mind me saying so. And now these two! It'll have to be the Archangel Michael before I marry.'

'But you can't want to go on wrapping up Dr. James's powders for ever?'

'Lord, no. That's hardly a livelihood. I tell you, Miss Kathryn, when once the baby is born, we are going to think again. Unless we do contrive to find something in the theatre, of course. I'd still like that best of all. Just you wait till the new season opens, and then we will see.'

'Yes.' Doubtfully. 'But in the mean time, do be careful, Beth.'

'No need to talk to me like a mother.' Beth took her arm, and the words out of her mouth.

'My mother did that when I first came to service. Don't forget, I did jump out of the window that time Mr. Morewood came after me.'

'So you did. What a long time ago! Oh, Beth, do you think the boys are all right?'

'As all right as they ever will be, with Morewood for a father. You know as well as I do, miss, that the Comyns are bound to have got in touch with him. You'd be crazy to write him.' They had talked of this before.

'I know, but I do worry about Roderick and Jeremy.'

'I promise I'll write for you, to him and Mrs. Goldfern, just as soon as the baby is born.' Beth was proud of her handwriting these days. 'It will be quite a different story when young master's born.'

'Will it? I have the horridest feeling, Beth, that they will still contrive not to pay me the income they should.'

'Oh, so have I,' said Beth cheerfully, then sobered as they entered the church door.

Kathryn had a loving letter from the ladies at Ross that week. The fine weather had done Janet good, Lavinia wrote, sounding much more cheerful than in her last letter. They had done some more work on *The Gest of Sir Cradock* and were thinking of venturing it again to some more sympathetic publisher. Perhaps dear Kathryn could advise them, now she was

375

moving in the publishing world herself. And she enclosed a draft for ten pounds on Mr. Coutts' bank: 'For baby clothes; how we wish it could be more.'

Kathryn sat down that afternoon to thank them for the letter and the money which was indeed a godsend, though she was sad to think of the many small economies it must entail in the little household at Ross. As to Sir Cradock, she suggested that they send it to her. 'I could show it to Mr. Newbery when he comes back from his summer holiday and get his advice. I am sure he would be helpful.' She wished she was sure he was going to like her own little stories, with which she grew increasingly dissatisfied as the hot days and hotter nights dragged on. Baby Liz still cried a lot in the night, and tempers in the household grew more and more frayed.

'We must get out of here,' said Beth as they dressed one September morning after a night when Silas Reynolds had walked the screaming baby to and fro in the hall, presumably after being ejected from the bedroom with her by his wife. 'You need your sleep. And so,' with a glance in the glass, 'do I.'

'I'll ask around the square.' But Kathryn did not say it hopefully.

'And I'll ask the girls. I wouldn't mind being nearer in, if it was all the same to you.'

'Of course.' Kathryn did think she would miss the fields, specially after the baby was born, but felt increasingly guilty because Beth was contributing steadily to their expenses while she had merely had Newbery's one payment and the ladies' blessed ten pounds.

She had no luck in the square and returned, downhearted, in the early afternoon to find with surprise that Silas Reynolds was at home.

His wife was screaming at him. 'Quit your job? You can't have; you're not that much of a fool.'

Kathryn heard the furious voice from the front parlour as she quietly closed the front door and moved to climb the stairs.

But Peggy Reynolds had heard her come in. 'Do you know what he has done?' She appeared in the doorway, red with rage. 'This fine husband of mine! He's quit his job, just like that, because they thought fit to sack his uncle. Fool of a man! Who does he think he is to decide who should get a frank and who not?'

'But it's a matter of principle, don't you see?' Silas Reynolds looked hagridden. 'Uncle knew the system was being abused. I'm sorry to say it, but Members of Parliament were actually selling franks for free letters, to strangers. How is the Post Office to run if people cheat it so?'

'I don't know,' said his wife. 'And I don't care. Where are you going to get another job? Tell me that, pray, Silas Reynolds.'

'Uncle thought —'

'I don't care what uncle thought! Have you thought at all where our next meal is coming from?'

'They gave me two weeks' pay . . .'

'Two weeks!' Furiously. 'You think you'll find another position in two weeks! With times so bad, and you with no influence! Oh, why didn't I listen to father? He said you'd make a mull of things, and he was right. I must have been out of my mind when I agreed to run away with you. Now I'll tell you something, Mr. Conscientious Reynolds. I had a letter from father last week. He misses me, he says. I can go back any time I want. And I'm going; now, this minute. Your lady friends will look after you, no doubt.' With a sneering glance for Kathryn. 'And that precious Baby Liz you dote on so . . .'

This brought Kathryn into the conversation. 'You can't do that,' she said quietly. 'You haven't thought about how it would look, Mrs. Reynolds.' She knew it was useless to appeal to finer feelings the woman did not have. 'If you go, Beth and I will have to move out; the baby will starve. I don't think your father would like that to happen to his grandchild.'

'Oh.' She thought for a minute. 'It's true; he did say something. Very well, I'll take Liz, but you'll have to give me the money for the coach, Silas Reynolds.'

She had gone by the time Beth got home. 'I couldn't stop her.' Kathryn was close to tears. 'What in the world are we going to do, Beth?' She had never felt so helpless.

'It's all right, Miss Kathryn.' Beth put a loving arm round her. 'Don't you fret about a thing. It's my turn to look out for us now, and I shall. I know just what we are going to do; I'd been thinking about it anyway; now my mind's made up. I'll go right down and give in our notice to Silas. We have to stay tonight, but we shouldn't any longer, nohow. It would be as much as our reputations were worth.' Laughing. 'Funny really. All this fine talk about reputation: and just look at the way the fellows go on! Now you get into bed, Miss Kathryn. We don't want all this ruckus bringing on young master early; that would dump the fat in the fire. I want you safe out of here before he's born.'

Kathryn was glad to obey. The day had indeed been exhausting. But she must stay awake to find out what Beth was planning.

She could not do it, and woke at last, late, to find Beth already gone.

'She's out, mum,' Susan told her. 'She said to let you sleep and she'd be back about noon.'

'She's not gone to work?'

'I don't reckon so. She had her best bonnet on. Mr. Reynolds is out too and I'm to make you some milk porridge.'

'Just the thing.' The cooler night and long sleep had done her good and she ate the porridge with relish, wondering all the time what in the world Beth could be doing.

But Mr. Newbery would be back soon. She went heavily back to the attic, sat down to revise her story of *The Hopeful Troll,* and found it almost impossible to concentrate on her work. Over and over her mind wandered away to the question of what Beth was arranging in town. For the first time in her life, she felt herself adrift, helpless, out of control, and it frightened her. The baby was kicking again, which was a relief, because he had turned quiet in the course of that scene with Peggy Reynolds and she had been getting anxious. She got up to stretch herself and breathe cool September air at the front window and saw Beth hurrying home across the square.

'It's all fixed.' Beth entered the front door as Kathryn reached the bottom of the stairs. 'The carriage is coming for us later this afternoon. You're looking better, thank goodness. Had a good sleep? Did Susan look after you?'

'Yes to it all. But, Beth, the carriage?'

'We are entering a new walk of life,' said Beth. 'No more milk porridge and water gruel. And no attic either. But there's one for you, Susan.' She turned to the girl who was standing in the kitchen doorway, eagerly listening. 'If you want to come.'

'Want to, miss? Course I want to.'

'Then that's settled. You pack up your things while we pack ours.'

'But where are we going, Beth?' Kathryn turned to face her when they reached the attic. 'You must tell me now.'

'We're going where we will be looked after, and about time too. You can't have the heir to Comyn's in the street, nor yet in the Bridewell, which was the way it was beginning to look. Just for once, Miss Kathryn, you must be ruled by me. It's not what either of us planned, but one has to make the best one can with what offers. You taught me that, miss, bearing with Mr. Comyn the way you did, and you taught me a lot else too, without knowing you were doing it. Now, it's my turn to think for us both and I don't reckon we'll either of us be sorry for what I've done. Nor yet young master, when he comes along. Not long now if you ask me. I remember a look my mother used to get. So come along, Miss Kathryn dear, get packing, do.'

'But, Beth, where are we going?'

'To a little house, with a little garden, in a little court, west of the Haymarket. You'll like it, miss, I promise you will.'

'But the rent, Beth? Food? Have you gone quite mad?'

'No, I reckon maybe I've come to my senses. It's no use sitting around waiting for the world to do you favours; that way you get nowhere. Leastways, when it offers you something, you'd better take it. I nearly missed this on account of a lot of starched notions. Some ways I'm grateful to Peggy Reynolds for making me jump in. We're going to run a salon, you and I, if that's the way you say it.'

'A salon? Beth, you're joking.'

'Not a bit of it.' Beth had pulled her shabby portmanteau out from under her cot and was folding shifts into it. 'I went along to the Theatre Royal at Covent Garden last week, that night I came home late. They're getting ready for the season there, see, they open end of the month. My goodness but it was all go. I'd dearly like to have worked in the theatre.' Wistfully. Then, brightening: 'But I believe he was right; it wouldn't do for you and me and the baby.'

'Who was right, Beth? What are you talking about?'

'The gentleman. Mr. Scarborough. I was talking to the man at the box office, see, asking if he knew if Mrs. Inchbald or Mrs. Siddons was back. Mrs. Siddons has gone to Ireland, he told me. He didn't know about Mrs. Inchbald, asked this gentleman who was buying a box for the season. Lots of gents there were, ever so elegant. They made the fellows I've been going with seem like a lot of nothings. So this one asked me why I wanted Mrs. Inchbald, and I told him, and he said right away he might have a better idea for us. And he took me to the Bedford Arms in the piazza and bought me a cup of the best coffee I ever drank and told me about it. And I told him about us. And it is a good idea, Miss Kathryn, and no need to look so shocked either; it's not what you are thinking. Not at all.'

'It had better not be. Beth, a total stranger — How could you?'

'I liked him, miss. He's out of the way somehow. You will too, I am sure of it. The case is, he's a nabob, rich as you please. The box keeper whispered me about him when we were going off together. He's just back from India, see, and I reckon he's lonely, poor fellow, and not the kind goes to houses of accommodation. No family, seems like. And what he said was, he felt right guilty about the way he'd made his money in India. Grinding the faces of the

383

natives, he said it had been, and he came to himself one day and wanted no more of it. Lucky thing he'd made his money by then,' said practical Beth. 'He's ever so well dressed, miss, nothing but the best, and a way with him like someone who knows where he stands. You know?'

'Indeed I do. But none of this explains why he wants to open a salon.'

'Nor why he picked on me,' said Beth. 'That puzzled me, tell you the truth, but never mind, he did. The thing is — I never was much of a hand at telling a story — the thing is, he wants to make up for all his goings on in India, so he's thrown in his lot with Mr. Wilberforce and that campaign of his for freeing the slaves you used to talk about. And what he says is, they need somewhere to meet, informal like, that's quiet. You know what the taverns are like; they're all the same; violence and women and pickpockets. He wants something more like a private house. He spoke of someone called Mrs. Montague, seemed to think I ought to know who she was.'

'I see. She's one of the bluestocking ladies; runs a salon in the West End. But why the Haymarket? Everyone knows what sort of people live there.'

'He says he wants to draw his group from every walk in life — Mr. Wilberforce and his friends live across the river at Clapham; the new bridge will be handy for them, and then it's kind of midway between Parliament and the City. And I'm not sure that being handy for the theatres doesn't have something to do with it too. He was ever so interested when I told him I had seen Kemble as Richard III. You'll like him, Miss Kathryn, I promise you will.'

'And we are to run his salon for him?' Kathryn could not help liking the idea.

'Yes, a free hand, he said. He won't live there himself, nohow. He told me that first off; to get things straight like. Our house; our salon. Well, Miss Kathryn, who could say no to that?'

'You really believed him? It could so easily be just the kind of thing everyone warns of. We go there, and the next thing we know, we're in the stews.'

'You won't think that when you've met him. Anyway, what do we have to lose? We can't stay here; not on our own with Silas Reynolds, even if we wanted to, which we don't. Come on, Miss Kathryn. Finish your packing. It's not the end of the world, remember, if you don't find you can trust him. We're safe in town by then; you're so near your time, you could go to the Goldferns for help. We'll be much nearer them, see?'

'That's perfectly true.' This had struck Kathryn too. And besides, once the baby was born, she meant to get in touch with Mrs. Comyn. No more need to hide. And Thomas's mother had a right to know about her grandson.

'This is a chance in a million, Miss Kathryn! You know you've always wanted to work with Mr. Wilberforce. Fancy us running a salon! And snapping our fingers at the Comyns.'

This brought Kathryn to another objection. 'But, Beth, did you tell him about the baby? I won't be much use for a while.'

'Course I did! He's easy to talk to. And it's me he's hiring, remember.' Beth's colour was high, her eyes shining. 'Just think of him picking me out like that.'

'Oh, Beth —' Now Kathryn was worried on another count. Was Beth building too high hopes on this chance encounter? Might she really be thinking of marriage with this philanthropic nabob? Well, she told herself, more surprising things had happened. Men did make amazing marriages. If the Duke of Clarence could set up house with an actress, surely Beth could marry a nabob? Anyway, she must obviously meet this romantic stranger, sum him up for herself. And, as Beth said, there really was no reason now why they should not go to the Goldferns for help if things went wrong. She turned to her packing with a will.

The carriage, arriving prompt at its hour, proved to be not the hired hackney Kathryn had expected but a brand-new private coach. All the neighbours came out to watch as the civil footman loaded their baggage for them. Kathryn had not been into town since July and she enjoyed the drive through the bustle of Long Acre and across Leicester Fields to the top of the Haymarket, where the market was over for the day and the evening crowds of strollers out already. She had forgotten how noisy London was, out in the comparative seclusion of Red Lion Square. Street cries, the creak and groan of carriage wheels, the furious shouts of coachmen at anyone who blocked their way, it all blended into a cacophony that made her shrink into herself.

'Nearly there.' Beth had noticed, and spoke cheeringly as the carriage swung across the broad market place where the strong sweet smell of hay testified to its morning business. 'It's quiet where we are going. You'll see.'

It was hard to believe, but she found it true. As the carriage made its slower way down a narrow side street the noise died away behind them. 'Here we are,' said Beth, and they turned into a cul-de-sac and stopped outside a low, old-fashioned, timbered house. 'I told you you'd like it,-Miss Kathryn.'

The footman came round to open the door and let down the steps. Kathryn was glad of his friendly arm to help her alight. All her attention was for the house, which looked, she thought, as if it had strayed from a country village, from Windover perhaps. 'Oh, I do!' She turned to agree with Beth, turned back as the front door opened.

'He said he'd be here to welcome us.' Beth sounded immensely pleased with herself.

But Kathryn was not listening. She was watching with growing amazement as the familiar figure came down the shining white steps. It could not be; it was entirely impossible; it was Mark Weatherby just the same. And he was looking at her without a trace of recognition.

'How do you do, Mrs. Comyn.' He held out his hand, civilly as to a stranger. 'I am so glad you decided to come.'

His voice. Mark's voice, after all these years. And he did not know her.

Kathryn fainted.

24

Kathryn came to herself in a strong crescendo of pain.

'That's better.' Beth's voice, encouraging, strengthening. Beth's hand holding hers. 'Now, push when you want to, Kathryn. Push!'

It seemed to go on for ever, the pain and the struggle, the fight and the pain, but Beth was always there, sharing the battle with her. 'Shout if you want to; scream; mother says it helps.'

'Ma —' She remembered, suddenly, what had happened. Mark was here, in this house, he was Mr. Scarborough and he did not know her. But he was here. Thinking this, she forgot everything else, forgot to fight the pain, rose on a wave of it.

'There we are,' Beth's voice triumphant. And then, 'Oh, my goodness!'

'What is it? Beth, is he all right?'

'She's fine,' said Beth. 'But she's a girl.'

'Oh, I am so glad.' Kathryn fell into sleep.

She woke to evening light. Which evening? She was propped up on down pillows in an immensely comfortable bed. A bunch of country-looking roses on a polished chest near the casement window caught late sunlight. Everything in the room looked good, looked cared for. After that bleak attic it felt like coming home.

Home? Mark Weatherby. But he was Mr. Scarborough now. Beth was probably in love with him. And he with her? In a minute she would be crying. And she must not. Why?

'Beth?' Her voice came out faint as a kitten's mew.

Beth was with her on the instant. 'Here she is.' She had a bundle in her arms. 'I was going to wake you soon. She's getting hungry, our young mistress.'

'Charlotte,' said Kathryn. And knew this was why she must not indulge in tears.

Charlotte knew just what she wanted, and Kathryn felt the world change around her as the hungry mouth began to suck. 'She's mine,' she told Beth. 'Charlotte Pennam Comyn. No one will even want to take her away.'

'It's a mercy really,' agreed Beth. 'He said to give you his best congratulations, miss — Mr. Scarborough.'

'You called me Kathryn before. I liked it. But, Beth, what a mull I've made of things.

Is he angry?' What in the world was she going to do? But with Charlotte Pennam Comyn nuzzling away at her breast, she knew she would manage.

'Angry? Of course not. I told you he was someone special. Just says he's glad I got you here in time. We had his own doctor to you when I thought things was going on a bit long, but he said you were doing nicely. No, he's not angry, only a bit surprised.' Laughing. 'He had thought from what I said that you were a proper matronly kind of person, a respectable widow, do you see? A chaperone for me! And now he says it won't do at all, we have to find someone else. But he will, no need to fret, he gets what he wants, that one.'

Does he? Kathryn bent once more over her miraculous daughter.

Beth said she must stay in bed, and she was glad to. It gave her time to think before she faced Mark under this amazing new guise of Mr. Scarborough, Indian nabob. That he was Mark Weatherby, she had not the slightest doubt. He had looked older, in that brief glimpse, brown from the Indian sun, with an air of command her Mark had lacked, but he was her Mark for all that. Her heart had told her so even before he spoke, and her brain confirmed that all his behaviour was characteristic of the Mark she knew and loved.

Except that he had taken a fancy for Beth. Even talking to herself, as Charlotte peacefully sucked, she would not put it more strongly than that. He was hers. When he got his memory back, he would know it as absolutely as she did.

But what would she do in the mean time? And would he get his memory back? What had happened to him all those years ago, after she left him with her step-father on the cliff? Something terrible, she was sure, there and then. And all those stories Oliver Morewood had told her about seeing him in London in bad company had been lies. She knew it now; should always have known it. Morewood had done something frightful to Mark and had lied to protect himself. What a fool she had been to believe him.

But that was the past. What was she going to do now? She knew already that she was not going to tell Beth. How could she? And yet it made her feel horribly guilty even to decide this. Beth, who was such a true friend. Beth, who was maybe a little in love with Mark herself. And he with her? She would not think it.

Her thoughts went round and round like this as her body grew stronger, and Charlotte ate and throve and kept her calm. She soon discovered that if she let herself get anxious, Charlotte cried, or was sick, or both. So she lay in the comfortable bed in the room she enjoyed having to herself and let herself drift. Time, she thought. Time must settle this.

She longed to question Beth about Mark, but found she could not. How could she call him Mr. Scarborough when she knew he was Mark Weatherby? Just to do so, to Beth, would make the concealment worse, somehow. Luckily, Beth talked a great deal about him. He had not expected them so soon, she explained, having made his proposal in the most general terms. The house was not fully furnished yet; he did not think of beginning to invite people in until the season began and the world came back to town. 'But he's finding me a sad disappointment, I am afraid,' confessed Beth. 'He thought I would take over directing the upholsterers about the furnishings, all that, and, Kathryn, I don't know the first thing about it. How should I? Oh, I know chintz from calico, but as to what will make a room into a salon, I've no more idea than the man in the moon. I told him so, said he'd better send the men away until you are well enough to come down and see to it. I said you would know just how to go on. So, the thing is, do you feel you might come down tomorrow?'

'Of course I could. Not too early; I must feed the baby first, but I am longing to see the rest of the house.' She had enjoyed exploring the rambling passages and odd rooms of the first floor with its tantalising views of a tiny garden plot, lawn and dusty rose bushes lying between two arms of the house. It must have been a small inn once, she thought, with its own yard. Only the blank end wall belonged to someone else. 'It was clever of Mr. Scarborough to find this house,' she went on now, using the name for the first time.

'Lucky, he says.' Beth loved to talk about him. 'But then, he thinks he's a lucky man. I wouldn't just call it that myself. Do you know, he has not the least idea in the world who he is?'

'What?' Easy to sound amazed.

'He said he thought he ought to tell me; asked me to tell you. He might be anything, he says, gaol bird, highwayman, runaway apprentice. The thing is, he was picked up for dead by a boat crew come ashore for water. Up our way somewhere; that's why they called him Scarborough when he came to himself and didn't know who he was. Isn't it the most romantic thing? He might be a duke or a prince. Anybody!'

'Except that then he would have been missed,' said Kathryn. This was when she ought to tell Beth she knew who he was. How could she? It would involve them in a conspiracy of silence against him — well, not against, but around. It would not do. She was not sure why, but she was sure that it would not do. Mark must remember by himself, without interference. And she knew capable Beth well enough to know she would be bound to interfere, to try and remind Mark of himself. 'But what happened to him, Beth? What did they do with him?'

'Pressed him, of course,' said Beth. 'You know how mad the navy is for men. He made light of it, but you could see he must have knocked them endways with what he could do. Started as able seaman, then they found he could write and reckon. He was promoted midshipman on the Indian station just before he got the wound that ended his service.'

'Wounded? Badly?'

'They left him for dead. But his luck held, he says. A Bombay merchant found him, saw there was life in him, took him in and had his own doctor to him. When he got better, he gave him work, put him in the way of making a fortune. Sounds like a fairy story, don't it, miss? But he says there was nothing to it. Bombay is full of younger sons who can't even count up to ten, poor things. Anyone with some education and some guts can make his way there. He's ashamed of it now, but the money's still there. Lucky for us!'

Kathryn woke early next morning after a restless night during which she had come to no decision whatever about how she was going to behave to Mark when she met him. She must make herself think of him as Mr. Scarborough, that was one thing certain. Charlotte was safely fed and down for her morning sleep well before the time named for him to meet the upholsterers with her. She very much hoped they would all arrive at the same time; it would make the first meeting much easier.

The ground floor of the house was in the same rambling, delightful style as the first floor, but here almost everything was still to be done. The series of rooms, opening into each other, would lend themselves admirably to the running of a political salon. There were inglenooks and window embrasures and small, odd closets for private conferences, and one handsome large room where she and Beth could hold sway over the tea and coffee urns. When Mark appeared, before his time, she was able to take a deep breath and plunge straight into a speech of thanks that led on to a practical discussion of colours and furnishings and, most important, lighting.

If she had allowed herself a deep, secret hope

that today Mark would recognise her, she was disappointed. He was charming, solicitous, civil as to a complete stranger. It was entirely horrible and she surprised both him and Beth a little by her almost desperate concentration on the furnishing problems before them. By the time the men arrived to take their orders, she knew exactly what she wanted and they received their instructions with respect.

'That's everything, I think,' she said at last. 'The next question is when you can have it ready.'

'Depends a bit,' said the foreman, scratching his head. 'Speed costs.' Turning to Mark. 'Times is hard, sir, as you well know. There's good hands a-plenty I could take on and get it done quick, if so be that's your wish, but it will cost you, sir, over and above what we have agreed already.'

'Then take them on, and do it. I shall be glad to be giving employment. And,' turning to Kathryn with a smile, 'I am sure you will want to have the work done as soon as possible. I can only apologise for the state of confusion to which you arrived.' He thanked and lavishly tipped the men, returned to Kathryn. 'And now, am I to be allowed to meet this good baby of whom Miss Prior speaks so warmly? I am sure a turn in the garden would do you both good, and I am sure too, judging by what I have just heard, that your advice there would also be worth its weight in gold.'

'Oh, I would like that!' She turned, as if to go up and fetch Charlotte, but Beth was ahead of her.

'No, you are not to carry her on the stairs yet. I'll fetch her from Susan.'

Extraordinary to find herself being ushered out through the garden door by Mark, to be suddenly alone with him. It was the last thing she had wanted, and yet it seemed perfectly easy; they were talking already like the old friends they really were. The neglected and mossy lawn must go, they agreed, it would never stand up to the use it would get when they opened the house.

'When do you hope to do so?' she asked.

'I thought by the end of the month, if you are strong enough. That will give time to get things going before Parliament reconvenes, to get people into the way of dropping in. It will all take a good deal of time, I imagine, even with two such charming ladies as yourself and Miss Prior in charge. Mr. Wilberforce was enthusiastic about the project when I put it to him in the summer, but I do not quite know how far he has got in canvassing for support among his friends.'

'I used to know him a little,' said Kathryn diffidently. 'And I confess I had been wondering just how you had presented the idea to him. I have not met him for some years, but I believe he has become quite fiercely evangelical in his views. And I have the greatest respect for that,' she hurried on. 'But if we are hoping for a broad consensus of opinion — to make the place pleasant enough to attract middle-of-the-road people — well, it can't be just coffee and tea, can it? And I rather think you should consider allowing some of the more innocent forms of play. It's the young, surely, who are most likely to be influenceable. And who need to be influenced for good, and they just won't go where there is no entertainment.'

'You are entirely right, Mrs. Comyn. Wine and a card room, you think? I know I can count on you and Miss Prior not to let things get out of hand. That is a most remarkable young woman, by the way. I think she is going to be quite as much of a draw as our card room. I have been looking all over town for an older lady to give gravitas to our venture, but I confess that so far I have failed to find anyone who would not be just a confounded wet blanket — Forgive me!'

She laughed. 'No need to apologise. But surely my widowed status, and little Charlotte . . . There is something very respectable about a widow and an orphan.'

'That's what I thought until I met you, Mrs.

Comyn. And I do hope you will not take that as anything but a compliment. But as it is, you do not chance to have an aunt very much like yourself only older, tucked away in the country somewhere?'

'Goodness,' said Kathryn. 'I wonder if they would.' Smiling at the thought. 'I know two remarkable elderly ladies who have lived at Ross — down on the Welsh border — all their lives. Something like the ladies of Llangothlen but on a slightly less aristocratic level. Darlings they are, and one of them is my aunt. They have translated a Welsh romance, *The Gest of Sir Cradock,* and want a publisher for it. We could invite them to town and get a few publishing booksellers here to meet them; maybe persuade them to stay. I am sure you mean to add a leaven of literary and maybe stage figures to your politicians? And ladies? I have a letter somewhere that I have never delivered, to Mrs. Inchbald, and another to Mrs. Siddons; might they not add a certain tone to your evenings?'

'I should just about think they would.' He sounded suddenly his old self, young and enthusiastic. 'What a lucky day it was for me when Miss Prior caught my eye at Covent Garden. And here she is, with Miss Charlotte.'

Miss Charlotte distinguished herself by

smiling at Mark, and though Beth pointed out afterwards that it was only wind, it made him her slave on the spot. But he was Beth's slave too. Once the strain of the first meeting was passed, Kathryn saw this all too clearly. He consulted her, but looked at Beth. And no wonder. More and more, seeing Beth in company, she was aware of the strange magnetism she had for men. No wonder she had never needed to pay her way when she was working for Mr. Newbery. For a man, to see her was to wish to serve her.

Busy with Charlotte and the whole new life, she had forgotten about Mr. Newbery, now realised he must be back in town, and sent him the little batch of stories that she had finished before Charlotte was born. In a civil note of apology for her dilatoriness and Beth's sudden leaving, she also mentioned *The Gest of Sir Cradock* and her new circumstances, inviting him to call.

He came one bright October morning and she was able to entertain him in the first of the downstairs rooms to be finished. But he brought back her stories.

'You do not think they will do?' Her heart had sunk at sight of the familiar, beloved little bundle as he took it out of the deep pocket of his greatcoat.

'I am delighted to find you so comfortably

settled.' He did not answer her directly, but it was an answer just the same. 'And Miss Prior is well? And the baby? No need to ask if you are. I have never seen you in such looks.'

'Thank you.' Mechanically. He was holding the pitiful little bundle out to her. 'You think they won't do at all?'

'Mrs. Comyn, I am truly sorry to have to say it, but I think it the act of a friend to tell you that this may not be the direction in which your talent lies. The trouble is, you have so much to say, Mrs. Comyn; you have tried to put too much into these little tales. And children don't like to be preached at.'

'Oh!' It hit her hard. 'Do I really preach?'

'I'm afraid so. Just look at this one about the faithful nymph. You have been reading Miss Wollstonecraft, I believe, and perhaps share her views about the position of women in our society. Very well; I have some sympathy with them, but a children's book is not the place where they should be aired. Ah —' taking her hand, 'don't, pray, look so down, Mrs. Comyn. I have another suggestion which I truly hope may prove to be something very much more in your line. And as to the small advance I made you against the children's project, you are not to be fretting yourself about that. I have the greatest admiration for your clear mind and mean to ask you to help me in various editing jobs in the course of the winter, if that will be agreeable to you.'

The disappointment was so great that she could only nod wordlessly. What a fool, what an over-confident idiot she had been.

'May I bring a friend of mine to call on you?' He had taken assent for granted. 'I think that you and he will deal admirably together, and be of use to each other. You may have heard of him; Mr. Clement?'

'The man who is editing the new Sunday paper? *The Observer*?'

'That's the one. He's having a hard enough time of it, I think. Money's tight, the Sabbath day observers are dead set against him; he's still trying to find just the note he needs. He was saying to me, just the other day, at the Shakespeare Head, that he was seriously thinking of looking for a woman contributor. Someone in the Wollstonecraft line, he said, only, she is in Paris, so that cock won't fight. Well, Mrs. Comyn, rubbing his white hands, 'when I got your note it seemed like a miracle. This salon Mr. Scarborough proposes — and what a romantic tale that is! But it will place you right in the heart of things. You will hear everything, see everyone of importance on the progressive side. I don't rightly know how Clement stands on the question of the slave trade, but you could ask him. Anyway I know he means to leave a great deal of latitude to individual contributors, within the general outlines of policy. Now, might not that really suit you a great deal better than writing little fables for children, Mrs. Comyn?'

'Oh, yes.' She clasped her hands to hide the fact that they were shaking. 'But, Mr. Newbery, you cannot be serious?'

'Never more so. When I told Clement about you, he could hardly believe his ears. May I bring him to see you? Oh, and by the way, I would very much like to see this *Gest of Sir Cradock* your friends have translated from the Welsh.'

'So long as I have not had a chance to put my preaching into it?' But she could say it cheerfully now. 'Do, please, bring Mr. Clement to call. I cannot begin to tell you how much I like the idea of writing for his paper.'

'I thought you would. It won't pay well, mind you; he's having a hard enough time of it, but —' his eye travelled thoughtfully around the luxurious furnishings of the room, 'I imagine that will be no great hardship to you.' He rose. 'Do give my kindest respects to your delightful friend Miss Prior. They miss her sadly in the warehouse, they tell me, but of course you are infinitely better placed here.'

Was he hoping for an explanation of the change in their circumstances? The hinted query made her a little anxious, but his call had reminded her of other commitments. When Beth joined her a little later she looked up over Charlotte's head to say, 'You did write to Mrs. Goldfern and Mr. Morewood, didn't you? To tell them about Charlotte?'

'Yes. The very next day. I told you I would.'

'That's all right then. I don't suppose we'll hear a word from Morewood, but I'll call on Mrs. Goldfern presently.'

'Not until you are stronger,' said Beth.

'No, there's so much to do. But I must write to Mr. Transome, tell him where to send my allowance. We'll be rich women, Beth, all of a sudden, able to pay our way.'

'As if Mr. Scarborough would care,' said Beth.

25

That autumn was one long Indian summer, and work in both house and garden went on even faster than had been promised. But word of the new venture got out faster still. Kathryn was not at all surprised to find how many friends Mark had made in the short time he had been in London, and they all of them called, on one pretext or another, so that she and Beth found themselves hard at work entertaining the great world before they had even started inviting it.

Mrs. Inchbald was back in town now, and she called and brought her friend, Mr. Godwin. Since Kathryn had read and enjoyed both Mrs. Inchbald's novel, *A Simple Story,* and Mr. Godwin's *Enquiry Concerning Political Justice,* the visit was a highly successful one, and both authors promised to come again soon, and bring their friends.

'But when is Mr. Wilberforce coming?' Kathryn asked Mark one afternoon of St. Martin's sunshine when she had taken Charlotte into the garden for her daily airing.

'I wish I knew.' Mark had been admiring the newly completed paving. 'He seems to be totally absorbed into the Thornton group out at Clapham. They have a new minister there, a Mr. Venn, and I believe are still hoping to get permission to send missionaries to India, despite the rebuff they received in Parliament this spring. For myself, I wish Wilberforce would concentrate on his campaign for the abolition of the slave trade. It is always a mistake to fight on two fronts at once, as I am afraid the allies are finding in France.'

'I suppose it was a terrible blow to him when his bill for abolition lost its way in the House this spring,' said Kathryn. And then, 'Is there bad news from France?'

'The worst. The Queen is on trial for her life, and there are gloomy tales abroad about the plight of the counter-revolutionaries both in Lyons and in Toulon. Sometimes I wonder if I ought to be doing something more positive about the state of the world, Mrs. Comyn.'

Her heart sank, and yet it was just like Mark. 'What exactly had you in mind?' she asked. 'Not, surely, to fight?'

'That's just it.' He needed to talk about it. 'I don't rightly know. It's odd to come home to one's own country a stranger. And with all this money. It's a great responsibility. I feel I have a duty — don't laugh at me, Mrs. Comyn — a duty to society.'

'I wouldn't dream of laughing,' she said. 'I respect you for it. But there is so much that needs reforming. It seems to me,' diffidently, 'that in some ways it might be worth thinking of things nearer home than Mr. Wilberforce and the slave trade. Oh —' hurriedly, 'it's totally barbarous, I know. But, think a little, Mr. Scarborough.' It was the first time she had used the name to him. 'How did Mr. Wilberforce get the money he is lavishing on his campaign against the slavers?'

'Very much the way I got mine.' It was almost a groan. 'By other kinds of oppression. I have heard things about conditions in these new factories, as they call them, up in the north that are not very pleasant.'

'And I have seen things here in London that have horrified me. Miss Prior and I were on the edge of the abyss when you came into our lives. I looked in, and what I saw shocked me. Frightened me. We were safe enough really. I had friends to whom in the last resort I could turn. But think of the young women who have no one. I tell you, it is the whole system that needs changing. What kind of country is it where seats in Parliament can be bought and sold — like women? Oh dear.'

Charlotte had begun to cry. 'Forgive me, Mr. Scarborough.' This time the name came more easily. 'I'm getting excited, preaching at you, and Charlotte does not like it.'

'I do,' he said.

It gave her the opening she had wished for. 'There is something I have been wanting to discuss with you. When Mr. Newbery brought me back my poor little stories the other day he suggested that I might feel able to write a column for Mr. Clement's paper.'

'*The Observer?* You didn't mention that. I was so very sorry about the stories.'

'Thank you. So was I! I haven't mentioned the other thing, because I have been waiting for Mr. Clement to call. But he's like Mr. Wilberforce, a man with a great deal on his mind. The thing is, if he should want such a column, would you have any objection to my writing it?'

'Why should I?'

'Because it would inevitably be based on topics I picked up here in your house. Mr. Newbery made it clear that my value to Mr. Clement would lie in the fact that I was living here, at the centre of things. I must have your permission before I even think of doing it. In case he ever comes to ask me.'

'But of course you have my consent; you must know that. I can think of nothing you could say that would not be infinitely valuable, Mrs. Comyn.'

'Oh, thank you.' She bent over Charlotte to hide the sheen of tears in her eyes. This knowing him and not knowing him was almost more than she could bear. And that was nonsense. What else could she do but bear it?

The French guillotined Marie Antoinette that October and along with this black news came alarming reports of a new reign of terror in Paris. Worst of all, the new Committee of Public Safety had rounded up any remaining foreigners and thrown them into prison. Even vocal sympathisers with the revolutionary cause like Helen Williams and Tom Paine were swept into gaol, and Kathryn was anxious about Mary Wollstonecraft. And the rest of the news was no better. There were horrible tales about the fate of the counter-revolutionaries who had been forced to surrender at Lyons.

'But it is all rumour.' Kathryn was delighted when Mr. Clement called at last, and plied him with questions. 'Is it true that you have your own sources in Europe, Mr. Clement?'

'A friend here and there.' He was a tall man with a long, serious face. 'But one has to be cautious how one uses the information they send, for fear of their being identified by it. And one must respect the wishes of Government here, naturally, or one pays the price.

But they are grateful, sometimes, for information I am able to pass to them. Connection is all important in journalism. I can reassure you, by the way, about Miss Wollstonecraft; she is safe enough, I understand.' Something slightly dry in his tone. 'She seems to have acquired American citizenship.'

'How?'

'By marriage, presumably.' He rose to go. 'I will be happy to receive a few sample pieces, Mrs. Comyn, as a ground for discussion, but I must warn you that our views at *The Observer* are a good deal less drastic than Miss Wollstonecraft's. You will bear that in mind, I trust. I had thought of something to interest the ladies so that they insist on their husband's bringing the paper home instead of reading it at the coffee house.'

'You don't think the ladies might be interested in public affairs?'

'Heaven forfend!' Smiling down at her. 'I am sure I can count on you for just the light, feminine touch that is needed, Mrs. Comyn.'

Mark found her still fulminating half an hour later. 'Gossip and frippery, that's all he thinks females care about. Wants me to write about! And there I was flattering myself I had a chance really to say something, to do some good in the world. Oh, dear!' Laughing at her own vehemence. 'Now Charlotte will have

411

hiccups again and Beth will scold.'

'I am sure Miss Prior is incapable of scolding. But as to Mr. Clement, I am truly sorry if his visit proved disappointing. Do you not think you will be able to give him what he wants?'

'I don't know if I want to. But I suppose I must try.'

'I think you should, you know. After all, the experience of writing for a newspaper should be an immensely useful one, and who can tell what might not come of it? What about an article on Mrs. Inchbald and her work? Might not that prove both satisfactory to Clement and interesting to you? After all, if they won't let you in at the front door, there is always the side gate.'

'Oh, thank you. The very thing. And perhaps a piece about the poor Queen of France? She seems to have behaved with the greatest dignity at the last.'

'And then, dare I suggest a piece about the slave trade? From a lady's point of view.'

'I wonder what Mr. Clement would say if I wrote about the female slaves here in London.'

'I think perhaps you should wait a while before you venture into that.'

'I am very sure you are right, but what a scandal it is.'

She wrote a note to Mrs. Inchbald that very evening asking if she would agree to such a piece, and Mrs. Inchbald called a few days later, bringing a friend with her. 'I have brought Mr. Holcroft to see you,' she explained. 'Because I am sure you two will like each other. I think you have a great many ideas in common. I know you share an enthusiasm for the works of Miss Wollstonecraft.'

'I am delighted to meet you.' Kathryn greeted him warmly. 'I long to see your play, *The Road to Ruin,* but I must tell you that I will find *The Follies of a Day* hard to surpass.'

'That's one for me.' He shook her hand warmly as if in contradiction to the words. '*The Road to Ruin* is all my own work, whereas I have to confess that the *Follies* is a shameless translation from M. Beaumarchais. I don't remember how many times I had to visit the *Théâtre Français* before I had his *Figaro* by heart, but it was worth it, and I am delighted you approve of the results, Mrs. Comyn. But tell me, do, about this newspaper project of yours. Mrs. Inchbald says you are thinking of writing a piece about her and I cannot imagine a more interesting subject.'

'Oh, spare my blushes!' Mrs. Inchbald's warm smile was for Kathryn, who was beginning to understand why everyone loved her. 'I've been lucky, that's all. And I do work hard.'

'And shares her earnings with a parcel of indigent relatives,' growled Holcroft, who was obviously very fond of the charming actress.

'But you are not to say that, Mrs. Comyn, if you should decide to write something about me,' protested Mrs. Inchbald. 'My poor sisters cannot help it that they have been less lucky in life than I have. It's a hard world for a woman.'

'That's what I want to write about,' exclaimed Kathryn.

'Then you will have to do it very cleverly, or you will lose your audience,' warned the older lady. 'You must sugar the pill, Mrs. Comyn, if it is to go down. But by all means come and see me in my little attic in Leicester Fields and I will be happy to tell you about the ramshackle life I lead.'

'Cleans her own grate in the mornings, while the carriages of noble ladies stand waiting for her in the street,' put in Holcroft. 'Won't take help from anyone. Or anything else.'

'I take advice from you in great indigestible helpings,' protested Elizabeth Inchbald. 'And from all my friends. But now, Mrs. Comyn, are we not to meet your charming friend Miss Prior, who seems to have set the town in such a blaze?'

Beth joined them a few minutes later, and as always the conversation changed. She would talk of people for ever, and of plays and politics in terms of people, but abstract ideas baffled and bored her, and Kathryn was not surprised when Elizabeth Inchbald soon rose to take her leave, confirming the visit she was to pay her next day, 'to hear the story of my life'.

'What a beauty she must have been,' said Beth when the two guests had left.

'Still is surely?'

'She must be forty if she is a day, but my goodness how elegant! And makes her own clothes, they say; lives on twopence halfpenny in a garret and sends her earnings to her family. And still carrying a torch for that prig John Philip Kemble, I cannot imagine why. Holcroft was looking April and May at her, didn't you think, and they say Godwin the philosopher fancies her as well. Not bad at forty!'

'Beth, are you really setting the town in a blaze?' Kathryn had not meant to ask it so bluntly, but Mrs. Inchbald had made her a little anxious.

'Doing my best!' Beth laughed. 'Oh, Miss Kathryn, to see your face! But we want Mr. Scarborough's venture to be a success, don't we? Lord, they are a simple lot, the fellows.

I thought it was just the cits were so easily led by the nose, but it's the lot of them, ask me. I reckon if Mrs. Jordan can land herself a royal duke with nothing more than a good voice and a fine pair of legs, I should do better with all that you've taught me. Added to what I have by nature. How surprised my mum would be! Lord, what a scold she gave me that time I had to jump out the window to get away from Mr. Morewood. "You bring it on yourself Beth," she said, "with your taking ways." No need to look so anxious, love. I can handle them now, see, the fellows. And don't you be worrying your head about Mr. Scarborough, either, Miss Kathryn. He'll get over it any time now; it hit him hard at first, well, it does, but it don't last, not with men like him. They get bored, see. Or I do! They want me to listen to them talk about life, liberty and the pursuit of happiness, or the greatest good of the greatest number, and they see me yawn, and sooner or later, that's that. But there's plenty others about will do me a treat and I'm waiting for just the right one, and proper grateful to you for the chance, Kathryn, and the training, which I won't ever forget.' And then, with the peal of delighted laughter that made men her slaves: 'And no need to look so Friday-faced, neither. I know what I'm doing. The world's going to be my oyster. You're not going to see me work and slave for a lot of ungrateful kin, like Mrs. Inchbald. Nor for a drone of a husband like Mrs. Siddons, come to that. Poor thing, no wonder she's ill; one child after another and working up to the last moment each time.'

'Are you sure Mrs. Jordan is any better off? She seems to have to work pretty hard, for someone with a royal lover.'

'Breeches parts in the ninth month,' agreed Beth. 'Don't you worry yourself about me, I'm studying form, see, as the racing fellows say. When I take the plunge, it won't be for pennies. And I'll see there's a lifeline somewhere handy.'

'Beth, this is a most shocking conversation. I wish I would hear from the ladies at Ross.'

'You think they'll come and make me a good girl? Don't you believe it; they're much too comfortable where they are, those two. They taught me a lot. Decided what they wanted, and got it.'

She was proved right when a parcel arrived for Kathryn a few days later. It contained *The Gest of Sir Cradock* and a loving, apologetic note from Lavinia. Dear Janet was much better, she wrote, but there was no question of her being able to face a winter journey to London. 'I am sure you will be able to find a more suitable companion in town.'

'Easy to say!' Kathryn was bitterly disappointed. 'But where?' She had not realised how much she had been counting on the two ladies' bracing common sense. And it was disconcerting to recognise that Beth had been right about them. They were not going to throw their bonnets over anyone else's windmill.

But their letter reminded her that she had had no note of congratulation from Mrs. Goldfern. Had she perhaps not liked having Beth write to her? It seemed unlike her, but Kathryn thought it high time she called on her. Besides, the Goldferns would have news from Hull and she was also beginning to be surprised at receiving no answer to her letter to Transome about her allowance.

Her reception at the house in the Strand was cool. There was no sign of the little boys, who had been part of the pleasure of her last visit. Mrs. Goldfern received her formally, in the drawing room, alone.

She listened civilly enough to Kathryn's apologies for the delay in calling, then came straight to the heart of the matter. 'I have to tell you, Mrs. Comyn, that I never had the letter you say your friend wrote to me. Such news as we have had of you has been the merest gossip. You and this nabob of yours are the talk of the town, as you must know.' No mistaking the disapproval in her tone. 'We have naturally been anxious about you. But there is more to it than that. I am only sorry neither my husband nor my father-in-law is here today. They have been very much wanting to hear from you.'

'Good of them,' Kathryn began, but was interrupted.

'I think you do not quite understand. Of course we were relieved to learn that you were so comfortably circumstanced, but you must see that, as men of business, their first anxiety has to be for Comyn's Bank, and the debt it owes our house. They made the loan to *you*, Mrs. Comyn.' No mistaking the note of reproach.

'But it is being repaid. Mr. Transome —'

'You mean you know nothing of what has happened since you disappeared so strangely?'

'Nothing at all.'

'Then I had better tell you. When you did not return from York, Mr. George Comyn was sent for. He has moved into the house, Mrs. Comyn, sent Transome packing, and refused payment of our loan.'

'But he can't.'

'He has. What were you thinking of Mrs. Comyn, to disappear like that.'

Kathryn told her the whole story. Or almost all of it. And realised as she did so, what a dubious business it must all seem when you left out the vital fact of Mark Weatherby. No wonder Mrs. Goldfern still looked disapproving.

'You should have come to us,' she said at last. 'We would have looked after you.'

'I know.' It was unanswerable. 'I'm ashamed, now. But it all happened so fast; I was so dreadfully frightened. I see now that it was inexcusable, what I did. It seems to justify everything people say about women being unfit for business. But, you see, Mrs. Goldfern, it wasn't myself I was afraid for, it was the baby, for Charlotte. Oh, for the first time I wish she had been a boy. Then we could fight them.'

'Of course,' exclaimed the other woman. 'You don't even know about that.'

'About what?'

'Your husband's will.'

'What about it?'

'Mrs. Comyn, when you vanished like that, causing such a commotion, your Scarborough lawyer, Mr. Renshaw, heard about it and came forward to point out that, as he drafted it, your husband's will referred not to "son" but to "child" throughout. Mr. Salmon at Hull had misinterpreted the will. Whether wilfully or otherwise, who can tell? Your daughter is heir to Comyn's Bank, and you have control of it until she comes of age.'

'Oh, my goodness,' said Kathryn. And then: 'Dear Mr. Renshaw. But what a pity he didn't tell me! He never did tell me things, come to think of it, just arranged them for me.' She thought about it. 'I suppose they have all been hoping, up there in Hull, that I have died in childbed, or at least sunk without a trace. No wonder I got no answer when I wrote to Mr. Transome. I'll get in touch with Mr. Renshaw at once, ask him to act for me. And, Mrs. Goldfern —'

'Yes?'

'Try not to think too hardly of me. I did truly act, as I thought, for the best.'

26

Emerging, sadly chastened, from the house in the Strand, Kathryn sent the carriage home. 'I'll walk,' she told the astonished coachman. She had to think, face the fool's paradise in which she had been living. 'You and your nabob are the talk of the town.' Not her nabob, Beth's nabob. And not a nabob at all; Mark Weatherby. What would he do when he became aware of the storm of gossip that seemed to be loose about them? He would propose to Beth, of course; she knew her Mark well enough to be sure of that. And Beth would take him, like the sensible girl she was.

And I shall go back to Hull and dragon it at Comyn's Bank. It was as obvious as it was miserable. She had only to announce that since Charlotte was the heir she was going back to take charge. Left alone with Beth, Mark's proposal would follow as a matter of course. She would just have to pray that he would never remember.

She brushed away a sprinkle of tears as she

reached the house that felt so insidiously like home. She was trying to decide how to begin her story when Beth greeted her with a tale of her own.

'Mr. George Comyn is here.' She helped Kathryn out of her pelisse. 'In blackest mourning. He wishes to see you. Urgently.'

'Tell him he must wait until I have fed Charlotte.' And then, as they climbed the stairs: 'Mourning? Why?'

'His wife died in childbirth, poor lady. A boy. Dead too.'

'No!' All else forgotten. 'Oh, Beth! Oh, Charlotte!' She picked up the hungry baby and put her to her breast. 'So much to say, Beth dear, but later.' She owed Charlotte her full attention.

'At last!' George Comyn had been pacing up and down the elegant empty salon. 'Dear cousin, I am so happy to see you safe. We have all been nearly out of our wits with worrying about you. But you are safe? You are well? And my little cousin?'

'Quite well, thank you.' She felt the full force of his charm focused on her and wondered what was coming next.

'We have to scold you, you know, for giving us such a fright. My poor aunt was quite distracted with worry, and everything at sixes and sevens at the bank. But now I am come, Cousin Kathryn, to help you as best I may out of this imbroglio in which you find yourself. Oh, quite innocently, I know you well enough to be sure of that. But, little cousin, the gossip, the scandal . . . It has made my aunt quite ill; I am afraid she takes the gloomiest view. Well, you know my Aunt Comyn. She has been saying terrible things about you, she and that Mr. Jones. I won't sully your ears with them. I blame it all on that young upstart Prior. Led you astray, of course, you in your delicate condition. You were always an impulsive child, dear Kathryn, and I never could help but have a soft corner in my heart for you. And now, I am here to save you from the consequences of your folly!' A dramatic sweep of the hand. 'You see me in black, cousin. My poor Anne is dead, like your Thomas. We are both alone, you and I. And I am here to speak the devotion I have always felt. To offer you the protection of my hand, my name,' working himself up, 'my heart.'

'But I already have your name, Mr. Comyn.' This was the man who had plotted to put her in a lunatic asylum. If she had not known, might he have convinced her? 'And your bank.' Sweetly. 'Did you think I had not heard about the surprising comeout over Thomas's will? Lucky for me that I chose to pay a call on Mrs. Goldfern today, and she told me what has been happening up in Hull. Can you really have been hoping that I would not find out? That I would sink without trace into the morass of London? Well, I have not done so, thank God, and I learned the truth this morning. No time yet to decide what to do, but while I am deciding, I do strongly recommend, Cousin George, that you reinstate Mr. Transome, and the repayments of the loan I secured from Goldfern's.'

'I said that was a mistake.' He muttered it more to himself than to her, the wind quite taken out of his sails.

'You were quite right.' Cordially. 'You have let yourself be badly advised, Cousin George. For the family's sake, I would as soon forget about it, but only if you can contrive to get rid of Robertson and Peters without too much scandal and get things back on to their old footing at Comyn's. I hope Turner is still there?'

'For the moment.'

'On the contrary. For good. Or,' smiling for the first time, 'until my Charlotte reaches the age of twenty-one and can make her own decisions.'

'You cannot mean to come back and run the bank yourself! Have you any idea what the talk about you has been like in Hull this summer? Vanishing without trace! Like a servant girl who has lost her character. And then bobbing up here in town, running a house of ill repute.' He stopped, alarmed himself at what he had said.

'I would not repeat that in front of witnesses, Mr. Comyn. Mr. Scarborough was in the navy; I think you would come poorly out of a meeting with him, if you came out of it alive at all. As to the rumours you speak of, I can imagine who has enjoyed spreading them. I think you had better go back to Hull and apply yourself to contradicting them. There is going to be an accounting, and soon.'

'You really mean to come back?'

'I think I shall have to. I have a duty to the bank, as well as to my daughter. Whether I shall stay is another question. And now, I think we have said enough. You know my terms: I recommend that you go home tomorrow and set about meeting them.' She had never seen a man so deflated and could almost have felt sorry for him if she had not remembered what he had planned for her. He had really expected to charm her into an instant marriage that would solve all his problems, had very likely got a special licence in his pocket. Frightening to think that, granted her own wretched circumstances, he might even have fooled her if she had not known what she did. As it was, she wondered how much he really understood about what Robertson had been doing to the bank. Not much, probably; he had never been trained to business. So would he be able to cope with Robertson and Peters? She rather thought not. It was more and more obvious that she must go back to Hull, but first she must get the Goldferns' advice. She wrote a quick note, asking for an appointment next morning.

The clock on the chimney piece struck the hour. Time to dress for the evening's callers. And no time to say anything to Beth tonight. Tomorrow she would face facts, plan, act. Today, she would allow herself one more happy evening.

In fact, guests started flocking in even earlier than usual. Mr. Clement was one of the first and delighted her with high praise of the piece she had sent him about Mrs. Inchbald. It was just what he had hoped for, he said, and he wished to commission her to write similar articles about other prominent ladies. 'I am sure you will find them eager to talk to you once they have read your *Mrs. Inchbald,* which I propose to run next Sunday.'

But next Sunday she would be in Hull. Here was her chance, and she could not take it. More and more she felt that she was moving through the evening as through a dreadful dream. And there had been no chance of a word with Mark, who had arrived with Godwin and Holcroft, all of them talking eagerly and angrily about the result of the treason trial in Scotland. Three men, Palmer, Skirving and Muir had been on trial for their lives there, not for any act of violence, just because they had belonged to Constitutional Societies and published books and pamphlets urging parliamentary reform and justice for all.

'If they are guilty of treason, so are all of us.' Clement turned away from Kathryn to hear what Godwin was saying.

'Found guilty,' said Godwin. 'Transportation for fourteen years! And to be treated like common felons. No books to be allowed for the terrible voyage to Botany Bay, no stores beyond what every criminal gets. It is a new barbarism, the behaviour of a Nero, a Tiberius, not an English Home Secretary. I am writing a letter to the *Morning Chronicle* to this effect. If it results in my imprisonment by Mr. Pitt's spies and bullies, I trust you will visit me in my cell.'

The speech was greeted with a round of applause. 'Is it really so bad?' Kathryn turned to find Mark beside her.

'I am afraid so.' He was looking very grave indeed. 'Afraid too that I take a risk in allowing so inflammatory a speech to be made in my house. I have been sure for a while that Mr. Pitt has one of his spies among our guests. I had been wondering whether I should warn you and Miss Prior. Now I feel it my duty to do so.'

'A spy? Here? One of our friends?' She looked about the crowded room. 'Impossible!'

'I am sorry.' He took her arm to guide her into a small side room where they could talk unheard and she felt the inevitable, shameful thrill at his touch, was amazed that he did not feel it too. But he was going soberly on: 'I had an unexpected guest today. I think I will not tell you his name. A man high in Pitt's confidence. One who must know what he is talking about. He had come to warn me, he said, as a stranger in town. He knew all about me, Mrs. Comyn, my story, my loss of memory. That was frightening in itself. They had gone to a great deal of trouble to investigate me . . . All of us.'

'You mean Beth and me too?'

'I am afraid so. He threatened me with what might happen to you two. Oh, in the politest possible manner!' She felt his controlled rage eating him up. ' "Such a charming pair of young ladies," ' he quoted furiously. ' "No one would wish to see them suffering the indignities of the Bridewell; still less on trial for their lives." '

'Our lives?' She could not believe her ears.

'The penalty for High Treason, Mrs. Comyn. Sympathy with the King's enemies. Your interest in the fate of Miss Wollstonecraft; my casual visits to Mr. Hardy and to some meetings of his Corresponding Society; our friendship with men like Godwin and Holcroft and Horne Tooke. In Government's eyes it all adds up to dangerous conspiracy.'

'I can't believe it. They must be mad.'

'Not mad; frightened . . .'

'Not half so much as I am,' said Kathryn. 'There's Charlotte to think of.' Imagine Charlotte in the Bridewell. 'And Beth?' She hardly dared ask it.

'Crime by association. What are we going to do, Kathryn?' He did not even notice that he had used her name, but she did.

'What did your sinister guest propose?'

'That I think of some pretext for closing the house. Go out of town for a while. Anything, he said, to close down this hotbed of conspiracy.'

'He called it that?'

'Yes.' They were silent for a moment, listening to the angry babble of voices from the main rooms.

'And his spy is out there; will report on what is going on tonight?'

'Yes. He told me so. Of course, we neither

of us expected this appalling news from Scotland. He gave me a week.'

'But you think this might make it less?'

'Don't you?'

'Yes.' She had seen curious glances directed at them from the vociferous crowd in the main rooms. 'We ought not to stay here longer. Can you get in touch with your visitor?'

'He told me to.'

'Ask him for three days. And — Mr. Scarborough —' She had so nearly called him Mark.

'Yes?'

'Do you think this is why Mr. Wilberforce and his friends have kept away?'

'Of course! Fool that I am. What a mull I've made of things. Of everything. My caller told me something else. Something I should have realised myself. He showed me a disgusting paragraph from *The World*. I'm ashamed to tell you about it, but I think I must.'

'No need. I've heard about it too. Scurrilous talk about the three of us. We have been very stupid, you and I. We should have known what the world would say. I blame myself the most. I tried to get my friends from Ross to come, did nothing when they refused. I've let myself live in a fool's paradise, and now we must all pay for it.'

'Miss Prior most of all.' His eyes were on Beth, where she stood in the midst of an admiring group of men. 'I won't sully your ears with what was said about her. I have to marry her, Mrs. Comyn. It's the only answer. I thought I should speak to you first, as being in some sort responsible for her.'

'Yes,' she said. 'You could say that.' It was what she had known would happen, and she did not know how she was going to bear it. He must not see her face. She moved away from him, back into the main salon.

'You won't tell her what I've said.' Following her. 'About this paragraph in the paper. I wouldn't want her to think that was why —'

'No, of course not. I'll not say a word.' Was this how one's heart broke? Quietly, politely, standing in a corner of a crowded room.

'Mrs. Comyn! I have found you at last.' Mr. Newbery interrupted, eager hand outstretched. 'I have just finished *The Gest of Sir Cradock*. It seems to me just the thing to catch the public's fancy in these troubled times. I should like to bring it out as soon as possible. I trust you are empowered to negotiate on your friends' behalf.'

'Yes, they gave me full powers.' She was aware of Mark beginning to move away, longed to stop him, tell him to think again.

How could she? Impossible.

'Good.' Newbery beamed at her. 'Then shall we say forty pounds?'

'Forty pounds?' Pulling herself together. 'For a poem that took my friends many years to translate? And that you think just the thing to catch the public's fancy? Dear Mr. Newbery, I think you must be making fun of me. How many copies were you thinking of printing?'

'Oh — as to that, I had not just decided. A first printing of fifteen hundred maybe, to see how the wind blows?'

'I don't think my friends would care for that at all. Perhaps you would be so good as to let me have the manuscript back in the morning. Mr. Godwin was telling me, just now, that he thought Mr. Johnson would be very much interested in *Sir Cradock*, and you know what a practical enthusiast he can be for a work. When my friends gave me full powers, they meant me to get the best bargain for them that I could, Mr. Newbery, and I intend to do so.'

'Dear lady, you take a man up so quick! Of course you are right to want to do the best for your friends. We have not quite understood each other, I believe. What I meant was a first payment of forty pounds and then a further figure to be negotiated if the thing should take, as we all hope it will.'

'That's more like it,' said Kathryn. They both knew he had meant nothing of the kind. 'I shall be down your way tomorrow morning, Mr. Newbery. May I come and see you when I have finished my other business, and we can settle the terms. But I think my friends would expect me to hold out for a larger first run, and some kind of undertaking about the necessary — oh dear,' smiling at him, 'I do dislike the word, but the necessary puffing, Mr. Newbery. Some tantalising hints in the papers ahead of publication? Forgive me if I seem to be teaching you your business, but we both know what a difference that can make. The public needs its appetite whetting.'

'I wish you were a man, Mrs. Comyn. I'd offer you a partnership.'

'What a pity.' She turned and left him, her eyes searching the room in vain for Mark. But Beth was still surrounded by her admiring group, though Kathryn thought its numbers had diminished slightly. Tonight, everyone but the most frivolous was concerned with the implications of the news from Scotland.

The three of them usually took a last glass of wine together after their guests had left, to discuss the evening and plan for the morrow, but tonight Kathryn felt she could not face it and made a pretext of anxiety about

Charlotte. 'I think I'll go straight up,' she told them. 'It's been a long day, and I have to visit the Goldferns first thing in the morning, and Mr. Newbery after that. I think he is going to take *Sir Cradock*.'

'That's wonderful news.' Mark stood there for a moment, visibly irresolute, looking from her to Beth. Had she meant to give him his chance to propose tonight? Get it over with? If she had, she was regretting it already.

'Talking of good news —' Beth was in sparkling good looks tonight, untouched apparently by the undertone of gloomy anticipation that had run through the rooms. 'But time enough for that in the morning. You look exhausted, Kathryn dear. I'll take you up. Good night, Mr. Scarborough.'

'Good night.' If he minded the lost chance, he did not show it. 'I'll call tomorrow afternoon, if I may, Mrs. Comyn. We must decide what is best to do. And I shall hope to see you too, Miss Prior.'

'Well, of course.' With her sunny smile. And then, when he had left: 'There's trouble?'

'Yes. But that's for tomorrow, Beth dear. I really am a little worried about Charlotte. Susan says she has been restless all evening.'

Beth was never an early riser, and Kathryn was out of the house before she appeared. It was fortunate that the Goldferns had asked

435

her to come early; it would give her time to fit in her call on Mr. Newbery. But when the carriage emerged from their quiet backwater into the noise and bustle of the Haymarket, she wondered if she ought not to have ordered it for even earlier.

No use fretting. The Goldferns would wait. And Mark's coachman was an expert driver and seemed to be on the best of terms with the brawny labourers who were manhandling the huge bales of hay that gave the market its name. No doubt they got together of an evening in some dirty comfortable local tavern. And plotted revolution? She very much doubted it. She must decide whether she was going to tell the Goldferns about the extraordinary threat against her household. She thought not. How could she tell them without telling them also about Mark? And that she could not do. The first person to be told about Mark must be Mark himself. And how could she do that? It would be to ask him to take pity on her, renew his old proposal. That had been difficult enough yesterday. Today, in the light of his declared intention of proposing to Beth, it was, simply, impossible.

She was only a little late and her apologies carried them through the first awkwardness of the meeting.

'No need,' Mr. Goldfern senior interrupted

her when she began to apologise again for not getting in touch sooner. 'My daughter-in-law has explained. And we had an unexpected caller yesterday afternoon. Mr. George Comyn, quite bursting with apologies and explanations. You seem to have given him the fright of his life, Mrs. Comyn.'

'I did my best.' Was this going to be easier than she had feared?

'He blames it all on everyone but himself. He explained — oh with such charm — that he was nothing but a child in business matters. And distracted — he said — by the death of his wife. He had always known Robertson as your husband's right hand. Naturally he took his advice in the crisis caused by your disappearance.'

'I should have thought of that, should I not?' Ruefully. 'Mr. Goldfern — both of you — let me say, once and for all, how deeply sorry and ashamed I am at all the trouble I have caused. And poor Mr. Transome.'

'Don't waste your sympathy on that broken reed, Mrs. Comyn. We owe you an apology there. If he had stood his ground, none of this would have happened. We should have had more sense than to send a figures man to somewhere action might be needed.'

'That's just what Beth said.' Surprised.

'Acute of her. Did you write to Mr. Renshaw, Mrs. Comyn?'

'Not yet. I thought I had best talk to you first. But I really ought to be up there myself, don't you think?'

'We had been hoping you would decide to go. Renshaw will need your backing, and you and Miss Charlotte do owe him something for the wording of that will.' Smiling. 'I think we have to assume that your husband simply did not notice what it meant. Is that going to worry you?'

'Not in the slightest.'

'Good. But, yes, I do think you should go up yourself, Mrs. Comyn, if you don't mind it too much. It will not be very pleasant, I am afraid. By what George Comyn told us, the talk here in London is nothing to what they have been saying in Hull. You have your mother-in-law to thank for that, I take it.'

'I am afraid so. She never did like me.' She looked at them both for a moment, thinking about it, facing it. 'I got Beth to write to her about Charlotte's birth, have had no answer.'

'Yes,' said the younger Mr. Goldfern, 'but remember my wife did not get the letter your Beth wrote her. Forgive me, but does she write well?'

'No. I've been teaching her. Stupid of me. So that means nothing. But what it all comes down to, doesn't it, is that the sooner I get up there and start facing down this slanderous talk, the better. It won't be pleasant, and it serves me right.'

'I'm very glad you feel like that.' The older Mr. Goldfern smiled at her for the first time. 'My son and I are convinced that your presence, and Miss Charlotte's, will work wonders in Hull. I imagine you do not know, how should you, that things at your bank have been a great worry this summer. To us: to everyone. One more muddle; one more scandal, and it is finished. I think it a great instance of the public spirit, the town spirit of the citizens of Hull, that it has not collapsed in the course of the summer. I am sure you know enough about the volatility of public opinion to understand this. These rumours of Jacobin plots against the Government have done the greatest harm to public confidence. And so will the Government repression — to call a spade a spade — that is bound to follow. You have heard, perhaps, of the outcome of the Scottish trials, Mrs. Comyn?'

'I have indeed.'

'Well there you are. It needs just one more thing — a French victory at sea, for instance; the disastrous evacuation of Toulon which, frankly, we look to hear of every day — and Comyn's is finished. No inheritance for Miss

Charlotte, and a disaster for the people of Hull.'

'And a considerable inconvenience for us,' put in his son dryly. 'So we have asked Mr. Comyn to wait a few days in the hopes that you will feel able to accompany him, Mrs. Comyn, give him the benefit of your support. We thought that if you would also allow us to send an express message to Mr. Renshaw, so that he could meet you in Hull, things might get settled, once and for all, on a sound basis. Mr. George Comyn was talking rather wildly about contesting the will, but I hope we managed to convince him that that could mean nothing but disaster for everyone. There is no chance the bank could survive such a dispute.'

'No wonder he asked me to marry him.' It surprised Kathryn to hear herself saying it.

'He did? The ideal solution. But do I take it you did not feel able to accept him, Mrs. Comyn?'

'No.'

'A great pity. But perhaps even more of a reason why you should consider going north with him.'

'You mean, I owe it to you.' She faced the bleak truth. 'It's good of you not to put it more forcefully, Mr. Goldfern. Of course I must go. But Mr. Comyn will have to wait a week or so. I cannot possibly go sooner.' She rose to take her leave.

'My wife was hoping you would take a luncheon with her and the boys.' The younger Mr. Goldfern had pulled back her chair for her.

So she was to be forgiven. 'How I wish I could, but I have business to transact with Mr. Newbery. Give Mrs. Goldfern my kindest regards and say I shall hope to call on her before I leave.'

'One other thing.' This was the older man. 'Did Mr. Comyn tell you that Windover Hall is for sale again?'

'Windover? No!'

'We were wondering, my son and I, if you might not consider buying the house back. It would be an ideal place to bring up Miss Charlotte, and you would be near enough to Hull to keep overall control of the bank.'

'Near, but not too near, you mean? But, dear Mr. Goldfern, what in the world do you suggest I buy Windover with? I may need to ask you for funds for the journey north.' Nothing would induce her to let Mark fund her.

'But, Mrs. Comyn, you do not seem to understand. You are the mother of the heir of Comyn's. My son and I will be happy to advance any funds you might need for so practical a purpose. You are simply to make your wishes known and leave it all to us.'

'And go north.' If it was a bribe, she wished to have the terms clear.

'Well, yes.'

After that, dealing with Mr. Newbery seemed like child's play.

27

Kathryn was late home, and both she and Charlotte were ravenous, but Charlotte must come first. The house had been quiet when she came in. Beth had gone out early, the servant told her, and Mark had not arrived yet. It gave her a breathing space, and she was grateful.

It was so much to give up. She put Charlotte down in her cradle and moved over to look out of the bedroom window at the sheltered garden where a few last, bleached roses spoke of the hopeful autumn days when she had walked there with Mark. She had been so sure that his fancy for Beth (and hers for him?) would pass, that presently he would remember. Shame on her, she had simply let things go, waiting for the happy day.

And this was what had come of it. Perhaps she should be grateful for the duty that called her north. At least it would spare her the purgatory of watching their happiness. Among all the wretchedness, perhaps the worst thing of all was how totally she must lose them both, even as friends. She could not risk Mark's remembering after he married Beth. She must buy Windover, go there, and stay there. She crumpled up the list of women's names Mr. Clement had given her the night before and threw it away. No hope of writing for the papers from the wilds of the north. All gone, she thought. Everything I tried for, everything I hoped for. Except the bank, and even there I am wanted only at a safe distance.

Charlotte let out a whimper and was sick. She picked her up, cleaned her up, and took her out into the garden, to walk up and down, up and down, on the new paving stones.

Susan found her there. 'Mr. Comyn has called, ma'am. He says it is urgent.'

'Mr. Comyn?' What now? 'Take the baby up, Susan. She's colicky today, poor lamb.'

'And no wonder,' said Susan. 'I had Mr. Comyn put in your little study, ma'am, so you wouldn't be disturbed.'

'Thank God you are at home.' George Comyn held out a shaking hand. 'There is shocking news from Hull. I came to you directly.'

'The bank has failed?' Shamefully, she had a moment of pure relief. That would free her.

'No, not that, though it might come to that. It's my aunt, poor lady, Mrs. Comyn. A terrible story — a paralytic seizure — I don't know how to set about telling you.'

She shut the study door behind her. 'Best sit down, Cousin George, and begin.'

'Yes. Thank you.' He mopped his brow with a shabby handkerchief and she thought he was going to seed since the death of his wife. 'You remember Mr. Jones?' he asked now, surprising her.

'Mr. Jones? I should think I do. He made a scene at the will reading.'

'That seems to have been the start of it. He had expected a handsome legacy.' Was there a hint of reproach in his tone?

'I saw to it that the servants got the legacies I thought they deserved; I considered Mr. Jones Mrs. Comyn's affair.'

'So did he. He has been making her life a misery all summer, only nobody knew. Nobody but those friends of hers the Misses Harris and from what I hear they actually seem to have taken his side. What could she do, poor lady, with the three of them all exclaiming against her? She seems to have paid him considerable sums as what he called compensation, but his demands simply grew with each payment. He planned to build a chapel out at Hessle, I understand.'

'Yes, that would make sense. Oh, poor Mrs. Comyn. So what happened?'

'That housekeeper of yours — Sally?' She nodded. 'Yes, Sally heard him shouting at the old lady and went in to find Mr. Jones praying, the Misses Harris in hysterics, and Mrs. Comyn stretched speechless on the floor. She has not spoken since. They sent for me, of course.'

'And you came to me.'

'Naturally.'

So much for the one more week with Mark she had thought she could allow herself. 'I cannot possibly be ready today.' She was talking as much to herself as to him. 'And we will have to take it in easy stages because of the baby. Send a man ahead to order horses for us and let them know at Comyn's that we will be there on Monday.'

'Sunday travelling?'

'Yes, Mr. Comyn.' Her tone was a warning. 'And now, if you will excuse me, I have all my arrangements to make.'

'But, Mrs. Comyn — Kathryn — the carriage? I rode down. You will be bringing your own?'

'Not my own, Mr. Comyn. Mr. Scarborough's, like this house. I thought that was what all the fuss was about. You cannot seriously imagine I am going to help myself to his carriage, as well as leaving him in the lurch the way I must? Think again, pray, and hire one for us. Comfortable, mind, for Charlotte's sake.'

He was crimson with embarrassment now, and muttered something about the cost of living in town and his pockets being to let.

'Now I've heard everything!' With something between a sob and a chuckle. 'You expect me to leave everything, my affairs . . . my friends . . . to go to the help of a bad-tempered old lady who has done all she could to make life unpleasant for me. And I am to pay the shot. Is that what you are trying to say?' And when he merely nodded miserably. 'Very well.' She sat down at her writing desk and scrawled a quick note to Mr. Goldfern senior. 'Take that to Goldfern's in the Strand. They will give you what you need. And I shall expect you at nine tomorrow, with all arrangements made. And for goodness sake don't waste my time with thanks.'

What a virago I am turning into, she thought ruefully as she rang for a servant to show him out. Poor Charlotte will be sick again.

When George Comyn had gone she sat a little longer in the quiet of her study, facing it all. This was almost the last time she would sit here. It was all over. If she had known at the time that these were the happiest months of her life — the only happy months of her life? — would she have lived them differently? She thought not.

Now she must set about saying her farewells gracefully, getting it all over with, freeing Mark and Beth for their life together.

And here was Mark, as if her thoughts had called him up. So much to say to him, but how? Where to begin?

But he had a tale of his own to tell. 'She refused me!'

'Beth?' She could not believe her ears.

'Yes. She laughed at me! Said she was too happy to scold, or she would have.'

'Laughed at you? Scold? Happy? I don't understand.'

'No more do I. I asked her if there was someone else, and she laughed harder than ever, and said no. Not the way I meant. And more than that she would not say, just went on laughing and told me to go home and think things over. We met in Leicester Fields,' he explained. 'I cannot imagine where she had been, so early in the day.'

'You proposed to her in Leicester Fields?' Kathryn had a sudden vivid memory of the two of them sharing a roll there. 'Not perhaps the most romantic of places to choose.'

'I did not feel romantic,' he told her, looking, oddly, a little shamefaced. 'You think she may have noticed that my heart was not in it? That I should ask her again? In more suitable circumstances? You make me ashamed; I'm afraid I had rather taken it for granted that she would be glad to have me.'

'As well she might!'

'My wretched wealth! You must know as well as I do, Mrs. Comyn, that some of the ladies who have graced our evenings have come largely because they have marriageable daughters. I suppose it must have helped keep the scandal-mongers at bay. Oh well, one advantage of it is that I can at least settle something on Miss Prior.'

'You don't mean to ask her again?'

'I do not. It would have been a disaster, and I respect her for recognising it. I bore her to death, poor girl, when I talk about what interests me. I just wish I knew why she laughed so much.' He had not liked it. 'But no matter for that. I have done my duty by her, she shall have a dowry from me, and I am a free man again. Mrs. Comyn, you, who understand so much, will understand why I had to ask Miss Prior first — Her case is worse than yours . . .'

'No,' she interrupted him. 'Please don't, Mr. Scarborough. Stop there, leave it, there is no need. My future is taken care of. I'm a rich woman too, or at least Charlotte is. There has been no chance to tell you. I have to leave tomorrow, go back to Hull where my duty lies.' She explained swiftly about Thomas's will and his mother's illness. 'I have to go to her; I'm all the kin she has except for George Comyn, who is a broken reed if ever there was one.' She had not mentioned George's proposal. 'But you can see, as a widow, living with her sick mother-in-law, making sense of her dead husband's bank, I shall be a perfect pillar of respectability. No need for you to sacrifice your future to me.'

'But I want to. You don't understand . . . It's not a sacrifice, it's why I made such a poor job of proposing to Miss Prior. Oh! Do you think that is why she laughed? Because she knew? She's no fool when it comes to people, our Beth. Oh, I was mad for her at first, like all the other men. There is something about her, some witchcraft, I don't know. But, Mrs. Comyn, imagine sharing a breakfast table with her! Trying to read the newspapers!' He ran a distracted hand through his hair. 'I am doing this all wrong. How can I explain to you? I thought for a while that it was Beth I was coming to see, when I came so eagerly to this house, found myself so happy here. But it was you I wanted to talk to!'

'Along with Mr. Holcroft and Mr. Godwin and a few others. Thank you for the compliment, Mr. Scarborough.'

'Why do you keep putting me off? Why

450

won't you let me speak . . . tell you? Is it my past you are afraid of? The time I can't remember? I have thought a great deal about that; hoped when I came to London that someone would recognise me, tell me my name, who I am. But if they haven't, after all this time, surely I can safely assume the past is dead, will stay that way?'

Now was the moment to tell him. And she could not. Why? It was, simply, impossible. To tell him now that she had known all the time . . . He would like it even less than being laughed at by Beth. Time, they must have time. She saw, suddenly, what she must do. 'Mr. Scarborough, you must see that it is too soon! You asked Beth this morning. It's still morning! How can you? Let it go for a while. Please. When I have found out how my mother-in-law really is, I mean to buy back my family home, Windover Hall, settle there with Charlotte. If you still remember me, come spring, come and visit me there. I shall be glad to see you.' Perhaps the place would bring back his memory. It was most certainly worth a try. If he came. If he had not found someone else. How could she put him off like this when everything in her cried out to fall into his arms, tell him the whole story? But, there it was; she could not.

'I shall come. I shall most certainly come.'

He took her hand, bent to kiss it, met her eyes in a long, strange look. 'What is it?' he asked. 'What is it about you?'

She had been vaguely aware of noise in the hall outside, now, suddenly, the study door burst open and Oliver Morewood strode into the room, two footmen ineffectually trying to prevent him.

'Found you at last!' He stank of spirits. 'Rich little bitch now. Nabob's whore; everything handsome about her, and not a stiver for her starving little brothers left to rot in the gutter.' He loomed over her, red-faced, threatening, then looked beyond her and saw Mark, advancing furiously upon him. 'You? Back from the grave?'

'You will apologise to the lady at once —'

Mark's angry words were cut off by Morewood's first, clumsy blow. After that, the fight was short, bloody and unscientific. Kathryn, screaming at them to stop, at the footmen to stop them, saw Morewood land a lucky hit on Mark's cheek almost in the moment that Mark floored him with a right-handed knockout blow. Everything was quiet for a moment, as he lay there motionless and Mark stood, staring down at him, breathing heavily.

'Oliver Morewood,' he said at last. 'I hope I've not killed him.' And then, turning slowly towards her. 'Kathryn?'

'Mark.' Their hands reached out, met, held.

At last he turned to the footmen. 'Take him away,' he told them. 'Revive him. Keep him handy. He must answer for this. And shut the door behind you.' Still holding both her hands in his he watched as they obeyed him. 'He'll live, thank God.' He smiled down at Kathryn. 'Oh, my dear love, you knew all the time?' He was looking back over the months they had been together. 'That's why you fainted! That day you came. I thought afterwards it was unlike the Mrs. Comyn I was getting to know and love.'

'Not half so much as you loved Beth.' She could say it now.

'Oh that! It was the strangest thing. I think I begin to understand it now. I heard her speak, you know, before I saw her, that day at Covent Garden. The voice went straight to my heart. But then nothing else was right. She talks like you, you know.'

'Yes. She told me once that she had formed her speech on mine. She's a great mimic, our Beth. Oh, Mark, I am so glad she refused you!'

'Not half so glad as I am. But I still wish I understood why she laughed so. We must tell her first, in case she needs telling, which I rather doubt. How soon can you marry me, my dearest love?' Their interlocked hands had been exchanging messages all this time, now he pulled her gently towards him.

'Not yet, alas.' She held back a little to say it. 'Poor Thomas only died this spring. Mark! I have to go north tomorrow. I promised George Comyn.'

'You won't go with him, my love. You will come with me. It solves everything, don't you see? Mr. Pitt's spy. The closing of the rooms. The scandalous tongues. We'll face them out together, be a nine days' wonder and enjoy it.'

'I think we can face anything together —'

'Oh, Kathryn.' She thought there were tears in his eyes. 'When I think of what you have had to face alone . . . There is so much I want to know: your mother; Windover —'

It reminded her of something. 'Windover is for sale. The Goldferns have promised to advance me the money for it. Will you like that?'

'Windover.' Both their thoughts were back on that windswept cliff. 'I shall like it above all things. But I shall buy it for you, not the Goldferns. My gift to my bride. We'll live there, won't we?'

'Would you like to?'

'With you and Charlotte? More than I can say. It's the strangest thing, Kathryn; I feel as if everything in my life was falling into place at last. With you at its heart, my only love.'

A small, loving pressure on her hands challenged her to query that 'only'. 'I have been racking my brains as to what to do,' he went on, 'since I received that threatening message from Mr. Pitt. Do you know what I had decided?'

'No?' This was the purest happiness she had ever known, standing here, her hands in his, waiting for his kiss.

'I was going to find myself a country town that needed a daily paper, and start one. And that's what we'll do, Kathryn, shall we? I've had enough of London. I hope you have too. With the world as it is, it's time, I think, to cultivate one's own garden. And I am sure it will prove a more useful way of spending my money than keeping open house for a lot of London wits and gossips. So — we will live at Windover, and I shall start a daily paper for Hull. Will you like that, Mrs. Weatherby? Will you grace it with an article when the fancy takes you?'

'Oh, Mark, you know I will.'

Now at last he pulled her close for a kiss that spanned the long, lost years.

'I hate to interrupt.' Beth's voice. 'And I do heartily congratulate you both, but Charlotte is crying, Mr. Morewood is threatening assault and battery in the hall, and Mr. Comyn says he must see you urgently, Kathryn.'

'I'll deal with them.' Mark was still holding Kathryn close. 'Have I your permission to tell Mr. Comyn, love?'

'You can tell the whole world,' said Kathryn. 'I'm the happiest woman in it.' One last, light kiss and he was gone. And she must break the news to Beth, whom she still felt she was betraying. What was going to become of Beth? But what she said was: 'Beth, why did you laugh so?'

'When the poor fellow was making such a mull of proposing to me? And in Leicester Fields too! Kathryn, love, I do hope I didn't hurt his feelings, but really you should have seen his face! A schoolboy taking his physic would have looked happier. And I was in such a seventh heaven myself you see. And I owe it all to you, Miss Kathryn dear.' It was ages since she had used the formal address.

'I don't understand —'

'No, why should you? It was all such doom and gloom last night, I don't believe you even noticed Mr. Kemble came.'

'Mr. Kemble? No? And —'

'He said he'd heard talk of me . . . Asked me to come to Drury Lane this morning, read a part or two with him. He says I'm a natural, Kathryn. I'm to join his company, a guinea a week to start, but he says it's just the start. Kathryn dear, can you do without me?'

456

'We will do our poor best, dear Beth.' Mark had rejoined them. 'It's wonderful news. Kathryn, I've given Morewood a good fright and let him go. And George Comyn merely wanted more money, so I sent him to the rightabout too. Told him I am taking you north. And I've told Susan to bring Charlotte down. I want to meet my daughter.' He turned to Beth. 'Kathryn and I are going to Hull tomorrow,' he told her, 'to look after the old lady and straighten out that bank of hers — and to silence the gossips, I hope. Will you live in this house and look after it for us, dear Beth? Let us visit you when we come to town? I thought we would have one more splendid evening tonight, announce the closing of the rooms and maybe hint at our engagement. Kathryn will explain.'

'I'm sure she will,' said Beth, with a sparkling, teasing glance for them both. 'So masterful!'

But they were in each other's arms again, and did not hear.

The employees of THORNDIKE PRESS hope you have enjoyed this Large Print book. All our Large Print titles are designed for easy reading, and all our books are made to last. Other Thorndike Large Print books are available at your library, through selected bookstores, or directly from us. For more information about current and upcoming titles, please call or mail your name and address to:

THORNDIKE PRESS
PO Box 159
Thorndike, Maine 04986
800/223-6121
207/948-2962